BOB THANKS FOR THE
MICKEY MOUSE PANCAKES
HOPE YOU LIKE THE
BOOK

9/25/15

Daryl Bettaux

The Bengal Ruby

An adventurous love story

Darryl Bettencourt

ISBN 978-1-4958-0600-1
Library of Congress Catalog Card Number: 2015948739

Published August 2015

INFINITY PUBLISHING
1094 New DeHaven Street, Suite 100
West Conshohocken, PA 19428-2713
Toll-free (877) BUY BOOK
Local Phone (610) 941-9999
Fax (610) 941-9959
Info@buybooksontheweb.com
www.buybooksontheweb.com

DEDICATION

I would like to dedicate this book, **The Bengal Ruby**, to my wife Sheryl, who has been my dedicated wife for 50 years. She has put so much effort in raising our three children, Amy, Jody, and Paul, who I also dedicate this book along with my nine Grand Children: Isaiah, Elizabeth, Luka, Joshua, Samuel, Christopher, Nathaniel, Katelyn, and William.

My wife Sheryl is a loving Christian, and it shows wherever she goes. Sheryl has been such a Christian example to me, and our children, and grandchildren. I could think of no better person to be at the top of the dedication list to this book, than my wife Sheryl. Thank you so much honey, for the wonderful person that you are.

Love Darryl

A special thanks to

George Marshall

For inspiring me to write, and become an author.

A special acknowledgment to my friend

Louie Borba

In 1966 I was considering a job in a Mechanical Engineering department; I was hesitant for the wages seemed low. But Louie advised me to take the job for it was in my field of education. I took the job and later extended my education. I had a very good and fun career for 43 years in Engineering. Thanks to those simple words that Louie Borba said. "**TAKE THE JOB**" Thanks again Louie for those words. A friend Darryl.

PROLOGUE

The story begins in the year 1957, when a man named Ray Johnson who was born and raised in California, on a ranch in the Sacramento Delta, was on his way for the adventure of his life. Being raised on a ranch in this area where people come across many different animals, it wasn't really a surprise Ray's passion soon became hunting and shooting. Ray was considered by everybody who knew him to be a very good rifle marksman.

In time, Ray graduated from high school and went on to college. Ray finished college with a BS degree in engineering and eventually landed an engineering job in Lodi, California. In college, he met a young lady named Shannon Doritee, also from Lodi California. She eventually became Ray's girlfriend and became a big part of his life, their relationship getting more serious with each passing time. Ray's passion for hunting never left; in fact, he pursued it even more, and he also got Shannon interested in shooting and hunting.

Even before college, Ray acquired an interest in the big cats of the world; his favorite was India's Bengal tiger, feeling they were superior in all aspects compared to the other big cats, even the African lion. Ray's love for hunting and his admiration for the Bengal tiger started him on a quest to India to hunt for a Bengal tiger trophy. With that came the hard part: getting the trip planned, picking a reliable tiger hunting guide, getting the hunting permits, and saying goodbye to his mom and dad, his best friend Joeseph Alexander, and his newly wedded wife, Shannon.

Ray had two loves: his passion for Shannon, and his admiration for the Indian Bengal tiger. One led to marriage, while the other led to an adventure of a hunt for the Bengal tiger in India. Originally Ray thought he would marry Shannon after his hunting trip to India, but being too much in love, they got married about ten months before his trip to India.

Ray found a guide by the name of Baasim Sharma, a well-known guide and hunting outfitter, especially known for Bengal tiger and leopard hunting. Ray researched him thoroughly before he made the decision. Baasim came with excellent references. He made sure Ray understood that Bengal tiger hunting was dangerous. When Ray had made all the arrangements, the date for departure was fixed on May 1, 1960.

The hunt was to take place close to the surrounding area of Ken River, a tributary to the large Yamuna River feeding the famous Ganges River in India. The area had a large number of wild animals, prominent among them the Bengal tiger, along with ruins of castles and villages on its banks.

During the hunt Ray made many friends, including an elephant named Baha, which means Beautiful. As the adventure continued, Ray, Baasim, and Baha encountered many obstacles and dangerous situations along the way. Ray soon found out that nothing was easy on this hunt for the Bengal tiger.

There was a lot of worry back home when there was no communication from Ray by a certain date, a date which they all had expected to hear from him. Family and friends were soon switching into panic mode. A devastated Shannon was starting to think she had lost Ray forever, but she had plenty of support all around her.

The governments of India and the United States were made aware of Ray being missing. Shannon and Ray's family kept in constant communications with India's government and the United States embassy in India.

Ray was having an exciting, if at times dangerous, adventure, as he pursued his dream Bengal tiger. Especially with all the things happening with the villagers, Ray was worried he would never see Shannon or his mom and dad again.

Shannon had a very loyal friend, Denise Silva, who later married Joeseph Alexander, Ray's best friend. Both Ray and Joeseph built their houses on their family farms at the Sacramento Delta, right next to the Sacramento River. Living close to each other, Shannon and Denise were together very often. It really was a coincidence that both couples were married to best friends, and they definitely enjoyed each other's fellowship on the farms.

Shannon loved Ray's parents, Mary and Paul Johnson, regarding them as the kindest people she had ever met. Thus, it was extremely hard for Shannon when Paul, her father-in-law, died in her arms. Before he died, he whispered something in Shannon's ear that later she would share with others, when the time was right.

Ray's parents were also very happy to have Shannon in their lives. They would always refer to her as their daughter, and to them she was like a queen.

Ray eventually made it back from India to the Sacramento Delta in California. In the end, Ray unfortunately never got the chance to accomplish what he had intended, which was to get a Bengal tiger trophy. Instead he felt he got something way more precious. Now you have to read the book *The Bengal Ruby* to find out what it was that proved to be, in the end, more precious than a Bengal tiger.

After Ray returned from India, exciting things ensued in the next twenty years. Ray and Shannon had a son they named Tiger. Ray and Shannon's best friends, Joeseph and

Denise, had a daughter, Annie. Tiger and Annie grew up together spending their time hunting on the ranch. They were the best of friends throughout their young life.

Life was going smoothly on the Johnson ranch until that day Paul died in Shannon's arms. Shortly thereafter, Mary also died. The deaths of her beloved in-laws sent Shannon to an extended period of grieving. When that was over, she lived on with all the happy memories she shared with them.

The story ended in 1980 through an announcement by Shannon recalling the time Paul Johnson whispered something into her ear just before his death. This last announcement was to be a cause for another happy moment at the Johnson ranch.

CHAPTER 1

BORN TO HUNT

I t was always like Ray Johnson was doing something related to hunting on his parent's farm next to the Sacramento River. When he was a teenager in high school, he received his first 22 caliber rifle, a Marlin 39A lever action. He always called it the Cadillac of 22 caliber rifles. He always liked a scope on his Marlin 39A, because it provided for better accuracy.

Ray's friend Joeseph Alexander always said Ray was a true marksman, the only person he knew who would sight in a 22 rifle at 75 yards. Joeseph would then add maybe that's why he could call his Marlin 39A a Cadillac, for he was also a near-Cadillac marksman.

Ray would often shoot squirrels at 75–100 yards. He would hunt muskrats and shoot them in the nose to avoid damage for the stretched and dried pelts, fur intact, that he would then sell for money. He trapped muskrat, mink, and beaver when he was in high school. Aside from trapping, he also hunted muskrat in the canals near the farm, calling and luring them into position for a good shot at their noses.

In one year of his trapping operation, Ray managed 150 muskrat, 6 minks, and 2 beavers on a Christmas break. He would send the pelts to a furrier to receive payment.

Ray was a true outdoors person, always trying to outsmart any animal if he could. He believed it takes a good hunter to get a shot at any animal, for they can hear, see, and smell better than any human. Ray felt you really have to know the animal you are hunting to get an advantage, and that became his challenge to get a shot at any animal.

Graduating from high school, Ray still thought only about hunting. He always had a special passion for the big cats of the world, and as he read and studied about them, he came to the conclusion that the Bengal tiger was the king of cats. He admired their habits, beauty, and the bravery of the tiger as equal to none. Ray felt they fear nothing, including man; a tiger has no fear of man, when some animals just try to avoid man, and that is what makes a Bengal tiger so dangerous to hunt.

Finally, Ray dreamed of going to India to hunt a Bengal tiger as a trophy to put on the wall. He never let anybody in about his dream for quite a while, young as he was.

It was while Ray was in third year college when he remembered his lifelong dream, turning his mind to consider what caliber hunting rifle he would choose to hunt his first Bengal tiger. With that, he started to research the guns and caliber that would be the best for hunting the Bengal tiger in India. Winchester had come out with a 338 Winchester Magnum, which he felt comfortable with. After looking at the ballistics chart, it showed to be very flat shooting out to 200 yards and had high impact level of energy (knock down power). With this, Ray knew he would not have to compensate his aim point out to 200 yards. It was considered good for all Africa plains animal such as lions and the Bengal tiger, though short of being a good choice for elephants or rhinos which are considered thick skinned; however, this is not to say it would not kill an elephant or a rhino, if for some reason you had to in self-defense. Ray had made his choice of a rifle and the caliber that he would use for the hunt.

Finding himself with a little time one day after school, Ray travelled to a little town called Isleton (population 1200), located along the Sacramento River just about 3 miles south of his parent's farm. He was there to order a high-powered rifle from a local sporting goods store called Chins Sporting Goods and Hardware. The store was filled with various fishing and hunting equipment.

Ray's family had bought all their guns from Mr. Chin, having known them for many years. The Chins were of Chinese descent, all great people and good citizens of the community. It was a privilege to know them. Ray went into the store to place an order for a 338 Winchester Magnum model 70 Winchester rifle.

Mr. Chin commented, "Ray, what are you going to do with such a large high-powered rifle—go to Africa or something?"

Ray replied, "This one's for a dream of mine, Mr. Chin. Maybe in a year or so I will let you know what it is and what I'd done with my dream."

Mr. Chin stated, "Fair enough, but it is going to take six months to get the rifle since it is a new model."

"That's okay, I am in no hurry."

Ray was almost done with his third year of college at Cal. State Sacramento where he was going for a BS degree in mechanical engineering. Ray was still living at the farm with his parents, for at times his dad needed help around the farm. He commuted to college 40 miles away, not a long distance by any measure.

One day at the college's student lounge, Ray met a young lady: Shannon Doritee, from Lodi California, a mere 25 miles away from the farm. Finding they hit off pretty good, they dated often, until they found themselves together all the time. Ray thought Shannon was such a great gal and fun to be around.

Eventually Shannon asked Ray, "Would you like to come with me and meet my parents sometime?"

He responded, "Yes, that would be great." Ray was wondering what was up, but he did like Shannon so much, he couldn't say no.

So one day Ray did go with Shannon to meet her parents. In the living room, Shannon introduced Ray to her mom and dad, Elizabeth and Bob.

Shannon's mom acknowledged Ray and said, "Bob and I have heard a lot about you from Shannon, and it's been all good." With that, Ray started to feel more comfortable with Shannon's parents, and they all then conversed more freely.

Bob told Ray, "We own and operate a 100 acre vineyard in the Lodi area." That gave Ray a lot to talk about since he was around agriculture all his life.

"My parents farm in the Delta. They raise either tomatoes or corn, depending on the commodity prices my dad sees fit after negotiating with the tomato canneries," said Ray.

Ray liked Shannon's parents, and he was hoping they were okay with him, though he told himself only time would tell how they really felt about him. Ray did know that their grape vineyard was in one of California's largest grape and wine producing areas, which meant it was a very valuable piece of real estate. Ray knew someday Shannon would want to run the vineyard operation; it would be in her nature to do so, and it would enable her to help her parents when they got older.

Another time, Ray asked Shannon to go with him and meet his parents at the farm. Shannon was excited at the thought he wanted her to meet his parents. Ray let his mom and dad know beforehand that he would be bringing Shannon to meet them.

Once at the farm, Ray introduced Shannon to his mom and dad, Mary and Paul. Immediately he could tell both his parents loved Shannon, for after they started talking it was like he was not even around. It did not escape Ray that his parents were paying so much attention to Shannon, who in turn appeared to genuinely enjoy talking to Ray's parents mainly about what her parents did and how long they had been in the area; Shannon appeared very comfortable conversing with them.

Afterwards, Ray guided Shannon around the ranch, showing her where he hunted and the shooting range that he used to shoot at targets and sight in his rifles. She was amazed at the size of the bullfrogs in the pond and the canal.

Ray told Shannon, "I often go frog hunting with my friend, Joeseph. We'd eat the legs—by the way, Shannon, frog legs are considered a delicacy in restaurants."

"I guess you learn something every day. You know, Ray, frogs are really ugly, it's a good thing you only see the legs," replied Shannon.

After touring the ranch, Ray and Shannon headed to Sacramento, dropping her off at her apartment near the college. Ray and Shannon kissed and held each other tightly, both sensing their relationship had gotten really serious. They both said goodbye to each other and Ray left for home.

One day while Shannon and Ray were talking about just anything they could think of, Ray suddenly asked her if she would want to go to the ranch and shoot his favorite 22 Marlin 39A rifle at the shooting range he had shown her before.

"I would love to try shooting," said Shannon. With that, both were off to the Johnson ranch for some shooting.

At the shooting range, Ray set up the targets and the sandbags to support the rifle on the shooting bench. He gave Shannon some instructions on how to view through the scope, place the crosshairs on the target, and squeeze the trigger until the gun went off. Shannon shot five five-shot groups, and Ray felt she did pretty well for a target 50 yards away.

Seizing the special moment, Ray could not help himself anymore to tell her, "Shannon I really like you a lot. No—much more than that, Shannon, I have fallen deeply in love with you."

Tears welled up Shannon's eyes, and they stood there hugging and looking at each other. They both knew then this was to be a relationship, that someday they would be one with each other.

"Shannon, in three years you will have your master's degree in business. In a year I will have my BS degree in mechanical engineering. All of it looks good, but there is something I feel I need to share with you, one I feel is a very important item," Ray said.

Curious, Shannon asked, "What is it, Ray?"

Ray paused for a while before telling her, "It is about my dream to go to India to hunt a Bengal tiger someday."

Shannon found herself looking at a seat to think about what Ray told her. Shortly she gave him a nod, to indicate that she accepted and understood his wish.

"Ray, your honesty means so much to me. I can see your passion for hunting, and you must know by now that I would always want you to be happy. Ray, I want to make you the happiest man in my life."

"Thank you, Shannon. Also, you are the only person that knows about this, so please do not say anything, for I would not want to make my parents nervous or worried." Shannon agreed.

After target shooting, they packed up and headed back to her apartment. Getting out of the car, Ray took Shannon into his arms, looked into her beautiful blue eyes, and gave her an emotional kiss. Shannon could just feel the relationship on fire, and it's going to be hard to put out. Not to say she was against it: as a matter of fact, Shannon thought that the hotter the fire the better, and she certainly would not be the one to try to put this one fire out.

Entering the apartment, Ray asked Shannon, "Did you like shooting my rifle?"

"Yes, it was fun. I can't wait to go shooting again."

Ray was smiling. "Maybe someday you will have your own rifle." Ray gave her a hug and a kiss, and he then left for home.

Pulling into the yard at the farm, Ray went into the house and greeted his mom with a hug. His mom asked if he had a good day.

"I had a great day, Mom. Shannon shot targets today and she did very well—and I also told her that I had fallen in love with her."

Ray's mom didn't quite know how to respond, but eventually asked him, "Did Shannon like shooting—and more importantly, does she love you?"

"Mom, we are both in love, and it's just the greatest feeling I have ever had; and yes, she loved shooting." After a brief pause, Ray asked his mom, "Mom, what is your opinion of Shannon?"

"Son, she is a great woman. Don't let her get away. She has a precious personality. I am sure she will be a great asset to this family." Ray thought that was good to hear from his mom.

Ray's mom told him that Mr. Chin had called. "He said to tell you that your rifle just came in. I didn't know you had ordered a rifle."

Ray didn't respond to his mom's comment and she didn't seem to care.

Approaching dinnertime, Ray's dad, who had been out in the field working, entered the kitchen area where Ray and his mom were. After Ray's dad cleaned up, they sat down to eat. Ray and his parents proceeded to discuss the day's events.

Ray's mom directed her talk to Paul. "Paul, something happened to Ray today that is real exciting for our family."

Paul smiled like he knew something. "Well, I suppose it has something to do with Shannon. I have seen them out at the shooting range, and they looked like they were having a good time."

"What Mom is alluding to, Dad, is that I told Shannon that I am in love with her, and we are both so excited. And she also likes shooting."

Ray's dad smiled even more, sitting in deep thought, before he said, "Well, Mom was right, this is a great day for the Johnson family, and Ray, thank you for picking Shannon. You don't know how much I was hoping she would be the one for you." Just then, a thought suddenly occurred to Ray's dad. "Are you trying to get Shannon hooked on hunting?"

"You know, Dad, I believe Shannon will be a hunter someday, so yes, and the plan is working."

Paul sat back in his chair smiling while looking at Mary. "Mary, it seems there is going to be another hunter in the Johnson family."

Ray's mom was looking back at Paul. "You know, that thought also occurred to me. One thing for sure, she will be the prettiest hunter in the Sacramento Delta."

Ray mentioned to his parents, "If I was to take a night class at college, I would be graduating this coming June. I really want to get it over with."

His mom with a grin said, "Your dad and I are both so proud of you for all that you have accomplished."

At this point, Ray was ready to retire for the night, mindful of a busy day ahead. "Good night, Mom and Dad, see you in the morning."

With no school for Ray on Saturday, he decided to pick up the rifle from Mr. Chin's store. Getting there, he saw Mr. Chin at the counter and they greeted each other.

Mr. Chin was in a good mood, announcing, "Ray, are you here to pick up your cannon? It did come in."

"That's right," replied Ray.

Looking around, noticed a 39A Marlin on the gun rack. Ray asked Mr. Chin, "Do you have any four-power rifle scopes?"

"Yes, I have a Bushnell Banner; they are good scopes especially for the money."

"I will take the 39A, the scope, along with the 338 Magnum rifle, and two boxes of 338 magnum ammunition."

"Ray, you already have a Marlin 39A, I sold it to you years ago."

"Mr. Chin, it's a gift for someone really special."

"Is it for a gal named Shannon?" Mr. Chin, smiling at Ray, asked.

"Yes, how did you know?"

"Ray, your mom and dad have been telling people that they really like Shannon; I believe that's her name."

Ray confirmed that it was her name, then wondered if Mr. Chin was still offering hunting safety classes, "Do you still offer those hunting safety classes? Shannon could use one to get a hunting license."

"I offer a class on Saturdays," Mr. Chin replied.

Ray paid for all the items and said goodbye to Mr. Chin. Going out the door, Ray turned and said, "Mr. Chin, you may meet Shannon some Saturday in the near future."

It was still early, so Ray called his friend Joeseph to come over so they could go out and sight in his new 338 Winchester Magnum.

While waiting, Ray mounted a Redfield 3-9 variable power scope on the new rifle. Ray had previously bought the scope for this rifle when it went on sale. Redfield scopes were high priced, but have a very good reputation for reliability, which Ray needed for what he was planning to do.

Joeseph pulled into the yard. Ray had already loaded the pickup truck with all the gear, so they headed out to the rifle range at the back of the ranch. They set up the target and put sandbags on the bench for rifle support, as commonly done to sight in rifles and target shooting.

Seeing the 338 Winchester Magnum cartridges, Joeseph said, "What are you going to hunt with this monster?"

"You'll know soon enough," Ray replied as he boresighted the rifle by looking through the barrel with the action removed. This was just to get the bullet on the target, so you can then use the scope adjustments to zero in your rifle. The target was set up at 100 yards. Ray's point of aim would be to zero it at ¾ inch high at 100 yards. This would give a good point of impact at 30 yards to 200 yards with no trajectory compensation for distance, a common practice.

Then came the big moment: Ray loaded the rifle with four cartridges and positioned the rifle on the sandbags, aimed, and fired. He felt it was a hard recoil but manageable. From that shot he made the appropriate scope adjustments. He did this about four more times and felt he was ready for a three-shot group to determine if the point of impact was where he wanted it. He shot a three-shot group, a 1 inch group, and impact point was right where he wanted it to be. So the rifle certainly was not a lemon for what he was planning. He needed reliability and accuracy, and Winchester model 70s are noted for both.

Ray asked Joeseph. "Do you want to shoot my rifle? The recoil really isn't that bad."

Joeseph quickly said, "No way will I put my shoulder to that abuse."

"Yes, it is sort of abusive" Ray admitted.

Soon they were back at the ranch house. Joeseph was still wondering what his friend was going to hunt with that monster.

Ray told him, "Joeseph, this is for a dream that I have had for years. I will tell you someday in the near future."

"Okay, Ray. just curious and anxious to know. I know it has to be something big."

CHAPTER 2

SHANNON BECOMES A HUNTER

R ay told his mom and dad that he planned to graduate in June, though he thought he would do it in January. He wanted to graduate early to have extra time to start planning for his hunting trip to India. His immediate goal was to look for a hunting guide notably experienced in going after a Bengal tiger.

Ray needed to look at traveling plans and get familiar with good Bengal tiger hunting areas in India, hunting permits, and passports.

Ray researched the weather in the central part of India, learning that the average temperature is 90°F from April to late June, summertime in the country; he wanted to avoid the monsoon season with its heavy rains. Ray considered May 1, 1960 a good date, but he knew this will all be decided when a hunting guide is contacted.

One of Ray's biggest concerns was how his parents were going to respond about the trip, and that he would be gone about sixty days. Being close to his parents, he thought it would be hard on them not having him around for that period of time. But with Shannon around, he thought maybe she could plan to help his parents through the situation.

Hanging out with Shannon at the campus one day, Ray remembered the rifle he bought her.

"Shannon, I forgot to tell you I bought you a Marlin 39A 22 caliber rifle the other day. Would you like to go Saturday and sight it in?"

"Oh, Ray, I can't wait! My own rifle to go hunting with!" Ray was happy she used the word "hunting," and he hadn't even mentioned it.

"It's set then, Shannon. If you could drive to the ranch, I will see you about 9:00 AM. I think it would be good for you to get used to the levee roads and the trip through Isleton."

"That would be fine." They hugged, kissed, and said goodbye, big smiles on their faces.

As he was leaving, Ray said, "Shannon, I have to go downtown Sacramento to do some shopping. I will see you Saturday."

After shopping in Sacramento, Ray headed for home. Inside he greeted his mom with the usual hug. His mom was busy cooking dinner as Paul came in from the field.

"How are things going today, Dad, is the tomato crop still looking good?" Ray asked Paul.

"I have had better days, son. I had trouble priming the pump on the Sacramento River. I believe the shaft packing is going to need to be changed. But as far as the tomato crop is concerned, it is going to be a good yielding crop." Dinner ready, the three of them sat down to eat.

"How is Shannon doing these days? Haven't seen her in a while, is she okay?" Paul asked Ray.

"She is fine, Dad. In fact she will be here in the morning. We are going to sight in her new rifle."

"I heard you bought her a rifle," Paul replied.

"How did you know I bought her a rifle, Dad?"

"Mr. Chin. He told me you bought Shannon a rifle and most likely a hunting safety class through him for a hunting license."

"News really travels fast," Ray replied.

Ray realized they were having a favorite meal of his. "Mom, this tomato beef roast is great as usual. Someday you should tell Shannon how to cook this special recipe of yours."

"Is there any particular reason why you would want Shannon to have the recipe?" his mom asked him with a smile.

"Well, someday she may be cooking it for me," Ray replied, laughing. Equally, his mom and dad's faces were all smiles. His reply was good music to their ears.

"I couldn't believe when I told her about the rifle, the first thing that came out of her mouth was she couldn't wait for her own rifle to go hunting with. I truly believe Shannon will be a hunter," he told them.

"So anyway, we will sight in her rifle tomorrow morning."

Ray hoped Shannon would like hunting, that she would come out to the ranch often to visit and to hunt—what his parents would need to fill the void when he was in India. He hoped to discuss the matter later with Shannon.

Saturday morning, Shannon drove into the yard at the ranch house. Ray went to greet her with a hug and a kiss before proceeding inside to say hello to Mom and Dad.

"Hello, Shannon. It appears you are the owner of a new rifle," Ray's mom greeted Shannon, smiling.

"Oh, Mom, can you believe Ray bought me my own rifle! How are you doing this morning? Is Dad already working in the field?"

"Shannon I am feeling fine, and yes Paul is already working in the field."

Shannon took Ray by surprise when she referred to his parents as Mom and Dad. Ray knew it must have made Mom extremely happy, and she probably could hardly wait to tell Dad.

After a short conversation Ray said, "Well, Mom, Shannon and I are going to sight in her new rifle. I know she is excited to get going."

"Oh, Mom, I can't wait to go hunting. I also want to share with you that I have fallen in love with your son."

"Thank you for sharing that with me, Shannon. I will certainly tell Paul what you just shared with me—and Shannon, Ray has also shared the same feeling toward you with Paul and me."

Ray noted the word "Mom" again; it's a wonder Mom's buttons didn't pop off her dress this time. Ray was extremely happy on how this morning started off.

Shannon and Ray were soon on their way to the rifle shooting range at the back of the ranch, having already loaded the pickup truck with all the things they would need.

"Why don't you drive; you'll get used to it, and you may find it fun driving around the ranch."

At the shooting range, Ray took Shannon's rifle out of its case. She was excited.

"This is a 22 caliber rifle, Marlin 39A. You should use 22 long rifle hollow point ammo for hunting, as the hollow points always makes better kills. It expands more as it hits the animal, creating more damage; also, it is more humane since the animal will die faster." She seemed to understand the concept of what he was saying.

Before Ray had her load the rifle, he instructed her in all the safety rules of handling a gun. As she had shot his rifle before, she knew her way around the use of scope. Ray set up targets, also putting a tomato on the ground. Now close to Shannon, Ray looked at her blue eye and gave her an emotional kiss.

"Shannon, it's so wonderful to be in love." Shannon was speechless, tears in her eyes.

"Shannon, this is your gun. Let's see you sight it in," he told her at last.

"Okay, Ray, let's go for it."

Ray had her shoot three times at the tomato. He noticed it was shooting low and to the right. Ray explained to her that each click on the scope meant 1/8 inch at 50 yards, which was where the targets were set, and if shooting low she needed to click up; if shooting to the left, she needed to click to the right. Shannon caught on very fast and she eventually zeroed the rifle in on the target at 50 yards.

After sighting in the rifle, Ray told her, "I think it's best for you to sight in at 50 yards, since you are a beginner."

Ray next introduced a 22 caliber Magnum Marlin bolt action rifle to Shannon. Since her 39A rifle was a lever action, Ray had to show her how a bolt action worked and the safety latch, and how to load cartridges into the clip. It was already sighted in, so he had her shoot at the five targets that he had put up at 50 yards. She did very well.

"This one appears to be a more accurate rifle," she told him.

"Yes, you can shoot up to 100 yards with this rifle."

"Shannon, when I am gone to India, feel free to use the 22 Magnum on a coyote if you spot one; as they are bigger, they require more killing power, and the 22 Magnum has more killing power than the 22 long rifle. Also, if you want to make longer shots at Cottontail rabbits or ground squirrels, this would be a good rifle to use."

Shannon then started shooting at objects other than targets. Ray set out some tomatoes at 50 yards and 75 yards.

He told Shannon, "Holding a rifle steady is difficult in actual hunting conditions, especially when hunting small animals that require a more steady hand from the shooter." Ray showed her the prone position and the sitting position, often used and taught by the military; again, she easily understood the two concepts. She decided to try the prone position and use her new Marlin 39A-22.

"Shannon, shoot at one of the tomatoes positioned at 50 yards." After trying five shots and never hitting a tomato, she appeared a little frustrated.

"You have to be calm, and you have to squeeze the trigger slowly. You must not jerk it, for any movement of the barrel caused by a trigger jerk can have a large effect on the aiming point." She was ready to try again. One shot had the tomato blew apart; she shot at four more tomatoes and hit them all. Ray was amazed at her early success at shooting in a true field hunting condition.

"Shannon, I am so proud of you!" Ray told her. "I want you to shoot at a tomato at 75 yards. What do you think you are going to have to do?"

"I will have to aim higher, as the rifle was sighted in at 50 yards."

"That's amazing, Shannon. Look at the trajectory chart. How much higher would you say your aiming point will be?"

After looking at the chart, she said, "1¼ inches."

"That's right. Go ahead and give it a try. Remember, longer distance requires better control by the shooter; also squeeze, not jerk the trigger for better control." She took four shots and hit three tomatoes.

Ray knelt down to her and she turned her face towards him. He gave her a kiss and said to her, "What do I have here—Annie Oakley?"

She responded, "No, you have Shannon—who is Annie Oakley?"

"Annie Oakley was a famous female sharpshooter. She was in the Buffalo Bill Cody's Wild West Shows in the

1890s. She performed all over the USA using a 22 caliber Marlin 39 rifle like yours to show off her skills in shooting."

Shannon also got to her knees, looking straight into his eyes. With her arms around him, she pulled him tightly close to her and gave him a kiss that he would remember forever.

"Shannon, that was one heck of a kiss! That was the most wonderful feeling ever in my life!"

"Ray, this has been a wonderful day; I love you more every time I am around you," she told him.

"The day is not over yet. I also love you more as we spend more time together, and I believe God has a plan for both of us." Shannon was wondering what Ray meant when he said the day is not over yet.

After getting over the kiss, Ray told Shannon, "I have one more shooting exercise for you to do today."

Shannon was wondering what was to come next. Ray went to the pickup truck, took out the Marlin 22 Magnum rifle, and handed it to Shannon.

"Do you remember I told you this rifle is capable of 100 yard shots? Well, I have a Cottontail rabbit target that I am going to set at 100 yards. There will be two cardboard boxes and one will have the Cottontail rabbit target on it."

Ray then took the boxes with the target and set them about 5 feet apart about 100 yards away. He came back to where Shannon was waiting; she loaded her cartridges into the clip and inserted it into the rifle, before going down in the prone position ready for the task. This time, Ray lay down beside her, his arm on her back to comfort her.

"Shannon, this rifle has a 3 to 9 power scope. Because of the distance, you should set it on 9 power, and since it was sighted in at 50 yards, you should aim 1¾ inches high." Shannon understood everything Ray was saying.

"Shoot at the rabbit target on the box on the left, and remember to aim high," he reminded her.

One shot and she said, "I hit the rabbit."

"Good shooting, Shannon." At that point, Ray just had to hug and kiss her. "You are almost ready to hunt." She then turned to Ray and gave him one of those kisses again.

After getting over the kiss, Ray told her, "This next target is going to be a tough one; a 3 inch diameter tomato sits on top of the box on the right. I hope you are up to the task; if you hit it once in three shots, you are ready to hunt." Ray just had to give her a kiss before she sighted in on the tomato.

"Ray, you and I are sure in a kissing mood today."

"Looks so. Well, go ahead shoot the tomato off the box. Remember you only have three shots to hit it." Ray was smiling as they lay next to each other; she sighted in on the tomato and pulled the trigger.

"I knocked it off the box—I am a hunter!" she exclaimed. Shannon didn't say another word for about 30 seconds, turning to Ray, tears flooding her beautiful blue eyes.

"Shannon, why are you crying?" Ray asked her, smiling.

She answered, "I saw a message pop up after I shot the tomato off the box."

"Well, Shannon, what does the message say?" She started to read the message on the cardboard box through the lens of the 9 power scope.

"To Shannon from Ray: Shannon, this has been a beautiful day; we are both full of emotion towards each other. Today I propose to marry you, so we could spend our life together. Shannon, look at me now and give me your answer."

"The answer is so simple and easy. Ray, I have dreamed of being your wife for quite a while; today you made my dream come true, so yes—yes—yes, I will marry you and be your wife!"

She planted another emotional kiss on Ray, caressing him much longer this time. Ray asked for her hand, pulled out a diamond ring, and slipped it onto her finger.

"Shannon, this is the start of my commitment to you. I will always love you." Like two love birds, the two of them started to settle down.

Shannon had a question, "Ray, when and where did you get the ring?"

"Remember the day I dropped you off at your apartment and I said I had to go down town Sacramento to do some shopping?"

"Yes, I remember," she replied.

They were ready to go back to the ranch house when they heard and saw a pickup truck coming down the dirt road next to the tomato field.

"Oh, it's Mom and Dad! They usually come out once a day together to look at the tomato and cornfields, to see how the crops are coming along."

The pickup truck stopped right where Shannon and Ray were.

"Well, how are you two doing today," Paul greeted them. A look at Shannon and he asked, "What's wrong? You look like you have been crying. Did Ray do something to you?"

"Yes."

Ray's dad came out of the pickup. "Ray, what the hell did you do to Shannon?"

"Hold on, Dad! Your son just made this the greatest day of my life," and she held up her hand showing the engagement ring that she just got from their son. Ray's parents were beside themselves. They walked over to Ray and Shannon, and all four hugged each other like this was the greatest day ever on the Johnson farm.

"Paul, I think we just gained a daughter, and if God wills it, we will have grandchildren in our lives," Mary said, smiling.

"Well, shall we all go home to for lunch and celebrate this occasion?"

Riding their pickup trucks, they drove back to the ranch house. Ray took out the guns and ammo out of the pickup truck, taking Shannon inside the house and showing her the gun safe in his room, giving her the combination.

"I will give you the keys to the house and my pickup truck, and I will let my parents know at the appropriate time before I leave for India," he told her.

Making it back to the kitchen, they saw Mary busy making lunch, while Paul watched the news.

"Mom, can I use your phone? I need to call my parents to let them know that Ray and I would be over to visit them later today?" Shannon asked Mary.

Sure—go ahead, Shannon, you are welcome to use anything in or around this house or ranch. We all want you feel comfortable around this family," Mary told her.

"Thanks, Mom, you have always made me feel comfortable and treated me so good," Shannon replied.

On the phone with her parents, Shannon didn't give any details about the visit to surprise them. Ray sat there listening, hoping it would be a surprise they would be okay with, for he never did get any hint he was acceptable to them.

After Mary called everybody to have lunch, the four of them set around the table conversing about many things.

"Shannon, have you called your parents? You know someday we need to meet them," Mary addressed Shannon.

"Yes, I did. Ray and I will visit them about 4 o'clock, and most certainly our two families should meet, especially now." It was getting close to 3 o'clock.

"Well, Mom and Dad, I think we will be heading off to Lodi to visit Shannon's parents, to give them the latest news about Shannon and me."

Shannon gave Paul and Mary a big hug, saying, "Thanks so much for welcoming me into your family and letting me share your son with you. Oh, by the way, Mom, if you could give me your recipe for the beef tomato roast that Ray likes to talk about so much, maybe I can try my hand at cooking. I will probably need guidance from you on that. Goodbye, and I love you both."

Ray and Shannon started their trip to Lodi about 25 miles away. On the way, they kept talking about the wonderful day they just had, a day full of excitement and all those kisses.

Ray was thinking, *Shannon you sure hit it off with my parents. I believe my parents think this day is the most exciting day on the Johnson ranch, and a new era in the Johnson family, and I want to thank you for being the main part of it.*

Shannon's mind was in another world. "Oh, Ray, we can't forget we need to go see Mr. Chin so I can take the hunting safety test for my hunting license. I can't wait to meet him!" she told him.

Ray was getting a little nervous approaching the grape vineyard where Shannon's parents lived. He hoped they would accept him into their family. He knew the time was getting close for him to find out what their reactions would be, for they were now pulling into the driveway. Shannon seemed perfectly calm, so maybe it's something he didn't need to worry about.

Out of the car, Ray looked at Shannon and gave her a hug and a kiss. Shannon just looked at Ray with those passionate blue eyes. She smiled at Ray, knowing he was probably nervous.

Into the house, Shannon called out, "Hey, Mom, Dad, Ray and I are here! You guys okay?"

Shannon's mom came out to greet them both. "It's good to see you both. Haven't seen Shannon for a week or so. Ray, how have you been? Haven't seen you for a long time!"

"I have been fine, real busy. Don't know if Shannon told you, but I plan to graduate engineering school in June."

"That's great, Ray, what an achievement!"

Shannon had been thinking, *Oh, no, he's going to tell them we are engaged to be married!* breathing a sigh of relief when it did not happen.

"Where is Dad?" Shannon asked.

"He will be coming in shortly. He is out in the vineyard but he knows you both are coming. He is anxious to see you, especially Ray, since we haven't seen much of him lately. He thinks a lot of Ray."

Ray was relieved to hear Shannon's mom's comment. It was good news to his ears. Shannon was smiling. Ray was starting to think that maybe Shannon had been preparing her parents that their relationship was getting serious.

Soon Shannon's dad walked in, giving Shannon a big hug, before shaking Ray's hand.

"Well, did you two have some fun out at the ranch today?" Shannon's dad asked.

"We sure did, Mr. Doritee. I gave Shannon a rifle and I am teaching her shooting and hunting methods."

"Shannon did mention it, and she was so excited about hunting. It certainly sounds like fun to me. And Ray, let me tell you something: you can just call us Dad and Mom."

Ray was then sure Shannon had talked to her parents about their serious relationship. He certainly was more comfortable with the situation, feeling accepted.

The four of them sat in the living room conversing about anything that came to mind. Shannon's dad and Ray mainly talked about farming, while Shannon and her mom were having a good old Mom to daughter talk. Shannon did not want to expose her ring finger yet, wanting to surprise her parents with the news. Ray just didn't know how and when she was going to bring up the subject.

Shannon got both her mom and dad's attention by saying, "At today's shooting lessons, Ray set up a Cottontail rabbit target on a cardboard box 100 yards away and told me to shoot at it, and I hit it."

"Well, Shannon, that must have been exciting," her dad said. Ray was thinking, *Here it comes*, and he started to get tears in his eyes—and he was not one given to crying.

Shannon then continued where she left off telling her parents, "Ray also set up a cardboard box at 100 yards with a 3-inch diameter tomato on top of the box; he told me I have three shots to hit it for me to be ready to hunt."

"Well, what happened?" her mom asked, excitement in her voice.

Shannon replied, "Dad, Mom, I hit the tomato off the box on my first shot and ecstatically yelled, 'I am a hunter!' But Mom, Dad, come sit beside me to share with me the most wonderful event of my life. After I shot the tomato off the box, I noticed something pop up after the tomato went flying, and it had a message."

"What did the message say, Shannon?" both her parents asked.

"It said, 'To Shannon from Ray: Shannon, this has been a beautiful day; we are both full of emotion towards each other. Today I propose to marry you, so we could spend our life together. Shannon, look at me now and give me your answer.'

"Mom, Dad, I gave him my answer: 'Yes—yes!' He then asked for my hand and slipped this ring onto my ring finger, and said, 'This is the start of my commitment to you.'" With that, she showed the engagement ring to both her parents, who were then sitting beside their daughter. In a short time, the whole family was in tears of happiness, Ray included.

Ray talked about how grateful he was to be able to share their daughter Shannon with them.

"Dad, Mom, I can't begin to tell you how much Shannon means to me, and I am so grateful that you both think I am okay for your daughter."

"Well, Ray, you had very good references. When Shannon said the two of you were getting serious and that she loved you so much, Dad and I went to Isleton to get some character references. We received only positive comments about you, as well as your mom and dad. I even recall one especially interesting conversation with Mr. Chin and his wife who owned the sporting goods store where you buy all your guns," Shannon's mom said.

"Mr. Chin told us, 'We have known the Johnsons for years, and I will tell you if you can't like the Johnsons you can't like anybody. If you need help and the Johnsons found out, they would be at your door to find out how they could help.'"

Dad told Ray, "We just wanted to make sure you were okay for our daughter, and you passed the test."

"Thank you for the vote of confidence. I have always been sincere with Shannon from the beginning of our relationship, and that's how it will be forever. I look forward to being part of your family, and I can say Shannon is loved and welcomed by my parents also."

Ray ended the visit by saying, "Well, I think Shannon and I will head back to the ranch for her car. She has school tomorrow. Oh, and please don't hesitate to call my parents. I am sure they are anxious to talk and meet with you." Shannon and Ray gave both of them a hug and went on their way.

Driving back to the farm, Shannon and Ray were excited about her parents' response to their engagement.

"We need to go see Mr. Chin about your hunting license," Ray said.

"This Saturday morning would be okay with me," replied Shannon.

"Okay, let's make it 9 o'clock Saturday morning." It was late when they pulled into the driveway at the farm, so Ray gave Shannon a kiss and said, "Drive carefully."

About that time, Ray's mom came out the door and said, "Shannon, be careful driving on the levee road, By the way, we talked on the phone with your mom and dad and they are excited about Ray like we are about you. Good night, Shannon, and have pleasant dreams tonight."

CHAPTER 3

SHANNON IS NOW A TRUE HUNTER

After the excitement at the Johnson ranch, Ray found himself with a lot of things to do: graduate college, get Shannon hunting with confidence and other details so she would enjoy the sport. Ray was hoping Shannon would come to the ranch to hunt and visit his parents while he was on his own adventure with the Bengal tiger in India. At some point, Ray had to decide how and when he would announce his impending trip to India.

One morning, Ray decided to call his friend Joeseph Alexander and let him know about the news of him being engaged to Shannon.

"Hey, Joeseph, this is Ray. How have you been, I haven't talked to you in a while."

"We sure don't see each other as much anymore since we both started college. Of course you have Shannon in your life. You know, I have never met Shannon," Joeseph said.

"Well, Joeseph, I proposed to Shannon last Saturday while giving her some lessons in shooting and hunting," Ray said.

"Then congratulations to you both! So you are trying to make Shannon a hunter—I don't know why, but it really doesn't surprise me," Joeseph replied.

"I plan on having Shannon over for breakfast on Saturday morning about 9 o'clock. After breakfast I will take her down to Mr. Chin's to take the hunting safety class so she can get a hunting license. Why don't you come over for breakfast? I know Mom would enjoy seeing you."

"I will be over on Saturday. Oh, Ray, you think your mom could have linguica and eggs for breakfast? You know that's my favorite sausage. Hopefully Shannon will like it."

"I will tell Mom about the menu for Saturday morning. Goodbye Joeseph, see you Saturday." After hanging up the phone, Ray talked to his mom about the breakfast with Shannon and Joeseph.

"I will cook linguica and eggs. Joeseph loves linguica. I hope Shannon likes it; if not I can always cook something else," said Mary, excited.

"Mom, Joeseph did mention if you could cook linguica and eggs."

"I love that boy like he is my own son, just like his mother loves you, Ray," Mary replied, laughing.

Later, Ray called Shannon. "Can you come over Saturday at 9 o'clock for breakfast? You will meet my longtime friend and neighbor, Joeseph, who would be with us. After breakfast, I will take you down to Isleton to take the hunting safety test for the hunting license."

Shannon was excited. "That sounds like a great Saturday morning! Looking forward to be there. See you Saturday at 9 o'clock. Oh, Ray, do you think we could do a little hunting if I get my license?"

"We can certainly give it a try. Okay, Saturday it is! I love you." And they hung up the phone.

Saturday found Ray in the kitchen talking to his mom and dad about Shannon all excited about taking the hunting safety test.

"I have given Shannon the gun safe combination. I also want to give her the house and pickup truck keys just in case I am not around and she wanted to go hunting, is that okay?"

"Oh, most certainly, Ray. If you can't trust Shannon, who can you trust?" Mary replied.

Ray and his mom discussed the arrival of Shannon and Joeseph for the linguica and eggs breakfast. A thought suddenly occurred to Mary.

"Ray, is Joeseph seeing any gal on a regular basis?"

"I am not aware of him seeing anyone, or at least he hasn't mentioned anyone special to me."

Just then, Ray noticed someone approaching. "Oh, here comes Joeseph!"

"Hi Mom, Dad, how have you two been? Always happy to be here and touch base with you both. I hope Shannon doesn't think it is strange that I call you Mom and Dad," Joeseph greeted them.

"Joeseph, believe me she won't think it's strange. She herself started calling us both Mom and Dad early on, maybe about the first or second time she met us."

Ray said, "It was the first time, Mom. I thought your buttons were going to pop off your dress when she called you Mom."

Joeseph just had to say, "Doesn't surprise me. You both are so loving I don't know anybody that doesn't like the Johnsons."

"Joeseph, remember this: the same is true of your parents," Paul reminded him.

Seeing Shannon arrive, Ray went out to greet her with a hug and a kiss. Inside they proceeded and Ray introduced Shannon to Joeseph. Ray explained to Shannon that Joeseph and he were neighbors, Joeseph's parents owning the ranch just down the road, both of them growing up together. For his part, Joeseph congratulated Shannon on her engagement to Ray.

"Shannon you are fortunate to be part of the Johnson family, as I am sure Ray is a lucky man to be part of your family. I really envy you both," Joeseph concluded. With that, Mary started serving breakfast.

"What kind of sausage is this? It sure smells and tastes good," Shannon said about the food after a while.

"It's Portuguese linguica; you know, Mom Johnson is Portuguese and she really has some good Portuguese recipes," Joeseph said, smiling.

"Now, Shannon, if you don't care for the linguica, I will cook you ham or Bacon—whatever you choose," Mary added.

"Actually, Mom, I find the flavor good. I have never had a sausage compare to this ever. It's great," Shannon replied.

Joeseph was grinning hearing that. "Well, Shannon, when you and Ray get married, don't forget to have me over for breakfast some time."

"We won't forget, Joeseph," Shannon answered.

With everybody just generally conversing and getting along, Shannon asked Joeseph, "Are you attending college somewhere?"

"I am attending UC Davis, taking up agriculture focusing on row crops," Joeseph replied.

"Well, that sounds interesting," Shannon replied. "My best friend also studies at UC Davis, also majoring in agriculture, though her main interest is with wine and grape production for her parents' vineyard in the Lodi area."

"What's your friend's name?" Joeseph seemed compelled to ask.

"Denise Silva."

"Oh, she is Portuguese!"

"Yes, full blooded. You know, thinking back, Denise's mom may have cooked linguica and eggs for Denise and me. But I will tell you one time she cooked this soup that had beef and spices, and you ate this bread covered with mint that she had poured hot broth over. So it really was soggy spicy bread with a mint flavor, and it was so good!"

Hearing Shannon's story, Ray's mom and dad smiled from ear to ear.

"Mom Johnson makes it, too," said Joeseph, grinning, "and Shannon you are right, it is great flavored bread and meat. It's called *soupas*. Maybe you can get the recipe from Mom someday and give it a try. I sure hope you both get married soon so I could have another place to have *soupas*."

"I believe the sooner the better," Ray said.

Shannon had a big smile at Ray's remark, but nobody else seemed to catch on to what Ray had just said.

Still smiling, Shannon went on to say, "I had already mentioned to Mom she needs to teach me how to cook some of her favorite recipes. And sure, Joeseph, you will always be invited for *soupas*."

From the ongoing conversation, Ray realized that Joeseph appeared to be very interested in Shannon's best friend Denise Silva, and Shannon was easily giving information about her. Ray was thinking he would put money on the table that somehow Joeseph will find Denise at college, but considered it was just a thought that he had.

With breakfast done, Ray told everybody, "Well, Shannon and I have to go to Isleton to see Mr. Chin about the hunting safety test."

"While Shannon is taking the test, could you drop by the hardware store and pick up some nuts and bolts?" Paul said. "Also, I need some items from Isleton Auto Supply. You may ask Kate or Sam for a filter for my pickup truck—here's the list."

"Sure, Dad; I always enjoy talking to Sam or Kate. They just always seemed to want to talk a little with me," Ray replied.

Soon Ray and Shannon were on their way to Isleton, about 3 miles away. Approaching Isleton they turned left, went down the grade from the levee road, and emerged in Isleton's Chinatown, where Mr. Chins Store was. They stopped in front of the store.

Looking at Shannon, Ray said, "Well, aren't you getting excited about getting a California hunting license?"

"I sure am excited!" she answered.

"Ray, back at breakfast table, what did you mean about getting married the sooner the better?" Shannon was smiling as she waited for Ray's answer.

For a moment Ray sat there looking at Shannon, before he managed to say, "At one point I thought we could get married after my hunting trip to India, but I don't think we can wait that long."

"Why?" Shannon asked, smile still on her face.

"Shannon, every time we hold each other and kiss, you know yourself we both get very sexually aroused."

Still holding her smile, Shannon said, "That's a good sign, Ray; a woman should get her man aroused, borne of our love for each other, and you know the whole world wouldn't come to an end if we did make a mistake before we were married. But I know where you are coming from: for ourselves, our parents, and our God, we should try to refrain from premarital sex."

With that, Ray quickly scooted over to Shannon, grabbed her, and gave her a kiss. "Oh my God, we better quickly go in to see Mr. Chin for your hunting safety test."

Out of the pickup truck they went and headed to Mr. Chin's store. "I can't wait to meet the Chins after hearing so much about them," Shannon said. As they walked through the door, the bell rang to let the owners know a customer had entered.

Coming out, Mr. Chin quickened his pace when he saw it was Ray, walking by him and right to Shannon, giving her a hug.

"Oh, Mrs. Chin and I couldn't wait to meet you! You picked a good man and a wonderful family! We have known the Johnsons forever. You will be so happy to be part of the Johnson family. Shannon, all of Isleton knows all about you. Ray's mom and dad have told everybody about you."

Mrs. Chin, aware of Ray and Shannon's presence, made her way out to greet them—discreetly calling the fire department before doing so. In a short while, Shannon heard a horn blow five times.

She said, "What's that?"

Mr. Chin said, "That should mean fire in town; today, however, they come to Chin's sporting goods to put out fire."

"I don't see any fire," Shannon said.

"Well, when you kiss Ray maybe fire gets too hot and needs to be extinguished—really, Shannon, this is Isleton's way of welcoming you to our community."

"Mr. Chin, Shannon and I were just talking about the fire," Ray said, laughing.

Outside the fire trucks came, along with some people from the community to show Shannon a welcome banner from the town of Isleton.

After all the excitement, Ray said, "Well, Mr. Chin, Shannon wants to take the hunting safety test so she can get her hunting license—can she take the test this morning?"

"Certainly," Mr. Chin said. "I will give her the test. If she passes, I will issue her a hunting license."

While Shannon was taking the test, Ray made his way to the hardware store and Isleton Auto Supply to get the items that his dad put on a list. Once done, he went back to Chinatown to see if Shannon had finished taking her test.

Walking into the Chins' store, Ray saw Shannon having just finished. Mr. Chin had corrected the written part, and she had passed the gun handling part.

"Shannon passed both parts and can now purchase a California hunting license," Mr. Chin confirmed. The license paperwork was soon filled out, and Ray paid for the license. Ray and Shannon bade goodbye to Mr. and Mrs. Chin and headed to the pickup truck.

When they got into the pickup truck, Ray pulled Shannon to him and said, "Good job—you did great!" kissing her.

Shannon smiled, "That was pretty good, Ray, you really aroused me."

"Good—that's what men are supposed to do with their women." Shannon smiled and they headed back to the ranch.

It was about lunchtime when they went inside and found Mary with some sandwiches. The three sat down to eat.

"Where is Dad?" Ray asked.

Mom answered, "He said he would be late for lunch from irrigating the corn. Shannon, did you get your hunting license?"

"I did, Mom—I also got a fire truck welcome from the Isleton community fire department. Mr. Chin told us the fire trucks came to put out the fire after Ray and I would kiss. Can you believe he said that?"

"Could be something you two need to think about. I know you both will be very careful, won't you?" Mary replied thoughtfully.

"Yes, Mom, we will be careful," both replied slowly in their low voices.

In a moment, Ray turned to Shannon. "Well, you got your license—are you ready to actually go hunting now?"

"Let's go!" Shannon replied.

Both were soon at the gun safe, Shannon opening it.

"Take what rifle you want," Ray said from behind her.

Shannon took the Marlin 39A-22—her rifle, followed by the right ammo. Back to the pickup truck, Shannon drove to where Ray directed her.

"Let's try the road next to the pond. Sometimes there are jack rabbits or cottontail rabbits there. If you get a jack rabbit, we just leave it to the scavengers, but if you get a cottontail rabbit, we will take it, and you will have to learn how to dress it out so we can eat it."

"Oh, that sounds interesting—what do you mean *dress it out?*"

"You have to skin it, gut it, and cut the head off. If you get one we will freeze it for they aren't very big, so you need quite a few to make a meal. So now are you ready for it?"

"I guess I am as ready as I will ever be."

Approaching the pond, Ray noticed a cottontail rabbit right away.

"Stop, Shannon, turn the engine off...! Look, down the road is a cottontail rabbit,"

"Ya!" Shannon said, "What do we do now?"

"This part of hunting is called stalking," Ray started. "The rabbit is too far away, so we have to get closer," he finished.

Ray quietly told Shannon, "There is a slight curve in the road. If we get low and stick close to the willow bushes on the right of the road, then we will approach the rabbit. When we get to the point where we can see the rabbit just around the curve, we will estimate the distance to see if you should take the shot or not, so let's go."

As it was her hunt, Shannon went first; at the end of the curve, they saw the rabbit was still there.

"Shannon, how far do you think the rabbit is?"

"I think it's about 75 yards."

"Okay. It's your shot—how high are you going to aim?"

"About 1¼ inch."

Ray thought, *Great, she remembered the trajectory table.*

Shannon got on her belly and scooted out just enough to see the rabbit. She took aim and shot. Ray couldn't see the rabbit, but Shannon looked back at him and gave a thumb up sign, meaning she got the rabbit.

Shannon was excited about her first kill as a hunter. Ray raised her up, pulled her into his body, and gave her a long passionate kiss.

"Now Ray, we can't get aroused like this when we are hunting," Shannon teased him in a firm voice.

They continued on the hunting adventure and down farther on the same road, they spotted another cottontail rabbit. Shannon said, "Looks like about 100 yards."

"Shannon, that's a long shot for a 22 caliber rifle, but it could be done. You are going to aim about 5½ inches high at that yardage."

Shannon got down in the prone position, Ray following next to her. She made her shot, and Ray could see she got the rabbit.

"Good shot."

"I know it was a fabulous shot," Shannon corrected him, smiling, looking at Ray eye-to-eye. She followed that by laying him over and giving him another arousing kiss.

"Shannon, I thought we weren't going to do that anymore."

"I know, Ray, but look, I think the rabbits sort of like seeing us out here kissing—look down the road, what do you see?"

Ray looked and said, "Two rabbits."

"What are they doing?"

Ray looked and said slowly, "I believe they are mating."

Shannon said with a big smile, "Ray, do you remember that old phrase—monkey see monkey do?"

"Well, we are not monkeys ... I think we'd better go dress out the rabbits."

"Okay," Shannon said with a mischievous grin.

Ray and Shannon were having the most of their time together before they drove back to the ranch house.

Ray showed Shannon where he kept his Buck knife for skinning, and proceeded to show her how to dress out a rabbit, washing and then wrapping them in tin foil so they could freeze them.

While they were at it, Mary came in and asked, "What did you guys get?"

"Got me my first two cottontail rabbits, Mom! Next time maybe we can have a barbecue," Shannon tinge of pride in her voice.

"Sounds good to me. I will teach you how to make a Portuguese solution that tenderizes and gives them an excellent flavor. It's good for barbecuing."

"It's getting close to dinnertime—can you stay for dinner?"

"Thanks for the invite, Mom, but I had better be going to Lodi to visit my mom and dad. I want to tell them what an incredible day I had with your son."

Ray walked Shannon out to her car.

"I hope you had fun today," Ray said. "You got a warm welcome from the Isleton community, met Mr. and Mrs. Chin, got your hunting license, met my best friend Joeseph, and got two cottontail rabbits."

"Shannon—I really hope you like it out here at the ranch. I have been thinking … while I am in India … do you think you could come out here and be around while visiting with my parents? It would help fill the void with me not being here."

"Absolutely, Ray. I want to be like a daughter to them. They are an important part of my life, as you are." With that they hugged and kissed, and Shannon left to see her parents in Lodi.

Driving to Lodi, Shannon's thoughts lingered about how lucky she was to have Ray and his mom and dad in her life; it's like a dream come true in a young girl's life. She felt it's truly amazing how God guided them together. Shannon wished her best friend Denise Silva would be as lucky;

she, after all, a pretty and smart gal. Shannon truly hoped someday a special guy would spot her.

Pulling into her parents' driveway, a thought flashed across Shannon's mind. Ray's friend, Joeseph, who she thought came across as very genuine, sounded like he was interested in meeting Denise. The questions he asked—about her name, her major at UC Davis—seemed to indicate it. And they did share common things about them that Shannon felt by next week Joeseph was going to figure out a way to meet Denise.

Shannon realized there was nothing to do except let things fall into place naturally. Finally she wondered who was going to get the phone call first when Joeseph and Denise did meet—she or Ray.

Shannon walked into the house. "Anybody home?" she called out.

"We are in the kitchen Shannon, just come on in here!" her dad replied.

"Shannon, how did your day go out at the Johnsons' farm?" her parents asked.

"Just great, Mom, I officially became a hunter today. I shot two cottontail rabbits, learned how to dress them out, then got them ready for the freezer. When I get some more we will plan a barbecue over at the Jonhsons'. I also got to meet Mr. and Mrs. Chin, had a fire engine welcome at the town of Isleton, and met Ray's best friend, Joeseph Alexander."

"Shannon, that's a lot to get done in a day!" her mom responded.

Just then the phone rang. Shannon's dad answered it. "It's Denise, Shannon; she wants to talk to you."

On the phone, Denise said, "Shannon, haven't seen you for a while—how is everything?"

"Everything is going just great—can't complain—how about you?"

"Oh, school is school, just the everyday grind. I like my major. I believe I can be of great help to our vineyard operation in the future. UC Davis is such a great school for learning agriculture."

"Glad to hear that from you, Denise," Shannon replied. "Oh, I should tell you I had linguica and eggs for breakfast today. Ray's mom is Portuguese and she also makes that same dish your mom makes."

"What, *soupas*? Does Ray like it?"

"He sure does! There's something else: his best friend, Joeseph, was there for breakfast, and he also loves Portuguese cooking."

Shannon caught herself thinking, *Oh, the cat might be getting out of the bag*; she really didn't want to bring Joeseph into the picture at this time. There was a period of silence on the other end of the phone, but Denise broke the silence and slowly asked Shannon, "Does Joeseph seem like a good guy?"

"Yes. He is very pleasant person to be around. His parent's farm is just up the road from Ray's parents' ranch."

"Is he attending school now?"

"Yes. He majors is agriculture...." Another long silence on the phone.

"Well, where does he go to college?" Shannon forgot how she got on the subject of Joeseph, but she knew she had to respond to Denise's question.

"UC Davis...."

"Did I hear you right? UC Davis...?"

"Yes, Denise—he goes to UC Davis."

Denise seemed to settle down. "Well, it's a small-small world, Shannon. It sure seems like you are entering into a great family, and I can't wait till you and Ray get married."

"Denise, you will be by my side when that day comes."

"I will certainly be honored—oh, Shannon one last thing: what's Joeseph's last name?"

"It's Alexander."

After they hung up the phone, Shannon felt certain Denise and Joeseph would be searching for each other at their school—she just couldn't help having that strong feeling.

And it turned out Shannon's mom heard a lot of her conversation with Denise to ask, "What's up with Ray's friend Joeseph and Denise?"

"Well, Mom, at breakfast today Joeseph asked a few questions after I mentioned that Denise was a student at UC Davis. On the way down to Lodi, I had a feeling Joeseph is going to find her next week. Now this call. We will see how it plays out from here on. I just wonder who is going to get the first phone call, Ray or me."

CHAPTER 4

RAY MAKES AN ANNOUNCEMENT
⊂━◆━⊃

On her way back to her Sacramento apartment, Shannon had plenty more time to think about her fun-filled day, especially that part hunting with Ray out on the Johnsons' ranch. It was a day she would long remember in her young life. She knew Ray had so much to think about. How was he going tell his family and friends about his upcoming trip? How would they manage to come up with a wedding date? Additionally, there was the matter of graduation in June.

Somehow, Shannon was certain they would be married before his hunting adventure to India; either that or their sexually charged encounters finally had the better of them. They just knew they couldn't last much longer before they engage in premarital sex, something they were fighting very hard to avoid. But because he said the sooner the better, referring to marriage, she knew the meeting with both families was just on the horizon.

Shannon felt it would probably happen when he finally brought up the topic of his hunting trip to India. He most likely would have everybody know that Shannon had agreed, having disclosed his dream long ago to her, right after he told her that he had fallen in love with her, and in return getting a positive response from her. Shannon understood his passion for hunting, and she wouldn't want to deny him that once in a lifetime adventure even though she knew it would be dangerous, that she could even lose him. Shannon didn't want to think about that even happening, but she knew the reality of such chance was there.

Shannon retired to her apartment to Ray calling in to see if she got home safely.

"I have a busy schedule this week. I have a job interview with a Lodi Company for an intern mechanical engineering position on Tuesday, and a big engineering test on statics and dynamics on Wednesday," said Ray.

"Okay. Do you know when will we see each other then?"

"I thought I could stop by your apartment after my test on Wednesday, your last class that day being at 10 o'clock—is that right?"

Shannon answered, "That's right. I will plan on seeing you Wednesday then."

"Yes. Okay, see you then. I will miss not seeing you for a few days, but I will be calling you to keep in touch. I love you."

It occurred to Ray the most he had not seen Shannon lately was two days; over three days had become a long time not to be together.

Meanwhile, Shannon was also wondering how she was going to survive not seeing Ray for more than three days. She thought of doing something special for him to surprise him when he walked through the door.

Ray and Shannon had finally reached that point when being apart that long had become so hard for them to endure, such painful situation, for they were just too much in love.

For two days Ray studied hard for his test on Wednesday, and prepared for his job interview in Lodi on Tuesday.

Sunday around the dinner table, Ray told his mom and dad, "The next few days are going to be hard not seeing Shannon until Wednesday. I have a job interview on Tuesday, and I have to study on Monday and Tuesday for an engineering test on Wednesday. And I have classes, but I guess I will get through it."

"What's the name of the company and where is it located?" Paul asked.

"The name of the company is Lodi Molds Inc., in Lodi. They are looking for an intern mechanical engineer that they can later hire permanently. But that really is okay, especially for what I have planned after I graduate college."

Ray's dad's curiosity got the best of him and he asked, "What's this plan you have after college that you mentioned if I may ask?"

"Oh, I will be letting everybody know in the near future." Ray was hoping his dad would stop the questioning at that point, and he did. But Ray noticed Paul had a smile on his face when he asked the question, as if he knew something, but then again his dad almost always appeared to be smiling, so Ray just sort of passed it off.

"You know, Dad, one of my professors recommended me for this job. He feels people from a farm environment make good mechanical engineers. He just feels they have been around and seen a lot of equipment."

"That's quite true; you also have repaired a lot of equipment and seen good and bad designs in such equipment, which definitely gives you some hands-on experience."

After dinner, Ray excused himself and headed to his room to study for his upcoming test and prepare for his interview.

Monday saw Ray off to school for his classes and thinking of all the tasks ahead of him on his way home. Mainly, he couldn't get his mind off Shannon and not being able to see her until Wednesday. He pulled in the driveway at the ranch, went into the house, and greeted his mom and dad and asked, "How are things going today?"

Ray's mom answered, "Oh, we are doing fine; by the way, Shannon called. She wanted you to call her at her apartment."

Excited, Ray went to his room and phoned Shannon. When Shannon answered the phone, Ray said, "Hello—honey, I can't stand not seeing you! In other words, it's been horrible. Shannon, we have got to get going on the wedding plans."

"Ray, we can talk about it more on Wednesday. I am about bursting at the seams as you are, not being able to see and touch you, but we have to control our emotions—though I am not sure I can or want to." The last statement passed right over Ray's head.

"Well, remember I have a job interview tomorrow and a test on Wednesday. I will be at your place around 11 o'clock on Wednesday morning. I will see you then and we can spend the rest of the day together. I will probably be exhausted, but I am sure you can revive me with a kiss or two."

"Ray I will try my best to get you going, especially after you have rested a little." Hanging up, Ray was wondering what she meant by *especially after you had rested awhile*.

Tuesday morning Ray attended his morning classes, then headed to Lodi for the job interview. At the Lodi Mold front desk, Ray introduced himself and told the receptionist, "I am here to see Mr. Fred Sunday for a job interview."

"I believe Mr. Sunday is expecting you. I will let him know you are here, Mr. Johnson. Please have a seat. I will let you know when he is ready to see you."

"Thank you," Ray said.

Ray felt a little nervous while waiting, but it soon passed with time. He was also wondering if taking time off for India would hurt his chances at the position being offered. Nevertheless, he felt the need to be truthful about this trip. For one thing, the good recommendations from his college professors at Cal State Sacramento were reassuring. He was soon feeling pretty good, reminding himself to just answer any questions truthfully, which would be the best anybody could ever expect.

Soon the receptionist was back for Ray. "Mr. Sunday is now ready to see you, Ray. I will take you back to his office—just follow me." At Mr. Sunday's office, she made the introductions. Before she left, she told Mr. Sunday, who was the engineering manager, "Ray appears to be a very polite young gentleman for the brief time I got to know him."

Surprised at her statement, Ray replied, "Well, thank you for the compliment, but I have to admit I am as nervous as a cat on a hot tin roof."

"If Fred makes you nervous, just let me know. I can probably straighten him out," the receptionist told Ray.

"Ray, Liz means what she says and she has straightened me out a few times, so what she says is true."

The interview went quite well, Mr. Sunday explaining the job position being offered in more detail. It would start out as a part time job to see how well Ray could take on the projects that he would be assigned. It would be about a year before the company would make up its mind whether to hire him on as a permanent employee.

Ray saw an opening to discuss his trip to India. "Mr. Sunday, I have to tell you about a trip that I have set myself to do. Starting in the month of May 1960, which would be about nine months after I have graduated, I would like to take about a sixty-day leave, to go on my dreamed adventure; do you think that would be okay?"

"That would be just about the time we would be making you an offer of some kind, so that would be okay. By the way, what are some of your future plans, if I may ask?"

"Well, I am engaged to be married. I hope to get married in July, but my girlfriend, Shannon, and I still have to work out the details about it."

"Did I hear you say Shannon? Is she by any chance a Lodi gal who goes by the full name Shannon Doritee?"

47

"Yes, Mr. Sunday, that is my precious gal from Lodi. Do you know her?"

"You know, Ray, it's a small world indeed. I have known Bob and Elizabeth for a long time—I own a small vineyard next to theirs. I have watched Shannon grow up into the fine gal she is today. Ray, you are a lucky guy. Excuse me, Ray, I have to call Liz up front.

"That's funny, she doesn't answer."

Standing in Fred's office doorway was Liz, the receptionist. "Fred, I was way ahead of you: I had already called Elizabeth to confirm that Ray was who Shannon was engaged to. I thought I remembered the name Ray Johnson and I was right; see, Fred, you must admit I am a pretty good judge of character." Fred and Ray both smiled at her after she said that.

Liz wasn't done yet; asking Ray to stand up, she then looked at him from head to toe. "You are a fine specimen of a man, Ray. I believe you are lucky to have Shannon, and she is lucky to have you, too. I will leave you both now so you can both finish your interview."

"Ray, your professors all gave you high recommendations for this job," Fred said to continue the interview. "One of your professors mentioned you came from a farming operation. He knew farm boys usually make good mechanical engineers, being always around machinery."

"Ray, that is what I call valuable hands-on experience, and I personally believe in that so much. From my perspective, I look at a successful engineer as one who has experience, natural ability, and capacity to apply his education to enhance his experience and natural ability; it just isn't about education alone."

With that, Fred brought Ray to the engineering department, before proceeding out to the shops to look at some of the equipment that was being made. He wanted to show Ray how the manufacturing process worked at Lodi Mold Inc.

"Does this type of machinery interest you to the point you would like to work here?" Fred asked Ray.

"Yes; one thing that interests me is the extensive use of hydraulics here. I love hydraulic systems, especially coming from the farm." The plant tour over, both of them headed back to Fred's office and sat down.

"Well, Ray, after our interview, I will not have to think about it anymore from the Lodi Mold Inc. position. If you like what you see here, you can start after your graduation; if you need time to think it over, take your time."

Ray sat there for a moment. "Fred, I guess I will be seeing you after graduation. I am looking forward to working here and hope I can do a good job for Lodi Mold, Inc."

The two shook hands and Fred said, "Stop by Liz's on the way out and tell her to get the paperwork ready for you to start work after graduation. Oh, and give Shannon a big hello and kiss for me."

At the front desk, Ray told Liz, "Goodbye, Liz. It's been a pleasure meeting you. I will tell Shannon that I met you and Fred. Shannon will be very excited."

Heading back to the ranch, Ray felt very good about the interview. He was glad Fred was okay with the time off for his adventure trip. He was also pleased he didn't pursue any details on his adventure. He was also happy that Liz and Fred both knew Shannon, and appeared to have a very good opinion of her. Ray just couldn't wait to have her in his arms, Three and a half days seemed like an eternity, but only another day and he would be at her door. Right now he had to get home and hit the books for the big test tomorrow.

Ray was just pulling into the driveway to the ranch house when his dad pulled up. They got out of their vehicles, greeted each other, and asked how each other's day had gone.

"How did your interview go today with Lodi Mold Inc.?" Paul asked his son.

"It couldn't have gone better; they want me to come to work after graduation." They both went into the house where Ray hugged his mom as usual.

"Well, Mary, Ray landed that job at Lodi Mold Inc.," Paul said.

"Also, Mom, guess what occurred during the interview: when we got on the subject of my future plans and I mentioned I am engaged to a gal named Shannon, Fred, the engineering manager, asked me if her name was Shannon Doritee. I said yes, and it turned out he has a vineyard right next to the Doritees

"Not only that, the receptionist knew them also. She called Shannon's mom to confirm I was the one engaged to Shannon, thinking my named sounded familiar. She came to Fred's office unannounced, asked me to stand up so she could give an approval check. As she left, she told Fred, 'See, Fred, I am a good judge of character,' and Fred just smiled as she left."

"Well, Ray, sounds like you had a good day," Mary said.

"Mom, Dad, I feel like I am the luckiest guy on earth to have Shannon and both of you in my life—what more could God give me?"

"Well, son that goes for the both of us to, we as parents are also very lucky to have you and our new daughter in our family."

After dinner, Ray went to his room to study before retiring for a good night's sleep.

Ray felt comfortable and ready in the ensuing test day. His mind, however, was somewhere else: how he was going to greet Shannon when she opened the door at his visit. He knew the situation was going to be a big emotional one at her apartment. He was thinking Shannon and he had to have the meeting of parents today to announce the wedding plans. Ray was also considering it would be a good time to get the tiger hunt to India announced. Anyway, that had to be a subject that would be discussed today with Shannon.

Finally the test was over. Even though exhausted, Ray pulled up to her apartment, went to her door, and rang the bell. It seemed like an eternity before she finally opened the door, but there she stood in front of him.

Ray looked at Shannon. "You are a beautiful sight." He then grabbed her, brought her tightly to him, and they just kissed each other time and time again, seemingly unable to get enough of each other. "Oh, I know what I forgot!" This time he grabbed her by the hips, raised her, and gave her kiss near her belly button then lowered her down to head level before giving her another kiss.

"Fred Sunday said to give you a kiss for him."

"That felt special you kissing me on my belly. I guess I wore the right skimpy tank top and short shorts today— actually it felt pretty great." They both smiled. "How do you know Fred Sunday?" she asked him.

"He was the one who interviewed me for the job. One thing led to another, until he mentioned he literally watched you grow up. The receptionist Liz also knew you—and by the way I got the job."

"Oh, Ray what wonderful news." With that, Shannon pulled him into her tightly, giving him such long passionate kiss to cover the time they were apart, before they started to calm down a bit.

After a while, Shannon said, "Ray, why don't you lie down and rest. I know you must be tired, especially after the test. If you want, you have a bathing suit here. You may want to slip it on and be more comfortable. It's sort of warm anyway."

"That sounds like a good idea; I will do that and then get some sleep on the sofa."

"Okay, Ray. While you are resting I am going to try get a suntan out by the pool. You just rest—I will be back." Giving him a kiss, she went and changed into her swimsuit and left; by that time Ray was already fast asleep.

After some time, Ray started to stir a little. He finally opened his eyes, only to see and feel Shannon by his side. At first he thought she had no clothes on, but came to make out a sexy bikini bathing suit. Shannon had tucked her body between the back of the sofa and Ray's body, a rather close fit which was probably exactly what Shannon wanted. Ray was now starting to think that's why she wanted him to have his bathing suit on—Shannon was probably thinking for today the more skin showing the better.

Ray was now pretty much awake, and Shannon was starting to sense it. Opening her eyes, she said to Ray, "I love you so much ... are you getting excited right now?" Then before he could answer, she shifted her body so it was about half on him and gave him a kiss.

Then Ray said, "I am so happy we are together right here and now. Shannon, my love for you will never end. These few days not seeing you or touching you has been torture, but now we are together."

After that remark, Shannon gave him such a passionate kiss, like someone lighting a fuse to a stick of dynamite. It was becoming obvious that they were moments away from sexual intercourse.

"I am ready, but are you ready for this?" Shannon finally managed to say.

"Shannon I am more than ready," Ray replied, smiling.

So together they consented to have a sexual relationship, and what little clothing they had on started to rapidly come off. What they tried to avoid in the past now proved to be beyond their control.

They were just moments away from changing their life forever. They were just moments away from engaging in sexual intercourse, when ... the phone rang!

Startled, the two of them fell off the sofa. Trying to catch her breath, Shannon staggered on her way to answer the phone. Ray couldn't believe what had just happened. He could overhear what Shannon was saying over the phone. "Oh, hi Mom, how are you doing? Yes, Mom, Ray is here. Oh no, you didn't interrupt anything that we were doing. Ray and I were on the sofa just talking. Oh, you want Ray and me to come to dinner on Friday at the ranch at about 5 o'clock, and my parents would also be there. That's so nice of you to invite my parents! We will be there, Mom, and thanks for calling. Please tell Dad hi, and we will see you Friday."

"Well, honey I guess you might say we were saved, or interrupted, by the bell." Looking at her, Ray couldn't resist giving her another kiss on her belly before doing the same to her lips.

Ray and Shannon then decided to talk about future plans.

"Shannon, this Friday's dinner may provide an opportunity for us to announce our wedding plans and my hunting trip to India. Does that sound okay to you, Shannon?"

"It sounds like a good plan."

"Let's see: I am going to graduate in June, which is a month away—maybe the first part of July is best for the wedding? Of course you have to work it out with your parents, but let's put the date as one possibility."

"I think it's a good date. We will see once we pursue it after the announcement Friday. I will explain to my parents why the sooner the better, as you say, so they could understand our position. I think they would want to try to meet our needs."

Ray truly hoped everything would be okay when he also announced the tiger hunting trip to India on Friday. "How do you think your parents will react to my going on a hunting trip to India?" he said.

"I will explain to them it's been a longtime dream of yours, and that you told me about it the first time you told me you loved me. I accepted it, and they will have to understand," Shannon replied through teary eyes.

"I just hope nobody is going to be upset with me."

"Ray, I will defend you always. I also must thank you for wanting to get married before your trip. That means so much to me."

"Shannon, I felt we had no choice. Right now we can look forward to our wedding day and our honeymoon when our life together will really begin, and shall never end. Together we will show our love for each other on our wedding night." By now Shannon's eyes were flooding with tears, unable to see how those words came out of his mouth.

"Well, I have to go home now. I won't mention anything about our forthcoming announcements on Friday. We will save everything for that night, and it will be a great night," Ray said.

Shannon responded with another caress and a very romantic kiss. They had better control this time, especially now that the wedding day would soon be announced.

"Tomorrow Thursday I'll just head home after my evening class. I will come to your apartment on Friday. Shannon, our love will hit a milestone on Friday." He gave her a kiss, said goodbye, and headed home.

Once at home, Ray greeted his mom and dad. Dinner was about to be served.

"Mom, I got your message at Shannon's apartment about you having Shannon's parents over. Would it be for dinner?"

His mom answered, "Yes. I thought it was about time we got our two families together—is that okay?"

"Mom, the timing couldn't be better! Thanks for planning the dinner, should be an enjoyable evening." After dinner, Ray went into the living room and watched some TV. Tired as he was, he soon excused himself, said good night, and went to bed.

Friday finally arrived, and Ray and Shannon met at her apartment after classes. Shannon was so excited as she said, "Today will mark the beginning of a new era in our lives, Ray, where both our families will hear from us about our future plans. This will be an exciting day for both our parents. I am so glad your mom and dad chose this day that God has made to bring us all together. Ray, I believe God had your mom call right when we were in need of a little guidance. I think we were saved by the bell, as you put it, God causing it to ring at that special time."

"I believe you are right in everything you say," replied Ray.

Walking together to their cars to head to the Johnson farm, a thought suddenly occurred to Ray. "With all the excitement and our busy schedule lately, I forgot to tell you how I thought for sure Joeseph would have called to say he had met up with Denise. I guess it wasn't meant to be."

"I did talk to Denise about Joeseph. By what she was asking, I also thought for sure she was in pursuit mode. Perhaps you are right it's not how it was meant to be for them." With that they both got into their cars and made their way to the ranch.

At the ranch house, Ray and Shannon realized Shannon's parents were already there. That got them smiling—and kissing—before they went in.

"Shannon, this I hope will be a great night," Ray said while holding Shannon's hand.

They made their entrance into the living room and greeted the parents with hugs, kisses, and handshakes. They then all started to have some general conversations about the week's events.

"My friend Liz called me about Ray being interviewed at Lodi Mold. She wanted to know if you were the one engaged to Shannon. So Ray, how did the interview go?" Elizabeth Doritee said.

"It went very well—I got the job, and I can start work after graduation in June." Everybody congratulated Ray on his new position.

Soon, Ray's mom announced dinner was ready. "Let's all proceed to the dining room. We are having Portuguese *soupas* tonight. The Diorites have had it over at Denise's house, so I felt comfortable having it tonight. Mind you, not everybody likes the soggy spicy bread. But that is not the case now, so everybody just have a seat. We'll have dinner served shortly."

After being seated, Ray noticed two extra place settings, and promptly mentioned it to his mom.

His mom acknowledged the error and said, "Guess I just miscounted."

Everybody went about eating then, when Ray and Shannon suddenly felt two pairs of hands on their shoulders. Turning to look back, they were surprised to see Denise and Joeseph together standing behind them.

Shannon asked, "Mom, how did you plan this?"

"Oh, it was simple: I asked Joeseph to come over tonight. Of course he said yes, and he asked if he could bring a girlfriend. I said yes that would be fine, hope she likes soggy spicy bread and he said she's Portuguese. I then knew it was Denise, I knew it would be a big surprise to the both of you."

Joeseph and Denise were only too happy to join the occasion. They didn't know what the evening announcement would be, but they would be part of Ray and Shannon's wedding.

Ray was starting to get a little nervous. He knew the time was fast approaching to make the announcement.

Dinner over, everybody made their way back to the living room. Shannon just had to ask Denise, "How did you and Joeseph find each other?"

"We just kept asking our agriculture professors for each other's name. Since our majors were both agriculture, we thought there might be an outside chance one professor would recognize one of our names, and eventually it paid off. It turned out we actually had a common class together, though it was such a big forum type class with about 125 students in it, all of them assigned seat numbers.

"One time Joeseph went up to the professor and asked for the seat assignment of one Denise Silva. The professor did not want to give Joeseph the number, but Joeseph told him he had an important message that he needed to give her. So the professor bent the rule and gave Joeseph my seat number."

"After class, he went to me and asked, 'Are you Denise Silva?' I told him 'Yes,' and I asked, 'Are you Joeseph Alexander?' and he smiled and said, 'Yes.' Joeseph mentioned, 'Our friends sort of set this up,' even though it wasn't a direct set up, but he believed you and Ray both thought it was going to bring us into contact with each other, and it happened. Anyway after that, we just kept seeing each other," Denise concluded.

"I hope you are happy?" Shannon asked, smiling.

Denise whispered in Shannon's ear, "I really like Joeseph a lot. He is a neat guy. I hope he thinks the same about me. We saw a lot of each other this week, and we have a lot in common." Shannon just smiled and gave Denise a hug.

As conversations in the living room started to wind down, Ray felt that the time had come, and he discreetly whispered into Shannon's ear, "Maybe it's time to announce our plan." She softly nodded in agreement.

Ray managed to get everyone's attention and started out by saying, "Tonight, Shannon and I would like to make an announcement about our future plans. We think that having both our families here and two of our best friends just makes this an ideal time.

"This past Wednesday, Shannon and I had a chance to discuss wedding plans. After some time, we both came to one conclusion: we would like to get married right after I graduate college in June. The date we are looking at is July 1. This date, of course, would have to be discussed between Shannon and her parents. It would be a little more than two months from now. This is what we both would like."

For her part, Shannon said, "Mom, Dad, this weekend we can talk more about it."

"Well, why the big hurry?" her mom asked. She and Shannon's dad were smiling.

"Mom, Dad, Ray and I are so much in love. We feel it strongly when we are together, that as Ray has put it, the sooner we do it, the better for us," Shannon replied.

At that point, everybody just clapped their hands, acknowledging that they all understood.

"Well, Paul and I will help in any way that we can. I just want to let the Doritees know: just ask and we will be there for you, and also we are easy to please, especially when it comes to Shannon being part of our family," Mary announced, smiling.

"Thank you so much. We also look forward to having Ray in our family. We really can't wait to get these two married," Shannon's parents said to acknowledge Mary's words.

Sitting there listening to all the comments, Ray thought to himself, *Well that's the first hurdle*, and he felt it went well. Now comes the one that's going to be a little hard for everyone to understand. He knew he had to be careful presenting his hunting trip to India.

Taking Shannon's hand, Ray slowly chose his words. "I have one more announcement to make. Months ago when I had Shannon out shooting targets for the first time, and until that time we realized our deep love for each other, I felt I had to tell Shannon a longtime dream of mine.

"As some of you know, I have this passion for hunting. Specially, I always have this love for the big cats of the world. The one I most admire are the Bengal tigers, these creatures that fear nothing, and are one of the most cunning animals of the world.

"When I told Shannon my desire to hunt the Bengal tiger for a trophy, she understood me completely and made no objection to pursue my wish. I thus made sure Shannon knew what I had in mind. My plan is to leave for India in May 1960. For that, I will shortly plan out the details to make the trip a success."

Shannon felt she had to say something. "I know tiger hunting can be dangerous, so I will need all your support while I wait for Ray to return. He will be gone for about sixty days, less if he had luck getting his trophy early. I will be here a lot with Ray's parents to try to fill the void of him not being around during that period of time. I hope you all will support him, as I do, to carry out his one-time adventure."

"Son, I always knew how much you loved the Bengal tiger," Paul said. "One day at the Chins' sporting goods, Mr. Chin told me you had bought a very large caliber rifle. Wondering what you were going to do with such a rifle, I put the facts together in my mind and saw you were probably going to India for the Bengal tiger. As Shannon will support Mom and me as we will support her while you are gone, I ask all of you here tonight to show your support for Ray's adventure to India."

Shannon's parents didn't have anything to say, probably anxious to talk to Shannon about it privately.

The evening at the Johnsons finally came at an end, and everybody started to leave for home.

Before leaving, Joeseph and Denise approached Ray and Shannon. "So that's what that Winchester 338 magnum rifle you bought was for," Joeseph said, addressing Ray.

"By the way, thank you so much for bringing Denise and me together. By the way, do you think Denise and I could use your shooting range? Denise appears to be interested in learning how to shoot."

"Of course—any time," Ray replied.

Shannon knew then that Denise had Joeseph's heart in her hand. Denise had to be excited at the conversation that just went on. Finally, Joeseph and Denise made their way home.

Meanwhile, Ray walked Shannon to her car. She was going to her parents to talk about this evening's announcements.

"Shannon, I thought everything went pretty good tonight," Ray said. "I'm sure you will be talking to your parents about everything that happened tonight."

"The wedding plans will be the priority that we will be working on," Shannon replied. "Just think, Ray, about two months from now we will be on our honeymoon."

"The sooner the better. We will just have to remember to unplug the phone," Ray said, smiling.

CHAPTER 5

WEDDING PLANS ARE TAKING PLACE

On her way from the Johnson Ranch, Shannon thought about the questions her parents might have about Ray's hunting trip to India, which was completely understandable to her. Shannon was comforted by the thought that her parents were reasonable beings who would always want her to be happy.

After pulling into her parent's driveway, Shannon soon made her way into the house.

"Hi, Mom! Hi, Dad!"

Upon hearing her, her parents greeted her at the entry with hugs and kisses.

Once inside, Shannon was the first to speak. "Well, what a night! I hope you are both okay with how things went at the Johnsons."

Shannon's mom thought about it. "You know, Shannon, today has been a long day for everyone. I think we all need to get some sleep and talk about it first thing in the morning," she replied.

Shannon agreed and they all retired to get some good sound sleep and much needed rest.

Back at the Johnsons' house, Ray and his parents were discussing the evening and how it went. They all were pretty excited about the upcoming wedding plans.

"I thought everything was fine the way you presented the announcements, but I don't know how Shannon's parents took the Bengal tiger hunting trip to India," Paul started. "I guess time will tell, but I thought Shannon's statement about your hunting trip to India was pretty convincing on how she felt. Son, Shannon is a great gal; you lucked out when you found her."

"I know Shannon will talk to her parents about the hunting trip. I sensed they were a little disturbed about that, but like Dad said, time will tell," Mary added, smiling.

Paul suddenly felt tired. "Well, it has been a long day. I am going to retire for the night and see you both in the morning."

Ray stayed up with his mom. He felt he could use the time to have a good mom-to-son conversation.

Mary spoke first.

"Son, you have been such a great gift to us—and now with Shannon to be in our family, it's like a dream come true. What I mean is that Dad and I could only have one child because of medical reasons. Through you, we will have Shannon. Our next dream would be for Shannon and you to give us some grandchildren in our lives. It would also be great if someday Shannon and you could build a house on the ranch—that is, if you both want it, too. That would just be another dream that would come true, especially with grandchildren around. But we know God is the one who can make dreams come true."

"Mom: first, thank you so much for having this dinner tonight. It let Shannon and me tell everyone close to both of us what our plans are. It was something we knew was in the near future, but when you called and gave Shannon the news about the dinner, that opened the door for us to announce our plans here tonight."

"Ray, I am glad I made the call that day. I just felt a need to do it that day," Mary said.

"The call came just in time, Mom—thanks again," replied Ray.

The comment made Mary recall feeling she probably interrupted something when she made that call. Mary understood only too well what a meeting at an apartment could bring after a prolonged separation, but she felt that was over with and done; besides, it's their life. They love each other, and things can happen. Ray and his mom said goodnight and they both retired.

Saturday morning at the Doritees, breakfast time, Shannon and her parents were talking about last night's announcements.

Shannon started out by saying, "I know you probably have questions about the wedding plans being so soon, and Ray's hunting trip to India, so I would like to explain if I could.

"At this point in our relationship, things can get very emotional. The other day after his test, Ray came over to my apartment. Remember we haven't seen each other for over three days; with the situation being what it was, I will be honest with you we were moments away from having a sexual relationship."

"Oh, Shannon, Ray doesn't come across as being that aggressive."

"Actually, Mom and Dad, I was the aggressive one."

Shannon's parents both responded, "Oh, really? So what stopped you?"

"We got a phone call from Mary Johnson telling us to come over for dinner Friday, and that you both were going to be there. So you might say we were saved by the bell, but I will tell you we both tried to avoid a sexual relationship, but that day it was almost impossible. Ray and I both then thought it would be a good time to tell everybody about our plans at the Johnsons on Friday night."

Shannon's parents now understood why they wanted to get married in a short time.

"Well, Shannon, that makes perfect sense for you two to get married as soon as time would permit. We will start getting our plans ready for a July 1st wedding." With that, they all hugged each other.

The issue of Ray's hunting trip came up as the next topic of conversation.

"Shannon, are you really okay with Ray's hunting trip to India?" Shannon's dad said.

"Yes, Dad, I am okay with Ray's trip to India. Please let me explain why. First, Ray was up front with me about his desire to hunt the Bengal tiger, this being his lifelong dream. You see, Ray is a victim of timing: he had this dream for a long time, and then he met me and fell in love with me, as I fell in love with him. That was a dilemma that he faced. He wanted his two loves: hunting the Bengal tiger, and now this passionate love he has for me, as I with a passionate love for him."

"Mom and Dad, I hope you understand I couldn't take his love to go hunting for the Bengal tiger away from him, even with the thought of maybe losing him. I know hunting a Bengal tiger in India can be dangerous, and while he is gone I know I will be a nervous wreck until I see him and hold him in my arms."

"Well, Shannon, you know everybody will support you while he is gone. Like Ray's dad said Friday night, we all should show support for Ray's adventure trip to India," replied Shannon's dad.

"Thanks, Mom and Dad, for all your support—you have always been such great parents and I love you both."

Shannon's mom was smiling. "Shannon, I believe you have made a good choice in Ray, and as for you being part of the Johnson family, you can tell the Johnsons are so excited about you being in their family, just as we are so excited about Ray being part of our family. Your dad and I can't wait to see Ray and you married; and if you both agree we can have grandchildren, it would be the most precious gift we could ever receive."

"Mom, I am sure we will be working on that. I know Ray and I will want children. Well, let's get started working on my wedding plans."

As Shannon and Ray had already picked July 1, 1959 for their wedding, Shannon's parents agreed to the date. The next item was how many guests to be invited; they agreed on 100 people, which they thought was reasonable. Next, they would use St Paul's Lutheran Church and their minister. It was the church that the Doritees attended in Lodi. Then they thought the Lodi American Legion hall for the reception would be a good choice, along with a sit-down dinner to be catered by a local catering service. The flowers would be provided by a local florist, the Lodi Flowers. Within a few hours, they had a wedding plan in place.

"Mom, I will run the plan by the Johnsons."

Shannon called the Johnsons, and Mary answered the phone.

"Hi, Mom, this is Shannon. Mom, I was wondering if you, Dad, and Ray would be available this afternoon. I want to come up and show you what we came up with as a wedding plan."

"That's fine, Shannon. You guys are really on this and that's great, so yes come on up, we will be here waiting."

Later at the Johnson Ranch, Shannon, Mary, Paul, and Ray sat down and talked about the wedding plans. Being easy to please, the Johnsons agreed to everything, and thought it looked great.

"Ray, the next thing would be to get the wedding announcements coming. I want you by my side when we pick the wedding announcements. Maybe we can go after school to a place in Sacramento that I know does wedding announcements."

"Okay, Shannon, I will meet you at you apartment on Monday."

"Next, I will have to go with my mom and dad to get fitted for my wedding dress—and Ray, you can't come with me to do that." She smiled and gave him a kiss.

"Shannon, since you are dressed in Levi's, would you want to do some hunting? I think you could use a little break in the action."

"That sounds great!" And they both went to the gun safe, took out the Marlin 22 and the 22 Magnum, and the ammo.

Ray turned to his mom and dad. "We will see you both a little later." They then went out to the pickup truck. Shannon was to be the driver. As they drove out onto the ranch road, Ray noticed that somebody was using the shooting range.

"Wonder who it is—let's go see!" Shannon said, smiling. They headed to the shooting range and pulled up close to the shooting bench. There, they were not surprised to see Joeseph and Denise. They all greeted each other with smiles and hellos.

"Well, our wedding plans are pretty much in place, and since you both are out here, the date of the wedding will be July 1, 1959," Shannon said. "So Denise, would you be my maid of honor?" Denise went to Shannon and they both hugged each other.

"Shannon you are my longtime friend. We grew up together and shared a lot of our life together as neighbors. I look forward to being in your wedding, and I can't wait to be your maid of honor."

It was Ray's turn to speak. "Well, Joeseph, you knew this was coming. It would be an honor for me if you would be my best man. You are the only person I would ever want.

We did so much together in this Sacramento Delta farming community and we will be friends forever."

Joeseph replied, "Ray I will be honored to be your best man. Shannon, remember to invite me over for linguica and eggs for breakfast and Portuguese *soupas* for dinner." They all laughed.

"Well, Shannon and I will attempt a little hunting now. Oh, I recall that on this very shooting range and this same shooting bench, something very special happened to Shannon and me one day. We will see you guys later."

At the shooting bench, Joseph and Denise just looked at each other, most likely wondering what their fate together would be.

Ray and Shannon driving down a ranch road were just delighted to be together, the same way their friends were enjoying each other. It just seemed to make their day.

"Shannon, drive real slow to the road by the pond; maybe some cottontail rabbits would be out."

Sure enough, there were two rabbits on the road. Shannon got out and took the 22 Magnum gun, thinking it might be a longer shot.

"Ray, you watch. I am on my own this time." With that, she stepped on the road and assumed a stalking procedure. Ray saw her get down in the prone shooting position; a little while later, he heard the shot, but he noticed Shannon was still in the prone shooting position; then another shot was fired and she got up, motioned to Ray to come over, and he did.

When Ray got to Shannon, she had a monstrous smile from ear to ear, "Well, did you get a double?" Ray asked.

"You might say that," Shannon replied. "When I got in position, there was a coyote stalking two cottontail rabbits, so I shot the coyote first, thinking the rabbit would be better in our freezer rather than in the coyote's belly."

Ray smiled. "You made a good decision," he said. "Let's go pick up the rabbit and the coyote. We'll take them back to the house so we can get a picture of you and the coyote."

"Ray lets first go by the shooting range and see if Denise and Joeseph are still there. I want to show her the coyote I shot."

Shannon and Ray drove to the shooting range. Joeseph and Denise were still there when they pulled up to the shooting bench. Shannon blurted out with excitement, "Hey, Denise, Joeseph, come over here! I want to show you something!"

They all went to the back of the pickup truck and Shannon showed them the coyote and the cottontail rabbit. "I was stalking the rabbit and saw the coyote doing the same. I shot the coyote first and then the rabbit." Joeseph, Denise, and Ray were so excited for Shannon having handled the hunting situation beautifully.

"Shannon, in the near future I believe there are going to be two gal hunters out here hunting—as soon as I can get my hunting license," Denise said.

Shannon, full of excitement, replied, "Denise, I can't wait for that day to come! So what prompted you to pursue hunting?"

Denise, with tears in her eyes, answered, "Well, Shannon and Ray, there must be something magical about this ranch and this shooting bench. Just moments ago, I was told by a man named Joeseph that he was in love with me. Shannon, I know this sounds familiar to you." Needless to say both Ray and Shannon were excited about the news.

After hearing the exciting news, Ray and Shannon went back to the ranch house. Ray took a picture of Shannon and the coyote before Shannon dressed out the rabbit and put it in the freezer. Back inside the house, Shannon told Ray's mom and dad about getting a coyote and another rabbit for the freezer.

"Well, Shannon that sounds like you are really becoming a hunter," Ray's dad commented.

"It's been another terrific day out here, but right now I have to get back to Lodi to see my parents," Shannon said.

Ray walked Shannon out to her car and kissed her goodbye. "I will call you tomorrow, and for sure see you Monday to pick out the wedding announcements," Ray said. "Drive safe to Lodi."

On her way back to her parents in Lodi, Shannon was thinking what July 1 was going to be like to be married, and she wished it was tomorrow. She was also thinking about Ray's trip to India, and how hard it would be to say goodbye, but she would have to endure a hard situation for the sake of her love for Ray. She was now pulling into her parent's driveway. She got out of the car and entered the house; her mom and dad were there to greet her.

"Well, Shannon, how did it go at the Johnsons?" her dad asked her.

"Everything was just fine. They are easy to please. Ray and I decided we would go Monday after school to pick out our wedding announcements. I would like you both to come also, so after we do the announcements, we could go to the bridal dress store and pick out, and get fitted for my bridal gown. I thought you both could come to my apartment about three o'clock and we could all go down town together."

With that, Shannon's parents broke down in tears. "Shannon, we can't believe our once little girl is getting married; right now it just hasn't sunk in yet," her mom barely managed to say.

Shannon tried to comfort them by saying, "Well, you know we will be a little bigger family, especially if Ray and I can have children. Can you even imagine the birthdays, the Christmas holidays with little ones around!" That helped put Shannon's parents in a much better mood.

It was about dinnertime, so the three of them sat down for dinner, and as usual, everybody wanted to know about today's activities.

"After I went over the wedding plans with Ray and his parents, Ray and I decided to do a little hunting today," Shannon said. "I got another cottontail rabbit, and you won't believe this, I also shot a coyote! You will see pictures of me and the coyote when Ray gets the film developed. It was so much fun! I felt I needed a break from all the wedding plans that we put together this morning, and it's always so great to be with Ray."

Shannon's Mom asked, "How do you view the relationship between Denise and Ray's friend, Joeseph?"

"Oh, Mom, that's another exciting thing that happened today! When Ray and I went out hunting, we noticed somebody at the shooting range. When we got there, we saw it was Denise and Joeseph. At that time it seemed appropriate to ask them to be maid of honor and the best man in our wedding. They both excitedly accepted."

"So really, Shannon, today you completed your wedding plan. It's great to have the two of them together when Ray and you asked them."

Shannon continued on and said to her mom and dad, "After I shot the coyote and the rabbit, Ray and I drove to the shooting range to see if Denise and Joeseph were still there, and they were. I asked them to look at what I got and they were excited to see the coyote."

"At that time, Denise told us she believed in the near future there is going to be two gal hunters out at the ranch as soon as she gets her hunting license.

"I asked, 'Denise what prompted you to want to become hunter?' And then Denise told us, 'Well there must be something magical about the Johnson ranch, and this shooting bench, for just moments ago a guy named Joeseph told me he was in love with me.'

"Denise and Joeseph have a serious relationship, and as Denise's friend, I am so excited."

Shannon's mom said, "Well, Shannon, you know your dad and I will wish the best for Denise. She has been a true friend of yours for years. You both grew up together, and you both did so much with each other. It was like you two were born to be together." They all were getting tired after a very busy day, and it was about time to retire. The three said good night to each other and went to bed.

Sunday came and it was sort of a relaxing day for both the Doritee and Johnson families. Ray made a phone call to Shannon and asked if it would be okay for him to come down and visit. Shannon replied, "Of course, Ray, you know you are always welcome at my parents' home. I will see you in a little while." After hanging up the phone, Shannon did mention to her parents that Ray would be coming down just to visit.

"That's great, I always liked talking to Ray," Shannon's dad said.

Ray arrived, greeted everybody, and gave Shannon a little hug and kiss as usual. Shannon said, "Why don't we all go into the living room." They all entered the living room and sat down. Shannon sat next to Ray on the sofa.

Feeling a need to start a conversation, Ray said, "Well, Mom and Dad, you really got some announcements Friday night at dinner. I hope you both are okay with everything, and especially with my announcement of the hunting trip to India. The last thing I ever wanted to do was offend you or anybody."

Shannon immediately entered the conversation by saying, with her arms around Ray, "Ray, I have told them the whole story and they are okay with everything—isn't that right, Mom and Dad?"

Shannon's mom was also quick to add, "Yes, Ray, we have no problems whatsoever with your trip. Shannon has assured us it was what she accepted because of her love for you, and that's all we needed to hear. Ray, we are both excited for this marriage to take place, so just maybe, if you both agree, you can give us the gift of grandchildren."

Ray looked at Shannon, who nodded as if to say, *Go ahead and say what you want.* "If God wills it, we will give you grandchildren and the sooner the better. It's really a no-brainer as Shannon and I will want to have children."

"I am sure God will give you children," Shannon's mom said.

"I am going to have to get back home. I will see you tomorrow at Shannon's apartment so we can pick out the wedding announcements. Shannon and you both can then go pick out her wedding gown. Shannon informed me I am not allowed to see the gown that she picks—anyway, see you Monday." Ray gave Shannon a goodbye hug and kiss, and soon was on his way back to the ranch.

Shannon proceeded to phone Denise to ask her if she could come to her apartment on Monday at about three o'clock. They could go to the bridal dress shop to pick out her maid of honor dress. Shannon did get a hold of Denise and she said she would be there. So now everything was set for Monday. Things were really shaping up for the July 1 wedding.

In the meantime, Ray made it home. His mom and dad had already retired, so he just stayed up and watched some TV. Ray's mind wondered off on the subject of where Shannon and he could go on their honeymoon. He had a favorite spot and he was not going to tell anybody where it was. He was just hoping Shannon would trust him to take her there, where he knew she would be surprised. He would have to talk to

Shannon about it in the near future. He now turned the TV off and went to bed.

Monday found Ray and Shannon in school. Ray knew Shannon would be at her apartment about one o'clock, time for his last class for the day. Ray thought he would go to Shannon's place and surprise her with an early visit. After he rang the doorbell, she opened the door and was surprised to see him so early.

"Ray, what a pleasant surprise! Well, come on in!" Going in, he lifted her up and gave her a very long kiss. "Ray! That was a fuse lighter; remember we have to be careful—unless you don't want to be careful, which would be okay with me," Shannon said with a smile. The two of them settled down and sat on the sofa, soon falling asleep together.

They had just woken up from their sleep when the doorbell rang again. It was Shannon's mom and dad, along with Denise. After greeting each other, Shannon said, "Well, first we will go to a stationary store to pick out the wedding announcements. Mom, Dad, why don't you follow Ray and me to the store."

To the stationary store they went, Ray and Shannon looking at various styles of announcements before settling on one, Shannon's mom and dad giving their nod of approval. The forms were then filled out so the announcements forms could be sent to the printer for printing, a task so simple and soon over with.

As the group was out on the street, Ray and Shannon went to the side for some privacy together. Shannon pulled Ray to her and told him, "Honey, this is where we will part for today. You will see me in the wedding gown on our wedding day, when my dad walks me down the aisle and presents me to you." Smiling now, Shannon continued, "Honey, we will be one after the ceremony. That will be thrilling, and we can have all the sex we want—do you like that?"

The words earned a big grin on Ray's face. "Shannon, that's going to be one joyous and thrilling day for you and me, and it's less than two months away." Ray then told Shannon, "I have been thinking about where we would go on our honeymoon. I want a very special place as a surprise for you, a place only fitting for the occasion—but would it be okay for me to pick the place that day?"

"That will be your choice, Ray. That will be the day when my name will change, and most of all when our lives will change. We will truly become one, and what a thrill that will be for both of us."

With that they said goodbye but agreed to get in touch later. Ray's parting comment was, "Have fun with Denise and your parents as you pick out your wedding gown. I will see you later."

The bridal dress store was just down the street. Shannon, her parents, and Denise walked to the store. Inside they introduced themselves to the salesperson at the order desk.

Shannon explained, "I am getting married on July 1st. I would like to look at your wedding gowns as well as a dress for my maid of honor." She gave Denise a big hug and said, "Denise, can you believe we are here doing this?"

With tears in her eyes, Denise said, "I am so thrilled to be here with my longtime best friend, and also with your mom and dad. This day is truly special, Shannon. I will remember it forever."

By this time Shannon's parents were also getting emotional, but smiling. Looking at the wedding gowns, Shannon found one that she really liked. She called her parents and Denise over to see what they all thought of it. After a while, they agreed it was a beautiful gown and quite fitting for Shannon. Shannon tried it on, and the seamstress came to make the necessary alterations to the gown, and soon that was done.

Tears in her eyes, Shannon looked at Denise, her arms around her friend. "It's the maid of honor's turn; you pick the dress that you want."

Denise told Shannon, "Well, it should be the dress that you want me to wear—it's your wedding after all."

"No, Denise, it's all your choice. You pick it out and I will accept what you pick. You know yourself, and we have never disagreed on anything."

"That is so true. All through our long friendship, we have always agreed on everything, and that is hard to believe." Denise went on to give Shannon and her parents a big hug.

In a moment, Denise was looking at dresses. In her mind, she knew the colors that she and Shannon liked. Stopping at one dress, she looked at the style and color, and felt this was exactly the one she and Shannon would like. She called Shannon over and said, "I would like to wear this at your wedding—do you think it would be okay?"

Tears flowing and standing face to face with Denise, Shannon answered her by saying, "You turkey, you know how much I love the color red—it is great, Denise!" Denise tried on the red dress, and she looked absolutely gorgeous in that red dress. Again, the seamstress came over and made the adjustments, and that was it for picking out the wedding gown and the dress for Denise.

"Everything would be ready in two weeks," the store clerk advised them. "By the way, you two gals are so cute and so pleasing to be around. Some guys are going to be real lucky to have you in their lives, and Denise, some guy better nab you quickly—I don't think you are going to last long."

Grinning, Denise replied, "Well, I am working on one right now." They all left the store and went to their cars.

Shannon said, "Mom, Dad, Denise can come with me. Mom and Dad, thanks for everything, and please drive carefully back to Lodi."

Shannon and Denise were left alone with each other.
"Denise, I have another task to get done today," Shannon
said. "I have to buy Ray's wedding ring."
Just down the street was a jewelry store, and a couple of
blocks later, they found themselves inside the store.
A salesperson came over to offer some help them. "I
want to look at men's wedding rings," Shannon said, and he
promptly showed her where they were.
Shannon started to look at some rings through the glass
display case. One caught her eye and she said, "Denise, look
at that wedding ring with a ruby mounted on it. I think Ray
would like that ring." She called the salesperson over and
said, "Could I see that ring with a ruby mounted on it?" The
salesperson handed her the box with the ring.
When she looked closer at the ring, Shannon noticed an
information sheet tucked in the box, so she read it to Denise.
"The ruby is considered the stone of love and passion. This
ruby was mined in the Bengal area in India."
"You are right. Ray would like that ring," Denise replied.
Shannon turned to the salesperson. "I will take this ring.
It is the right size, but I want it to be engraved on the inside
with these words." (The words were: *Love Shannon 7-1-59)*
The ring taken care of, Shannon and Denise were soon
out of the jewelry store and to Shannon's car, heading back
to Shannon's apartment. When they got to the apartment,
Shannon asked Denise if she could come in for a while just
to talk, so they both went in and sat down.
"This has been a wonderful day to be with you. I hope you
enjoyed it as much as I did. Denise, you are one of kind, you
are like a sister to me," Shannon shared with Denise.
"Shannon through the years we have been together many
times, but I must say this day is the most special to me.
Shannon, I want to thank you for including me in your plans.
Thank you so much from the bottom of my heart."

"Denise, I am going to share this only with you: I am trying to be a big girl, but I will need you like no other time when Ray leaves for India."

"I will always be there for you, and remember we will soon be hunting buddies."

"Oh, that's right! That Joeseph sure works pretty fast, but he certainly seems like a great guy."

"Yes, and I am so lucky he happened along, thanks to you and Ray. I have dated many guys, and most of them just want to have sex. Joeseph gives me so much respect it's hard to believe there are some still good guys out there," Denise replied.

Shannon smiled. "It must be typical of those farm boys in the Sacramento delta," she said.

After a while, Denise had to leave. "Shannon, don't worry; Ray is a good hunter with lots of experience. Everybody will be by your side when he is gone. I can guarantee it. I especially will be by your side no matter what. You just ask and I will be there for you.

"Well, I do have to go. I will be seeing you later. What a perfect day I have had with you, my longtime friend. Shannon, I love you like a sister, and that means I would do anything for you, and I do mean anything," Denise said.

CHAPTER 6

TWO GALS GO HUNTING

⊷⊷⊷

Three weeks have passed since the wedding plans were initiated. The time had come to contact all the people involved and take care of the things needed for the occasion: contacting the florist, choosing the flowers, choosing the dinner menu for the catering service, making arrangements with the Lutheran Church, and going to the pastor for marriage counseling. The wedding gown and the maid of honor's dress had all been picked up, and of course Ray's ring. Ray had already gotten Shannon's ring at the time he picked her engagement ring. Ray and Joeseph were fitted for their tuxedo, as did Shannon's dad and Ray's dad. Everything appears to be in motion and going forward.

Amidst all these, Ray was in the middle of finals at college, with one eye set at graduating in about two weeks. Afterwards, he would be starting his job at Lodi Mold Inc. He had a full load of things to do, but he seemed to handle the pressure very well.

At dinner, Ray was telling his parents he would be graduating in two weeks from the coming Saturday.

"Do you want a big graduation party?" Paul asked his son.

"I would prefer just family, Joeseph and his parents, and of course Shannon and her parents. Also include Denise and her parents, especially considering her ongoing relationship with Joeseph. Oh, please also invite the Chins. They are so special. I would like them to be here for the party—and that would be just about right for me."

"Okay, we will call everybody by phone. We will have a barbecue here at the ranch on that afternoon."

"That sounds great, Dad, Mom, thank you so much."

Ray decided to call Fred Sunday at Lodi Mold Inc., indicating to him the date he would be graduating college.

"Ray, why don't you plan on coming in that following Monday? I will have Liz get all the paperwork ready," Fred said.

"Thank you so much, Fred. I will be there on that Monday." They hung up the phone, and Ray felt a sense of relief that it was done and over with.

One thing Ray wanted to do was to go see the Chins at their sporting goods store. So he headed to Isleton and went into the store, where both Mr. and Mrs. Chin came out and greeted Ray kindly as usual.

"Well, Mr. Chin, I promised I would tell you why I bought that 338 Winchester Magnum rifle—I am going to go to India to hunt the Bengal tiger."

The Chins stood there in amazement, "Well, that will be one adventurous trip, Ray! When will the trip take place?"

"In May of 1960 is my plane's departure. Everybody is okay with me going—it has been such a longtime dream of mine to hunt the Bengal tiger."

Mr. Chin said, "You mean even Shannon is okay with the trip?"

"Yes. And I told her long before I told anybody else. But I know she will need a lot of support while I am gone."

"Oh, by the way, Ray, I gave Joeseph's gal friend a hunting safety test last week and she now has a hunting license. Looks like things are getting serious with them. I understand she is Shannon's best friend; she sure is nice and very cute. She mentioned that she and Shannon will be hunting together at your parent's ranch and the Alexanders' ranch; that should help Shannon get through the rough times when you are gone."

"Well, I did want to keep you updated: Shannon and I will be getting married this July 1st."

That gave the Chins a large grin on their faces. "Well, congratulations!" they said in unison. In a while, Ray was back to his pickup truck and headed back to the ranch.

Inside their house, Ray proceeded to call Joeseph.

"Hey, Joeseph, I was down to see Mr. Chin today. He told me Denise got her hunting license—so when do you think she will be ready to go with Shannon hunting?"

"Actually we just got back from hunting. She got a couple of cottontail rabbits, and so it was a pretty good day. She was using my Marlin 22 rifle. I taught her about stalking. She just got done dressing out the rabbits for the freezer. She did very well; I believe she could hit the trail with Shannon at any time, whenever they are ready. They could hunt on our ranch or yours. That gives them about 600 acres total to hunt on."

"That's great, Joeseph. Is there anything new happening?" Ray said, getting a little nosey.

Joeseph answered Ray's question by saying, "Ray, I believe something great is going to happen in a few days or in the near future."

"Okay, Joeseph, I won't pry anymore. You have a good day. I will let Shannon know that Denise is ready to go hunting when time permits." They then hung up the phone.

Ray had just gotten off the phone with Joeseph when the phone rang. It was Shannon. She sounded excited over the phone.

"I just got a phone call from Denise!" Shannon started. "She is so excited having gotten her hunting license. She even went hunting with Joeseph. He taught her about stalking to get a closer shot, and using the trajectory table for different distances other than the sight in distance. He also showed her

81

how to dress out the rabbits that she got, and then freezing them, just like you did with me."

"Shannon—slow down a little. You sound more excited than Denise."

"Ray, she is my best friend! I can't wait to go hunting with her." Shannon continued, "She wants to go hunting this Saturday with me, which would be okay since next Saturday you will be graduating and we couldn't go. Ray, it would be convenient if we could use your guns and I have my own— would that be okay?"

"Of course, Shannon. You really do sound excited."

"Well, I am excited! We have always done everything together. She will help me pass the time when you are gone, and that is important," Shannon replied.

"Okay, Shannon. You and Denise come out to the ranch on Saturday and I will drop by your apartment after classes on Wednesday, if that's all right."

"That would be great, Ray! I want you to stay for dinner if you can."

"Shannon, that sounds good. Would be your first time cooking something for me. I can't wait to see you on Wednesday—I love you so much." They then both hung up the phones.

It's Wednesday and Ray was done with his last class for the day and now he was headed to Shannon's apartment. Once there, he rang the doorbell. Shannon opened the door and Ray went in, lifting her up and giving her a kiss on her belly. She was wearing that very skimpy tank top again, and her belly was so inviting that he found he just had to kiss her there.

From Shannon: "Ray, that felt so good—do it again." And he did, but this time he kept kissing her at various parts of her body until he reached her lips. He then gave her a long and exciting kiss on her lips.

"If you are that excited, you just wait till we are on our honeymoon, which is now about a month away," teased Ray.

"Ray, you basically lit my fuse and it's so hard to stop, especially when we are here alone."

Ray gave her another passionate kiss before he said, "Let's save everything for our wedding night, Shannon. We can hold out." With that they both calmed down.

"Well, dinner is about ready. I cooked something very special for you, so let's sit down for dinner," Shannon said. She took a covered roaster out of the oven and Ray recognized the smell: it was his mom's recipe for the beef tomato roast.

Ray smiled. "This will be great, thanks so much!" he said. Shannon served the roast and they ate. Afterwards, Ray commented, "You did a great job, thanks again." Shannon got the desert out, and Ray could see it was a chocolate cake, and that was his favorite. Ray's response was, "Did Mom tell you that chocolate is my favorite flavor?"

"Your mom has been telling me a lot about things you really like."

After dinner, they went to the sofa and started talking about things that happened during the day. The subject came up about Denise going hunting with Shannon on Saturday.

"I am so excited about going hunting with Denise. I truly hope everything will work out for her and Joeseph," Shannon said.

"Shannon, I believe it will work out. I believe they were made for each other like you and me."

"I hope you are right," Shannon said, unaware that Joeseph had mentioned to Ray that something great was about to happen in the near future. As it was getting a little late, Ray kissed Shannon, thanked her for the dinner, and then left for home.

After school on Friday, Ray and Shannon arranged to meet at the student lounge around three o'clock. Realizing they both needed to eat, they placed their order and found a place to sit.

Ray asked, "Shannon, are you and Denise still going hunting Saturday morning?"

"Yes, Denise and I are spending tonight at my parents so we can take off in the morning for the ranch. It's closer from Lodi than from here. I think we will get to the ranch about nine o'clock."

"Sounds good. I will probably be in the field helping my dad fix an irrigation culvert. And I will probably see you two hunters roaming around looking for something to shoot. It should be fun for you both. Remember, you can also use Joeseph's parents' farm. The two ranches are connected by a dirt road in the back next to the Georgiana Slough."

"Ray, it's only a month away and you and I will share the same name," Shannon said, smiling. "It's going to be such a great day and a real great night, especially if we think how we will try from then on to make our children and give both our parents their most precious dream, grandchildren. I can't wait to get started."

Soon, Ray and Shannon were ready to head home. After giving each other a kiss, they both headed home to their parents.

Arriving at his parent's house, Ray went inside and said hello to his mom and dad.

"How is Shannon doing today? Is everything going okay. I would imagine you both are getting excited with the wedding about a month away," Mary asked.

"Yes, Mom, we are both very excited," replied Ray. "By the way, she made me dinner on Wednesday. We had your famous tomato beef roast, and she baked a chocolate cake—

you know how I love chocolate. She did a good job cooking, and she is really in good spirits," Ray added.

"Dad, Shannon and Denise are going hunting in the morning. I told her I would be helping you repair that irrigation culvert and I would be out in the field with you. She has the keys to the pickup truck, the house, and the combination to the gun safe, so she has everything she needs."

"Ray, I really appreciate you helping me tomorrow. I just can't do the things I use to do anymore. It's called getting older," Paul said.

"I understand, Dad. You can call on me any time. The day I say no to you and Mom, feel free to call a meeting so we can discuss my attitude. I will see you both in the morning. I am so tired I am going to hit the bed for some good sleep."

It was about nine o'clock on Saturday when Shannon and Denise went through the door and gave Mom a hug, and went to get the guns and ammo that they needed. As both came back through the kitchen, Mary noticed something about Denise that caught her attention, but she didn't say anything. After they said goodbye, they got into Ray's pickup truck and headed out to the back of the ranch. As they were driving, Shannon saw Ray and his dad working on the irrigation culvert, so they headed over to see them.

"Hello, Ray! Hi, Dad!" Shannon said. You guys are really into this job. You are full of mud and dirt from head to toe."

"Sometimes on the farm you will get downright dirty," replied Ray. "You will learn someday, Shannon."

"Just think, Shannon, someday Mom and I will be gone. When that happens, this farm will be yours to take care of; then again I think you would look cute full of mud and dirt. I wish I could live to see you look like that," Paul added.

"Dad, you say the word and I will be out here helping Ray with any job you ask him to do, and I mean that—okay?"

Paul just sat back and gave a big smile to his new daughter.

Paul asked, "Is Denise on the other side? I need to ask her something."

Scooting over and leaning across Shannon, Denise looked out the pickup truck window opening in the door and commented, "You guys really are dirty. That is a dirty, muddy job. But you are working with your son, so you really don't care—do you, Dad?"

"That's right, Denise; you really nailed us with that comment, for that's who we are: father and son. Looking at you hanging out that window, I sense this is going to be a very special day for Shannon and you together." Ray's dad had a monstrous smile on his face as he stared at Denise, who smiled right back and gave an inconspicuous nod at Paul.

In a moment, Shannon and Denise were back heading for their big hunting expedition.

As Shannon was driving to the back of the ranch towards the Georgiana Slough, where Ray had mentioned of a road that connected the Johnson ranch and the Alexander ranch, Shannon stopped the pickup truck.

"Well, Denise, where do you want to start hunting today, on the Johnson ranch or the Alexander ranch?"

"Shannon, let's just start here on the Johnson ranch."

"Okay" Shannon said, and continued driving. Just then, Denise saw a jack rabbit ahead. Shannon promptly stopped the pickup truck. They then got out, used some bushes as cover, and began a stalking procedure. When they thought they were close enough for a shot, they both lay down in the prone position, Shannon on Denise's right side. Denise was going to take the first shot. Shannon was going to be the backup in case Denise missed and the rabbit, for some reason, stayed, which can happen.

As they were lying down, a thought suddenly occurred to Shannon. "What do you think Ray's dad meant when he said we were going to have a very special day together?"

"I don't really have an idea, but we better get this rabbit."
With that, Denise settled down and started to aim.

Shannon said, "You are looking good—real, real, real good!"
Meanwhile, Denise was thinking Shannon must have seen
what Ray's dad saw when she was talking to him and she was
leaning out the pickup window opening.

"Well, here it goes," Denise said, and she fired. Shortly,
the jack rabbit did a few flips and then fell dead. Denise
told Shannon, "I got that turkey. Shannon, hurry, take aim!
Another one just came out." Complying, Shannon took
careful aim and squeezed off a shot, and down went another
jack rabbit.

Shannon told Denise, "Just look at that, we got a double
on our first hunt together! We both shot and hit our target—I
am so proud of us! My best friend, I believe we are looking
at enjoying our life together as hunting wives."

"Denise, I noticed that shiny ring on your finger just
before you shot. You hid it pretty good, until you put your
left hand around the rifle stock and I noticed the ring. Is that
what Ray's dad meant when he said we were going to have
a special day together?"

"Yes, he did see the ring when I was leaning out the pickup
window."

Hearing that, Shannon yelled out as loud as she could,
"Denise is engaged! Denise is engaged!"

Back at the irrigation culvert they were working on,
Ray asked his dad, "Did you hear somebody yell?"

"It was probably Shannon yelling after seeing Denise
wearing an engagement ring," Paul replied.

"Dad, how did you know," Ray asked.

"I noticed the ring when she was leaning out the pickup
window, but I wanted Shannon's best friend to surprise her
when they were alone. I bet your mom noticed the ring also,
but knowing your mom, she also wanted the two of them to

cherish the moment together. That's how it should be with friends."

Ray and his dad were winding up the job on the irrigation culvert, and were putting everything back in the pickup truck.

Ray said, "Dad, should we go find them so we could tell Denise congratulations?"

"No, let them enjoy the day hunting together, knowing they will spend their life together as best friends should do."

"Dad, you are right. Let's go back to the house and clean up. We are really dirty."

With that, they made for the pickup and went back to the house.

Ray and his dad walked through the back door and into the kitchen, where they greeted Mary. She had baked a cake and was about to put the frosting on it, along with other decorations that she was very good at doing.

"Mary, what's the occasion?" Paul asked.

Mary answered, "It's just a little celebration to congratulate Joeseph and Denise on the occasion of their engagement."

"Who told you, Mom?"

"I noticed the ring on her finger this morning as they were leaving to go hunting. I didn't say anything because I thought once Shannon noticed the ring, it would be appropriate that the two of them would celebrate Denise's engagement as best friends and hunting buddies privately."

Paul said, "I noticed the ring on Denise's finger when they stopped by while Ray and I were working on the irrigation culvert. I felt the same as you did: let them enjoy the moment together as friends."

Mary had finished decorating the cake, and everybody was excited. It came out so good, as usual, and was just right for the occasion.

"Oh, Joeseph called earlier and told me he would come over around two o'clock," Mary said. "He was excited to see how the two did on their hunting adventure; he doesn't know I was baking a cake to have a little celebration for them, honoring their engagement."

"Mom, you are so great and kind to others. It's the reason every young person will always end up calling you 'Mom.' You just watch—it won't be long for Denise to call you 'Mom.'"

"Ray, it doesn't cost anything to be kind to people. Anybody who enters our home is treated with respect and kindness by both your dad and me. That's just a natural thing we do, and I hope you will always show kindness to others also. Also, we both don't care what color their skin is; anybody is welcome in this house."

Being a poor sight to look at, Ray and his dad went to clean up and get some clean fresh clothes on. After this, they went into the living room and talked about the day's events. Joeseph arrived around two o'clock. Once inside, everybody congratulated him on his engagement to Denise.

"Thanks, all of you. I know I hit the jackpot when I met Denise, and I will always be grateful to both Ray and Shannon for that."

"I wonder how our hunters are doing right now. They have been out a long time. I saw the pickup roaming around between the two ranches. I can hardly wait to see what they managed to get."

"I will make a guess it's not going to be just cottontail rabbits; it's going to be a variety of animals," Ray replied.

Just then, Joeseph saw the cake that Mary had prepared.

"Mom, thanks so much for the thought, Denise will be surprised—and excited." Joeseph went over to Mary and gave her a monstrous hug. "I guess I should have expected it knowing that's just how you Johnsons are."

Meanwhile, the two hunters were still out vigorously hunting, and their hunting expedition is turning out both exciting and successful. At this point they were looking at California ground squirrels, of which they had located a pretty good size group in an area on Joeseph's parent's ranch. As they tried to approach these varmints, they soon realized these critters were pretty smart. They were tough to make a kill, as they often would make it into their holes before they died. Ray mentioned this to Shannon before, and so indicated 75 yards was about as close as one could get, and 22 Magnum rifle would be the rifle of choice. Since they only had one, they would take turns using the 22 magnum.

Spotting a squirrel on the levee, Denise was quick to position herself, took aim, and shot and made the kill.

"Good shot," Shannon said.

Soon, another popped up and Shannon got that one. By the time it was over, they had shot six squirrels. Denise had the 22 Magnum and they were just about ready to call it a day.

"Denise, look, a coyote is coming over the levee! It probably knows a lot of squirrels were in the area, and probably wanted some dinner."

As the coyote cautiously came down the levee, it noticed some of the dead squirrels. The coyote then stopped long enough for Denise to get a shot.

They both got up and hugged each other. Denise had gotten a coyote, which was a milestone for any hunter. They collected the squirrels and the coyote, depositing them at the back of the pickup. Filled with a sense of accomplishment, they called it a day.

Inside the pickup, Shannon and Denise looked at each other and agreed it had been a wonderful day for them.

"Shannon, someday if our future husbands would agree, it would be great if we could raise our families here," Denise said. "It would be like a dream come true for both of us."

"Denise, don't say it too loud—if Mary Johnson heard you say that, she would probably say, 'Where do you want us to build your houses?' It would be a dream of Paul and hers, I just know it." Soon they were headed back to the Johnson's house.

Back at the house, Ray, his parents, and Joeseph were anxiously waiting for the two hunters. When they finally saw the pickup approaching, everybody went outside to greet them. Ray and Joeseph greeted the hunters with a hug and a kiss.

Ray was quick to say something. "Did you both have fun?" he said. Turning to Denise, he added, "Denise, congratulations to you and Joeseph for your engagement. We were all excited to get the news. Much as you tried to hide it, Mom and Dad both noticed the ring but wanted you and Shannon to share the moment privately with each other. Shannon and I did not notice the engagement ring on her finger, and they said nothing to leave it as a surprise to Shannon. They both felt that's what Denise must have wanted."

"Thank you, Ray. As for the hunt, I know everyone is anxious to know how we fared at it, so I'll say you can now look in the pickup and see what your future wives got today." Heeding Denise, everybody went to look—and were smiling shortly.

"Well, you gals must have really been on a mission to get all these critters today," Paul said.

Shannon said, "Those are seven jack rabbits, four cottontail rabbits, six squirrels, and a coyote right there. The poor coyote must have been hungry at the wrong time, and too bad for him, my friend dead-eye Denise nailed him."

Remembering to get a camera, Ray took a picture of both Shannon and Denise with the game making the background.

"We must admit we had so much fun out here today," Denise said. "If our future husbands would agree, it would be great to raise a family out here. It would be like a dream come true for Shannon and me."

91

It wasn't long before Mary had her arms around Shannon and Denise, saying, "It would be like a dream come true for everybody. Especially the day grandchildren would be roaming around here. I am sure Joeseph's parents, and of course Dad and I, would all agree. All you have to do is say when and where, and the houses will be built." Joeseph and Ray both smiled.

Denise gave Mary a hug. "Mom, Dad—thank you so much for everything this ranch represents. There's just plain love all over the place, between you two and Joeseph's parents. I couldn't ask for better people to be surrounded by."

Ray was thinking silently of how he had told his mom it wouldn't take long for Denise to refer to them as "Mom" and "Dad."

"Well, we have to dress out four cottontail rabbits and get rid of the rest of these critters; you might say food for the scavengers."

"When you get done, you just come on in to get cleaned up a little and just relax—you both had a very busy day," Paul said.

Shannon and Denise proceeded to dress out the rabbits and get them freezer-ready. After that they headed towards the pond area where a lot of wildlife tended to be, placing the dead animals there before making their way back to the ranch house. Noticing Joeseph's parents' car in the driveway, Denise wondered what was up. After washing up at the porch area, they went into the dining room where everybody was congregating.

Denise went over to Joeseph's mom and dad and gave them a hug. "Mom, Dad, how are you both doing today?" she asked them.

"Denise, we heard you had such a day hunting with your best friend Shannon, and we're quite happy for you," they replied excitedly.

"Words can never begin to describe our most wonderful day together—it was a dream come true," Denise replied.

Joeseph's dad said, "Well, Denise, Mary told us how you would love it if you and Joeseph, along with Shannon and Ray, could someday live out here and raise a family. That would certainly be a dream come true for everybody here today. You just say when and it will happen. I know I speak for the Johnsons also. Also, remember that the houses will be built at no cost to you. It will be an honor for us and the Johnsons to do that for our new daughters, and of course our sons, and hopefully someday our grandchildren."

The words brought a flood of tears to Shannon and Denise's eyes. They could barely get the words to thank them, the emotions preventing the words from coming out.

Ray's mom thought it was time to bring out the cake that she had made to celebrate this day that Joeseph had asked for Denise's hand in marriage. Mary presented the cake to Joeseph and Denise.

"Denise, I noticed the ring on your finger this morning when you and Shannon were heading out to go hunting through the kitchen. You were trying not to make it visible, but I caught the sparkle of the diamond on your hand. I knew I had to think of something to honor you and Joeseph today, so I got busy right away when you both walked out the door."

Denise looked at the cake and read the words on it: "To Joeseph and Denise, on this special day that your commitment to marriage was found out. Congratulations from your friend Shannon and the Johnson family."

Soon everybody was enjoying the cake that Mary Johnson had made. After a while, Shannon and Denise decided they would head back to Lodi. They were going to stay at Denise's parents for the night.

93

Before leaving, Shannon made a suggestion to Ray. "Why don't you drop by my apartment after school on Monday? I will be there any time after two o'clock."

"I will see you then." He gave Shannon a kiss, and Shannon and Denise were then on their way back to Lodi.

On their way, Shannon said, "I really liked Joeseph's parents. I can tell they love you. What do you think of Joeseph and Ray's parents' offer to build a house we can use to raise a family out on the farm?"

Denise recalled, "Well, you did say if I let in that we would someday like to live out on the farm that Ray's mom would jump at the idea, and she did. Shannon, it's clear you and I will have sweet, loving in-laws. The other day Joeseph was talking about a wedding in February 1960, right after our graduation in January. Joeseph and I know our sexual emotions are sky-high, so the sooner the better it would be for us. He wants Ray to be the best man, before Ray took off for India in May."

"Well, Denise, I would say after today and with children living on the farm, we and our in-laws will have many joyous days ahead of us."

"Shannon, I have heard of daughters-in-law having strained relationships with their in-laws about grandchildren. In no way would that be the case—that would devastate Joeseph and Ray's parents, and that's never going to happen on my watch."

"I agree—I could never do that either."

After pulling into Denise's parents' driveway, the two friends were greeted inside by Denise's parents, who gave both a big hug.

Denise's mom turned to Shannon. "Well, I bet you both had fun hunting together. You must also be excited about Joeseph and Denise being engaged."

"Mom, everybody at the farm was excited," said Denise. "So much, actually, that Mom Johnson made a cake to have a small celebration. Mary spotted the ring just before we went out hunting but she didn't mention it. She thought Shannon and I should have that special moment together. Instead, she just started baking and decorating the cake for Joeseph and me, so when Shannon and I got back we could have a little celebration."

The two went on to share their hunting success for the day, adding that they would have pictures of everything they had shot when Ray had the film developed.

After a while the two excused themselves to get some rest after such a fun-filled Saturday.

On Sunday morning, Shannon, Denise, and her parents were back conversing with each other over breakfast.

"The coming Saturday will be a big day for Ray. He will be graduating college with a degree in mechanical engineering. On Monday he will immediately start work at Lodi Mold, Inc.

"I can't believe in about five weeks Ray and I will be married. That will be a great day in my life, and my best friend Denise sitting right here will be right by my side to share the moment. But it won't be long before she finds herself in the same situation."

Denise's dad said, "We are so happy seeing you in this very special time of your life, especially since you two grew up side by side all those years."

"Dad, yesterday as Shannon and I were hunting and having fun out on the farms, I mentioned to her how it would be like a dream come true if we both could live on the farm and raise our families there," Denise said. "When the Johnsons and Alexanders heard it, they simply asked us when and where we would like to have the house. Joeseph's dad added it would be a dream come true for them, too, making sure to say we will have a house built at no cost at all to us."

Denise had tears in her eyes but managed to say, "Mom, Dad, Shannon and I know all the parents involved in our future plans have a dream of their own."

"What's that?" Denise's dad asked,

"To give you grandchildren." Denise's mom and dad went over and hugged both Shannon and Denise for making such a commitment.

Denise's Mom then said, "You are both so right. I am sure your in-laws are every bit as excited as Shannon's parents like us to hear that."

Soon, Shannon and Denise bade goodbye to head back to Sacramento and Davis to get ready for school on Monday.

Once inside her apartment and relaxing in front of the TV, Shannon heard the phone ring and took the call. It was Denise, "Hi Denise. Is there something wrong?"

"No, no! I just thought I'd call you to thank you for the fun-packed weekend. And Shannon, I must say Paul and Mary just adore you like you really are their daughter, and they are just full of love for you.

"Denise, I have been blessed to have them and Ray in my life, but I have another person that I am also blessed to have in my life.

"Who is that, Shannon? I can't think of anybody else."

There was a long pause and then Shannon casually said, "Denise—Denise, you are the one I have been blessed with for all these years. You are my best friend, and I can always count on you—and I hope you have the same feelings about me."

"That's a no-brainer, Shannon, and you know it. We are close and loyal friends, and now look at the future and the fun we will have on the farms in the great Sacramento Delta."

CHAPTER 7

RAY'S GRADUATION

It was Monday, and Ray's graduation was less than a week away. Further, Shannon and Ray's wedding day was a little more than four weeks away, so things were really getting a little busy and you might say a little on the hectic side.

Ray's dad took care of all the food and drinks for Ray's graduation; they were going to have barbecued steaks that he had ordered from the local butcher shop in Isleton. Everybody was involved in getting the yard set up with tables and chairs; Ray's mom would take care of all the table settings, so everything seemed to be under control and ready to go. Ray wanted just friends and relatives of his mom and dad's family, which would include some aunts, uncles, and cousins, all of which would amount to about forty guests.

After his last class, Ray headed over to Shannon's. It was around two o'clock, the time they agreed to meet at Shannon's apartment. After Ray rang the bell and Shannon opened the door, they greeted each other with another long emotional kiss. They then went to sit on the sofa.

"I have only three days of school left before I receive my long-awaited degree in mechanical engineering. It has been long and hard, but I am finally finished. But Shannon, we are just beginning. Just think of that: in a little over four weeks, we will unite forever—I can't wait for that day."

Shannon responded with a very emotional caress and a kiss like she was trying to light Ray's fuse. "Shannon, you have to save all this for our wedding night when we both won't care about lighting fuses."

"I understand, Ray, but it's almost impossible for us both to wait."

After a while, they settled down a little better.

"I made an appointment for us to see the pastor of my church at four o'clock tomorrow after school," Shannon said. "I thought we could meet at my parents' house and meet with Pastor Green at church—is that okay?"

"Sure. I will be at your house around 3:30." Ray then remembered something. "Is it still okay for me to pick our honeymoon location?" he asked her.

"Sure, Ray, it's okay; just proceed with your plans," she replied. Smiling, she added, "I have only one request: make sure the room has a nice bed. I know it's going to be used with a lot of passion and often."

That got Ray smiling and shaking his head. "Shannon, I swear I think you are like a dog in heat."

That got them both laughing, and he pulled her to him tightly before giving her a long, passionate kiss.

"Why didn't you wear that skimpy tank top today?" he asked her, smiling.

"You want me to put it on? Sounds like you are trying to light fuses again," she replied.

"No, that's okay."

Their time together over, Ray was soon making his way out Shannon's apartment. "See you tomorrow at your house," he said before being on his way.

On his way, Ray considered how everything seemed to happen pretty fast—graduation, wedding, job, and the hunting trip to India. He decided planning for the hunting trip must come after graduation.

Back inside their house, he greeted his mom who was busy as usual; his dad was out in the field irrigating the tomatoes.

He realized his mom appeared anxious. "You look deep in thought, Mom—is something bothering you?"

"No, Ray, nothing is bothering me. It's just I am so excited to have Shannon in the family, especially after she mentioned the other day that maybe someday she would like to raise a family out here."

Paul had just entered the kitchen. Seeing Mary a little teary-eyed, he asked, "What's wrong, Mary?"

"Nothing, Paul. It's okay."

"Dad, Mom is too excited about Shannon and me raising a family out here someday."

Paul smiled. "Well, that makes two of us. I can't wait to get those grandchildren, go out in the field, and get them all dirty and muddy."

"Tomorrow, Shannon and I will see the pastor of their church to discuss our background and who knows what else. It's to give us an idea if we are compatible with each other," Ray said.

"Don't be surprised what the answer might be," Paul said. "Your mom and I were told by some pastor we would never make it, and we have been married forty-five years. Just be prepared but don't you two worry about it," he concluded.

The three of them proceeded to talk about other things, when Paul remembered something. "Ray, have you done any planning yet for your hunting trip to India?"

"I have already made inquiries about plane routes and the best areas for tiger hunting," replied Ray. "I will have to get serious about picking a guide next, and getting in touch with the proper Indian agency to acquire leopard and tiger hunting permits. I intend to take care of those right after the wedding."

At this time, Ray's mom had dinner on the table. While they were at it, talk resumed in the direction of Ray's graduation party.

"Well, Mom and Dad, this Saturday I will graduate—are you ready for the party?"

Paul and Mary were quick to respond with, "Yes, excited and ready we are!"

"Then I go to work, and July 1st Shannon and I will get married." At that moment, Ray remembered he had to make reservations at the Borg's Motel for his honeymoon room. "Well, Mom and Dad I think I am going to retire, but I do have to make one phone call."

"Okay, Ray. And tomorrow after Shannon and you get done with the pastor counseling, could you both come up to the ranch? Mom and I have something we would like to discuss with you both."

"Sure we will be here." Ray went to his room and called the Borg's Motel and made reservation for the Fourth of July weekend and then went to bed.

The next morning Ray grabbed a quick breakfast, said goodbye to his parents, and said, "Shannon and I will see you tonight after the pastor counseling session."

After school classes, Ray headed straight to Lodi and Shannon's parents' house. Inside he greeted Shannon with a kiss and said hello to her parents.

Shannon's mom told Ray, "You don't have to be nervous. Pastor Green won't bite. He might disappoint you with what his conclusion will be, but you need not worry about it. One thing Dad and I know is that you two were made to be together—there is no doubt about that."

Once at the church, Shannon and Ray proceeded to the office where the church receptionist first greeted them then took them to the pastoral office where Shannon introduced Ray to Pastor Green.

Pastor Green had them sit down and explained what the session was meant to accomplish. He told them that marriage is a sacred and important ceremony in the eyes of God, and

God wants it to be a lifelong commitment. He also went on to say that it is the church's responsibility to make sure the persons to be joined in marriage are compatible with each other. This is so they would truly have a chance to be married as man and woman for life. And if it was determined that they were not compatible with each other, it was the church's duty to recommend to the couple that they should not get married, for fear the marriage would end in divorce. But in the end it is the couple's choice. If they still wanted to get married, the church would perform the marriage ceremony.

After listening to Pastor Green's explanation, Ray and Shannon both felt relieved that the decision was still theirs; they knew they loved each other and it would be a marriage for life.

Pastor Green started the questioning, and Ray and Shannon gave him their honest answers. When it was over, Pastor Green told them, "The only area you are not compatible is your religious status. Ray, you mentioned you consider yourself a Catholic but do not attend church on a regular basis. Shannon is a Lutheran and attends church regularly, and I know that for a fact as her parents have attended this church for years. I also got from my questions that you are both in love, and at times during your courtship there were situations that you both became really emotional with each other. But you avoided premarital sex, as tempting as it was.

"Shannon, you were very truthful when you said Ray was in control and tried hard to always respect you and your parents, even though at times you often wanted so much to consent to premarital sex." Pastor Green continued to say, "Shannon, I believe Ray will be a fine husband for you, and Ray, I look forward to seeing Shannon and you in church and someday baptizing your children." Sitting across the desk, Pastor Green smiled at the two of them and concluded, "Not all counseling sessions do I feel this good about."

Ray and Shannon felt they were truly going to have a very blessed wedding. They ended the session with, "Thank you, Pastor Green. We will see you at the rehearsal, and then on the big day of July 1st."

Ray and Shannon felt quite relieved, especially after showing an open attitude with the pastor. They felt they gave him a sense of confidence after expressing their commitment to each other.

"I forgot to tell you my mom and dad wanted us to go up to the ranch," Ray told Shannon. "They wanted to talk to us about something. They never let me know what it was about, so would that be okay?"

"Sure, but I wonder what it's about. I certainly hope there is nothing seriously wrong."

"Shannon, if it was something serious, they would have told me about it." With that, Shannon and Ray took separate cars and headed to the Johnson ranch.

At the ranch, they found Mom and Dad in the kitchen and they all greeted each other.

"Let's all sit down for dinner; it is a real simple dinner tonight," Mary started. "It's something we occasionally do—breakfast at dinner time with linguica, eggs, and pancakes. I hope that's okay, Shannon," she said.

"We actually do the same thing at our house, Mom. We like the occasional change—it seems good to have a change every once in a while," Shannon replied.

"I suppose you two are getting pretty excited as July 1st gets closer," Paul said while they were having the meal.

"We're beyond being excited, Dad. By the way, I made our honeymoon reservations yesterday, so that's all set and ready to go."

Mary curiously asked, "Where are you going for your honeymoon?"

"Only I know that answer, and it's pretty special and appropriate," replied Ray.

Shannon always seemed to have a sense of humor, but sometimes people got the feeling she actually meant what she said.

"I hope it's not too far," she said. With a serious look on her face, she added, "Because if it's going be a long drive, we might have to begin our honeymoon in the car."

Ray and his parents managed a reserved laugh, kept in check by the thought that Shannon might be serious.

After dinner, Paul said, "The reason Mom and I wanted to talk to you both tonight was that we would like to let you know what we would like to give you as a wedding present. If you agree that it would be okay."

"Well, Mom and Dad, you know Ray and I are easy to please. We both would have a hard time not accepting anything you would want to give or do for us."

Ray somehow felt he knew what was coming, and he thought it might be a good idea to get the box of Kleenex right now.

Paul proceeded with what he wanted to say. "Shannon—the other night, you and your friend Denise mentioned that someday you both would like to raise a family out here in the Sacramento Delta. Well, Mom and I would like to make that dream happen by building you a house of your choice for your wedding present—if that would be okay with you both."

Ray was right all along in what he had been thinking. Shannon was so emotional she had trouble responding. She managed to look at Ray, and they both gave a nod of approval to each other. Shannon then went to them both and gave them a monstrous embrace. When she finally spoke, she could barely get the words out.

"Thank you so much for wanting to do that for us and your future grandchildren." Ray and Shannon just sat there and embraced each other tightly, and again they both said, "Thank you so much, Mom and Dad."

After things calmed down, Mary said, "Here is a magazine of home plans that you may want to look at. They are not detailed plans, but they are designed so a contractor can make the construction plans from them."

"If at all possible, and if you both could make a decision on what floor plan you both like, I would get a contractor involved right away, even before you are married. Then of course you both would have to pick a location on the ranch to build," Paul said.

Shannon just could not get over what had just taken place. Another thing also occurred to her. "Mom, Dad—what if something happens to Ray on his trip to India? Even though I don't want to think about losing him ... and then there is just me."

"Oh, Shannon, that's the important part. You are like a daughter to us. If something was to take Ray away from you and us, the house is yours, and even if you chose to get married again, the house is yours. Shannon, we cherish you as a daughter, please always understand our feelings toward you."

"Anyway, you decide what floor plan and don't forget the rooms for your future children. Once you pick the floor plan, construction will start; we would like to get the house finished before Ray leaves for India."

Ray and Shannon couldn't say thank you enough, grateful for the kind of start they will have in their new life together.

It was finally time for Shannon to head back to college. She thanked everybody before saying goodbye to them.

Ray walked out with Shannon and hugged her tightly. "Well, what do you think about today?" he asked her.

"Ray, it's been another wonderful day," she replied.

"I will see you tomorrow around three o'clock at your apartment. Maybe we can look at the house plans while we're there. It's also my last day of school. And then its graduation and the new job at Lodi Mold."

After Shannon left, Ray went back into the house and sat down with his parents.

"Mom and Dad, you are so nice to Shannon. I know she feels like she is a daughter to you both. I know she will be here for you whenever you need anything, especially when I am gone to India on the hunting adventure."

"Well, Saturday I graduate. Although the ceremony is at eleven o'clock in the morning, I have to be there about nine o'clock. Everybody else should get there about ten o'clock. After the ceremony, we can all come home and prepare for the party, and thanks Mom and Dad for doing the party," Ray said.

It was getting late so they all said goodnight and went to get a good night's sleep.

The next morning, Ray headed to school for his last day of college education at Sacramento State. Along the way, his mind was full of memories of the school and his professors. Ray silently acknowledged the personal milestone he had reached with Sacramento State, without which there also would not have been a Shannon Doritee in his life. Somehow, he felt it was God's plan for them to meet that day at the student lounge. He fondly remembered how he happened to notice this cute brunette, blue-eyed, 5 foot 6 inch gal, who basically turned his life upside down when he fell in love with her. Reaching the college parking area, he realized this was truly the last item in the memory of his college days. Soon life would take a different course—it was sad, but it also gave good feeling.

105

He attended all of his classes and said goodbye to his professors. The last professor congratulated him on his new job at Lodi Mold. "Mr. Fred Sunday called me to ask me what I thought of you. I told him it would be no mistake if he hired you, that Ray Johnson is one of a kind. It is that simple. He replied he didn't need to hear any more than that. I just thought I would share that with you, Ray. You know I always thought of you as one of a kind. Have a great career and, by the way, have a great wedding. I will be at wedding ceremony when you and Shannon Doritee get married."

Ray showed a puzzled look on his face. "Do you know Shannon?" he said.

"I have seen Shannon grow up from an infant to the young lady that she is today," the professor said, smiling. "You see, I am her uncle by marriage. I am Elizabeth Doritee's brother, so Shannon is my niece. Ray, sometimes this is a small world. You and Shannon have fun in it. My sister is happy to have you in the family and so am I, Ray. You have a good last day here at Sacramento State."

Ray just could not believe what he had just learned.

Ray was soon done for the last time with all his classes and was later at Shannon's apartment where he found her fair as ever.

Shannon smiled at Ray as he came in and closed the door. They kissed passionately, though mindful not to light any fuses, making sure to save everything for their wedding night.

"I've said all my goodbyes, but I couldn't believe who my last professor was," Ray finally managed to say.

"Who was he?" Shannon asked.

"He knew you and he said he would be at our wedding."

"Who is he?"

"He is your uncle."

"He is one of your professors—oh, I completely forgot about my mom's brother teaching at Sacramento State!" she said. "Well, I guess we learn something every day."

"Shannon, I can't wait to get the graduation over with. That would make our wedding day that much closer, and then we can go on our honeymoon and light a lot of fuses and we won't care." They then held each other tightly and kissed.

Shannon said, "That night will be special, I guarantee it."

Ray looked at her and said, "You going to wear something really special?"

"Yes, and you will like it—you will love to see me in it."

They smiled and kissed again. Shannon obviously had something up her sleeve, and Ray thought it best to find out on the night of their honeymoon.

"Shannon, did you have time to tell your mom and dad how the meeting with the pastor went, and the house my parents want to build for us as our wedding present?"

"I did tell them and they were so excited. They had nothing but compliments for your parents, for wanting us to have a great start in our new life together."

"I brought that house plan magazine. Maybe we could pick the house we would like. We can take our time, too, as there's nothing else going on today and seeing it's a big decision for us and our future."

The first thing they needed to work out was about the number of children and bedrooms. Deciding three children would be the most they would have, they therefore needed at least four bedrooms. There were many good-looking floor plans and exterior designs that they liked—after three hours, they finally made their choice. Next to consider was the location for the house, and they decided the north end on the Sacramento River side would be the ideal place.

They celebrated their final choice with another round of hugs and kisses.

107

"I can't tell you how excited I am to someday be able to enjoy ourselves on your parents' farm along with our kids," Shannon said, beaming. "Ray, I can't wait to have a baby and be a mom like your mom, every young person wanting to also call me 'Mom' after they get to know me."

Ray looked into Shannon's blue eyes and said, "I believe you are already starting to fill Mom's shoes. I know if she heard what you just said she would be so proud of you. Her philosophy is quite simple: show love and kindness to everybody and kind words will come your way."

Shannon sat there thinking about what Ray had just said. She felt so fortunate that God found a spot for her in the Johnson family.

"You know, Ray, it is so generous for your family to give us a house. I can't believe them putting that kind of money out for us."

"Shannon, they would simply tell you that everything is to be ours someday when they are gone, that they would rather want to see our family enjoy it while they are living."

"It's a wonderful way to put it like that, Ray. I have great parent's—I know they love me and I respect and love them greatly, but they don't compare to your parents in how they show love to everybody. They are truly special people."

"I am sure they would be honored if they heard what you just said. I will show Dad and Mom the house plan and the location we picked. I know they will be happy to start the construction as soon as possible."

Giving Shannon a kiss and a tight caress, Ray said, "I love you more every day that passes. I will call you tomorrow about some details on the graduation." Ray then started his drive home.

Back with his parents, he promptly showed them the house plans and the location on the ranch that they had chosen to build their house.

Looking at the house plan, Paul said, "It looks great. It also appears to be kid friendly." The comment made everyone happy and excited about the new house to be built. "I will contact a building contractor I know in Sacramento and get him going on this project. I will do that tomorrow," he added. "Well, in three days I graduate and I look forward to that day. Right now I am going to retire to get some sleep. Good night, I will see you in the morning," Ray said.

The next morning, Ray was talking with his parents about his graduation day. He told them he would have to leave early Saturday morning to get to the college campus at about nine o'clock, to get organized for the graduation ceremony.

"I will call Shannon to ask her if she could pick you both up that morning and take you to the college area where the graduation ceremony is to be held. She knows the campus well, and it would be less confusing for you both. Shannon should pick you both up at nine o'clock, for the ceremony will start about eleven o'clock."

Ray's parents agreed it was a good idea. He then called Shannon and told her the plan and she agreed to it, and he confirmed the same to his parents.

"Dad, Friday I will help set up for the party and go get the food and whatever else is needed for Saturday."

"Ray I have a friend with a good size barbecue cart. He will barbecue the steaks. You will recognize him when you see him. He is good at it. He has always been there when we could use some help. This should be a fun party. I have called everybody on the list and told them to be here at six o'clock."

"Well, Dad, it looks like everything is in place and ready to go."

On Friday morning, Ray, his mom, and dad set up the table and chairs. Recalling this was Shannon's last day of school, he called to tell her everything was set up for the party.

"I sure miss you the past two days. I'd drop by at the ranch if that's okay," Shannon said.

"That would be great—just come on over and the sooner the better—you know I don't like not seeing you for one day."

Mary was happy to learn of Shannon dropping by.

Soon Shannon was pulling into the driveway. Ray went out to greet her in his usual fashion—a passionate kiss and a tight caress. He then showed her how everything was set up for his graduation party and Shannon appeared to be quite excited.

"It will be a great day for you tomorrow. And then we will be married in a month. That really excites me."

Just then Ray noticed a pickup towing a barbecue cart coming down into the yard. Instantly he recognized it was Joeseph and his dad, and tagging along was Denise.

Ray and Shannon went to greet them, and Ray said, "So you are the friend Dad was telling me. I am so glad the Alexanders could be part of my party."

Paul and Mary went to greet everybody who showed up, thanking them for bringing the barbecue cart and for offering to do the barbecuing on the day of the party. Shannon and Denise were off to the side conversing about the upcoming wedding day. Denise was as excited as Shannon was.

Denise just had to ask a question, "Shannon, what are you going wear on your honeymoon in the motel room?" Shannon whispered in Denise's ear.

Denise's response was, "Really? That's what you are going to wear? Sounds good to me, and I know Ray really will enjoy that moment."

Ray asked Joeseph, "Are you going to help your dad with the barbecuing tomorrow?

"Actually I will. Denise also offered to help."

"Thanks so much. That's a big job and my family and I really appreciate that you all are helping out." Ray went over and gave the three of them a big hug and again said, "Thanks." They then positioned the barbecue cart and the three said goodbye and left.

Ray, Shannon, and Ray's parents were left at the ranch, and Shannon thought it was a good time to thank Ray's parents.

"Mom and Dad, did you look at the house plans and the place we would like to build the house?"

"We did, Shannon, and it looks great. I told Ray it looks kid-friendly and you already know what that means for Mom and me."

"Dad, Mom, when we get married, Ray and I will work on the kid project continually." Everybody paused and smiled. "I am serious, I want to have children and I want you both, along with my parents, to have grandchildren. For that's everyone's dream."

"Shannon, Mary and I will enjoy letting them get real dirty out in the field, like we did with Ray and his friend Joeseph. Hopefully you won't object," Paul said, smiling.

"Heavens, no! If God wanted everybody to be clean he wouldn't have made dirt. You just wait, Dad, someday I am going to help you repair or build an irrigation culvert, like you and Ray did a time back, and then you will see how I look all dirty and muddy—would you like that?"

"I will call you when a project comes up, especially when Ray is gone on his hunting trip to India. At times I probably will need some help around here."

Before leaving for Lodi to be with her parents, Shannon made sure to whisper in Mom and Dad's ears, "Thank you for the house. I love you both so much."

Ray walked Shannon to her car, said goodbye, and gave her a kiss.

Graduation day finally arrived. As he said, Ray left early to be at the graduation staging area by nine o'clock. At this same time, Shannon was at the ranch to take Ray's parents to the graduation ceremony. Once there and seated, they had to wait about 45 minutes for the ceremony to start. Looking at the engineering class listing, they saw Ray had achieved a 3.85 GPA, good to be in the top 5 percent of his class. Ray's parents were so proud. After about 10 minutes, Shannon's parents came and sat by Shannon. They came with Fred Sunday, Ray's new boss. Shannon introduced Ray's parents to him.

"We at Lodi Mold Inc. are certainly excited for Ray to join the company," Fred started. "You have raised a fine son you can be proud of. Just look at his GPA and his class standing, and just think about the wonderful young lady he is about to marry. That says a lot about where your son is coming from. I call it good upbringing."

The ceremony was starting. The students entered and were promptly seated, the speeches were given, and the diplomas were handed out. The ceremony was closed with a prayer. Shannon and her group finally found Ray in the crowd. They all hugged him. For her part, Shannon grabbed and gave him a long kiss, not bothering to care who was watching.

"Shannon, that was one fuse lighter."

"It was meant to be, Ray; only thing left is for the dynamite to explode."

"It will explode in a month," Ray replied, smiling. They smiled and hugged for a moment more before finally walking out the stadium to the cars. They were headed home for the party.

They were back at the ranch around three o'clock. Joeseph and Denise were already putting the charcoal in the tray, looking to start the steaks around five o'clock. The grill would hold at least sixty steaks, which should enable them to cook more than they really needed. Joseph's mom and dad had just pulled up; Joeseph's mom was going to help get the food onto the buffet table.

Joeseph's dad said, "It's 4:30. Let's light the charcoals."
At five o'clock the steaks were on the grill, and both moms
had everything on the buffet table.

The guests started arriving. Ray greeted and welcomed
them, introducing Shannon to those who hadn't met her
yet. At about six o'clock everybody was seated to eat. Ray
and Shannon made their way to each guest to hold a little
conversation with aunts, uncles, and cousins, and of course
the Chins.

In a moment, Ray decided to get the attention of all the
guests.

"I would like to thank you all for coming to my party
today. It is wonderful to see you here to help me celebrate
a milestone in my life. I would like to thank the Alexander
family and Denise Silva for helping out with my party.
Speaking of Denise and for those who don't know yet, my
best friend Joeseph is engaged to her. They will make a great
couple.

"I know Joeseph will be happy to finally have a lot of
hands to give him all the linguica and eggs and Portuguese
soupas that he could eat. My mom, Denise's mom, Denise,
and Shannon who wants to learn Portuguese cooking from
my mom should be enough help for him in that regard.
Saying that, let's congratulate Joeseph and his bride-to-be
Denise Silva."

After the applause, Ray proceeded to talk a little about
his bride-to-be. "By now you know her name is Shannon. I
met her at college in the student lounge, and it didn't take
long for me to realize I really had to marry this gal you see
standing next to me.

"Some of you know how hunting and shooting rifles is
my lifelong passion. Somehow I managed to get Shannon
interested in shooting and hunting also. But the story doesn't
end there. One day I set up some targets for her in which

one of the targets was rigged in such a way that if she hit the tomato off the top of the box, the proposal message would pop up. Shannon could then read the message through the rifle scope.

"I thank God that Shannon's first shot hit the tomato. As expected, she read my proposal and went on to accept me to be her husband. I then slipped the engagement ring onto her finger—and here we are today. Shannon and I plan on living on the ranch. Here where we will raise a family and give grandchildren to our parents."

Shannon felt she needed to say a little something so she said, "I have to share how everything on this Johnson ranch is so special. It's special because Ray's mom and dad are so special, for they show love and kindness to everybody that they meet. Any young person who walks into the house and converses with Ray's mom and dad will most likely call them Mom and Dad before they leave—that's how welcome they make you feel. You can ask Ray's best friend, Joeseph, or my best friend, Denise, who is standing by my side here tonight. They both call them Mom and Dad."

Shannon had one more thing to say. "I hope, Mom and Dad, that as time passes by and young people happen to visit us, they would also want to call us Mom and Dad. I am certainly going to try hard to make that happen."

Ray again thanked everybody for coming, making sure to add, "Shannon and I hope to see you all at the wedding on July 1st." The party then came to a close and the guests all started to leave.

CHAPTER 8

THE WEDDING JUST WEEKS AWAY

S unday after the graduation party, Ray relished the fact he was finally done with college and he can now give his full attention to Shannon, especially considering that their wedding was less than a month away. He was also looking forward to starting his new Job next day in Lodi. There was also the matter of his hunting trip to India, and he knew he had better start planning soon.

`Feeling the urgency to work out their plans, Ray decided to invite Shannon to the farm. Knowing Shannon was with her parents in Lodi, he accordingly gave her a call. Shannon's mom answered the phone.

"Hi, Mom, this is Ray. How is everybody doing after yesterday's party?"

"It was a wonderful party, Ray. Everybody seemed to enjoy it, along with your stories of personal experiences with each other and Shannon's words about your parents, of how people call them Mom and Dad because they show an abundance of kindness and love to anybody they meet. I saw people around me had tears in their eyes, confirming that's just how the Johnson family is, and I know why Shannon feels that way being around your family," Elizabeth said

"Mom, thanks for the kind words. I know my parents would be happy to hear you say that about them. But you know once Shannon and I are married we all will be one happy family. I just know that in my heart. Mom, does Shannon happen to be there?"

"Yes, I will get her."

In a moment Shannon was on the phone.

"Hi, Shannon, how are you doing? Hope you enjoyed the party yesterday."

"Ray, it was a great party. Everybody had a great time. Denise called me to say she was so happy being part of it. Now we have a big one coming up—I just can't stop thinking about that day, and I really, really, can't stop thinking about our honeymoon night!"

"I know, Shannon, I can't wait either. It should be a great and enjoyable honeymoon."

"I am telling you we are going to light so many fuses, and there is going to be so much dynamite going off that I am not sure the bed will hold up." There was a long pause and, still laughing, she continued to calmly say, "I know what you are thinking, Ray. I am like a dog in heat—well, you got it right, and I am getting hotter by the day."

"Shannon—when we leave our wedding reception, only you and I will know about fuses, dynamite, and a dog in heat. We will say goodbye to the guests and head to our honeymoon destination, and they will be clueless."

Ray felt the time was right to explain the purpose of his call. "Shannon, the reason I called is I was wondering if you could come up to the ranch so we could discuss our plans after we are married. We will have to make some decisions—so you think you could make it up here?"

"Sure—I will see you in an hour or less," Shannon replied.

Ray was in the kitchen drinking coffee and reading the newspaper when his mom and dad walked in and sat down at the table.

"That was a great party last night Ray, everybody seemed to enjoy themselves," Mary said.

"The Alexanders did a great job barbecuing the steaks," Ray replied. "I must say that Denise Silva is a pleasure to watch. She is a typical Portuguese hardworking young lady. Joeseph has latched onto a great gal."

"I have Shannon coming over this morning so we can discuss some items that have to get decided and planned for after we are married; one main item is where we are going to live."

"Oh!" Ray's dad said, "I got a hold of the contractor. He is coming to look at the site next week. Said he will start excavating the home site and start building in about three weeks. He feels by October or November the home will be done."

Ray was amazed. "Dad, you really got things going fast."

"Son, your mom and I can't wait to get Shannon and you living in your own house on this ranch. It means so much to us that Shannon wanted to live out here by Mom and me."

"Well, Mom and Dad, Shannon will be here in a little while. I can't wait to tell her about the house. She will be so excited!"

Ray and his parents were still in the kitchen talking when Ray said, "I see Shannon pulling into the driveway. I will go greet her and tell her about the house—she will be excited." Ray then went out and greeted Shannon with a kiss and the usual hug. In time he told her that their house would probably get started in three weeks, to be finished around October or November.

"Ray, your dad really got going quickly on that project!" Shannon replied. "I didn't expect that news."

"That's just how Dad works. Once he decides on something, then he follows it up with a let's-get-it-done attitude."

Ray and Shannon made their way to the house. Once inside, the first thing out of Shannon's mouth was, "Dad,

Mom—Ray just told me about the house getting started in three weeks to be finished in October or November."

Approaching them, she said, "Thank you so much! Now Ray and I can watch our future start to take shape as we watch our house being built. Thank you so much!"

"I hope you both will enjoy the house, and not leave those bedrooms vacant very long," Mary replied, smiling.

With a grin and a special look on her face, Shannon responded, "Mom, your son told me the other day that I am like a dog in heat, and I told him yes, and I am getting hotter every day. As you can see, I know we are going to try hard to fill those extra bedrooms once we are married. And when I get pregnant I would like you and my mom to help me decorate the baby's nursery."

"Oh, Shannon, I am so glad and excited that you would include me along with your mother; it would be an honor to be part of helping you with the nursery, which is sort of a woman's thing. And thanks so much for wanting to include me in your plan."

Ray and his dad just sat there smiling and listening to what they felt was going to be a great relationship between Shannon and Mary.

Mary felt she had to say a little more to Shannon and Ray. "Now let me tell you both: sometimes it takes longer to get pregnant than one would think. So don't get discouraged if it doesn't happen right away. Let's all just pray that God has a plan for you both to have children."

Ray thought it was a good time for him and Shannon to take a walk around the ranch, to spend some time alone. It would also give them a chance to discuss their plans after they were married.

So after he thought about it, Ray said, "I think Shannon and I are going for a walk around the ranch. Shannon, is that okay with you?"

"That's fine, Ray, I could use some exercise anyway." With that, they headed out the door and started walking. During their walk, Ray asked Shannon, "Have you thought about where we are going to live after we are married?"

"Actually, I have given it some thought; maybe we could rent an apartment in Lodi, especially since you will be working there. Then in about four months our house would be done and we would move to the ranch. By the way, next week I plan on moving out of my Sacramento apartment."

"That sounds good, Shannon, since I start my job on Monday. We could start looking for an apartment next week, so we would be all set after the wedding to have you move in. I will move in right after we find an apartment."

As Shannon and Ray continued their walk, they passed by one of the farm tractors. A thought suddenly occurred to her. "Ray, could I get up onto the seat of that Yellow Tractor?"

"Sure—that's a Caterpillar D-4 track type tractor."

Shannon got up onto the seat and asked, "Ray, how do I look?"

"Beautiful," Ray said, smiling.

"You know, Ray, I have driven an International TD6 track type tractor in the vineyard for my dad. I see International H Farmall wheel tractors over there—I have also driven them."

Shannon continued to observe some of the equipment in the vicinity. "Ray—while you are working and while you are on your trip to India, I could be of help to your dad if he needs me." Shannon got off the tractor. Ray pulled her close to him and held her very tightly.

"Shannon, we will have a great life out here. I believe you are going to enjoy it."

At the moment, Paul and Mary were looking out of the living room window watching Ray and Shannon. They couldn't help thinking how lucky the family was to have Shannon as a part of it.

119

"Seeing Shannon sitting on the D-4 tractor, I bet she told Ray if I needed help she could drive any of those tractors," said Paul. "She probably drove some tractors for her dad, but it's just a guess, Mary."

Mary responded, "Knowing Shannon, it's probably a good guess."

Back out by the tractors, Ray and Shannon were just resuming their walk. "With our kids out here next to their grandparents, there will be a trail from our house to theirs that our children will use a lot, probably to get a treat that Grandma and Grandpa will have in box. They will probably call it the treasure box."

"Well, Shannon at least they will know their grandparents; lot of kids never get to see their grandparents and that's sort of sad."

"You know, Ray, I have always meant to ask you, but kept forgetting: when you go on your hunting trip to India, how are you going to pay for it? I was just always wondering."

"I have fifty thousand dollars set aside for the trip. I believe it will cost thirty thousand, but I will know more after we are married and I start to put the plan together. By the way, I really have to get going on the trip plan right away after we are married," replied Ray.

Shannon was shocked by the amount of money Ray said he had. "That's a lot of money for somebody as young as you to have—how did you accumulate that much money, Ray? I don't mean to pry but I am just curious," Shannon asked.

"Shannon, you are going to be my wife, so you are not prying."

"About the money: for years my dad would give me 10 to 15 acres of tomatoes; if I took care of raising the crop, I would get the revenue off the crop. He just wanted me to know how to work and be responsible, and the money I received would be my reward," Ray said.

"Well, once again your parents came through to help make you the person that you are—hardworking, responsible, and very considerate especially to me," Shannon said.

"Shannon, my parents are successful because they believe hard work and kindness to others will always result in some sort of success. My parents live in a very basic house, live a modest lifestyle, and yet they are pretty wealthy people. Aside from that, they also sometimes use their wealth to help people in need, or loan money to people so they might achieve more success in their lives—and they are not jealous of others who succeed."

Soon Shannon and Ray were headed back to the ranch house. Ray recalled a Christmas letter that his dad once wrote.

"Shannon I am just going to tell you a portion of what the letter said. The letter went something like this:

Ray: someday when you get married and have a family and I will be a grandpa, I am sure there will be an occasion where the family will be walking down a street. I will be trailing behind just watching with joy in my heart seeing my family in front of me enjoying life. And then seeing every now and then you or one of your family members looking back to see if I was still there. And on some other similar occasion, one of you will look back to see if I was still there, and if I was not there, hopefully I will be a memory in all your family's hearts, for I will be gone and that's just part of life.

That was a touching letter, and soon we are going to become a part of that letter after we get married and raise a family. The letter brought to me the reality that the dad and mom I love will not always be here for me—but life and memories will go on."

The words made Shannon so emotional she just hugged him. "Ray, thank you for sharing such a touching letter.

121

It's something you don't always think about when you are young. But Ray the way your parents are …we will always remember them as long as we live, and they will be great memories."

Once they were back at the house, Paul said, "Well, did you both have a good walk? Shannon you looked pretty good on that Caterpillar D-4 Tractor."

"Dad, I told Ray if you ever needed any help I can drive a tractor and will always be here to help you. So please, always keep that in mind."

Paul smiled. "Shannon, I just told Mary you were probably saying something like that. I may have to take you up on that. But if you are carrying my grandchild, work will be sort of off-limits for you."

"I understand. Those little lives are too precious to take any chances, and as a mother to be, I would always agree to that," Shannon replied.

Before leaving back for Lodi, Shannon said to Ray's parents, "Next week Ray and I will look for an apartment to rent. I can have that to move in after the wedding. I can't tell you how excited we both are." Shannon then said goodbye, and Ray walked her out to the car, and hugged and kissed her.

"Will you need help moving out of your apartment?" Ray asked.

"No, Ray, it's a furnished apartment. I can handle everything, and Denise is going to help out. We will probably go out to lunch and do our girl thing."

"Well, it will be a fun day for you with Denise."

"Ray, when I close the door to that apartment for the last time, it will bring back a lot of great memories. There was the day I cooked you your first dinner, then there was the day you kissed me on my belly and worked up to my lips, which sent chills up and down my spine. And how about the time we hadn't seen each other for over three days and I had to manipulate everything that day. I convinced you to put on your swimming suit while you fell asleep on the couch. I slipped into a bikini and came back to lay by you while you were sleeping; you woke up and there we were. I had basically convinced you to have sex, and then the phone rang. Ray, those were great moments, but I am glad for that phone call; now, we will have a great honeymoon."

"Shannon, those really were great moments. I will always remember how I missed you so much over those three days."

"Oh, Ray, good luck tomorrow at your new job."

Ray said goodbye and Shannon was off to Lodi.

Ray went back into the house; his mom had prepared a quick dinner. While they were eating, Ray mentioned to his parents, "Mom, Dad, wedding bells are getting real close. Tomorrow I will start my career in engineering at Lodi Mold. I know I will like engineering as a profession, but my heart will always be right here on this farm. Shannon will most likely be involved with its operation, and also with her parent's vineyard. She will get a degree in business in January 1960, which will come in handy to run a farming operation."

"I can tell Shannon has farming in her heart—because, Ray, she has you in her heart, and she would do anything for you," Paul said.

Ray was really sort of tired but did say, "Mom, Dad, Shannon would also do anything for both of you. Well, I am going to get things ready for my job tomorrow, and then I am going to hit the bed for a good restful sleep. I will see you both briefly in the morning, good night."

Monday morning Ray was up early. He had a quick breakfast with his mom and dad, said goodbye to both of them, and then headed to Lodi.

123

Once he was at Lodi Molds, he went to the receptionist desk and said hello to Liz. She acknowledged that they had been anxiously awaiting his arrival.

"We have all the paperwork filled out for you; all you have to do is sign your name on three spots that are indicated on the documents," she said.

Ray signed the documents in the areas indicated and handed them back to Liz, who said, "Well, how are you and Shannon doing lately? You must be very excited what with wedding bells just around the corner."

"We can't wait! Yes, Liz, we are excited and so is everybody in our families."

"Ray, I will take you back to see Fred Sunday."

Once they were at Fred's office, Ray shook his hand.

"Well, Ray, welcome aboard! We are all excited to have you as part of the Engineering Department," Fred said.

"I am really excited to be here. I hope to be an asset to Lodi Molds, Inc."

Fred made a phone call to one of his engineers and asked him to come to his office; in a while, an engineer by the name of Ray Jensen entered Fred's office and was introduced to Ray.

"Ray I am going to start you working under Ray Jensen who has worked for the company for twelve years," Fred said. "Ray has a vast knowledge of all the equipment we produce. He will assign you various projects; as some of our production machines may have problems, you will be asked to look into the situation to try to solve the problem. This will be a joint type project: when you think you have a solution, you should discuss it; if you both agree, then you can go forward to fix the problem."

Ray Jensen then said, "I am looking forward to working with you. You come highly recommended—and Ray, feel free to ask any questions, we really work as team around here."

Fred then said, "Well, now would be a good time to take Ray to his new office and get him settled in and introduce him to our Engineering staff."

Meanwhile, Shannon and Denise were on their way to Shannon's apartment in Sacramento. She was going to move out and live at her parents until she and Ray were married in July. They arrived at the apartment and went inside.

Shannon looked around, then said to Denise, "This apartment will always bring back wonderful memories that Ray and I shared. There was the time we hadn't seen each other for over three days and we really missed each other; then he came over. I must admit I really tried to set things up. I knew he was tired so I mentioned that he had a bathing suit here, and if he wanted to put it on and take a nap on the sofa, it would be more comfortable. That he did and he fell asleep almost immediately—in the meantime, I slipped into...."

"Don't tell me, you slipped into a bikini?"

"That's right—and then while he was sleeping, I got between him and the back of the sofa; that's very skin-to-skin contact, right?"

"Shannon, you really wanted to have sex, didn't you? Poor Ray—how could anybody resist you in a bikini?" said Denise.

"Well, I also dosed off. When we woke up, he finally saw what I was wearing. I moved almost on top of him—by this time all fuses were lighted, and we were consenting to have sex. It was the most wonderful moment," Shannon said.

"Well, what happened?" Denise said, excitement mounting, as if she were listening to a suspense radio show.

"Denise, you are not going to believe this...but just when we were about to engage, the phone rang...."

Denise, laughing, said, "I thought that could only happen in a Hollywood comedy movie! Anyway, who called?"

"It was Ray's mom. She wanted to invite us over for dinner that Friday—remember when you and Joeseph surprised us that you had met, and we also made some announcements?"

"It was God's plan—but now just think how great your honeymoon night will be. Just make sure to disconnect the phone this time."

After the two friends brought Shannon's things into the car, Shannon took the keys to the apartment office and said goodbye to the manager. Shannon and Denise were soon off to Lodi.

At Lodi, most of Shannon's items went right into her room. Around five o'clock, the phone rang. Shannon answered it and it was Ray. He wanted to know if she could go with him to look for an apartment in Lodi.

"Yes, that would be great," she said. "I will get the newspaper and see what is listed. Okay, see you in a little while. Oh, Ray, how did the new job go?"

"I am going to like it here, great people to work with,"

Ray said enthusiastically.

Ray was soon on his way to Lodi. Denise had left and Shannon's parents were out of town. Once there, Shannon let him in with a big hug and kiss.

"Shannon, that was an arousing welcome; you must be having a good day."

"Ray, it's always a good day when we touch each other."

"You got that right; did you get a chance to look at the paper for an apartment?"

"Yes—there is an apartment complex on Lockford Street that looks pretty good; it's $110 per month, one bedroom, even has a swimming pool. It has refrigerator and stove but no other furnishings."

"Well, we have to buy furniture anyway for our new house, so that would be fine."

Smiling, Shannon said, "Remember we need a real good bed, right?"

"Yes, Shannon, we certainly wouldn't want it to break during our activities, would we?"

"Ray it's just something to think about and you know by now that's my favorite subject."

Ray and Shannon proceeded to look at the apartment that they thought would be just right for their short stay. They went to the office and asked the manager if they could look at the apartment. He gave them the key and the apartment number, and they went to look at it; after checking inside, they both agreed for a short stay it would work just fine. They looked at the pool area to see it was well kept and very clean. Back at the office, they signed the agreement papers and gave the deposit and first month's rent.

Ray explained to the manager, "I will be the occupant until after July 1st, then Shannon would also move in once we're married." After taking care of the apartment, they headed back to Lodi, where Shannon's parents were just back from their trip.

"Hi Mom, Dad—how was your trip to Monterrey?" Shannon said.

"It was beautiful as always. It really is one of my favorite places to visit."

"Do you go to Monterey very often?" Ray asked.

"When Shannon was younger we used to go to Monterey more often. Shannon loved to climb on the rocks by the ocean and watch the waves hit the rocks. It is just so beautiful! After you are married, Ray, you should take Shannon to Monterey someday—you would both have a good time."

Ray smiled and turned to Shannon. "Shannon, we should go there someday. I heard it's a great place for young newlyweds."

Shannon turned to her parents. "We just rented an apartment for Ray. After the wedding I will move in with him. Except for a stove and refrigerator it's not furnished, so we will have to buy some furniture; bedroom furniture should be the first on the list, with a sofa to follow. But we might as well get nice furniture for our new house, since it's scheduled to be finished around October or November. We can have the furniture ready to put into our new house."

"Well, Shannon and Ray, Dad and I were talking and we agreed we would like to buy your bedroom set as our present for your wedding—would you like that?"

Ray and Shannon were overjoyed by the gift from Shannon's parents. "Thank you so much. It would truly be a great remembrance from both of you," they managed to say.

"You pick it out and it will be our pleasure to give it to you. Make sure it's of good quality, one that would last a long time," Elizabeth said.

"Believe me Shannon will make sure it is good and strong," Ray said. "She knows it's going to be put to good use, and surely she wouldn't want it to break during our activities."

Shannon's parents had a monstrous smile on their faces after Ray's comments.

"It probably has something to do with giving us grandchildren," Bob said.

For the first time, Ray actually saw Shannon blush after her parent's remarks.

Ray gave Shannon a kiss and said, "Well, I have got to get home. Thanks again for the gift," he said.

Turning to Shannon, he said, "Shannon maybe tomorrow we can go shopping for the bedroom set, maybe at Breuners Furniture in Stockton. They carry very nice furniture, and it's close to Lodi. I will pick you up after work—does that sound okay?"

"That sure sounds good. I will see you after work." Shannon had another smile on her face as she whispered in Ray's ear, "Honey, it's going to be great picking out our bedroom set; but really more once we actually use it."

Ray smiled and said, "Well, I do have to get going."

Back at his parents' house, Ray found his mom putting the final touches to a waffles, eggs, and bacon dinner. It was one of those breakfast type dinners. Once seated, Ray told his parents about his new job, of how he really liked the people, especially the person he was working under, Ray Jensen. Ray believed he could gain a lot of good experience working for him.

"By the way, Shannon and I rented an apartment today in Lodi where she can move in after we are married. I will probably try to move in next week."

"Is it furnished?" Mary asked.

"No, Mom. We will have to furnish it, but when our house is done, we will have some furniture for our new home. Shannon's parents want to buy us our bedroom furniture as wedding present; we are excited to go shopping for it."

"That is so thoughtful of them," Mary said. "I believe that since Shannon is the bride it's good that it comes from her parents. I just happen to believe bedroom furniture is a woman's thing, especially the bed."

"You can say that again, Mom, Dad. I am telling you Shannon is obsessed with beds," Ray said, laughing. "Shannon and I—and I assume her parents, too—are going to Breuners Furniture in Stockton tomorrow after I get off work to pick out our bedroom furniture."

"While you are there, you might as well look at sofas that Shannon and you might like. Take what you like and consider it a housewarming gift from Dad and me, if that's okay with Shannon and you. Put it on layaway; Dad and I will go down and take care of the rest."

"Thanks, Mom.

"Well, I am going to hit the sack. I am tired and have to go to work in the morning. Again, thanks for everything you are doing for Shannon and me."

After work the next day, Ray was back at Shannon's parents' house. In time, the four of them were on their way to Breuners Furniture in Stockton.

As they were looking around inside the store, Ray spoke to Shannon. "We better have a good look at sofas, too. My parents want to buy us one for our new house."

"Oh, that is so nice of them again, but that's just your mom and dad." Shannon and Ray soon picked out their bedroom furniture, one that particularly met with Shannon's approval. After that, they went on to look at sofas. In time, they eventually picked one that they liked.

While Shannon's parents paid for the bedroom furniture, Ray advised the salesperson, "Put the sofa on layaway. My parents will be here tomorrow to pay for it. Their names are Paul and Mary Johnson. You can deliver the bedroom furniture at the same time."

"Are they from the Isleton area?" the salesperson said.

"Yes, do you know them?"

"Yes, they have shopped here in the past; sometimes it's a small world." The sales clerk then said, "Delivery will be Friday at four o'clock if that's okay."

"That's fine; Shannon will probably be at the apartment to take delivery."

"I will be there," Shannon said, smiling.

The four of them were soon back at Lodi, where again Ray thanked Shannon's parents for their gift. "I am so glad Shannon really liked what we picked. My mom felt bedroom furniture is really a woman's choice, and she was so happy you gave us the bedroom furniture."

"Your mom called me last night to tell me those same words that you just said," Elizabeth said. "Your mom is a very thoughtful lady. I can see that this family will get bigger and happier as time passes."

Ray said goodbye, and Shannon walked with him to the car. Shannon gave Ray one of those fuse-lighting kisses, and told him with a snicker, "Can't wait to try the bed."

Back at the farm, Ray greeted his mom and dad. "Well, we picked out our bedroom furniture and a sofa. If you can go to Brueners, it's on layaway under your name, with delivery instruction after you pay for it."

Mary said, "We will go tomorrow and pay for it. Did Shannon like it?"

"Yes, and she was so surprised when I told her."

CHAPTER 9

JUST DAYS BEFORE THE WEDDING

On Friday, Breuners was scheduled to deliver the furniture to Ray and Shannon's apartment. Shannon and Denise were already at the apartment waiting for the delivery truck. Around four o'clock the doorbell rang. Shannon opened the door to the delivery men from Breuners, who promptly brought in and set the bedroom furniture in the bedroom, assembling the bed frame along with the box springs and the mattress. Next came the sofa into the living room.

Shannon was in the bedroom observing the bed very carefully as it was being assembled. She couldn't hold it back anymore, so she finally managed to ask one of the men.

"Do you think this bed is strong and durable enough?"

Denise was laughing to herself about Shannon's question. The man had a puzzled look on his face, but he did give Shannon an answer.

"Well, I think you could breed an elephant on this bed, if that's what you are trying to know. You don't look like an elephant, so it should work for many, many years. Is that the answer you are looking for?"

That gave Shannon a big smile on her face. "Well, thanks, first of all for not thinking I looked like an elephant. My future husband would appreciate that. But the analogy was good and yes, I am satisfied with your answer. Thank you for your humorous attitude." Shannon signed the receipt and the men left.

Denise just started laughing and said, "Shannon I am sure glad you don't look like an elephant. I sure hope your bed doesn't break on your honeymoon and ruin your thrilling sexual experience with Ray."

Looking at the bed, Shannon proceeded to lie on it.

"Shannon, I know you are having a dream right now, but in a few weeks your dream will become a thrilling reality."

"Denise, I wish that day was right now."

Right then Ray walked in and said "Hi" to both Denise and Shannon. "Well, Shannon does everything look okay? Is the bed furniture to your liking?"

"Yes, it should hold up pretty good. The delivery person said you could breed an elephant on it, and since I am not an elephant, it should last a long time."

The sight of Denise laughing had Ray with a puzzled look on his face. "How did an elephant become part of the conversation?"

"Ray—you know, Shannon and beds," Denise said, laughing. "Well, I am going to leave you two alone now." Turning to Shannon, she said, "Oh, Shannon, we should try to go hunting sometime before your wedding, so think about a time."

Alone, Shannon and Ray went to look at the bedroom furniture. They hugged and kissed, but avoided lying on the bed, before they went and sat down on their new sofa.

"We need to buy a kitchen table and chairs, and some place settings of plates, silverware, and pots and pans," said Ray. "Since tomorrow is Saturday, maybe we could do some shopping in the morning."

"That's fine; we can go in the morning. You can come by and pick me up in the morning at about nine o'clock."

"I plan on telling my parents that on Sunday I would be moving to our new apartment."

Shannon was thinking about how Ray's parents were going to take the reality of life that their son, who had lived with them for twenty-three years, was now going to be gone. "If you don't mind, Ray, I will come up Sunday to be with you and your parents. I think it will be hard on them to see you leave. Maybe with me around it will make it easier. I love your parents so much and I feel that I can give them support if they need it."

"It would be great if you could be there on Sunday. It's moments like this that will always make our family happy and why I am so lucky that I found you and you accepted me to be in your life."

"Ray, the decision for me to marry you was so easy. Okay, Ray, I will see you in the morning and we can go shopping." They said goodbye, hugged and kissed, and were on their way.

Back at the farm, Ray greeted his mom and dad who were in the living room watching TV.

"Ray did the furniture get delivered to your apartment? I hope everything was okay, and I sure hope Shannon was happy with everything," said Mary.

"Mom, everything was delivered and Shannon appeared to be excited. Tomorrow Shannon and I are going to go shopping and look for items that we will need to finish setting up our apartment for real living," replied Ray.

Ray noticed that his dad was really quiet and appeared to be in deep thought. "Dad, you are pretty quiet; is there something wrong, or something we need to talk about?"

"Son, I was just thinking how things are really starting to change for your mom and me. One thing we both have to get used to is you not being here in this house. It's going to be an adjustment, but it will be fine because we will have Shannon as our new daughter in the family, and you know what we think of her," Paul said.

135

With teary eyes, Mary said, "It is just that you have been here for twenty-three years, so it will take some adjustments when you are not here. But Ray, the good part is we know your future looks so bright, and we couldn't be happier for you and Shannon."

Since they were on the subject, Ray thought it was the right time to tell them that Sunday he was planning to move to his and Shannon's apartment.

"While Shannon and I were talking earlier, we thought that I would move to the apartment on Sunday. Shannon wanted to be here thinking it will be hard on you to see me leave, and she wants to support you both. Mom, Dad, that's just how she feels, so she will be here Sunday."

Paul and Mary were now smiling. "I know that's how Shannon would think. But we also know in about four months you both will be living close by, and that will be great for us," Mary said.

With that the three of them all said good night and went to bed.

On Saturday, Ray was off to Lodi to pick up Shannon at her parent's house. Shannon's mom said to Ray, "Looks like another busy day for you and Shannon. It appears you are trying to finalize your apartment for real living. Have you ever shopped for groceries?"

"Actually, Mom, I have almost zero experience shopping for groceries."

Shannon immediately said, "That's okay, Mom, Ray and I will go together for groceries. It will be almost like we are married and that will be exciting." With that they were off to Lodi to do their shopping for their apartment.

At True Value Hardware, Ray and Shannon found most of the items they were looking for. Loading them into the pickup, they were soon back at the apartment. They liked the kitchen dinette set that came with six chairs, which meant they could have people over for dinner, something that was really important to both of them.

Next they were off to the grocery store. Once there, Ray was thankful he had Shannon along; he felt clueless, except when he saw the Portuguese linguica at the meat department.

"We have to have linguica and eggs. We'd invite Joeseph and Denise over for breakfast. Joeseph will be excited," Ray said.

"Well, it shouldn't be too hard to cook, but I will ask Denise to come and help me. She definitely knows how," Shannon said.

While they were shopping, Ray still couldn't believe the gal he had chosen to marry. For whatever reason, it was a proud moment in Ray's life; for him, it was like a prestart to making their home together.

Leaning over to Shannon and looking at her face-to-face, he whispered into her ear, "Just looking at you I get so emotionally aroused. I don't even have to touch or kiss you to get aroused."

Shannon just looked at him and said, "It's just one of those natural things, Ray. It is called love. Ray, it's going to come to a climax on our wedding day, which is three weeks away."

Ray and Shannon finished their shopping and went back to the apartment. After putting their groceries away, they stood together in their little living room. Shannon brought Ray close to her body and gave him a kiss, and they embraced each other for a long time.

Shannon gave Ray a little room and started to unbutton and take his shirt off. Ray was surprised by Shannon's action.

"Shannon, what are you doing?"

"Ray, I can't wait any longer! My emotions and sex drive are just uncontrollable at this moment. I feel we have to make love. I can't wait till we are married."

"Honey, calm down. We can wait, we have talked about this before and we just have to wait."

Shannon was now starting to take her blouse off.

In panic this time, Ray again said, "Shannon, hold on! We really have to wait for our honeymoon."

Shannon looked closely into Ray's eyes and gave him such soft kiss. She then said to him in a soft voice, "Honey this is why I really love you. I just put you through one hell of a test, and Ray you passed it."

"Shannon, what was this test about?"

"It's about you loving me, and not just the sexual part of what I have to offer. And let me tell you, Ray: after we are married, the only way we will be separated is if one of us dies. I will show no sympathy for any man or woman who will try to take you away from me. I hope all the world understands what I am talking about."

Ray was now very emotional and told Shannon, "We will have a wonderful long-lasting marriage, but let me tell you that was one hard test you just gave me. I am glad I passed, but I came close to flunking it because of my love for you."

"Pass or flunk, Ray, I will always love you. That is just plain and simple. I will die for you if I ever have to; I want you to always remember that."

After their emotional incident, Ray dropped Shannon off at her house, gave her a kiss, and reminded her to be at the ranch Sunday to comfort Ray's parents as he prepared to pack his things for his move to the apartment.

"I will see you in the morning. And Ray: after today, I love you more than ever," said Shannon.

Once back at the ranch, Ray told his mom and dad, "Shannon and I went shopping all day. The apartment is now ready for real living.

"Tomorrow I will start packing my things so I can move to the apartment in Lodi. Remember Shannon will be here in the morning while I pack things. I am sure Shannon will have some things to say that will comfort you both about me moving out of this house when I have been here all my life." Ray's mom and dad were seated a little teary eyed but not really emotional. Ray then told them good night and went to bed for it was getting late.

Sunday morning found Ray packing his belongings into boxes. His mom and dad were already up and in a relatively quiet mood. Shannon arrived and greeted them with a big hug before she went to Ray. After hugs and kisses, she turned to Mary and Paul again. Shannon started out by saying, "I know this is a big and emotional day in your lives to see your son move out after twenty-three years. It should be emotional, for you both love your son, and that is perfectly understandable."

Shannon paused a bit before she continued. "Let's all three go sit on the sofa."

At the sofa, Shannon sat between Paul and Mary. By this time Mary was really crying. Shannon was impelled to hug and hold her; she felt she knew what Mary was feeling, that she would be doing the same if Ray were her son. Shannon grabbed each of their hands and held them very tightly. "By now you know I deeply love you both as I do your son. But let's all remember Ray will always be your son. He has your blood running in his veins. Now I want to be Ray's wife, but all I am really doing is sharing what is yours—and he always will be yours." At that point Shannon gave them both a hug and kiss on the cheek, and they both seemed a little more relaxed.

"It's just such a milestone in our lives, Shannon," Paul said. "We will get through this emotional time, but that's just how it is and how it should be. The good part is that in October or November you will be back at the ranch in your new home, and that will be exciting for Mary and me," he concluded.

By now Ray had everything packed in his pickup and was ready to go. The four of them walked toward the pickup all tearful but with smiles on their faces. Shannon noticed that Paul was trailing behind. When she turned to face him, everybody stopped. Shannon went to Paul and said with a smile of happiness, "Dad, I just wanted to see if you were still following. Someday I will look back and you won't be there and that will be sad. But a lot of memories of you will always be in our hearts, that's just how life is," Shannon said.

"Shannon, Ray obviously told you about my Christmas letter; it is just how life is. Mary and I will not be with you forever. Thanks for bringing it up at this special time." Shannon just had to give Paul a hug of comfort on such a trying moment in his life.

Ray hugged his mom and dad and of course, Shannon, and left for Lodi. Shannon stayed a little while longer and asked. "Mom, Dad, will you be okay?"

After they acknowledged that they were fine, Shannon made her way to the apartment in Lodi. Mary and Paul stood there watching Ray and Shannon head up the levee, until the cars disappeared from their sight. This time they were smiling as they walked back to the house.

Once at the apartment, Ray and Shannon started to unpack Ray's belongings. Shannon was in the bedroom making the bed up.

"This bed is certainly nice and sturdy. We should have many years of service." Shannon had a big smile on her face as she looked at Ray, who made no response aside from a smile on his face, too.

"Shannon, I have an idea: since we bought some linguica, why don't you give Denise a call and ask her if she and Joeseph could come over tonight and have linguica and eggs.

It would be one of those breakfasts for dinner occasions; I know everybody does it every now and then," Ray said.

"That sounds great! I will call Denise right now." Shannon gave Denise a call and invited her and Joeseph over for dinner. Joeseph happened to be with Denise so they both agreed to come over for dinner. They were very excited, especially Joeseph who loved his linguica. "They will be here for dinner, and they were so excited."

It was about six o'clock when Denise and Joeseph rang the doorbell. Shannon answered the door for them.

"Denise, could you help me with the cooking? I really never have cooked much and could maybe use some guidance," Shannon said.

"Sure, Shannon. Let's get started. Just think: your first dinner for your best friends in your first home—it's almost like Ray and you being married." Shannon and Denise were having a wonderful time together knowing that sitting on the sofa were two men who soon would be their husbands. They also knew they would be living on two farms next to each other, where they could enjoy hunting, target shooting, and someday have children who would also strike a friendship. For Shannon and Denise, this was truly a dream that was about to become a reality.

Shannon and Denise had finished cooking and told Ray and Joeseph it was time to eat. As everybody got seated around the table, Joeseph was in heaven for the invitation. As they were all eating Joeseph commented, "Shannon, Denise mentioned she wanted to go hunting again before you get married."

"Yes, Denise mentioned it and I thought tomorrow would be a good day if it's okay with Denise."

"It would be a good day for me so let's plan on it," Denise said.

"If it's okay with you both, I would like to give you lessons in shooting a 30-30 Winchester Model 94 lever action carbine. It would be open sights—not a scope on it—and used for bigger targets, and would have more of a kick to your shoulder. I need to show you how to aim when using open sights," Joeseph said.

"Any particular reason you want them to learn to shoot the Winchester 30-30 carbine?" Ray asked.

"I thought both Shannon and Denise need to have a self-defense plan. With them eventually living out in the country, they may need to use a larger rifle either as a deterrent, or just plain self-defense against any unwanted intruder, for you just never know." They all thought it was a good idea, so Shannon, Denise, and Joeseph agreed to meet in the morning at the Johnson ranch. Ray had to work and couldn't be with them.

"Ray has a 30-30 carbine, so Shannon you can use his," said Joeseph. "I have a lot of ammo. By the way the 30-30 Winchesters 94 were always referred to as the gun that won the West."

"Should we be wearing a cowboy hat? Is that the rifle that John Wayne always used in his movies?" Shannon said with a smile.

"Yes, that's the rifle," Ray said. "You both should have fun learning how to shoot the 30-30 carbines. Pay close attention and get good at using them. You may really need to use them someday. You just never know when or why, but a situation could occur."

Dinner over and everybody had a good time, they said goodbye. Shannon was still there with Ray, just hugging and kissing each other.

"Ray since I am going to hunt and target-shoot tomorrow, we need to switch cars. I will need your pickup." Ray agreed and they switched car keys. "Well, Ray, I will be going now.

I know you are going to be lonely tonight. I sure wish I could be with you tonight, but we both know the reason why we can't. Good night. I love you, and have pleasant dreams on the bed," Shannon said with a smile.

The next morning Shannon, Denise, and Joeseph were at Johnson ranch. Paul and Mary were both gone so there was no one at the house. Shannon went in to get the 30-30 Winchester out of the gun safe; Joeseph had to show her which rifle to get.

Back to the pickup trucks they went heading for the shooting range, where Joeseph explained how to use open sights to aim at a target. He also had to show them how to load the rifle. To get used to shooting it, he had them use the shooting bench first. Joseph thought they caught on very quickly. He then set some boxes up and they shot at them without the assistance of the bench, which is called off-hand shooting. Shannon and Denise shot about fifty rounds each at boxes set at about 40 yards, and hit the target about 80 percent of the time.

Joeseph said, "You are doing very well. I am really proud of you both. I know you brought your 22 rifles so I will leave you two to go hunting—have fun."

Denise and Shannon were soon on their way. The hunting adventure earned them four cottontail rabbits that eventually ended up at the freezer. Shannon and Denise then headed back to Lodi.

While driving to Lodi, Denise told Shannon, "I believe we did real well with those 30-30 Winchester 94 carbines. We should be able to defend ourselves very well if a situation calls for it."

"I agree, whoever thinks they are going to take us on will have another thought; after we finish with them, they may not be able to think," Shannon said with a smile.

Time proved to be slipping away too fast. While Ray had his work to go to weekly, he and Shannon usually spent Saturdays out at the ranch to be with his parents. Ray's parents had adjusted to Ray not being there, but they were always excited when Saturday came. One day while Ray and Shannon were on their way to the ranch for one of their Saturday visits, they noticed some equipment at the north end of the ranch. Looking at each other, they proceeded to smile and kiss each other. Ray whispered in Shannon's ear, "They are starting to build our house."

"I can't believe it, Ray! Let's have a look at it—but first let's get your parents to come with us. I think they can make the walk."

Ray went to get his parents and they all walked to where the new house was being built. When they got there, everybody was so excited to see the foundation had been poured, and framing was getting started.

Ray told Shannon, "Our future lies here, and I couldn't be happier with a person named Shannon whom I chose to share the rest of my life with. Shannon, I will just love you forever, and thanks for wanting me in your life."

Shannon was so emotional she couldn't talk. She went to kiss Ray and gave Mary and Paul a hug.

She did manage to say, "Thanks so much for the gift. Dad, did you notice I looked back to see if you were still following and you were there?"

"I noticed, Shannon; thank you for looking. I guess the Christmas letter really meant something to you. Maybe it will always be our secret till the day I die."

The four of them walked back to the house and had some conversation, mainly about the wedding less than a week away.

Mary said, "Shannon this time next week you will be married and then Paul and I really will have you in our family. We both feel so blessed that you will eventually be living out here on the ranch."

Ray and his dad went out to the shop to get a Farmall Tractor ready to pull a trailer; it would be needed when they started harvesting tomatoes. That left Ray's mom alone with Shannon.

"Mom, I feel that I must tell you something that happened Sunday when Ray was moving into our apartment in Lodi. I started to be sexually aggressive with him—I had his shirt off and I was taking my blouse off, and he told me calm down we can't do this. I then gave him a soft kiss and told him he just passed one hell of a test. Mom, he passed because he loved me, and not what I was offering to give him."

"Shannon I am so happy for you both. I know we raised a fine son that does care about people, and I know he will love you through life forever, no matter the circumstances."

"Mom, next week we will be married; I dream of all the days we will have together, but I can't wait for our honeymoon night."

"You know, Shannon, your wedding day is approaching very quickly, and I know everybody can't wait to hear you called Mrs. Shannon Johnson."

CHAPTER 10

THE WEDDING

I t was Monday. In five days, the wedding ceremony will take place, and Ray and Shannon will be joined together as husband and wife. Shannon was at the apartment waiting for Ray to get home from work. She felt they really had to touch base with each other on a daily basis before the wedding. And she had some things to discuss with him when he got to the apartment.

Ray finally arrived at the apartment; he and Shannon greeted each other in the usual emotional way. They both went to sit on the sofa and started to talk about how the wedding was getting closer to reality.

Ray took Shannon into his arms and said, "Shannon, I can't wait to see you as Mrs. Shannon Johnson. It means so much to me that you are really finally mine."

"I have been yours for a long time, Ray, and I have loved every second of it. I still remember the day you approached me at the student lounge at school. It seems like it was just yesterday."

"You know, Shannon, our love just mushroomed to the point that here we are almost ready to get married, and hopefully start a family."

Ray and Shannon just sat there talking about all the past events that had happened in their lives after they had met and fell so deeply in love.

"Shannon, I will always remember that day at the student lounge. When you walked in and sat down, I said to myself, 'Wow, a blued-eyed brunette!' There was also a guy sitting at a nearby table, and he was really looking at you in what I thought was a serious aggressive look."

Shannon was smiling as Ray continued to say, "So, Shannon, I couldn't let you get away that day without meeting you. You know I am not a very aggressive guy when it comes to girls, but that day I just had the courage. I was scared to death to ask you if I could sit at the table with you. When you looked up, those beautiful blue eyes just sparkled as you first looked at me, but best of all you said 'Sure, have a seat.' Shannon, that guy at a table close by you probably forced me to go and meet you, as he looked like he was seriously looking at you. I thought I would never again have the opportunity to meet you. From that day on, I could never stop thinking about you."

Ray then moved closer to Shannon's face, looked into those irresistible blue eyes, and then told her, "I will always remember you that day in the student lounge," before giving her a kiss.

Smiling, Shannon said, "Well, Ray, I have something that I must share with you now. I had a gal classmate one day mentioned that she had a guy in her math class that really appeared to be a great catch for some gal. She talked to you often after class, so one day after her class, I had her point you out; after a while, I sort of kept tract of you and noticed you almost always went to the student lounge after that class. Later I asked my friend if she could somehow find out what your favorite color was, and she did find out for me."

Ray was really thinking now and said, "You turkey, you really set me up in the student lounge, didn't you?"

Shannon laid him on the couch, looked at him, and gave him a long, romantic kiss. She pulled away from him and said the story hadn't ended yet, so she continued, "Ray, remember the guy who was sitting at the table next to me that you thought was giving me some serious looks?"

"Ya, I remember him."

"Well, that was my gal friend's boyfriend, and I asked him to look like he was seriously going to make an attempt to meet me."

"Well, your plan worked—and worked well," Ray said with a smile. "The way you looked that day—you were a beautiful young gal that I really thought would never give a farm boy like me a chance."

"I wore a pretty short red dress that day after I found out your favorite color was red—by the way I also knew you were a farm boy. When you approached me and asked if you could sit at the table I was at, I knew my plan was working. When I looked up at you and I said, 'Sure, have a seat,' at that instant I knew I had you in my heart, and I was never ever going to let you go."

"Shannon, you had everything that turned me on that day, and that's all there is to it. Thanks so much for the plan, it worked for both of us. If we have children, someday I hope we can share this story with them, for it really is a great story. And in a few days we will have each other forever. And that will be a start of a new chapter in our lives."

"My parents are inviting everybody over on Thursday night for a get together, and you might say it will be a briefing on the wedding," said Shannon. "Joeseph and his parents, Denise and her parents, your parents will all be there. We will go over a few things. It really is simple, for it's not a big elaborate wedding. Everybody is to be there at seven o'clock, so Ray tell your parents and let the Alexanders know."

On Tuesday, Shannon again waited at the apartment for Ray to get home from work. She had already cooked him a dinner so they could eat when he returned.

Ray finally got to the apartment, walked in, and there was Shannon, acting like a wife, giving him a hug and a kiss. Ray said, "Shannon, we are getting to practice our premarriage routine."

"Ray, there is one item we just haven't got to yet," she said, smiling.

Ray smiled back at her and said, "I know what item you are talking about. We will save it for our wedding day." Ray then gave Shannon a smile and a long kiss. "It's almost here—just four more days."

At dinner, they talked about Denise and Joeseph. They were wondering when their friends would announce their wedding day. Shannon said, "Denise hasn't mentioned anything about a date."

"Well, we will just wait and see. I am sure it will be before I leave for the hunting trip to India."

"Ray, I can guarantee it will be before your trip to India, as Joeseph wants you to be his best man."

Soon Shannon was getting ready to go home. Before leaving, she gave Ray a casual kiss and said, "Goodbye, honey; have sweet dreams tonight as you sleep in our bed alone."

Ray just shook his head and smiled at her, waving at her as she left for home. He was always amazed at her personality and her ability to strike a little humor into the conversation whenever it pertained to sex with him.

On Thursday; everybody was at Shannon's parent's house to discuss the final plans of the wedding on Saturday. Everybody was talking with each other when Shannon's dad got everybody's attention.

"I would like to tell everybody involved in the wedding some of the final details. The rehearsal will be Friday at St. Paul's Lutheran Church at seven o'clock. Pastor Green will be officiating the wedding ceremony. I have asked the

Alexanders to take care of the guest book, and the Silvas to hand out the wedding programs and welcome the guests"

"The church will provide a vocalist and the organist," Elizabeth said. "The reception would be held at the Lodi American Legion hall, with a band for some dancing if some wanted to dance. And Denise, Joeseph—don't forget the rings."

"I thank you all for being part of the wedding, especially Ray's and my parents for giving us such a wonderful start," Shannon said.

"Oh, during the reception, Ray and I will change clothes, wave goodbye, and head to Ray's choice for our honeymoon. If you need to phone us, the number is…that's tough, we will take no calls. We will be busy finishing our wedding rites," she concluded.

"Shannon only worries about one thing on our honeymoon," Ray said. "Denise here can tell everybody what Shannon's worry is."

"Shannon's primary concern is the bed better not break," Denise obliged to say.

Everybody laughed, which told them the meeting was over. The Doritees served cake and punch as refreshments.

Denise and Joeseph managed to get everybody's attention. Denise told everybody, "Since we have all of you here tonight, Joeseph and I thought we would announce our wedding date. We have decided that November 1st would be the day. Our parents have already agreed to that date. We would also like to ask Shannon and Ray to be our maid of honor and best man in our wedding."

Ray and Shannon both agreed and responded with, "Yes, they would be happy and excited to be in the wedding!"

Shannon just had to ask Denise, "Remember what the most important part of marriage is?"

Denise, smiling, answered Shannon's question, "A strong bed, one that you could breed an elephant on; you taught me well, Shannon."

Joeseph had a puzzled look on his face. How did an elephant fit into the conversation, but he just passed it off and didn't respond to the comment.

Everybody finally made their way home, after saying thank you and goodbye. Ray stuck around a little longer and gave Shannon's mom and dad a hug of thanks, saying, "You don't have to take Shannon too seriously when she jokes about the bed having to be strong."

"Ray, I am not joking! You will see Saturday, Sunday, and Monday during our honeymoon if I am joking." Shannon was smiling as she looked at Ray, her blue eyes focused on him. Grinning, she added, "Ray, have sweet dreams tonight when you are sleeping in our bed without me."

Ray held Shannon tightly to his body, gave her a romantic kiss, and left for his apartment. He drove in a happy mood, knowing things were about to get to the point where he and Shannon could start living their life together. They could just love each other every day.

Ray also knew he needed to get started on putting a plan together for his hunting trip to India after the wedding. The trip to India had to be his priority, along with keeping Shannon happy.

On Friday, the excitement started to build up with Ray and Shannon. Having taken six days off work, Ray was at the apartment. The doorbell rang and there was Shannon, who couldn't stay away, and entered the apartment.

Knowing it was soon to be their time, they just talked about how Saturday was going to be a great day for them, and especially the honeymoon, when they would finally engage in something they had never done before. They were excited about their honeymoon and couldn't stay off the subject.

They were sitting closely together on the sofa when Ray said to Shannon, "I can't believe in another day we will be together forever. Shannon, it is like a dream that has finally come true. At one time I didn't think I had a chance to ever even meet you, and now here we are about to be married."

Again, they were getting sexually aroused to the point they almost couldn't stop. When they came to their senses, they pulled away.

"Ray, we can wait another day, but just think what we almost did just now," Shannon said. "But tomorrow we won't have to stop, and Ray it will be a thrilling time for us both."

Around seven o'clock, everybody started arriving at St Paul's Lutheran Church for the wedding rehearsal. Pastor Green was there to greet everybody. In time he gave them all the instructions on the wedding ceremony, adding, "I need everybody here at ten o'clock. The ceremony will start at 11:30 am. I expect to introduce Ray and Shannon to the guests as Mr. and Mrs. Ray Johnson at twelve o'clock. I refer to it as a *High Noon* wedding." Ray and Shannon stood there holding hands with big smiles on their faces. The pastor reminded Denise and Joeseph not to forget the rings. He also reminded the Alexanders they would handle the guest book, while the Silvas would greet and hand out the wedding programs to the guests.

Pastor Green informed them that the church would provide the organist and a solo vocalist to perform at the ceremony. He then had them stand in the appropriate standing positions and went over the program until everybody felt comfortable.

Soon the rehearsal was over. Pastor Green dismissed the wedding party, telling Ray and Shannon, "Well, Ray and Shannon, after you leave here tonight, the next time you will see each other is when Shannon's dad walks her down the aisle. Shannon's dad will give his daughter's hand to you, Ray, so she can be your wife forever. In God's eyes, that will be a joyous occasion, and may God bless you both. I will see you tomorrow."

Walking out to their car, Shannon and Ray were very emotional, especially Shannon, who was thinking about her dad giving her away to Ray. Shannon looked at Ray and said, "Those are profound words when you think of my dad giving me away."

Ray hugged Shannon to comfort her. "Shannon, those words are precious, seeing how he agrees with the choice that you have made. And remember, Shannon, he is giving you to me to be my wife, but you will always be his daughter, and nobody can take that fact away from him." Shannon was a little more relaxed after Ray's comments.

They were standing in the church parking lot facing each other. "Shannon, I love everything about you," Ray said. He lifted her up and gave her a kiss on her belly, saying, "Remember those days?"

"I will never forget the first time you did that. It sent my emotions through the roof. Ray, you know many times I was ready to give you my body, but you wouldn't take advantage of me. Thank you for giving me that respect. I know it was hard for you."

"Shannon, tomorrow we won't have to worry about any of those premarital sex issues. They will all be in the past."

Ray and Shannon gave each other their last premarital kiss and said goodbye to each other. But Shannon blurted out, while smiling, "Ray, have sweet dreams tonight in our bed without me! I love you and I will see you at the altar tomorrow."

On Saturday, everybody in the wedding party was promptly at the church. The men had their tuxedos on, ready for the ceremony. In the bride's dressing room were Shannon and Denise trying hard to avoid tears. Denise told Shannon, "We have to save the tears for after the ceremony; we don't want to smear our makeup—and Shannon, we can do it."

"Denise, I love your red dress. You are a beautiful, trusting friend." That statement almost brought them a flood of tears, but they made it through the incident without crying. Shannon looked at the clock and told Denise, "Its 11:20. This reminds of a movie about a sheriff who was in a difficult situation that was to take place at twelve o'clock. The sheriff asked the township to help him, but they were cowards and refused. He had to go it alone. In the movie, they kept showing the clock ticking towards twelve o'clock."

"I am no coward," Denise replied. "I will always help my best friend through any circumstance that may occur, and you know you can count on me."

The guests had all arrived and were now seated. Joeseph was ushering Ray's parents down to their seat. He whispered into Mary Johnson's ear, "Mom, this is a great moment for you and Dad. You are about to gain a daughter. I know you will both be happy."

She whispered back, "I know, Joeseph; she will be like a daughter, just as you are like a son to me." Joeseph just smiled and went back to usher Shannon's mom to her seat.

Joeseph ushered Elizabeth down the aisle. As he seated her, he whispered to her, "Congratulations, Mom, you are about to gain a son named Ray."

Smiling, Elizabeth replied, "Joeseph, you called me 'Mom.' I am honored to be like Mary. You have made my day, thank you." Joeseph then headed back to take his place besides Ray at the altar.

At 11:30, the ceremony was about to get started. The church usher knocked on the bridal dressing room door and told Denise and Shannon to come to the church narthex. Denise and Shannon looked at each other, smiled, and said, simultaneously to each other, "Here we go, it's almost *High Noon!*"

Ray and Joeseph stood at the altar waiting. Just then, the narthex door opened, the organist started playing, and Denise started walking down the aisle. Taking her place to stand, she gave both Ray and Joeseph a big smile. Of course Joeseph was just so excited, for that was his future bride-to-be. The Narthex doors were now closed again.

Next, Shannon and her dad took their places in the narthex. Shannon's dad told Shannon, "Honey, this is one thing only a dad gets to do, take his daughter down the aisle, to give her away to her new husband-to-be. And Shannon, it's this moment only that you and I can share, and I will cherish it forever." At that moment, the organist started to play "Here Comes the Bride," and the usher flung the doors open. For the first time, Shannon and her dad could see all the guests, the candles on each pew, and at the end standing by the altar were Pastor Green, Denise, Joeseph, and Ray.

Before they began their walk down the aisle, Shannon said softly to her dad, "Thanks for everything you and Mom have done for me, and Dad let's take this trip that only a daughter and her dad can ever take. Let's go, Dad." With that they started their journey to the altar. Shannon was full of smiles as she passed the guests. Finally they stopped. She looked at Denise and gave her a wink and a smile.

The pastor then said, "Bob, do you give your daughters hand in marriage to Ray Johnson?"

"I do with no reservation. Ray is a welcomed addition to our family." He then gave Shannon a kiss, took her to Ray, and brought their hands together. "Take care of my daughter, Ray." Bob then went and sat down by Elizabeth. They both had smiles on their faces.

Pastor Green then proceeded with the ceremony in a normal fashion. Ray and Shannon were facing each other; they had already given each other their wedding rings.

"In a moment the church bell will ring twelve times indicating high noon," Pastor Green reminded the two. "Ray and Shannon, always remember that last ring of the bell, for it will tie you together as one. The two of you should always protect each other in whatever situation that might occur, no matter what the danger is, for God will be by your side and give you the strength to endure. This Marriage is sacred to God—always remember that."

By now Denise was smiling through tears. Soon the church bells started to ring; on the twelfth, Pastor Green said, "It's high noon: Ray and Shannon, I now pronounce you man and wife. Ray, I think it's time that you give Shannon a kiss." Shannon lifted her veil up, gave a thumb up sign, and they both engaged in a long kiss.

Shannon whispered to Ray, "Did that arouse you?"

"Just like old times, but we are going to do something about it later," he replied.

The pastor asked them to turn to the guests as he said, "I now would like to introduce to you Mr. and Mrs. Ray Johnson."

The wedding party was soon headed out of the church, greeting the guests as they were coming out. After the pictures were taken, everybody headed to the reception.

All the guests at the reception and were at this time seated, waiting for the wedding party to arrive. When it did, the last to enter was Ray and Shannon, who were all smiles as they waved to the guests applauding their entrance. The wedding party proceeded to the head table and sat down; at that time, the food was served. Later, the cutting of the cake and a toast was given by Joeseph and Denise.

Denise was soon giving a talk about the two newlyweds. "By the way: for all you young people, if you are not planning on getting married soon, don't go to the shooting range on the Johnson ranch; things can happen quickly over there, and a wedding like this can be the result," she said. She held up her hand and pointed to her engagement ring. "But if you want to be courageous, ask Ray and Shannon if you and somebody of interest could use the shooting range. I know they would let anybody use it, for they both know the results could be a good thing. It happened to them, and it happened to Joeseph and me."

After the toast was made to honor Ray and Shannon, the newlyweds started to visit with the guests. As they were making the rounds to each table, they came upon one where, to Ray's surprise, he noticed the gal who set up the situation at the student lounge, where Ray and Shannon met for the first time.

"Ray, I didn't tell you, but how could we not invite these two who set you up so you could meet me."

"Well, I remember Gail! I could never figure out why she asked all those questions. But I fell for it hook, line, and sinker!"

"Ray, this is Gail's boyfriend, Bob."

Ray acknowledged Bob with a handshake, "Well, you were the other half of the scheme. I have to say, Bob, you were really convincing on how you were looking at Shannon that day, and I knew I had to make a move and make it fast."

"Ray, Shannon, seeing you both here today, I am so glad it all worked out. By the way, I also like hunting and shooting," said Bob.

Bob's words had Ray thinking, *Oh, here it comes*, while squeezing the hand of Shannon, who had a big grin on her face.

Smiling, Bob said, "Ray, do you think it would be possible for me to take Gail out to your shooting range sometime so I could teach her how to shoot?"

Gail was smiling through tears, recalling Denise's words about the shooting range. Ray said, "You two have a lifetime pass to the shooting range; after all, look what you have done for us."

Ray and Shannon were finally done visiting with all the guests. Shannon whispered in Ray's ear, "It's time; let's go change and get going to our honeymoon destination."

"We do have to get going." With that, they waved to the guests and prepared to leave for their honeymoon destination.

They changed to their going-away outfits. The car was already packed and all the guests were waiting for them. The parents wished, along with Denise and Joeseph were there to wish them well.

"You treat Shannon gently, you know she's not very big, so don't hurt her, I love you both," Denise said, smiling. "Oh, Shannon, hope the bed holds up."

Ray and Shannon were soon off to their honeymoon.

As they were driving, the two discussed various things that have happened in their lives, one of which pertained to Bob and Gail going to the shooting range.

"Well, that's a no brainer. Bob will use that as a starting point to enhance their relationship, and they will be engaged in a short time." Ray leaned over while driving and gave Shannon's a quick kiss. "By the way, I love the red dress you chose for our honeymoon getaway. It is very sexy," he said.

"I am glad you noticed. Hey, why did you have to bring up sex? Now I am in heat again. You know we have been on the road for almost two hours. How much longer do we have to go?"

"About half an hour more," replied Ray.

As they were driving along, Shannon noticed that they had passed Fort Ord Army Base. She now knew what vicinity they were headed for, but didn't say a word to Ray. They were then entering Monterey.

"Ray, I love you—you know you have picked an area that I have loved for years," Shannon said.

"We aren't there yet," Ray replied. As they drove around next to Monterey Bay, Shannon noticed the Fisherman's Wharf sign, and then a sign that said Lovers Point.

"Ray we are about ready to experience the long-awaited event in our life. That event will bring us together as one and give us a thrill in our life that we have never experienced before."

"Well, Shannon, we are here at Borges Motel and it's just across the street from Lover's Point that looks over Monterey Bay. Are you okay with the choice I made?

"I didn't know when I picked it, but got a hint that day when your parents returned from Monterrey and stated that you used to come here often, and you always loved it here at Monterrey. But I had already made plans before I even learned that you liked Monterey Bay, so I was pleased to learn that you liked it here," Ray said.

"Ray, lets hurry and check in so we can go and try and make a baby. This is exciting and I can't wait much longer!"

Off they were to the Motel office to check in, and were greeted by the desk clerk who said, "Ray Johnson and the previous Shannon Doritee; first, congratulations on your marriage today."

Shannon asked, "You remember both of us?"

"Yes. Shannon, both your parents visited here often, especially when you both were really young. Very recently your mom and dad were here and mentioned you were getting married to a young man named Ray Johnson on July 1. When Ray made the reservation, I called your mom and told her that I believe your honeymoon was going to take place right here at Lover's Point."

"So our parents know we are here. I can't believe what I just heard, but it's okay," Ray said, amazed.

"Both your parents called me and told me to tell the two of you to enjoy your honeymoon. Ray, your mom also told me to tell you both don't worry, she won't call you on your honeymoon."

All the news made Ray and Shannon happy and excited as they finished checking in. After securing the keys and room number, they thanked the desk clerk. Before leaving, Shannon just had to mention, "Well, I don't mean to appear to be in such a hurry, but Ray and I have got to go and try to make a baby. I believe I am in heat. Oh, by the way, are your beds strong and durable?"

The desk clerk took everything in stride, though he appeared to be amazed at what Shannon just shared, "Honey, I believe you will be fine in the room."

Ray stood listening to Shannon and the desk clerk's conversation. He loved his new wife's approach about what was to be their first lovemaking experience. He knew Shannon was always open about the subject, and could care less about how others would take such comments. To Ray that was Shannon, and that will always be Shannon, and that's the woman he married and would love forever.

With their luggage, they went to locate the room. When they found the room, Ray unlocked the door, turned, and looked at Shannon. In an instant he grabbed her, gave her a very emotional kiss, and carried her into the room and laid her down on the bed. Ray smiled at her and said with a smile, "Are you still in heat? I hope so because I am very aroused about this present situation."

Shannon got off the bed, stood up, and faced Ray; they then kicked off their shoes, still face-to-face. Looking at

Shannon's beautiful blue eyes, Ray said. "Shannon, what do we do now?"

Smiling, Shannon said, "Ray, I will guide you. I know you like this red dress as it's your favorite color. I am going to turn around and I want you to unzip my dress and pull it down." Shannon turned back to face him; by this time, Ray was really sexually aroused. Shannon said, "I can tell you like what you see." At that point, Shannon unbuttoned Ray's shirt and pants and had him take them off.

"Shannon, you have nothing on under your dress."

Shannon responded, "Well, Ray, I thought that I might be in a hurry at this special time to make love, so I felt the quicker the better."

Ray smiled then grabbed her, lifted her up, and gave her a kiss on her belly button. He worked up to her lips and gave her a kiss that lighted her fuse, and he laid her gently onto the bed, and they made love. After they were finished they lay on their backs, having a conversation about how wonderful it felt to finally make love.

Shannon with a smile said, "Ray, that was way more thrilling than I would have ever dreamed. I hope I satisfied you."

"You were great. And we didn't break the bed."

"Ray, I am not so sure. I think we are lying at an angle."

"Shannon, you are having hallucinations."

They remained hugging and kissing lying in bed, and enjoying the comfort of each other. They finally fell asleep in each other's arms.

It was now morning so they both got dressed and went out to Lover's Point where they enjoyed the view of Monterrey Bay. They had breakfast at a nearby restaurant next to the motel. After breakfast, they went for a walk and found a rock formation. They both like climbing in the rocks and watching the wave come in.

Ray and Shannon's honeymoon was quickly coming to an end. On the last night after making love and lying in bed and talking, Shannon brought up the subject of becoming pregnant someday, that they should make love real often.

Ray asked Shannon, "What do you consider 'real often'?"

Smiling, Shannon said, "Everyday"

"Shannon, I would like to be able to do that, but for a male it may be impossible."

"Okay, I will give in on that a little—six times a week."

"I will give it a try. I love you, Shannon, and it certainly won't be hard to give it a try." Grinning, Ray continued, "You know, Shannon, you always worry about the bed breaking; well, what about Ray breaking?"

"Oh, Ray, you can outlast any bed!"

The morning the honeymoon was over, they said goodbye to the motel desk clerk and headed home to Lodi.

When they got home to their apartment, they called everybody and let them know the honeymoon went well. They were ready to really start their life together as Mr. and Mrs. Ray Johnson.

CHAPTER 11

RAY STARTS PLANNING

R ay and Shannon were now getting into the routine of everyday living as a married couple in their Lodi apartment. Shannon was becoming an excellent cook and Ray was really enjoying married life. Each day he would tell Shannon he loved her more and more every day.

It was late August. Ray's Job at Lodi Mold Inc. seemed to be going extremely well; he was told by Fred Sunday that everybody was extremely pleased with his work and the contribution he was making to the company. He was told that the permanent position was his when he gets back from his hunting trip to India.

One Saturday Ray and Shannon made arrangements to meet Joeseph and Denise at Ray's parents' ranch, to see Ray's parents on their usual Saturday visit to the ranch. When Ray pulled into the driveway, they noticed Joeseph and Denise were already inside visiting with Ray's parents. Ray and Shannon went inside and they all sat down to talk about the week's events. Shannon mentioned to Denise and Joeseph, "Would you want to come and see how our house is coming along?"

Denise said with some excitement, "That sounds great!" They all went outside and decided they would walk to the sight. As they got closer to the construction site, Shannon noticed some equipment just north of their house. "Ray, do you see what I see?"

"Shannon, looks like we are going to have some neighbors just 300 yards north of us."

Denise and Joeseph had big smiles on their faces: they were going to live next to their longtime friends, where both families could enjoy fishing and hunting together, and whatever else the outdoors had to offer.

Ray's and Shannon's house was coming right along and looked to be on schedule. Ray asked Joeseph, "When is your house scheduled to be finished?"

"I think about the latter part of December, if the weather holds out long enough to get the outside done, so the inside could be worked on under any weather condition."

The four of them started to walk back to Ray's parents' house. Inside they sat with Ray's parents to converse with each other. Ray's dad asked, "Ray, have you started any planning for your hunting trip?"

"Actually, Dad, I have got my passport and visa paperwork coming. So I have got that done. Oh, I also got in touch with our State Department if it could ask Bob Jones, the US embassy consulate in New Delhi, India, to provide a list of some reputable tiger and leopard hunting guides he could recommend. He was going to look into it for me, and get back to me in about five days."

"Son, you have got to keep on it; time flies sometimes."

Shannon was quietly telling Mom and Denise, "After about two months I am still not pregnant. It's a little discouraging, but Mom I remember you telling me it's not always easy to get pregnant. Be assured we are trying very hard to give you grandchildren."

Ray's dad looked at Shannon and Denise. "Shannon, Denise, I was wondering if I could ask a favor of you two gals since you are both here?"

Shannon and Denise immediately turned to Paul and Shannon asked, "Dad, what is it you want us to do?"

"Well, since the tomato harvest is about to begin and Ray is working, I was wondering if you two could distribute the empty boxes when the trucks bring them."

Denise said, "Dad if I remember my Spanish, I believe we could be called the two amigos, and we can do it. Just give us a little guidance, and Dad, I guess we should include you, so really we are the three amigos."

Paul smiled and put his head down, his hand on his forehead, and then raised his head to look at his precious new daughters. And then he said, "Okay, you two, we will start on Monday morning. You will be working among Mexicans that came to work here. They are wonderful hardworking people just trying to make a living for their family back in Mexico. Always treat them with respect, and I know you will."

Shannon then just felt compelled to say, "You know, Dad, I have learned one thing from you and Mom; you will always show respect to any nationality. When we have children, I will make sure they have that same mentality."

Ray and Joeseph had a big grin on their faces when Denise called themselves the two amigos; they came across as being able to do any task together as friends.

Joeseph, smiling, said, "Ray you haven't seen these two amigos perform their shooting skills with the Winchester 30-30 carbines. I have been working with them once a week—they are outright good. I wouldn't want to be on the other end of that barrel if they were mad at you, or if you were a person that had any thoughts that they didn't like."

Turning to Shannon and Denise, he announced, "Let's all go to the shooting range and show Ray how you two amigos have a new acquired skill to shoot the 30-30 Winchester carbines."

The four of them got the guns, ammo, and a lot of tin cans, before they squeezed into the seat of Ray's pickup. They appeared to really enjoy being packed in the pickup like sardines in a can. At the shooting range they all got out. Shannon and Denise were getting ready to show their shooting ability with the Winchester 30-30 carbine.

Joeseph set up seven cans for each of them at about 25 yards.

Each rifle was loaded with seven rounds of ammo to shoot. Joeseph then said, "Are you gals ready?" When they gave thumbs up and a nod, Joeseph gave the order, "Fire away!" In less than 10 seconds, every can was hit.

Ray couldn't believe the performance he had just seen with the lever action 30-30 Winchester carbines. They each hit every can they shot at. Ray went up to Shannon, gave her a hug and a kiss. "Well, I believe nobody better mess with you two amigos, unless they plan to die."

"Ray I just think it's good to have experience shooting an open sighted rifle for self-defense at a close distance, and shooting fast and accurate," Joeseph said.

"We may never need it, but if we have to use our shooting skills, I feel we are qualified to do the job. Especially if somebody pushes us into a corner that we don't like being in," Shannon said.

"You know, I believe we forgot one thing when we were shooting," Denise said, smiling.

"What did you gals forget?" Joeseph said.

"Our John Wayne western cowboy hats," Denise replied, smiling.

The shooting demonstration done, they all headed back to the ranch house. They went inside to say goodbye to Paul and Mary. They walked out together, but before Shannon got into the car, she went back to Paul and Mary.

"Mom, Dad, I know it's hard for you to see us leave on these Saturday visits. But in few months that's all going to change when we move into our new house and start our life out here." She gave them both a hug, and then said, "See you Monday, Dad. I am anxious to help you with the tomato harvest. Denise and I are so proud that you asked us to help."

"The Alexanders and us are so lucky to have you two gals in our family. I guess I could have said you two amigos as Denise so graciously stated. I feel that the amigo name, meaning you two as friends, is going to stick around here forever. I love that kind of name calling, and Mom and I love you both. See you Monday morning."

Everybody was headed home. While going back to Lodi, Shannon mentioned to Ray, "Your parents appear to be lost without you being around. It will mean so much when we can get moved to the ranch. I know it will change their mood."

"I know at times Mom and Dad looked a little depressed during our visit, but their mood changed when Dad asked if you and Denise could help him when the tomato harvest starts. And you both said yes so enthusiastically."

At the apartment, they went inside and turned on the TV. They were sitting together on the sofa when the doorbell rang; Shannon got up and answered the door.

"It's for you! It's a telegram from the United States embassy in New Delhi, from Mr. Bob Jones. Ray you have to sign for it," Shannon told Ray.

Ray got up and signed for the telegram. It had some information on hunting guides especially noted for Bengal tiger and leopard hunting. Bob Jones stated he personally would recommend SHARMA HUNTING OUTFITTERS. The reason was he knew several hunters who had used them; they were considered good, they could speak excellent English, along with many Indian dialects that people use in the villages. The telegram had a list of five guide and hunting outfitters along with their addresses. Bob Jones also included in the telegram the address of the embassy in New Delhi. He stated communication would have to be done by telegram to any of the addresses listed. Phones in this era of history are almost nonexistent here for international calls. Bob Jones did state not to hesitate to get in touch by telegram if ever Ray needed help.

Ray went back to the couch to sit by Shannon. He gave her a romantic kiss and said, "Are you okay, with this? You know it's just getting started."

"I wouldn't have it any other way. You have to live this dream out. It's important for you. I will support you all the way on your trip to India."

Ray gave her another arousing kiss. "I think I know what you are thinking."

"Ya, Ray you do know me and my emotions—and yes, we have to try our bed. Let's go try to make a baby!"

"Well, Shannon, nothing like ending an evening on a loving note," Ray replied.

Sunday morning found Ray relaxing while going over the list of five hunting guides that Bob Jones had given him. One of the guides that really caught Ray's attention was Baasim Sharma and his brother, Aadesh Sharma of the SHARMA HUNTING OUTFITTERS. One item that Ray really liked about them is that they spoke excellent English, and speak and understand almost all of the dialects spoken in India. To Ray this was important. Besides, Bob Jones knew hunters who have used them and they came with good recommendations.

He brought Shannon in on the decision making process, and she agreed and mentioned, "Ray, you should send them a telegram so you can start communicating with each other."

"I will start to draft a telegram and go to the Post Office and send it tomorrow." With that decided, they headed to church, of which they attended most every Sunday.

Later in the afternoon after they got home from church, Ray told Shannon, "I am going to start writing what information I need from the SHARMA HUNTING OUTFITTERS. Then I will send a telegram to them. I will give them my address so we can communicate, and tell them I would appreciate a response as soon as possible. I am going to include items like my planned date to leave is May 1, 1960; price they charge and what area would the hunt for the Bengal tiger take place. And he should include any other items that he thinks would be beneficial for me to know about on such a hunting trip."

Shannon then came over to Ray, got real close, and hugged him tightly and kissed him. Ray could sense what was next. "Honey, I feel like its baby-making time."

"Okay, let go do it, Shannon. I know when we start talking about my trip it's hard on you, and you feel a need to make love as often as possible." So off they went, and just showing how excited they were in their new married life.

Later in the evening when they were eating dinner, Ray mentioned to Shannon, "Well, you two amigos get to help Dad tomorrow. I hope it all works out."

"I can't even begin to tell you how excited Denise and I are about tomorrow; being able to help your dad is an honor. I will pick up Denise about seven o'clock in the morning and head to the ranch."

Ray looked at Shannon and said, "Honey, my dad is so grateful that you two will be there to help, and I know you both will be well compensated for your work."

"What do you mean—you think he is going to pay us?"

"Shannon that's a no-brainer; of course he is going to pay you. My dad wouldn't have it any other way."

"I don't think Denise is expecting to get paid, and I certainly think your parents building us a house is more compensation than I deserve."

"Not in Dad's eyes; you are worth way more."

"Well, I hope we can do a good job for your dad."

"I have confidence that you both will do a good job. Well, maybe we should go to bed. It's work for you and me tomorrow, and you have to get up earlier than normal."

Shannon said to Ray with a big grin, "Going to bed sounds like a wonderful idea to me." So they both were off to the bedroom.

Monday morning came and Ray and Shannon had a quick breakfast. After giving each other a kiss, Shannon was off to pick up Denise and head to the ranch. Ray was getting ready to leave for work. He grabbed his draft of the telegram that he was going to send to the SHARMA HUNTING OUTFITTERS later today on his lunch hour. Ray went to work, and as planned went to the Post Office and sent the telegram to SHARMA HUNTING OUTFITTERS in New Delhi, India.

After work, Ray thought he would head to the ranch to see how the two amigos were doing. Ray knew it would be a long day for them, as that's how farmers operate when they are harvesting a crop. When he got to the ranch, he got into his pickup and headed out to the tomato field. He stopped where his dad was and asked, "Well, Dad, how are the two amigos doing?"

"They are doing great, but you won't recognize them."

"Why is that?"

"They are both covered with dirt. I bet they are itching all over, but I can see they enjoy it out here, and most of all they enjoy each other. And Denise, well, that little Portuguese gal is hard to beat, nothing will stop her. Joeseph's dad was out here watching them work and he told me, 'I don't think anything or anybody can stop those two when they get focused on something.' But anyway, son, go out and give Shannon a big kiss—if you can see her lips."

With that, Ray made his way out to where they were distributing boxes for the tomato pickers. Shannon did not notice him when he got there; when he got close to her, he startled her for an instant. And then she went to him and with a smile, gave him a romantic kiss, and said, "Ray, this is great out here! Denise and I love it. It's great to do good hard work. I believe we are just about done for today. Your dad said the tomato crop is one of the best he has raised."

"So did you get to send your telegram to the hunting guide?"

"Yes, I did. That's a start. Hopefully he will respond soon," replied Ray.

Denise came up to Ray and said, "Well, I think the two amigos are doing okay. Ray, being able to speak Portuguese, I was able to talk to the Mexicans—the language is so similar. Your dad was amazed when I started talking their language. You know, Ray, Shannon and I being out here with your dad made us both realize what a kind man your dad is. He is so good to the Mexicans, and you can just see that he appreciates them. And now he can use me to get that point across to them because I can speak to them, and I am proud to be able to do it. These are good people just trying to make a living for their families back in Mexico, Ray; that's how your dad views it, as do I, and I believe Shannon does, too."

"Shannon, I am going to head back to Lodi. I will see you in an hour or so." He gave her a kiss and said, "You two drive carefully." Ray was on his way, but did stop to see his mom briefly; he walked in and said, "Well, Mom, how are things going?"

"Son, it couldn't be better. Having Shannon and Denise working along with Dad has been the highlight of our lives. Joeseph's parents are beside themselves, especially when they happened to hear Denise speak to the Mexicans in Spanish."

"Well, Mom, great to hear that.

"I have to get home now. I just stopped by to say hello. I have already seen dad. He also seemed pleased at how the two amigos did today. I know Shannon will be tired when she gets home. After she cleans up I will take her out to a little restaurant called the Broiler in Lodi. It's a simple little restaurant. I will see you, Mom."

After Ray made it back to the apartment, Shannon walked in shortly after.

"Well, what a day I had," she said. "It was hard but it felt great. I am going to take a shower and get cleaned up. I don't think I have ever been this dirty."

"Honey, let me take you to the Broiler for dinner after you get cleaned up."

"That sounds great! I didn't feel like cooking tonight being so tired. Your dad said it will take about two weeks to finish the tomato harvest. Your dad is such a great man; those Mexicans just plain adore him for how he treats them."

Shannon came out all cleaned up, and Ray came to her and gave her a gigantic hug and kiss, thanking her for helping his dad. He told her it meant so much for his mom and dad to have both her and Denise around. They then went out to dinner, and a little later returned back to the apartment.

"Ray, I am going to have to go to bed. I am so exhausted." With that off they both went to bed and fell asleep in each other's arms.

After both had said goodbye the next morning, Shannon proceeded to pick up Denise and go to the ranch. Ray was wondering if and when he would be getting a telegram from SHARMA HUNTING OUTFITTERS.

At home from work Wednesday, Ray had just sat down when the doorbell rang. Ray answered the door and saw it was the telegram carrier. Ray excitedly signed for it and paid the fee.

Ray went to the sofa and began to read the telegram.

INDIA POSTAL SERVICE TELEGRAM

FROM BAASIM SHARMA OF SHARMA HUNTING OUTFITTERS

MR. RAY JOHNSON I EXCITEDLY RECEIVED YOUR TELEGRAM DATE YOU HAVE IN MIND AROUND MAY 1 1960 IS A GOOD TIME TO GO HUNTING WARM BUT NO MONSOON RAINS FEE FOR TIGER AND LEOPARD HUNT 28000 DOLLARS EVERYTHING PAID AFTER YOU ARRIVE HUNT FOR 4 WEEKS MAX MY SUCCESS IS 80 PERCENT HUNT WOULD BE KEN RIVER AREA BEST TO HAVE BANK TRANSFER MONEY TO BANK OF NEW DELHI INDIA ONE MONTH BEFORE ARIVAL HAVE GUNS AMMO AND EQUIPMENT SHIPPED AIR FREIGHT TO OUR ADDRESS I PROVIDE SKINNING SERVICE TO PRESERVE ANIMAL SKIN FOR TAXIDERMIST TO MAKE TROPHY MOUNT IF YOU DECIDE TO USE ME AS YOUR GUIDE I WILL TAKE CARE OF HUNTING PERMITS THROUGH INDIA BIG GAME DEPARTMENT WHEN TRAVEL DATES AND FLIGHT NUMBERS ARE FIRM I WILL PICK YOU UP AT NEW DELHI AIRPORT AND MAKE RESERVATION AT HOTEL PLEASE SEND TELEGRAM TO CONFIRM EVERYTHING IS OKAY ALWAYS BAASIM SHARMA

Ray felt good about how fast the SHARMA HUNTING OUTFITTERS responded to his telegram. He liked what area the hunt would take place. He had already researched the places to hunt, and the Ken River was identified as a good Bengal tiger and leopard hunting area. Ray was really pleased with his first contact and would be sending a telegram to SHARMA HUNTING OUTFITTERS in the near future.

Ray was relaxing and watching TV when Shannon walked in, dirty as ever from her day's work at the ranch.

"How did the day go at the ranch?" he asked her.

"It went great; four loads of tomatoes went out today, so your dad was pretty happy at how things went today. I am going to take a shower and clean up. I will be out in a little while."

"Wait a minute—I need to give you something." He walked over to her, grabbed her tightly, and gave her a kiss. "Shannon, we always have to do this, and I don't care how dirty you are."

With sex in her smiling eyes, Shannon said, "Ray, we have been so busy lately we have sort of got out of touch a little, but we will get back on track tonight."

"Sounds like a lovely plan to me."

After Shannon was all cleaned and freshened up, she came and sat by Ray on the sofa.

"Honey, I received a telegram from the hunting guide today. I would like you to read it and get your opinion," Ray said.

Shannon did as Ray suggested, and when she was done she told Ray, "I am very impressed. I believe you got a good person. He was prompt in getting back to you, gave some good advice on things to do, and they pretty much take care of everything. He stated the actual hunt duration is a maximum of four weeks, which means most likely you could be back home in six weeks or less, which is less than you originally thought. And you know that makes me happy."

"I am going to send a telegram back to him and tell him for now everything looked fine. I will also be working on airplane reservations. Are you still okay with this?" Ray said.

"Yes, I am okay with everything," and she gave him a long and passionate love kiss. Ray automatically knew what that meant; she was in one of her sexy moods. By now, Ray and Shannon could communicate their desires without even talking to each other. Their love for each other was stronger than ever and growing every day. The only thing missing in their marriage was Shannon was still not pregnant. Ray was starting to think maybe for now God had a different plan, especially since he had a hunting trip planned.

The next morning, Shannon was off to the ranch and Ray was getting ready for work. He was planning to send a response to Baasim Sharma to thank him for the telegram, and that everything looked good. He was going to work on travel plans, and would let him know when he had them all in place.

Ray enjoyed his work very much, and his supervisors appeared to be happy with his progress. On his lunch hour, he went to the Post Office and sent a telegram to SHARMA HUNTING OUTFITTERS, stating everything looked okay.

Ray thought the initial planning for the hunting trip was taken care of and he felt it was a good start. He would start to concentrate on the airplane reservations, and what route he would take to get to New Delhi, India. He felt Shannon was still okay with the trip and showing support. He knew it was going to be hard on her as the trip got closer to reality.

CHAPTER 12

MARRIED LIFE ON THE RANCH

It's mid-September and Shannon and Denise were done helping Ray's dad with the tomato harvest, which also saw the two of them being named the two amigos. They loved the title; after all, they were the best of friends and soon will be living next to each other on the two ranches, and will probably tackle any task that will come their way.

Joseph and Denise's wedding was to take place on November 1 and all the details had been taken care of. The two were really excited to get it done and over with. They would also graduate at the end of December from California UC Davis with degrees in agriculture, really a perfect degree for two whose parents were in the agriculture business, not to mention getting older and needing all the help they could get. With their house coming along, they are really starting to see their life taking shape.

Ray and Shannon were enjoying and loving their married life, but Shannon, disappointed about not being pregnant, was considering a visit to the doctor. Meanwhile they were excited about moving into their new house in October, and being by Ray's parents at last.

One night at the apartment, Ray and Shannon were talking about Ray's trip to India.

"Have you made or thought about your travel plans yet?" she asked.

"I have looked into some airlines. I think TWA airlines is the one I would like to use. It is big in international travel, and they go to just about every big city and country, and New Delhi, India, is on their list. I am going to start looking at reservations maybe tomorrow."

Shannon came close to Ray, gave him one of those kisses, and said, "Honey it's time to go to bed."

Ray responded with, "Honey, are you still okay with the trip?"

"Ray, you will find out in bed."

As they lay there after lovemaking, Shannon asked Ray, "Honey, would you mind if we went in to see the doctor on why I can't get pregnant?"

"Make an appointment; I think it's time we look into it. It's so important to both of us." They then fell asleep in each other's arms.

In the morning Ray was off to work. Shannon and Denise were to meet and have lunch at the Cosmopolitan Restaurant in Lodi. They felt a little quiet time together would be good, especially after their exciting time helping Ray's dad during the tomato harvest. At the restaurant, they found a nice quiet corner where they had a good talk as friends.

"Well, did you enjoy helping Ray's dad in his tomato harvesting operation?" Denise asked.

"Yes, Denise, I hope your experience was as good as mine," replied Shannon.

"I certainly enjoyed working with Paul. Seeing him work with the Mexicans showed me what a kind and loving man he is," said Denise.

"I agree with you completely. As good as my parents are to me, they never came across as treating others with kindness and love like Ray's parents. That is a characteristic they just don't have."

"I have exactly the same feeling about the Johnsons."

The subject of Ray's trip to India came up when Denise asked Shannon, "How is Ray's trip coming along? Is it pretty much planned?"

"He has communicated with a Hunting Outfitter called SHARMA HUNTING OUTFITTERS. The guides' names are Baasim Sharma and Aadesh Sharma. They are brothers. Baasim will be Ray's guide. He has sent Ray a telegram with all the information on what Ray needed and what they provide. The USA embassy consulate in India, by the name of Bob Jones, recommended him as he knows hunters who have used this guide, and he comes with good references.

"Ray is now working on the air travel reservations. He should be done pretty soon with all the trip plans and airlines ticket purchasing."

"How are you taking this trip? Is it still okay with you? I know it will be hard on you when he leaves, but you know Joeseph and I will be by your side while he is gone?"

Shannon said with a grin, "When the subject comes up, I give him a robust kiss and we automatically know what's next. Denise, I am going to love him to death before he leaves."

Lunch was almost over. "I almost forgot: could you come over to the apartment after lunch?" Shannon said. "Ray's mom and dad are going to be there. They wanted to talk to us two amigos. Ray's dad will never forget that name we are tagged with. He just plain loves to hear the name the two amigos."

"Sure, we are about ready; we can head to the apartment now."

The two friends were soon at the apartment conversing when the doorbell rang. It was Paul and Mary. Shannon and Denise greeted them with a hug and a kiss.

"Well, how are you two doing today?" Paul asked. "Hopefully you are resting after two weeks of hard work. I have to say you two gals—or should I say you two amigos—

did a great job. I really needed your help since Ray has a job, and you two gave me the help I needed."

Shannon went to Paul and said, "Dad, who wouldn't want to help a man who has helped many in time of need?"

Denise was listening to a very emotional exchange of words between Shannon, Paul, and Mary. Denise knew Shannon was strongly attached to Ray's parents and rightfully so, for they are good people who are hard to find. Denise wondered how Shannon would take the day of reality when Paul and Mary were no longer with them. Shannon would need a lot of loving and consoling attention, and she wanted to be that person to help her through that time when it came.

Just then, Paul turned to Denise. "And you, Denise, you just broke my heart when I saw you could talk to the Mexicans, changing your accent and speaking Portuguese, and they understood. I could tell they enjoyed you. They liked you both, I could tell by their facial expressions. You two came through when I needed you. You said yes when I asked you for help. You never even asked what you were going to receive for your work; I could tell you just wanted to help."

With tears in her eyes, Shannon looked at Denise and said, "You and Mom have given Ray and me a wonderful start. Giving us a house is way more than I need."

"The house is another story," Paul said. "Helping me without hesitation is what good families are about. You are like a daughter to Mom and me, a daughter we could never have. And Denise, you are also like a daughter, and soon you two will be living next to Mom and me, and we can't wait for that day to come."

Denise went to be next to Shannon and said, "You know, Mom, Dad, Shannon and I are so lucky to have you and the Alexanders in our lives. We are so lucky to be close neighbors as we start our families out here along the Sacramento River. It sets a stage for a great future for all our families."

Mary came over to both Shannon and Denise and gave them a hug. "Well, the reason we came over was we needed to thank you both for helping and give you this payment for your labor," she said, then handing them each a check for $3000. At the bottom of the check was little note that said, "Thanks to the two amigos, love Mom and Dad."

Denise and Shannon said, "Thank you so much."

"Well, Mary and I have to be getting back home," Paul said, and they left to go back to the ranch.

After Paul and Mary left, Denise told Shannon, "Shannon, you really are like a daughter to Ray's parents. You can just feel the emotion they have for you. It's so obvious they love you so much and want to do anything for you."

"Denise, the feeling is the same from me to them. I don't know what I am going to do when someday they are gone from my life. I know life must go on, but it will be hard for me at the beginning. I do know one thing," Shannon said.

"What's that?" Denise replied.

"My husband and you, my best friend, will be there to help me through the grieving period."

Just then Ray walked in from work and said, "Hi!" and gave Shannon a hug and a kiss. Smiling, he asked, "Well, did you both have a good lunch today? I am sure you had plenty to talk about."

"We had a wonderful lunch," Shannon replied. "Your parents came over to share something with Denise and me, along with some loving words, and with this," she added, showing Ray the check.

Ray smiled. "Not bad for two weeks work," he said.

"Did you get to do any trip planning today?" Shannon asked him.

"Yes I did. I contacted TWA airlines. The route and flight numbers are set, and they are sending tickets by mail, which should be here in about four days," Ray replied.

Shannon went to Ray—and at that time Denise decided to leave, for she knew Shannon and Ray needed some time together alone, especially whenever anything came up that was related to the hunting trip. Shannon looked at Ray with her blue eyes sparkling and gave him an earth-shattering kiss. "Ray time is getting closer as every day passes," she said. With emotions running high, they both knew what this moment meant, so they were off to their lovemaking.

"Shannon, are you still okay?" Ray asked.

"Yes, I will be fine. It's getting hard, but the day you leave will be the hardest day in my life. But I will get through it. I have all kinds of support, and I wouldn't have it any other way."

"Well, I hope you will be all right. I plan to leave May 1 and arrive at New Delhi, India, on May 4. I will leave San Francisco for Oahu, Hawaii, Tokyo, Japan, and then to New Delhi, India. When I get the tickets and flight numbers, I will send a telegram to Baasim Sharma and let him know the dates of arrival and flight numbers. Everything is set right now," said Ray.

Later in the evening, Ray asked Shannon, "Honey could you do a little shopping for a nice metal locket and a put picture of you in it so I can carry it with me when I go on my tiger hunt to India?"

"I will do that tomorrow," she replied, and gave him one of those lovemaking kisses, and they went to bed for the evening.

Ray and Shannon had been to the doctor to look into why Shannon could not get pregnant. After the doctor did some tests, the report that came back indicated everything was normal. The doctor advised them to give it more time and one day a surprise would happen. Ray and Shannon were relieved by the report. They also remembered what Ray's mom had said about getting pregnant sometimes taking time. Later in the week, Ray received the TWA air travel tickets, flight numbers, and the dates and times of departures and arrivals. The next day, he sent a telegram to Baasim Sharma to let him know what day and time he would arrive in New Delhi. In the telegram, Ray asked for a response back, to verify he had received the message.

Shannon had resumed college, commuting to Sacramento on a daily basis. Joeseph and Denise had also started school, all three graduating college at the end of December.

One day after work, Ray was at the apartment with Shannon when the doorbell rang. It was a telegram from Baasim Sharma stating that he would pick Ray up at the New Delhi, India airport, and was looking forward to meeting him. That was about seven months away; time was closing in, but Ray was in pretty good shape as far as planning. He would have to think about what he was going to air freight to SHARMA HUNTING OUTFITTERS ahead of time. He also had to make a shipping container to put all the items that he would need.

"I am really impressed with Baasim," Shannon said. "He really responds very quickly, appears to be a very organized and thorough person. It really makes me feel relieved knowing he will take care of you, and that's important to me."

"Well, Shannon, he did come with good references, but you are right: he has been very responsive to my telegrams."

It seemed amazing to Shannon and Ray how quick time was going by. Friday night when Ray and Shannon were lying on the sofa, the phone rang. Ray answered it.

"Oh—hi, Mom! How are things going? I am glad everything is going good. Yes, Mom, we will be coming up tomorrow for our usual Saturday visit. You have something special that you and Dad want to show us? Okay, see you in the morning."

"Ray, what was that all about?" Shannon asked. "Sounds like something special. We have missed a couple of Saturday visits, so maybe something new has taken place at the ranch. Guess we will see in the morning what's so special."

On Saturday morning, Ray and Shannon arrived at the ranch, went inside the house, and greeted Ray's mom and dad.

"Why don't you two sit down for some breakfast; it's linguica and eggs," Mary said.

"Mom, that sounds great! And I am hungry," Ray said.

After breakfast, Ray asked, "Mom, what's so special that you and Dad want to show us?"

"Let's all get in the car and I will show you," Paul said.

"Well, your house is near completion," Paul said. "The salesperson for the flooring, carpet, drapes, and window blinds is there waiting so you can pick out everything that you want," he concluded.

Shannon was so excited that their house was near completion and they could move in soon. "Mom, Dad, thanks so much for this gift. It's beyond my wildest dreams that we will be in our new house, and living by you."

Past the driveway and after going out, Shannon went to Mary and Paul and hugged and kissed them and said, "Thanks again, I just can't believe what you have done for us!"

They all went into the house and looked at all the rooms. When they came to the children's rooms, Shannon got emotional and said, "Mom, Dad, this is where your grandchildren will be. Oh, by the way, Ray and I had some tests done and the doctor said there is no reason why Ray and I can't have children, but like you once told us, sometimes it just takes time."

"Shannon, that's wonderful news! I am really excited for you both, and also for Paul and me," Mary said.

Ray and Shannon were introduced to the floor, carpet, and window covering salesperson. Eventually they picked out everything they liked, and that was done.

"Oh, Shannon, Ray—Mom and I have another special item to show you both. I think you are going to love what's in the garage, so let's go see," Paul said.

Shannon and Ray were wondering what could possibly be so special about a garage. Approaching the door and opening it, Shannon found herself speechless for a few seconds before she managed to say, "Honey, look what we have—and it's red."

Paul and Mary had bought them a new 1960 Red Chevy Impala. Paul told Ray and Shannon, "We thought you needed a more reliable car, especially with Shannon commuting to college for another few months, and we didn't want her to have car trouble."

"Dad, that's a pretty good excuse but I am not sure that's the only reason."

Mary went to Shannon and whispered in her ear. "Ray's probably right, Shannon. It's just that we love you both and want to do as much as possible for you while we can."

"Well, what a morning! When do you think we can move in?" Shannon asked with excitement in her voice.

"The contractor said this coming Friday would be the day," Paul replied.

Shannon remarked with a smile and tears, "We will start packing. I suppose Ray will bring a farm truck and start moving on Friday. I am sure Joeseph and Denise will help. It shouldn't take too long." Shannon went to Ray and said with a very emotional voice, "Honey, shall we drive our new car back to Lodi and start to pack?" They thanked Mary and Paul for everything, got into the car, and left for Lodi.

When they got to their apartment, they were so excited about the house and the new car.

"Honey you can expect surprises like this. That's just how they are. They appreciate and love both of us, and want us to have a better life than when they first got married," Ray said. "My mom and dad had a real tough time in their young married life, but now that they have made it, they want to share it with us and sometimes with others."

"I know, Ray, that's why your parents and I have a real daughter-to-parents relationship. You know, Ray, how hard it will be on me when they pass on."

During the week, Ray and Shannon packed and readied things for the move to the ranch. Shannon called Denise to ask if they could help with the move, and of course Denise agreed. She and Joeseph would come on Friday morning to help.

Friday morning Ray brought the big farm truck to take everything to the ranch. Denise and Joeseph pulled up eager to start loading everything onto the truck. Just then, Denise noticed the red Chevy Impala and asked Shannon, "Did you get a new car?"

"Well, it was given to us."

"You don't have to say who gave you the car. I can make a good guess—Ray's mom and dad did, right?"

Shannon answered with a smile, "Ya, they did! Denise, it was a complete surprise. It is never ending what they do for us."

Denise with excitement went to Shannon, looked at her face-to-face, and with a smile said, "Shannon, they cherish you and always will, for you are the daughter that they never could have. So you might as well get used to surprises every now and then for the simple fact they love their new daughter."

Ray and Joeseph were listening to the two friends talk.

"You know, Shannon, you got to them early on when you started calling them Mom and Dad," Joeseph said.

"We better get loaded and head to the ranch," Ray said.

In time, Ray and Shannon were into their new house, getting comfortable and conversing about how living out on the ranch was going to be exciting, especially once Denise and Joeseph were married and moved into their house next door.

Time was moving real fast. Joeseph and Denise were married, December came, and Joeseph and Denise settled into their new house and enjoyed being neighbors to Shannon and Ray. Joeseph, Denise, and Shannon were finally college graduates ready to get their young married lives really going.

Ray was looking at the items he was going to put in the container that he was going to ship air freight to SHARMA HUNTING OUTFITTERS in New Delhi, India. Ray phoned Joeseph and asked if he could go with him to the shooting range to shoot his 338 Winchester Magnum, just to check and see that everything was still okay. Joeseph said he would be right over.

Joeseph pulled into the yard and Ray had everything ready to go to the shooting range, so they both headed out and got set up.

"Ray, the time is getting close for the India trip. Are you ready for it?" asked Joeseph.

"I am ready, and I hope Shannon will be okay when the time actually becomes a reality." Ray was loading his rifle and getting ready to shoot, but paused for a moment, tears welling in his eyes as he told Joeseph, "I don't know how I am going feel without Shannon being with me." He took three shots and saw the gun was sighted in like when he last shot it, so it was ready. He was also going to take a 336 Marlin 30-30 lever action for hunting small game, just in case they would need food, like small deer which India has an abundance of. The Marlin rifle shot perfectly, so both rifles were ready to ship.

"Ray be assured Denise and I will look after Shannon and your parents while you are gone," Joeseph said. "I will keep training the two amigos on shooting the 30-30 Winchesters. I don't want them to lose that skill. They are good but I want them to get even better."

"Joeseph you really want them ready for anything that may come their way, and they may need to have a forceful response," replied Ray.

"You just never know in this world what could happen. I want them to be up to the task if they are called upon to respond to any situation," Joeseph said with a smile. "Ray, I believe our wives will defend each other and even die for each other if a situation came to that; in other words, they would go down fighting."

"I believe you are right. Keep on training them. I guess we can go back to the house now." They packed up and went to the house. Ray said goodbye and thanked Joeseph for coming.

One night when Ray was on the sofa just talking, Shannon asked, "Have you made contact lately with your guide Baasim?

"You know, Shannon, it's the middle of February, and I do have to get a few things done by March," replied Ray.

Shannon went to Ray, got close to him, and asked, "What do you have left to do, honey?"

"I have to get everything into a container to ship by air freight, and then I have to get $40,000 dollars transferred to the Bank of New Delhi." Ray paused a little and said, "And then I have to get prepared."

"Prepared? Prepared for what?" Shannon replied, smiling.

Ray looked into her blue eyes and said, "To make love with you every day until I leave for India."

"Oh, Ray honey, that's one hell of a good idea! When do we start?"

"Shannon now let's not get into a rush about what I just said—we can start tonight, if that's okay with you."

"Well, the sooner the better! I can hardly wait to tell Denise!"

Ray had a surprised look on his face, and then commented, "You are going to tell Denise about us making love every night?"

"Yes! She is my best friend and we share everything with each other. That's the way it is with us and it will always be that way. I hope that doesn't bother you."

"I am fine with it. If you are okay with sharing everything with Denise, then it's okay with me." Ray was grinning from ear to ear and told Shannon, "Honey when you look at me with those blue eyes, I could never say no to you."

"I know, Ray; I figured that out a long time ago. You know what I am going to ask next?"

"Yes, I know, and the answer is yes."

CHAPTER 13

GOODBYE AND ON TO INDIA

It was the third week in February and Ray was trying to take care of all the last items for his hunting trip. He had the $40,000 transferred to the Bank of New Delhi, and a checking account was set up. He was now working on a container that he would use to ship by air freight all his hunting gear that he would need for his trip to India.

Ray was out in the garage finishing the shipping container. Shannon quietly walked up behind him, and he didn't notice her. She then slipped a locket and chain around his neck. Ray had asked her to shop for a locket to put a picture of her in it.

Ray turned around on his knees and looked up at Shannon. Yes, there was the beautiful blue-eyed brunette looking down at him. She came to her knees and gave him a long kiss and a hug that appeared she was not going to give up. It was a very emotional moment for both of them.

Ray had a tear or two and then managed to say, "I thought maybe you forgot about the locket."

"I could never forget something like that."

Ray looked at the locket. It had a ruby mounted in the center, and it was engraved with the words, *Ray, ruby is the stone of love. I hope you consider me your ruby.* Ray opened the locket and there was a picture of Shannon, while on the other half of the locket was a picture of a Bengal tiger.

"Thanks, honey, it's a great locket. It has everything that I love; it's a big locket with a real heavy chain. You must have picked it out based on some rough going, which is good since I will be hunting."

"I have to say it was hard to shop for it knowing why you wanted it." They then kissed. "It's getting late; I think we should go to bed."

The next morning came. Ray had taken the day off from work so he could pack everything into the shipping container. When he was done packing the container, he wrote the address on the shipping container, and he enclosed his new house address so Baasim would know where to send a telegram. Everything was set to go.

"Well, Shannon, everything is packed. I think it's still early. We should go to the San Francisco Airport and get it air freighted to New Delhi, India." Shannon agreed and off they went to San Francisco. They went to the air freight terminal and got the container paperwork filled out. When it was done, the container was on its way to India.

On the way back home, Shannon was pretty quiet. Ray noticed it and said, "Honey, are you okay? You are pretty quiet."

"Ray, I was just thinking how much I am going to miss you. If we don't hear from you by a certain date I will be in a panic, along with the whole family...," she paused, "and I don't know what I would do if that situation occurs."

Ray tried to calm her by saying, "You know I have a good guide, so I believe everything will be fine. He has been on many tiger hunts and knows the area very well."

They arrived home, went inside, and sat down watching TV. "I will send a telegram to Baasim Sharma tomorrow to tell him the container would arrive at the New Delhi Airport in about five days," Ray said. "The container would be delivered to his business address. I will ask him to send a telegram to our new address confirming the container was received."

The next morning Ray was up early, had a quick breakfast, and headed to work. Before going, he asked Shannon, "Well, what have you got planned for today? Anything special?"

"Denise and I are going hunting. Joeseph wants us to do some shooting with the 30-30 Winchesters. He wants us to do a little practice at moving targets. You know, Ray, he really is serious about us being able to defend ourselves if the need ever arises. It's like he suspects something is going to happen, and I suppose it's always good to be prepared. I will say we are pretty good with those Winchester carbines."

"I know you two amigos are real good. It will be a good deterrent against any person who is up to no good. I will send the telegram to Baasim today and you gals have fun. I will see you tonight."

Shannon gave Ray a gigantic hug and kiss and said, "Honey, have a good day. I love you—see you tonight."

A week later, a telegram came. Shannon who was home saw it was from Baasim the guide. He wrote:

INDIA POSTAL SERVICE TELEGRAM

I RECEIVED THE CONTAINER EVERYTHING WAS FINE NO DAMAGE RAY TELL YOUR FAMILY NOT TO WORRY I WILL TAKE GOOD CARE OF YOU NOTICED YOUR NEW ADDRESS RAY I WILL HAVE A SMALL SIGN WITH BAASIM WRITTEN ON IT SO YOU CAN FIND ME WHEN YOU GET OFF THE PLANE ALWAYS BAASIM

Ray got home from work, came in, and greeted Shannon with a kiss. "Did anything exciting happen today?" he asked.

"Got a telegram from Baasim. He said everything got there in good shape and to tell your family he would take good care of you."

"He really seems like a good guy. That statement made me feel so good. He realizes that families can be concerned about hunting a Bengal tiger."

"I believe he is a good guy just by his responses to my telegrams. Honey, everything is now set for my trip," said Ray.

They were approaching the month of April, which meant in a month Ray would be on his way to India. Ray and Shannon knew they would soon be separated for about six weeks—less if Ray had luck and got a Bengal tiger early during the hunt. Of course this was what Shannon was hoping for.

Time was really flying by, and May 1 was just a week away—and Ray would be off to India. After dinner, Ray called TWA Airlines to confirm that flight numbers and times were still good. TWA confirmed that everything was still as planned, and his flight from San Francisco would depart at 10:00 AM on May 1.

Shannon overheard the conversation. "Honey...," she said.

"I know, Shannon—let's go to bed. It's our favorite time of the evening." After they made love, Shannon whispered something into Ray's ear.

Ray's response was, "That sound great to me," and they fell asleep.

The next morning came. Ray had already taken off work until he was back from his trip to India. Shannon and Ray were eating breakfast when the phone rang. Shannon answered the phone. It was Ray's mom. Mary wanted to let them know that this Friday, Paul was planning to barbecue all the cottontail rabbits that Shannon and Denise had, and she was making the Portuguese solution to marinate them for a couple of days. She asked Shannon to come over to learn how to make the solution.

"Everybody is going to be here," Mary said. "It's sort of a going-away party for Ray, as he would be leaving Monday." Shannon hung up the phone. She had a very emotional look on her face at that time, realizing Ray's departure was really getting close.

"What's wrong, honey, are you okay?" Ray asked.

"It's just that you will be leaving real soon." Shannon was starting to feel the reality of Ray leaving, and it's getting closer, and she knows it's going to be so hard. "Ray, everything will be okay. I can handle it."

Shannon went over to Ray's mom to learn how to make the Portuguese marinade solution to put the rabbits in. When she got there, Mary had everything set up. Shannon greeted Mom with a hug and said, "Hi, Mom—so, we are going to make something that will make the rabbits tender and flavorful."

"That's right, Shannon. I am sure everybody will enjoy the flavor and the tenderness especially when we barbecue them." Shannon had tears in her eyes. Mary noticed.

"What's wrong, Shannon? Is it about Ray leaving on Monday?"

"Yes, I don't know how I am going to make it through that day; it's going to be tough."

"Shannon, it's going to be tough on all of us. We all have to be strong and let him go. Then we will have to support one another in a big way."

They continued making the solution for the rabbits. As they were putting the rabbits in the solution, Mary put her arms around Shannon. "We all will get through this, and everything will be fine in the end." Shannon then just started to walk home.

On Friday, Ray and Shannon headed over to Ray's parents' house and everybody was already there. Paul was doing the barbecuing, so Ray went around talking to everybody until he got to Mr. Chin and his wife. Mr. Chin opened the conversation by saying, "Ray, are you ready for the big cat hunt?" Mr. Chin with tears in eyes looked at Ray and continued to say, "Be careful, Ray, we all want you back here safely."

"I will be careful, Mr. Chin. I want to be back, too, and then maybe Shannon and I can have children."

After Ray had talked to everybody he made his way over to where Shannon, Denise, and Joeseph were seated. "How are you all doing tonight?" he asked them.

"Ray we are doing okay," replied Denise. "We were just talking about how it might be a good idea if Joeseph and I took you and Shannon to the San Francisco Airport on Monday morning so Shannon wouldn't have to drive back alone. We all know how she is going to feel after you leave."

"Oh, that's a great idea. Actually I was planning to ask if you could do that for us. I want Shannon back home safely," replied Ray, and that settled the matter.

Everybody was now eating, and for those who had never had rabbit cooked this way it was a tasty treat. Ray's dad got every body's attention.

"Well, you were invited here today to say goodbye to Ray and to wish him well on his trip to India. He leaves for India on Monday, which is just a few days away. We all thank you for coming."

Paul asked Shannon and Denise to come and stand by him before saying, "These are the two amigos who will have to support Mary and me while Ray is gone. It will be hard for all of us until Ray has returned safely back to California. So we all ask you for your support."

Joeseph got up and said, "Before we all leave this farewell dinner, I asked the two amigos to do an exhibition in rifle shooting. I had them get good at close range shooting using the Winchester 30-30 carbine. I wanted these two friends to be able to defend themselves with fast and accurate shooting."

Joeseph then set up seven cans in a row, with another can on top of each of the seven, which made a total of fourteen cans. He was going to have them shoot seven shots each. Denise was going to shoot the top can and Shannon would immediately shoot the bottom can after the top can had been shot off. This was to show their ability to shoot fast and accurate. The two amigos loaded their guns with seven rounds. Everybody watched as Joeseph gave the "Go" signal and, in 16 seconds, the fourteen cans were blown away.

Everybody clapped after the two amigos had done their shooting exhibition. Joeseph and Ray went to their wives and hugged and kissed them. Ray commented to everybody, "Well, anybody that picks a fight with these two—good luck, for they are probably going to need a doctor or a mortician."

Joeseph proceeded to say something about his longtime best friend. "You all should know by now Ray and I have been best friends for years. Ray, I wish the best of luck on your Bengal tiger hunt, and may God be with you and get you back safely to all of us here. And Ray, you know these two amigos can take care of themselves—and one never knows in today's world when and where they might have to go to use their shooting skills."

Soon everyone was leaving, and Ray and Shannon thanked everybody for coming. They said thanks to Ray's parents, for it was a great and enjoyable day.

Ray, Shannon, Denise, and Joeseph started walking home. When they got to Ray and Shannon's house, everybody was in tears.

"Well, we will see you guys," Shannon said, smiling. "Right now Ray and I have some things to do."

"You going to try to break the bed," Denise said, also smiling.

"Ya, we are going to give it a good test." Both couples said good night and went to their homes.

The next morning, Ray was doing some packing for his trip. He had sent all of his hunting gear in the container that he had air freighted to New Delhi, but he still had two suitcases full of cloth and general hygiene items. He had everything done at about noon time.

Shannon and Ray were on the sofa watching the noon news, but they were just so exhausted that they fell asleep. After a few hours the doorbell rang and awakened them both. Ray got up and went to see his mom and dad at the door.

"Ray, are you all packed and ready to go?" Mary asked softly.

"Ya, Mom, everything is ready. Denise and Joeseph will be driving Shannon and me to the San Francisco airport. I also made a list of all the contacts just in case you or Shannon has a need to contact anybody by telegram or mail. I listed the SHARMA HUNTING OUTFITTERS and the guide's name, and Bob Jones at the United States consulate. I also included the State Department embassy communicator."

"I believe Ray's guide is a great person," Shannon said. "He was kind enough to say in one of the telegrams to tell Ray's family not to worry as he will take good care of Ray."

"He sounds like good, reliable, and down-to-business person. Ray, you have applied for a tiger and a leopard permits—is that right?"

"Ya, Dad. Baasim has an 80 percent success rate, so he must be pretty good."

"We will see you tomorrow," Paul said. "You both get a good night's sleep. It's sure great to have you living on the ranch—it's so convenient." Paul and Mary then left for home.

With all the talk about the trip, Ray could sense Shannon was in her lovemaking moods—and so was Ray, and they both went to bed.

On Sunday morning, Shannon invited Ray's parents, Joeseph and Denise for breakfast, and of course it was linguica and eggs, which really pleased Ray and Joeseph. Everybody was now eating, but the mood was very quiet and Shannon sensed it. She looked at Denise who also was so quiet, like it was the end of time, or something.

"Okay, everybody, it's not the end of the world," Shannon blurted out. "We got to remember Ray is going on a trip that he has waited all his life. So damn it, let's give him the support that he needs, so tomorrow when he takes off for India he can feel that everybody is okay with him leaving. Let's show some excitement around this table. I won't have it any other way."

Ray's dad had a big and surprised smile on his face, and he said loudly, "Shannon, Shannon, thank you for restoring some family unity around this table. And you are right, we need to support Ray, and we will support Ray on his dream of hunting the Bengal tiger—so will we all support him?"

Everybody yelled out, "Ya! Ya!" That had everybody in a much happier mood. As for Shannon, she had a few tears falling as she hugged Ray although she was trying to hide it.

"Well, that was quite an outburst around this table," Ray said, smiling. "Thanks, Shannon, you brought this table to life. Thank you all for your support. I know you all support what I am doing, but there has to be some emotion to go along with that support. That's why my beautiful blue-eyed wife has a few tears right now, and I can understand all of that—it's because we all love each other, and that's as simple as it gets." Ray paused for a while and then said, "So tomorrow when I leave I will know you all support me, even if there are emotions, but I will have a good feeling about all of you, and that's what counts."

At that point, everybody said goodbye. Joeseph said, "Denise and I will pick you up about 4:00 AM for the airport."

Paul and Mary gave Ray a big hug and then said, "Be careful and good hunting. Hope you will enjoy your long awaited dream, Ray. We love you, and we hope to hear from you by the middle of June."

Ray and Shannon were alone to enjoy the rest of the day with each other; it was nice not to have any outside interruptions.

"Honey, it's getting late," Ray said, smiling. "Maybe we'd better retire a little earlier tonight. We have to get up early since Denise and Joeseph will be picking us up at 4:00 AM."

"That's right; and Ray, we have some last minute business to attend, too. Are you excited?" Shannon said.

"I am always excited about being close to you, Shannon, and I always will be. I will love you always; on my hunting trip, I will always have you on my mind, I will promise you that."

Ray and Shannon enjoyed their last night together until he returned home again, in about six weeks, and Shannon made sure she got every last ounce of love out of him that night.

The morning came and the doorbell rang. Shannon went to see Denise and Joeseph at the door. They came in for a little bit. Joeseph helped Ray with his luggage, and they all got into the car and headed to the airport.

On the drive to the airport, Ray addressed Joeseph and Denise. "While I am away, I would like to ask you both to take good care of my wife and keep an eye on my parents."

"Ray that's already taken a spot on my list of things to do while you are away," replied Joeseph.

"Thanks, Joeseph, and keep training the two amigos with those Winchester 30-30 carbines." There was a smile on everybody's face.

Shannon was very quiet and appeared to be in deep thought, which was understandable; after all, her husband was going to be gone for six weeks.

Soon they were pulling into the airport parking area; they found a parking spot and got Ray's luggage. They proceeded to the TWA airlines check-in counter for international travelers. Ray presented his passport and tickets; he received his boarding pass, checked his luggage in, and got the departure gate number.

They walked to the assigned gate number for his departure. Shannon and Ray walked to a window at the terminal and they could see the TWA airplane that Ray was to take. Shannon started to hold Ray very tightly. Ray could sense her emotions, but there were still no tears. Denise and Joeseph were standing twenty feet away to give them the privacy they needed.

Denise stood looking at her best friend go through a very agonizing moment in her life and was now just crying on Joeseph's shoulder as Shannon and Ray hugged and kissed. The gate attendant announced that boarding would take place in five minutes. Denise was crying so hard it would be hard for Shannon not to notice.

Seeing Denise, Shannon motioned to her and said, "It's okay, amigo, I will be fine." With those words, Denise found herself out of control emotionally.

Shannon was now facing Ray with her hands on his shoulders, as Ray's arms were also around her as they were talking to each other. Shannon held the locket that she had given Ray and that he was now wearing. She opened it. They looked at it and Ray said, "I will always have this locket with me. It will make me feel that you are with me on this trip, and will guide me through it. Shannon, it will remind me of my love for you and the Bengal tiger. I feel something great is going to come out of this trip, and it may not even be a trophy of the Bengal tiger."

"Honey, that locket holds a lot of the reasons we are together, especially our love for each other. There is some not so obvious information on the locket—someday you may notice it."

The gate attendant started to take boarding passes. Ray and Shannon walked to Denise and Joeseph. Denise was crying and trying hard to control herself.

"Goodbye, Joeseph; take care of everybody, and thank you always for being my best friend. And Denise, take care of your best friend for me—okay?" And he gave her a hug.

He turned to Shannon, lifted her up, and told her, "Honey, if we were not in public, I would give you a kiss on your belly button and that would light a fuse." He let her down and gave her a long kiss.

The gate attendant told Ray, "Sir, it's time to board."

Ray let go of Shannon, motioned to Denise and Joeseph, and said, "Goodbye, amigos, see you in about six weeks."

In time Ray was seated in the plane. After a while, he wondered what Shannon meant about a not so obvious information on the locket. Ten minutes later, the plane taxied out to the runway.

Shannon, Denise, and Joeseph watched as the aircraft turned, before finally taking off.

"I hope God will let me see him again," Shannon managed to say.

The three went to the car and started the drive home.

CHAPTER 14

RAY MEETS BAASIM

Ray had been on the plane for a couple of hours. The route to New Delhi involved stops at Oahu, Hawaii, Tokyo, Japan, and finally to New Delhi, India, approximately 10,000 miles. With the stops and layover time, Ray would land in New Delhi on May 3, about 7:00 AM New Delhi time.

Ray was taking off from Tokyo, Japan, heading to New Delhi, India. He was getting very excited to meet his guide, which would be in about another 12 hours. In the back of his mind he was missing everybody back home. He was wondering what Shannon meant when she said there was some not so obvious information on the locket he was then looking at. He just couldn't find any clues as to what she was talking about.

Ray decided to start a conversation with the passenger he was sitting next to, someone who appeared to be a Hindu and maybe from New Delhi. After he introduced himself, he asked, "Are you going to be staying in New Delhi or going on from there?"

The person who introduced himself as Acharya Sharma, a citizen of India, replied. "I live in New Delhi. I am returning from a trip of the United States." He then asked Ray, "What is your reason for going to New Delhi?"

"I am going to be trophy hunting for a Bengal tiger. It's something I have always wanted to do, and my hunting outfitters are in New Delhi"

"If a may ask, who have you contracted as your hunting guide?" Acharya said.

"I am using SHARMA HUNTING OUTFITERS. My guide's name is Baasim Sharma. Oh, didn't you say your last name was Sharma?"

"Yes my last name is Sharma. Baasim and his brother Aadesh are my nephews," Acharya replied, smiling. "Their dad was my brother. It was he who started the business but he died a few years back. The sons continued on with guiding tiger and leopard hunters. If I may say so, you made a wonderful choice. These guys are good."

"I just can't believe I ended up sitting by my guide's uncle. Sometimes this world doesn't seem that big," Ray observed.

"Which area are you going to hunt for the Bengal tiger?"

"The Ken River area is where Baasim is taking me." Ray was now pretty excited that he had somebody to talk to on the plane. He was anxious to carry on a conversation with Acharya.

"You are probably going to enjoy the jungle. If you get a chance to see a Bengal tiger, you will see how beautiful they are that you will probably have a hard time pulling the trigger."

"You could be right. I will have to see when and if that happens how I would deal with the situation. As you said, the Bengal tiger is a sight to behold."

Acharya and Ray continued talking about various items. He got on the subject of hunting in the Ken River area.

"You will probably come across those ancient castle ruins by the clan of Rajputs who used them to fight against the tribes of Mughals. You must be careful when you do, for some castles are occupied by gangs of robbers. My nephew Baasim knows all this, so I am sure he will guide you carefully."

Ray asked Acharya, "Are there villages along the Ken River, and are the people pretty civilized?"

"Yes, there are villages, and because of years of British occupation in India, most village people are pretty civilized and speak good English. But there are some that still believe in some old traditions and legends that have been passed down to them from their ancestors."

As Ray found Acharya so interesting to talk to, he tried to glean all the information he could out of him. The man himself appeared to be around sixty years old and very educated. "Acharya, if I may ask: what is your profession?" Ray said.

"I am a medical doctor, and I went to Stanford University Medical School in California. I started my education in 1940. The government of India paid for my education, as India has a large need for medical doctors."

"Do you know the Sacramento Delta? I happen to have been born and raised there."

"Ray—in 1941 I had a little time off from school. I went to a little town along the Sacramento River. I believe the town was called Isleton. I always liked to fish, and people told me that was a good area, especially for striped bass."

By now Ray had a big smile and commented, "I was raised 3 miles north of Isleton."

"This is starting to get exciting. Let me continue: I stopped at a sporting goods store in Isleton and went in to buy some bait. A Chinese man, Mr. Chin, waited on me. I asked him if he thought the landowners would let me fish off the river bank. His response was, 'I know one farm where if you ask, they will let you fish on their property. They are the kindest people that you will ever find. Their name is Paul and Mary Johnson. Their address is RT. 1 BOX 7 on their mail box.'"

Ray excitedly said, "You met my parents back in 1941? That is just plain unbelievable!"

"Mr. Chin was right: your parents are very kind. When I went down into the yard, your dad was just pulling up in his pickup. He got out and I introduced myself. I asked if it would be okay for me to fish off his riverbank, and your dad's response was, 'Oh, most certainly you can! Just park your car down here in the yard.'"

"Acharya, I was about four years old then. Where was I when you were talking to my dad?"

Acharya answered Ray with a smile, "In my arms. Your dad handed you to me and said, 'This is my son, Ray.'"

"So in 1941 you met me, and here we are almost twenty years later talking as if we had never met. This is an amazing story. I just can't believe what has transpired on this airplane trip to New Delhi."

"My nephews Baasim and Aadesh will be shocked when we get off the plane, meet them, and we explain what we have found out during our conversation on this flight."

There were about two more hours before they landed in New Delhi. Acharya thought he would like to share a longtime legend about the Bengal tiger. The legend was handed down over the years from his great grandfather, then to his grandfather who told him about the legend of the Bengal ruby.

"I would like to share the legend of the Bengal ruby with you, since you will be hunting the Bengal tiger," Acharya said.

Ray listened intently to Acharya as he started to talk about the legend.

"My ancestors told me this legend many times. It's about how Indian clans or tribes would trap a male Bengal tiger in the wild and give him a drug made from natural plants that would make him unconscious for a while. They then would have a large ruby mounted in a gold ring, which was attached to a chain, and they would place the necklace around the tiger's neck," Acharya said.

"What was the purpose of placing a ruby necklace on the tiger's neck?" asked Ray.

"It was to make a Bengal tiger friendly to a man. Once the tiger had made eye contact with the first man that he sees, the tiger was to protect that man from harm. So the tiger was pretty much around that man to see that no harm would come to him. After he had made eye contact with a human, he was to be considered a protector of his new friend, the legend says."

"Acharya, has anybody ever come across such a Bengal tiger with a ruby hanging around its neck?"

"As far as a ruby hanging from the tiger's neck is concerned, yes, there had been sightings. Even today some villagers still practice the tradition of putting a ruby necklace around the neck of a tiger, believing the legend that the tiger will be friends with the first man the tiger happens to make eye contact with. So we don't know if the legend is true or not, but the tradition of hanging a ruby from the tiger's neck is real."

"Have your nephews ever came across a tiger with a ruby hanging from a Bengal tiger's neck?"

"Not that I am aware of, but some villagers even today practice the tradition. It is considered a very sacred ceremony to put the ruby necklace around a Bengal tiger's neck."

Ray was amazed that such a tradition is still being practiced if only to try to make true the Bengal ruby legend.

"You would never know what villages practice the tradition as it is kept a secret. But I can guess you would find out quickly if you walked into a village with a ruby around a tiger's neck, and that village had members that practiced the tradition. Nobody seems to talk about the consequences of that situation, or if it has ever occurred. Oh, well, it's a legend, and maybe there is nothing to it."

The plane captain announced over the loudspeaker that they had about an hour before they arrived at the New Delhi Airport. Ray realized it was still morning in New Delhi. One of the first things he considered doing was to send a telegram to Shannon when he had a chance.

"Acharya, when we get off the plane I know Baasim will have a sign so I would know him. But if we walk out together, I will ignore the sign and let you introduce me to him; that should really surprise him," said Ray.

"That's how we will do it. I am sure my nephews will be together. That should really surprise them both and they will enjoy hearing our story. I plan to take them and you to dinner tonight after you get settled into your hotel."

"Sounds good; should be fun to talk to your nephews. I feel like after talking to you they aren't even strangers."

The captain announced they would be touching down in about 5 minutes. Ray was starting to get excited and a little nervous as the plane touched down and taxied to the terminal. The airplane then prepared for the passengers to exit. Ray and Acharya walked down the stairs and then to the passenger terminal. Ray saw Baasim with his sign, and Baasim and Aadesh had noticed their Uncle Acharya. They went to greet and hug their uncle and Baasim shortly resumed looking for Ray.

"Oh, let me introduce to both of you an acquaintance I made on the flight," said Acharya. "This is Ray Johnson from California."

Baasim immediately gave Ray a handshake and a hug. "What a coincidence that you two would meet," he said.

"There is a lot more to this story; we will talk about it later. You won't believe it when you both hear what happened about twenty years ago," Acharya said.

"Ray, let's get your luggage and get you to the New Delhi Hotel," Aadesh said and soon they were driving to the hotel. "Tonight I want to take everybody to dinner, and that means all the children and your wives," Acharya said. "I want Ray to meet everybody, and then we can tell everybody what happened twenty years ago."

At the New Delhi Hotel, everybody went in with Ray and helped with his luggage.

"Ray, we will pick you up in the lobby tonight about six o'clock," Baasim said.

"That sounds good," replied Ray. "Can you tell me where I could send a telegram, and how far the Bank of New Delhi is from here?"

"You can send a telegram right from this hotel. The bank is just down the street, about three blocks."

After they left, Ray used the time to relax, taking a nap for about two hours. He woke up feeling refreshed after a long and exhausting flight. Deciding it was time to send Shannon a telegram, he went down to the hotel lobby and asked the desk clerk, "Where do I go to send a telegram?" The desk clerk directed him to the customer service office, and there he found the person who could send a telegram to Shannon.

Ray sent the following message to Shannon:

SHANNON I AM ALREADY MISSING EVERYBODY ESPECIALLY YOU ON THE AIRPLANE I MET A PASSENGER BY THE NAME OF ACHARYA SHARMA I HAD A LONG CONVERSATION WITH HIM HE HAD GONE TO SCHOOL AT STANFORD AND HE ACTUALLY WENT TO THE SACRAMENTO DELTA TO FISH ONE DAY AND HE ACTUALLY MET MOM AND DAD AS THAT'S WHERE HE ASKED PERMISSION TO FISH AND BELIEVE IT OR NOT HE HELD ME IN HIS ARMS THIS WAS IN 1941 BUT SHANNON HE IS ALSO THE UNCLE TO MY GUIDE AND HIS BROTHER LET

211

DAD AND MOM KNOW ABOUT ACHARYA AND HIS VISIT IN 1941 SHANNON THIS MAYBE THE LAST COMMUNICATION FOR A WHILE ONCE WE START THE HUNTING TRIP IT MAY BE HARD TO FIND A PLACE WHERE TELEGRAMS CAN BE SENT LOVE YOU SHANNON LOVE ALWAYS RAY

The telegram sent to Shannon, Ray made for the Bank of New Delhi a short distance from the hotel. At the bank, he verified that $40,000 dollars was in his account; when that was done, he then asked for a book of blank checks, and he was all set to continue his venture. He went back to his hotel, deciding to rest a little more as he waited for Baasim to pick him up for the dinner. Walking back to the hotel, he couldn't help but notice the many impoverished people on the streets. It made him feel so lucky with what he had back home.

Back in his room, Ray sat on the bed and listened to the news on the radio. He was looking at his locket and at the picture of Shannon, trying to figure out the not so obvious information on the locket that she referred to when they said goodbye at the airport. He then dosed off.

When Ray awakened, he glanced at the clock and went down to the hotel lobby to wait for Baasim to pick him up. He was excited to meet the families. In time Baasim entered the hotel lobby and they greeted each other.

"My family is waiting outside in the car. We will meet my Uncle Acharya, my brother Aadesh, and his family at the restaurant," Baasim said.

The two made their way to the car parked at the hotel entry. "Why don't you sit with my two boys in the backseat," said Baasim. "They are anxious to meet you."

Ray got in the backseat and sat with Baasim's boys who were eight and ten years old. After entering the car, Baasim introduced Ray to his wife and two sons before he drove to the restaurant.

After driving along and while conversing with everybody, Ray was impressed how good they could speak English. After they pulled into the restaurant parking lot, Ray noted a very upscale restaurant and a nice environment inside. They were escorted to where Baasim's Uncle Acharya, Aadesh, and his family were seated; Aadesh introduced his wife and daughter to Ray.

Acharya started to tell everybody about the flight to New Delhi and his conversation with Ray.

"What I am about to tell you would seem like this was a made up story. But let me tell you in 1941 when I was attending Stanford Medical School, I made a trip to the Sacramento Delta to go fishing on the Sacramento River. Well, the spot I was advised to go turned out to be Ray's parents' farm. I met Ray's dad in the yard where I asked him if I could fish on his property, and this man sitting right here amongst us was about four years old when his dad handed him to me and said, 'This is my son, Ray.' Thus I met Ray about twenty years ago and here we sit around this table, and he just happened to choose SHARMA OUTFITTERS to guide him on his Bengal tiger hunt," Acharya said.

"I am proud to be amongst this family," Ray said, smiling. "I feel like I am part of your family. Your uncle and I had some wonderful conversations on the flight. I already sent a telegram to my wife and told her to tell my mom and dad about your uncle fishing on the Sacramento River and meeting me. I know they will remember the incident."

"All hunting trips are always very meaningful, but Ray this will be special to me," Baasim said.

"Ray, do you have a picture of your wife? I see a locket hanging from your neck," asked Aadesh.

213

"Yes," replied Ray, and took the locket off the chain and passed it around. Everybody thought Shannon was a beautiful woman, and they loved the words engraved on the locket.

As Baasim and his wife inspected the locket and the engraved message, he happened to turn the locket to look at the engraving on the back, and commented to his wife, "I really can't make out what it says; it must be a manufacturer's product identification." Ray was busy talking with everybody he never heard Baasim's remark about the engraving on the back of the locket.

By this time everybody had ordered what they wanted, and after the dinners were served and all were busy eating, Ray asked, "Well, Baasim, what are the plans for tomorrow?"

"I will pick you up in the morning about eight o'clock and we will go down to the shop. I have everything ready and packed in a trailer. It's about a 12-hour drive to the Ken River where we will pick up our hunting vehicle at a village."

"That sounds great," replied Ray excitedly. "I can't wait! Oh, by the way here is a check for $28,000 dollars for your fee. I thought while we are hunting your family will need money, so I decided I would pay it now." Ray noticed Baasim had a strange look on his face. "Is something wrong?"

"Ray, somebody has already taken care of your bill. Your bill has already been paid," said Baasim.

"Who would do such a thing? That's like giving me a gift of $28,000." Ray looked at Acharya at the other end of the table; he had a smile on his face as he looked at Ray. Ray could now sense it was Acharya who paid his hunting bill.

"Ray, please accept the gift. It is something I really wanted to do for you."

"Why do you want to do this for me?" asked Ray.

"Ray, let me explain: sometimes people do things like this when they feel they would like to help someone in need.

But in this case, Ray, it goes back to 1941 when I met your parents on my fishing trip to the Sacramento Delta."

"You want to give me this gift because my parents let you fish on their ranch?"

"No, Ray, I need to explain a little more. I went back fishing about four times and your parents were so kind to me, always wanted me to stay for dinner, and I would."

"That's just how my parents are; anybody is always welcome at my parents' house."

"Yes, Ray, I know that is your parents' mentality, a wonderful attitude to have. But on my last fishing trip to your parent's ranch, I had to say goodbye as my studies at Stanford were becoming really intensive and starting to come to an end. As usual I had to stay for dinner—by the way your mom is a wonderful cook," said Acharya.

"Acharya, an act of simple kindness doesn't mean you should do this for me."

"Well, let me tell you here tonight: what I got from Ray's parents that night when I had dinner with them was a learning experience. It was that a true giver of a gift is one who really gets the joy of giving something to someone. After dinner that night, Ray, your parents smiled as your dad handed me an envelope. I opened the envelope to see a check for $2000 and a note saying, 'Acharya, it is with joy in our hearts to give you this for all your hard work to become a medical doctor. We both hope that our paths will cross again someday.' That, Ray, is the reason I am happy to give you this, and I hope my nephews learn from this night about giving with joy."

"Well, to you, Acharya, and your nephews and their families—thank you so much for a memorable evening that I will never forget. By now my dad and mom both have probably read a telegram that I sent, and my mom and dad are probably smiling that our family's paths have crossed."

215

Soon everybody was ready to depart, as tomorrow would be a big day for Ray and Baasim heading out for the adventure that Ray had always dreamed of.

Baasim took Ray to the hotel and said, "I will pick you up in the morning, Ray, you have a good night's sleep."

"Okay, Baasim, see you in the morning."

In the hotel, Ray headed to the customer service desk and sent a telegram to Shannon telling her what happened earlier, and to make sure his mom and dad were informed. Ray then proceeded to his room. At first he found it hard to fall asleep at the excitement that will start in the morning, though he finally did after a while

CHAPTER 15

THE HUNTING JOURNEY BEGINS

Back at the Johnson Ranch, Denise was over at Shannon's enjoying breakfast with her friend. It was almost ten o'clock. Shannon brought up that this was the fourth day without Ray, and she was starting to wonder why she hadn't received a telegram yet. "I hope nothing is wrong over there in India. I would expect to hear from Ray by now," she said.

"I am sure everything is okay. A telegram is probably on its way as we speak." Just then there was a knock at the door.

Shannon went to answer the door. It was the mail carrier. "Hi, Shannon, I have two telegrams for you. They came within six hours of each other," the mail carrier said.

Hearing the word "telegram," Denise rushed to be by Shannon's side.

Shannon read the telegrams, and with a big smile told Denise, "You won't believe this when you read these telegrams." While Denise was reading the telegrams, Shannon got on the phone and called Ray's parents. Mary answered the phone.

"Mom, Denise and I will be right over; just got a telegram from Ray and everything is okay. Mom, is Dad there? He is? Good, tell him to stay. He has to be there when you read the telegram. Mom, we will be right over," Shannon said.

Denise finished reading the telegrams, and her comment was, "Wow, what a story! Paul and Mary will have no idea that this could happen after twenty years."

Denise and Shannon were soon in the pickup and heading to Ray's parents. They arrived to see Mary and Paul anxiously waiting to read the telegrams.

Shannon handed Paul the first telegram and he proceeded to read it out loud. When it was over, he said, "It is hard to believe that after twenty years, Acharya—who came here fishing and held Ray in his arms—meets Ray on a plane and is Ray's guide's uncle. That is hard to believe."

"Here is the second telegram," Shannon said. "It is a very touching and emotional telegram. But Mom, Dad, this is how you come across to everybody you meet; that's why after falling in love with Ray, I fell in love with you both. You two are a hard act to follow when it comes to your kind attitude to all people. Dad, please read the telegram."

Paul proceeded to read the second telegram; after he did, he became very emotional that he could hardly talk to Mary. Finally he told her, "Mary, remember when Acharya said goodbye to us on his last visit and we gave him $2000, seeing what a big achievement it was for him to graduate from Stanford University? He said he learned from us, that because of our kindness and how we gave him that gift, he called us a joyful giver."

Well, Paul, what are you leading up to? We always give from our heart."

"With joy in his heart, Acharya gave our son something, because of what he learned from us. He wanted to let his nephews and their families know how good it feels to do it with that attitude."

"Paul—what was the gift he gave Ray?"

"He gave Ray the hunting guide fee, which amounted to $28,000."

"Oh, my God! I bet that was hard for Ray to accept at first, but once explained he was probably fine with it," said Mary. "Paul, you told Acharya that someday you would hope our paths would cross again—with Ray there, our paths indeed crossed with Acharya."

" I hope I can meet Acharya someday, I believe we are destined to meet," Shannon said. With that, Shannon and Denise took their leave and went back to Shannon's house.

Back in New Delhi, Baasim had picked up Ray and they were at the SHARMA HUNTING OUTFITTERS' office and shop.

Baasim explained to Ray what was about to take place, informing him that the trip to the Ken River would take about 12 hours driving time to the village, where they would pick up their hunting vehicle.

"Ray you have a leopard and a Bengal tiger hunting permit. I have been in touch with the Indian Department of Game; I asked them if there were any incidents of leopard attacks at villages, on humans or livestock," Baasim said.

"What did the department have to say?" asked Ray.

"They told me a small village 5 miles south of a village named Bamitha has had a lot of leopard attacks on the village's livestock. They also said the villagers would probably welcome a hunter who could shoot and kill this rogue leopard that has killed a total of eighteen goats and six sheep in the last year."

"Baasim, is it on the way to where we will pick up the vehicle that we will use for the main part of the hunting trip?" asked Ray.

"Yes. It's about 20 minutes out of our way. I have done this type of thing before. Ray, it will be of great help to the village people, and you might get an Indian leopard," Baasim said.

"Sounds good to me, I am ready to go," Ray replied.

"Well, we better get going then. It's a long trip, and we will need to stop after about 6 hours where we can get fuel and something to eat. Ray, could you get your gun out of its case and have it handy? You never know, we might spot a leopard in an open area stalking an animal and not paying attention. You may get a shot—it would be a rare situation but it has happened," Baasim said.

As Ray took out his rifle, he thought he would strap on his 44 Magnum revolver too, in case something happened that he would need a handgun. They then hooked up the trailer with all the gear and supplies. Just then, Ray noticed something strange about the trailer.

"The vehicle we will use for the hunt must have an entirely different type of hookup; I notice there are two types of towing hitches," Ray said.

Baasim told Ray, "Yes, the hunting vehicle is completely different, used especially for hunting in the jungle type terrain. You are really very observant to notice that; nobody on previous hunts has ever commented on the trailer hookup. I can't wait to show you the vehicle. I know you will like it, and it's made in India."

Soon Ray and Baasim were off heading towards the Ken River, and possibly a side trip to try to get Ray a shot at an Indian Leopard. As they were traveling down the road, Ray couldn't help but notice the beauty of the Indian countryside, and it got even more beautiful as they went east.

As they were driving along, Ray thought he would ask Baasim about the legend of the Bengal ruby. "Baasim, your Uncle Acharya told me about a legend of the Bengal ruby. I take it you have heard of the legend?"

"I have heard of the legend, but I have never come across a Bengal tiger with a large ruby hanging from its neck," Baasim replied. "However, I have a friend who is also a tiger hunting guide come across two tiger skeletons with a ruby necklace still around the tiger's neck as he was on a hunting trip. He assumed the tiger died of old age, and he thought it best to leave the ruby necklace on the tiger's skeleton."

"That's interesting; so that part of the legend is true. But it remains to be proved that the Bengal tiger with a ruby necklace hanging from its neck becomes a friend of a human it has made eye contact with," Ray said.

"As far as I know you are correct; maybe someday we will all find out if the whole legend is true," said Baasim.

"Baasim, what are the different animals that we may come across on this hunting trip?"

"For sure we will see deer, maybe a water buffalo, or even a sloth bear. Most likely because our hunt is along the Ken River we will see a mugger crocodile. We need to be cautious when we are at the Ken River water's edge. Mugger crocodiles are ambushers, and males can be 12 feet long and can be aggressive towards a man. They can also hunt on land, as they can travel over land very easily. So we must be careful where we set up our camp. The leopard, although not easy to come across, is the biggest threat as far as attacking humans is concerned. Leopards will actually go into a village and attack humans. They have no fear."

"What about snakes? Are they around where we will be hunting?"

"I have rarely seen a king cobra or an Indian python. Both these snakes will not come after humans unless provoked. The Indian python will come after a human only for defensive purposes, and not for food. They are a small version of the python species of snakes, and could not swallow a human, but they can kill you."

"Baasim, I have to admit I can't stand the sight of snakes."

"We will see elephants at villages where they are used for work on heavy jobs. They are mostly domesticated in the area of the Ken River. There are various species of monkeys, and of course the beautiful peacock and its loud high-pitched cries that make the jungle come alive."

Time was going by relatively quick, as they had been on the road for about four hours. Baasim told Ray that they would stop at a city named Gwalior. The city was very large, with about 1 million people. They needed to stop there to get fuel. They also needed to eat and relax for a while. Ray found himself relaxing until he finally fell asleep. Baasim awakened Ray when they were approaching Gwalior. Now awake, Ray looked around as they drove down what appeared to be a major street. Finally, Baasim pulled into a gas station and fueled his vehicle; afterwards, he took Ray to a restaurant where he usually ate when he was at Gwalior.

Seated inside, the two proceeded to order lunch. "What is good on the menu?" asked Ray.

"I like curry chicken. It comes with mashed potatoes and very flavorful broth. It is my favorite," replied Baasim. When the waiter came, they both ordered curry chicken.

"Well, you were right—this is an excellent lunch. I love that curry flavor," said Ray.

After resting awhile, they were on their way to Bamitha, a small village. After about two hours on the road, around three o'clock, Ray told Baasim, "Stop—do you see that man up the road? He is waving his arms. He looks like he might be in trouble or has a problem."

Baasim stopped the vehicle but told Ray, "Get your rifle ready. It could be a trick. He could be part of a robbery gang, so we will approach him very carefully." Baasim slowly brought the vehicle towards the man. About 50 yards away from him, Baasim stopped the vehicle.

"Let's get out slowly. Bring your rifle and your 44 Magnum revolver. We will approach and ask him what's wrong," Baasim cautioned.

"Okay, let's get out," Ray replied seriously.

As they went out, the man started to run towards them frantically asking for help. He was speaking to them in an Indian dialect; fortunately, Baasim could understand him.

"Baasim, what's he saying?" asked Ray.

"His wife is cornered by an Indian leopard. She is in a small cave in a rocky area. She is fending the leopard off with a tree branch," replied Baasim.

"Well, let's go help her. How far is she from here?"

Baasim later found out that the man could speak English. "Where is your wife?" Baasim asked the man.

"When we get through this grove of trees, there will be an opening and a clearing. Then you will see her and the leopard," replied the man.

The three of them ran through the grove of trees. Ray and Baasim followed the man until they came to the clearing. The man pointed to where his wife was cornered by the leopard. Ray immediately took his position, his rifle equipped with a bipod for front stock support.

"It looks like it is about 175 to 200 yards," he told Baasim.

Ray set his scope on 9 power and zeroed in on the leopard. He tried to do it fast, as the woman was screaming frantically. She was in a little hole in a cliff of rocks, poking at the leopard with a tree branch.

"Ray, hurry! Time may be running out!" Baasim said in a terrified voice.

"Baasim, I can see the urgency, but the leopard is moving from side to side and I can't get a good shot at him," replied Ray. Just then a thought occurred to Ray. "Baasim, when I say yell, yell out my name as loud as you can." Ray thought the leopard might stop moving because of the distraction. Ray was aimed at the leopard when he told Baasim, "Yell now!"

Baasim then yelled out, "Ray! Ray!" as loud as he could.

Through the scope, Ray could see the leopard stopped moving and raised its head to look around for the source of the loud sound. Ray pulled the trigger.

The leopard lay dead, and the woman was saved.

The three of them ran towards the woman who was still in the little cave terrified. Her husband hastened to her and tried to calm her down. Ray and Baasim were looking at the leopard to make sure it was dead. In a moment Baasim stepped away to calm himself down after such an incident.

Ray stood over the dead leopard, relieved that he was able to be calm enough to take the shot that saved the woman's life. Just then he heard what sounded like little rock falling from above the rocky cliff. He looked up to see a leopard about 20 feet up on a rocky ledge getting ready to jump onto Baasim. Just as the leopard was ready to jump off the ledge, Ray quickly drew and cocked his 44 Magnum in one motion and shot the leopard as it leaped toward Baasim. Baasim was not aware what just happened until he looked and saw that 5 feet from him lay another dead leopard. Ray was now on one knee head looking down, the 44 Magnum revolver still in his hand.

Ray looked up to Baasim and said to him, "My friend, do you realize what just happened here in just a matter of a minute?" Ray then stood up and holstered his revolver.

Baasim, along with the young woman and her husband, went to Ray and put their arms around him.

"Ray, I know what just happened here. You saved a young woman's life with a 200 yard shot. And you saved my life in an instant just when the leopard was ready to leap at me. With a quick draw, you shot the leopard that was ready to take my life."

Ray just stood there for a moment taking it all in. In a moment he said, "Is everybody okay? I hope so. This is something I will never forget."

"Ray, we will all remember what happened here today, as we will remember the marvelous shooting that you performed under tremendous pressure. You came through and saved our lives," Baasim said, smiling, before telling the man and his wife what he had just told Ray. Again, they all thanked Ray profusely.

"Well, it's not quite how I thought I would get my leopard trophy, but here it is."

"Ray, you need to say two leopard trophies," Baasim said, smiling. "I guess I better get busy and get the leopards skinned and prepared for the taxidermist. Ray, you just want a head to shoulder mount, right?"

"Yes, that will be fine, but Baasim I only signed up for one leopard permit."

"I will take care of it with the Indian Department of Big Game. I will tell them the story and that's all they need to know." With that the four of them walked back to the vehicle. Ray and Baasim had to go back out to where the leopards were and then skin and prepare the skins for the taxidermist.

Ray and Baasim were about to bid goodbye to the man and his wife who introduced themselves as Baahir and his wife Banhi Singh. Baasim introduced Ray and himself to them before explaining they had to drive out to get the leopards skinned and prepared for the taxidermist so Ray could have them mounted as trophies to always remember this special day.

Banhi approached Ray and said, "Ray, thank you so much for saving my life. I am forever grateful to you both. But you and Baasim must come to our village. It's not far—our village has to honor you for what you have done. You are both special—right, Baahir?"

"Yes! We need to honor you both, you must come. My wife Banhi would have very hurt feelings if she could not honor Ray for saving her life." He then told Baasim how to get to the village.

A smiling Baasim looked at Ray told them, "Okay, we will be there as soon as we take care of the leopards, and thank you for inviting us."

Banhi gave Ray a hug before she and her husband started walking to the village, occasionally looking back and waving goodbye. "See you in a little while at the village!"

Baasim and Ray got into their vehicle and returned to where the leopards were. Once there, Baasim took out the necessary tools to prepare the skin for the taxidermist. Ray was watching intently as he had never seen this done before. Before Baasim started skinning the leopards, he took a lot of measurements on each leopard to provide the critical dimension that the taxidermist would need.

"I would never have thought about having to give the taxidermist measurements," said Ray.

"That's a must as each animal is different in size," replied Baasim.

Baasim put an ID tag on each leopard's ear that would correspond to the dimensions on paper that he filled out. He proceeded to skin the leopards, applied salt to the flesh side, and folded the skin flesh side together. Baasim would have to repeat the salting process maybe several more times; eventually the skins would be turned flesh side out, folded, and the skin will then dry to be shipped later. Baasim explained the complete process to Ray, who was really interested. When they were done, they put the skins in a special container in the trailer, to be treated again later until the process was done.

Baasim and Ray were soon on their way to the village where Baahir and Banhi were waiting for their arrival.

"Baasim, what do think is going to happen at this celebration? How elaborate is it going to be?"

"My friend Ray, you will just have to wait and see," Baasim replied, smiling. "Ya, wait and see. As a hero to Banhi, I am sure she will arrange everything for tonight's event."

Ray started to get a little nervous approaching the village. Soon he could see Baahir and Banhi waiting to greet them. When Baasim and Ray got out, Banhi was the first to greet them, giving Ray a hug.

"Ray I am so thankful that you and Baasim could make it!" she said. "We have pigs and lambs being cooked right now for the celebration. I can never thank you enough and my villagers are anxious to meet you." Banhi then stepped back from them and with her arms extended outward, welcomed them to her village.

At that point, all the villagers clapped their hands and chanted, "Welcome to our village, Ray and Baasim!"

Banhi guided Ray and Baasim to meet the villagers; Ray thought that there were about 200 people in the village. As they were introduced to the villagers, Ray saw they could all speak English. He also got the impression that Baahir and Banhi were the leaders. The villagers were so thankful that Ray had saved Banhi's life, for she and Baahir were leaders of the village.

Ray then asked, "Are you the leaders of the village?"

Baahir answered, "Yes, we are like what you in the United States call a city manager or mayor. Banhi and I do the job together."

Baahir and Banhi then took Ray and Baasim to a village park where a lot of tables and benches were set up for big celebrations that the villagers would have. Banhi told Ray and Baasim, "We do have quite a few gatherings throughout the year; of course, today is a very special occasion. Let's sit down. It's getting close to the time of the feast." The four of them went to sit down at what appeared to be the head table.

"Banhi you most certainly didn't have to go through all this," Ray said, realizing how big the event was.

"Ray, you are a special guest. It's something we all want to do for you and Baasim. The villagers voted to have this celebration. I don't decide things on my own—we are you might say a small democracy."

"I just don't know how to thank you, but mainly I am just glad you are alive and we are here talking. I can't wait to send a telegram to my wife and tell her of this incident with the leopards and now the celebration."

Banhi, being sort of inquisitive, commented, "Ray, I noticed a locket hanging around your neck—is there a picture of your wife in it?"

"Yes, would you like to see her picture?"

"Oh, most certainly, Ray!" Banhi and Baahir both looked at Shannon's picture. Banhi, looking at Ray, said, "She is beautiful—blue eyes, dark hair, and medium skin color. Can she shoot as good as you?"

"With a certain rifle—probably better than me."

"Ray, I wish your wife could be here to see what we have planned for tonight. I believe she would be honored and proud of you."

The food was now ready so everybody got up and went to get their food. "Lamb is one of my favorite meats, and it sure looks good," he said.

Baasim wondered how the village would honor Ray. He had a feeling it was going to be very special—and something the whole village agreed to, for that's just how this Indian village operates.

After villagers and guests finished eating, Banhi stood up and called everyone's attention.

"Tonight I want to share with all of you how my life almost came to an end to day," she started. "There are three people that saved my life; I want to thank them here tonight. First is my husband Baahir who ran frantically to the road to get help. When he got to the road, he got the attention of Baasim, a hunting guide driving with a hunter down the road where Baahir was. They stopped and offered help. The hunter friend happened to be a man named Ray Johnson, who appeared to be anxious to help. I was fending off the leopard with a tree branch when I saw the three of them. I was too exhausted, but I saw the hunter lie down and aim his rifle. The leopard was moving back and forth waiting for a chance to kill me. I thought to myself, 'How is this hunter going to shoot the leopard when it is moving,' and I was about ready to give up from exhaustion, when I heard a loud yell, 'Ray! Ray!' The leopard stopped moving, raised its head—and then I heard the shot, and the leopard lay dead in front of me. That's what happened to me today," Banhi finished her tale.

The villagers all stood up and clapped their hands.

Baasim then stood. "The story doesn't stop there," he said. "My hunter friend, ever alert at the scene, also shot another leopard, by a quick draw of his revolver. He shot the leopard as it was leaping toward me. So you see, Banhi and I owe our lives to Ray Johnson."

Again the villagers stood up and clapped their hands to honor Ray.

It was Ray's turn to stand up and emotionally address everyone. "I believe the whole incident that took place today was God's plan. He put everyone in the right place at the right time—that's just how He works. I am thankful to God that he guided me to this place, and I ended up saving two lives, but I give Him the credit for all this."

"Well, Ray," Banhi said, "I would like one of our villagers to bring a gift for you, to thank you for the deeds that you, through your God, had performed today, that saved my life."

A villager brought a box to Ray, handed it to him, and said, "Ray, this gift was approved by all the villagers today for saving the life of our precious leader Banhi. It has been in this village for a long time, waiting for the right person to come along, and you Ray, are that right person. Baasim had told us you were married to a woman named Shannon, so we give this gift to you so you can give it to your wife Shannon. This is so she will also have a memory of what her husband has done for our village here today."

Ray then opened the box; he was speechless for a while as he looked at a necklace with about a one inch diameter ruby mounted in gold. He finally found some words to say, "You in this village are unbelievable to give me this valuable gift for my wife Shannon. It is such a big sacrifice from you all. I wish my wife could be here by my side right now; knowing her, this would bring tears in her eyes, while hugging every one of you and thanking God that two lives were saved."

Baasim, Baahir, and Banhi smiled at their new friend Ray, all of them happy for him.

"Ray tomorrow you leave, to continue on your adventure," Banhi said. "I know you have a good guide who will take care of you, but still I would remind you to be cautious of the Bengal tiger. It is such a dangerous animal, and I wouldn't want to lose you who have become like a son to me. I hope sometime in the future our paths will cross again, and hopefully your wife will be with you at that time."

Ray hugged Banhi. "Since I left California, this trip has been full of surprises. Indeed, I think our paths will cross again, and maybe even sooner than we would expect; we will have to wait and see. If not, I know my wife will want us to make a special trip someday to see you and visit your village."

"Ray, that would be so exciting for all of us in this village, and I hope it happens soon." Ray and Baasim were given a special place to retire for the night, and they all said good night.

Morning came and Ray and Baasim were soon on their way after saying goodbye to the hosts and the village.

"This is a part of my life that I will remember forever," Ray said.

CHAPTER 16

RAY GAINS A NEW FRIEND

R ay and Baasim were on their way to get the hunting vehicle. Baasim told Ray the driving time would be about 5 hours, and they would stop at a city named Chhatarpur to get some fuel and something to eat and rest a little.

"Since you got your leopard trophies, there will be no need to take the side trip to that village that has had some leopard problems. That will save us two or three days," Baasim said.

"I still can't believe what happened yesterday." Ray paused a little while, and then asked Baasim, "Would Chhatarpur be a place that I could send a telegram from?"

"It is a big city, and don't worry, I know right where to go to send a telegram," replied Baasim. "When you send your telegram, mention to your wife that this will be the last telegram until we start heading back from the Bengal tiger hunt."

"Do you think I should send the ruby necklace that the villagers gave me, or would it be better to keep it with me?"

"I believe I would send it to her. I have used air mail to the United States with 100 percent success. The Post Office has small mailing boxes strictly for air mail. That way, you wouldn't risk it getting stolen, or lost, or who knows what might happen when we are hunting for the tiger."

"Well, that's settled then. I will send it first class guaranteed delivery air mail and insure it."

"That is exactly what I have always done; it should be fine. Ray, tell Shannon to expect delivery of the package in about two weeks."

Ray thought it was a good time to ask some questions about the Bengal tiger. "Baasim, could you tell me about the habits of the Bengal tiger, like about things to look for indicating a tiger is in the area?" he said.

"Of course I would be happy to tell you about the Bengal tiger and some of its habits, and other facts besides."

"As a hunter, I have always taken an attitude to know as much as possible about the animal I am hunting," explained Ray.

"Ray, you are very unique. I like that you want to know as much as possible about the animal you are hunting. I can tell you come here with a lot of hunting experience, and it showed on how you took control of the leopard situation yesterday. I was in a panic and you were trying to get a job done in a controlled way, and you did it and saved two lives."

"Experience in the field had made me what I am. Having as much facts as I can get makes me feel like I have a slight edge in my pursuit in hunting the animal. I must admit, though, that I never have hunted in this type of jungle environment, or for an animal as big as this."

Around twelve o'clock, Ray and Baasim approached the outskirts of Chhatarpur. In no time, Baasim was securing fuel for the Land Rover, before proceeding down the street to the restaurant.

"This restaurant serves excellent food," said Baasim as they stepped out of the vehicle. "They also have American cuisine on the menu. It's a pretty famous tourist attraction, and they get a lot of American customers."

Once they were seated in the restaurant, Baasim spotted a friend who was also a Bengal tiger hunting guide sitting alone a couple of tables down from where they were. Baasim went over and asked him to join them. When he did, Baasim introduced Ray to Bishr Sarin.

The waiter came and they all ordered their lunch. Baasim asked Bishr, "How is tiger hunting going? Have you had good success this year?"

"It's about average, but this year I noticed something strange," replied Bishr. "Do you remember when we were talking about the legend of the Bengal ruby last year?"

"Yes, I remember that. You told me how you came across two tiger skeletons with a ruby necklace around their necks and how you just left the ruby necklaces where they were."

At this time, Ray found himself intently listening to the conversation, anxiously waiting for what was Bishr about to say next.

"Just on my last trip, I came across the two tiger skeletons— and Baasim, the ruby necklaces were gone from the tigers' skeletons."

"Do you have any idea what could have happened?" Ray asked.

"I have my own thoughts, but you have to remember it's just my opinion," replied Bishr.

"Well, I am anxious to hear your opinion," said Ray.

Bishr took a deep breath before replying, "I believe there are still some villagers who still believe in the legend. And they do their part capturing a tiger and placing a ruby necklace on the tiger's neck."

"So you believe some villagers have placed the ruby necklace on a tiger, and that completes that part of the legend. And now they are waiting for somebody to make eye contact with the Bengal tiger with the ruby necklace. And that will make the legend true if the tiger becomes a protective friend to that person."

"Yes, Ray, that's what I believe."

"Like I told Ray, maybe someday we will find out if the legend of the Bengal ruby is true," said Baasim.

After lunch, Ray and Baasim said goodbye to Bishr and headed to their vehicle.

Before parting ways, Bishr mentioned to Baasim, "Be on the lookout on the Ken River trail. I heard there are a lot of gang robberies going on lately, especially where the Ken River makes the sharp turn to the west. Make sure you have your guns handy. Anyway, the government issued a memo to all hunting guides; if you feel threatened, shoot them."

"Thanks for the information," replied Baasim. "We will be looking out for trouble. In any case, Ray here has shown us what an excellent marksman he is with a rifle and his 44 Magnum revolver. Anybody would be wise not to get in a shootout with him—this Californian can shoot."

Bishr said his final goodbyes and said, "Good luck to you both and be careful."

"There is a Post Office just down the street for our telegrams. You can then also get the ruby necklace air mailed to Shannon," said Baasim.

Inside the Post Office, Ray asked a clerk for the appropriate container to put Shannon's necklace in. Afterwards, he was back with the clerk and said, "I would like to send this air mail to California, USA. I would have it insured—how many days do you think will it take to reach its destination?"

"Approximately fourteen days," replied the clerk.

Ray also took care of the message for Shannon this way:

DEAR SHANNON IT'S BEEN 7 DAYS AND I SURE DO MISS YOU THE TRIP HAS BEEN FULL OF SURPRISES YESTERDAY I SHOT 2 LEOPARDS BY DOING SO I SAVED MY GUIDE'S LIFE AND A WOMAN NAMED BANHI WHO WAS CORNERED IN A SMALL CAVE AND KEEPING THE LEOPARD AWAY WITH A TREE BRANCH HER HUSBAND APPROACHED US FRANTICALY

ASKING FOR HELP WENT A LITTLE WAYS AND
THERE SHE WAS AND TIME WAS RUNNING OUT I
MADE A 200 YARD SHOT AND THEN WHEN WE GOT
TO THE SCENE AND EVERYBODY WAS TRYING TO
CALM DOWN ANOTHER LEOPARD 20 FEET HIGH ON
A ROCKY LEDGE WAS GETTING READY TO LEAP
ONTO BAASIM AND I GOT HIM WITH MY 44 MAGNUM
REVOLVER SO I HAVE 2 LEOPARD TROPHIES THE
MAN AND THE WOMAN INSISTED THAT WE GO TO
THEIR VILLAGE FOR A CELEBRATION TO HONNOR
ME FOR SAVING THEIR LEADER'S LIFE SO WE DID
GO I AM SENDING YOU A VERY SPECIAL PACKAGE
THAT CONTAINS A GIFT FROM THE VILLAGERS TO
THANK ME FOR WHAT I HAD DONE IT WILL GET
DELIVERED IN ABOUT 14 DAYS SHANNON I LOVE
AND MISS YOU DEARLY WE ARE NOW ON OUR WAY
TO PICK UP THE HUNTING VEHICLE AND THEN WILL
HIT THE TRAIL ALONG THE KEN RIVER SHANNON
THIS IS THE LAST PLACE I WILL BE ABLE TO SEND
A TELEGRAM I LOVE AND MISS YOU SAY HELLO TO
EVERYONE HOPE MOM AND DAD ARE OKAY

LOVE RAY

Done at the Post Office, Ray and Baasim returned to their
vehicle and started their drive down the road to go pick up
the hunting vehicle. Baasim told Ray it was about a two-hour
drive.

As they were traveling down the road, Ray said, "You
know, Baasim, just before we stopped for fuel and got
something to eat, you were about to tell me about the habits
and some facts about the Bengal tiger."

"That's right, Ray. I will start by telling you about the
tiger's senses.

"For one, it has excellent night vision—six times better
than a human's. Their day vision, however, is just about

equal to that of ours. They are excellent at judging distance, which helps determine when they should go for the kill. Their sense of hearing is the best they have, a big help to them in their hunt for food."

"I would have thought their eyesight would be their advantage in hunting for food," said Ray.

"You are right; their hearing and night vision are their biggest assets when it comes to hunting for food. The tiger's sense of smell is very good but not used for hunting. It is mainly used for interacting with other tigers as they leave urine traces for other tigers to smell, for the male to find a female that is ready to mate. Urine traces are also used to mark a tiger's territory, which is about 20 square miles for a male, and 17 square miles for a female. In general, the only time a tiger will enter another tiger's territory is for mating. They also mark their territory by shedding the bark of trees, a sign that I also find useful when hunting as we will be doing," said Baasim.

"What's a tiger's favorite food in the area we will be hunting?"

"One of the tiger's favorite foods is the sambar deer, which can weigh from 200 to 700 pounds, and the smaller chital deer, which weighs about 80 pounds. The area we will be hunting at has a plentiful amount of deer. The tiger will always go back to finish eating their kill, and when the animal is big, it will take some time to finish eating it, so they will even eat rotten meet," said Baasim.

"You mean when we are hunting, we could look for some tiger kills, and use that as a way to get a shot at a tiger," said Ray.

"That's right, Ray, but we have to be lucky to find a kill. First we need to find a tiger's territory and a convenient place to shoot from. We have to get there before sunrise and wait. Another way is to kill a deer and prop it up as bait. I have used this method with some success. Still, finding something that they have killed is the best way, as they will always return to feed on their kill," explained Baasim.

"How do tigers get other tigers' attention? Do they have a way of calling other tigers especially for mating?" asked Ray.

Baasim responded to Ray's question, "A tiger will roar to attract another tiger; its roar can be heard up to two miles away, and for mating, the tiger's roar will be used to locate each other. Mating mainly takes place in the spring, so our timing is good; if we hear a roar, we should pay close attention to where it's coming from," said Baasim.

"Well, Baasim, you covered lot of things to be on the lookout during our hunt. Thanks for all the information. These are things I as a hunter like to know," said Ray.

The two soon saw a sign that said, BAMITHA VILLAGE TWO KILOMETERS AHEAD. "Remember the village I told you about just south of the village of Bamitha that had leopard problems?"

Ray said, "Yes, I remember you said the leopard was killing their livestock; but I guess we won't be going there since I already got my leopard trophies."

"Actually, Ray, in spite of the leopard incident, we saved two to three days. Now we don't have to set up and find a shooting area for the next morning to wait and hopefully get a shot," said Baasim.

"That's right, our shooting area was within minutes away and we didn't have much time to get things done."

"Well, thanks again for saving my life," said Baasim, smiling. "I let Uncle Acharya and brother Aadesh know what happened through the telegram that I sent. We are only an hour away from the hunting vehicle. The Vehicle dealer has a place on the Ken River, so this will be your first look at it. By the way, the Ken River is a very clean river, not like the Ganges River."

After around an hour, they were pulling into the vehicle area. Baasim noticed Ray intently looking around, a puzzled look on his face.

"I don't see any vehicles here. It looks like an elephant zoo," observed Ray.

Smiling, Baasim said, "Ray, my friend—our vehicle for this hunt is *an elephant*; his name is Baha, which means 'beautiful.' He stands 10 feet 3 inches, and weighs 10,200 pounds."

"My gosh, he is a monster! I never would have thought we would be using an elephant. Now I understand why the trailer had a very unique hitch."

"Ray, there are advantages to using an elephant. I will explain it to you later." They were now pulling into the office parking area. They got out and went into the office where Ray was introduced to the owner of the elephant for rent business. Baasim filled out the paperwork and settled his account. It was obvious to Ray that Baasim had used this place of business before.

The owner told Baasim, "Let's take Ray out to meet Baha. Now let me tell you Baha is a great, kind, and intelligent elephant. Don't forget he can sense statements made that he may not like, and he may let you know about it with some action. It's nothing life-threatening, just his way of trying to let you know what he thinks of your attitude."

The three of them proceeded to the area where Baha was kept; when the elephant saw Baasim, he immediately came to him, putting his trunk on his left then right shoulder as a way of greeting. Baha then pulled away a little, placed the tip of his trunk on Baasim's forehead, and applied a little suction. "Ray, Baha just gave me a kiss," explained Baasim.

Ray laughed. Baha came to him and grabbed his hand with his trunk as if to introduce himself to his new friend. Baha then put the tip of his trunk on Ray's forehead and gave Ray one of his kisses. "Baha, your breath stinks real bad—and I mean bad, bad, bad," observed Ray. Baha's owner smiled, and he knew what was coming next.

Baha raised his trunk and let out one of those elephant screeching sounds as if to say he didn't like Ray's attitude. His trunk proceeded to pick Ray and lift him about six feet up, holding him in the air. Ray finally petted his trunk and said in a very kind voice, "Baha, I am sorry I said that. Could you please let me down now—please, please." Baha, being the intelligent elephant that he is, dropped Ray about six feet to the ground, and then let out one of those elephant screeching sounds, as if he were laughing at Ray.

Baha's owner and Baasim found themselves laughing at what they saw. "Well, my friend Ray, you just got yourself a welcome from your new friend Baha the beautiful," said Baasim.

In a sarcastic tone of voice, Ray said, "You call him beautiful? You got to be kidding." In an instant, Baha started to approach Ray again, but he immediately told Baha in a gentle tone of voice, "Baha, you are beautiful," and went to grab his trunk and gave him a hug. "Baha, you are my friend forever."

The words settled Baha, and the up and down motions of his trunk indicated he really liked and approved of Ray.

"You have now gained a true and loyal friend. He will do anything for you," said Baha's owner. "He will protect you from harm and be a true friend. Don't forget, though, that he will get you straightened out if you get out of line. He is a very loving animal; just like a dog is man's best friend, so is Baha."

"I am glad he likes me. He is starting to grow on me as being an exciting companion," replied Ray. He went to Baha, gave him a kiss on his trunk, and everything was starting to sink into Ray that he could be a friend of a 10,200 pound animal. Baha is even starting to look beautiful in Ray's eyes.

The three of them proceeded to a dining hall where all hunting guides and their clients are offered a dinner. As the three sat down for dinner, they discussed what would happen in the morning.

Baasim was leading the conversation. "We will first have breakfast while Baha is being fitted with a special harness to tow a trailer," Baasim said, adding how he told the elephant outfitter he would like to get going no later than nine o'clock if that's okay.

"That will be fine— gives me plenty of time," said the outfitter.

"I am anxious to see this elephant towing harness," said Ray. I imagine something like a horse-drawn wagon except a hell of a lot bigger." Suddenly something occurred to Ray. "Baasim, why are we using an elephant for this hunting trip?"

"We use an elephant because they are pretty much maintenance free. They eat and drink at their will, and are way more reliable than a vehicle like a Land Rover. At times they can provide protection to a friend, too. Ray, you always have good questions.

"By the way, what you said about the harness being like a horse drawn wagon is basically right—they have the same basic design.

"I think we can now go to the sleeping quarters to get a good night's sleep," concluded Baasim.

CHAPTER 17

TAKING THE KEN RIVER TRAIL

T he next morning, Ray and Baasim had breakfast and prepared to head up the Ken River. First was Baha's harness that Baasim took care of. Everything went as scheduled for them to leave by nine o'clock as planned.

Back in California at the Johnson Ranch, everything was pretty normal. Shannon was home and talking to Denise on the phone when the doorbell rang. "Denise, I have to answer the door." Shannon opened the door to see the mailman.

" I have a telegram from Ray," said the mailman. "Here is the pen you need to sign for it."

Shannon was so excited she was shaking so much. She couldn't hold the pen steady, but finally managed to sign for the telegram. She went back on the phone to tell Denise, but Denise was no longer on the line. A minute later, Denise came charging through the door.

"Shannon, I heard the mailman say telegram so I just came running over as fast as I could. Have you opened the telegram yet?"

"No, I am still so excited. Let's calm down first and sit on the sofa where I could read it."

Soon Shannon managed to read the telegram. "Can you believe what happened over there? And he ended up saving a woman's and his guide's life! I am so proud of him!" beamed Shannon.

Denise was right there by her friend's side. "That sounded like one hell of a situation and he took care of it. It appeared they had a celebration to honor him, and the woman wanted to send you a gift so you could feel proud of Ray—that's quite a gesture," she said.

"Well, he also got two Indian leopard trophies," replied Shannon. "I hope to meet the lady someday, and perhaps even go to their village. That would be something I would like to do." When Shannon was calmer, she remembered something. "Oh, I have to call Mom and Dad! Denise, let's drive over to the house and surprise them!"

Quickly Shannon and Denise drove over to the Johnsons' ranch house. They found Mary and Paul in the kitchen eating a late breakfast.

"Well, what brings you two over here this morning with those big smiles? It must be something exciting?" said Mary.

Just then Joeseph walked in. "I saw Shannon's car in the driveway so I thought I would stop in," he said. He went and gave Mary a hug and said hello to Paul.

"I just got a telegram from Ray; wait till you hear what happened," said Shannon, before proceeding to read the telegram. When it was over, everybody had big smiles on their faces.

"I bet the woman and Ray's guide were glad Ray was a good marksman—doesn't surprise me when it comes to shooting. We all know what Ray can do when it comes to that," Joeseph said.

"It sounds like the villagers had a big celebration for what Ray had done, and the lady was so thankful for Ray saving her life. I wonder what the gift is; bet you are excited, Shannon," Mary said with a smile. "I guess we will find out in fourteen days or so."

"That's one heck of a way to get two Indian leopard trophies. That's a lot of mental pressure on Ray when he shot the leopard at 200 yards, which saved the woman's life. I am pretty proud of my son," Paul said, smiling broadly.

"I guess we will not get any more telegrams until they return from their hunting trip. I miss Ray so much; I wish I could be there with him," Shannon said, tears welling up her eyes.

"Time flies fast, Shannon. Look, it's already been a week," said Joeseph.

"Hey, you two amigos, we need to go practice your 30-30 rifle shooting. I always want you to be prepared. Look what Ray just encountered; you never know when a need will occur to use those rifles," added Joeseph. Shannon and Denise agreed it sounded like a good outing.

Shannon asked Mom and Dad, "Is everything okay with you both? Do you need any help? I know you are starting to plant your crops."

"I will be planting tomatoes and corn again," replied Paul. "The price for tomatoes is higher than last year, so that's the plan." It seemed everybody had all calmed down and ready to continue their day.

Back in India, Baha was all hooked up to the trailer and ready to go. Ray was witnessing what this so-called hunting trailer looked like being towed by a 10,200 pound elephant. Ray and Baasim would be sitting about 5 feet high on a fold up seat, which gave them a good view of the surrounding area.

"There is a gun rack behind the seat," Baasim told Ray. "I believe you also brought a 30-30 lever action rifle. Ray, put that up behind the seat along with your other rifle, and also have your 44 Magnum revolver with you. You never know what we might run into going to the Ken River trail, and it's the jungle."

"How far will we travel today?" asked Ray.

"About 12 miles; it will take us around four to five hours. Then we will stop and stay for the night and relax."

Ray and Baasim climbed up onto the seat. Ray had already put his guns in the rack, so they were ready to go. Just then Ray noticed something.

"Baasim, don't you need a rein to let Baha know what you want him to do? That's what horses need so they know what do," said Ray.

"Baha takes word commands most of the time," replied Baasim, smiling. He paused and added, "His commands are: 'Go,' 'Left,' 'Right,' and 'Back.'"

"Well, let's get going. I am getting anxious," said Ray.

Baasim gave Baha the command, "Go, Baha." Baha didn't move. Baasim smiled.

"I guess Baha must have lost his hearing; or maybe he didn't like your attitude, Baasim?" said Ray, smiling.

"I bet if you go up and talk to him he might respond to some commands," said Baasim, still smiling. Baha let out the typical elephant screeching sounds. Ray got off his seat.

"Baasim, what possibly could I do to change his attitude? I just can't imagine what is wrong with him," pleaded Ray.

At that instant, Baha let out two more screeching sounds and proceeded to sit down on his hind quarters, as if to say he wasn't moving until somebody came and talked to him.

"You better go and talk to him," repeated Baasim.

So Ray went up to Baha, said in an angry tone of voice, "Baha, you are just like a 10,200 pound jackass. You get up, we have to get going."

Believe it or not Baha got up gently. Ray then said, "Now that's a good boy—thank you."

Baha put his trunk to Ray's forehead and gave him a kiss. In turn Ray gave him a hug on his trunk before going back to his seat.

"Baasim, I think we are ready to hit the road."

"I am surprised he was okay with your tone of voice, especially when you called him a jackass. I think he just wanted to see you and give you kiss."

"Actually, Baasim, after I said it with that tone of voice I thought for sure I would have to apologize, but let's see if he responds to your commands."

"You should sit to the far right in the seat. I always sit to the far left in the seat," said Baasim.

"Why is that so important?"

"Just look at what you are looking at from this seat if you were sitting towards the middle. When Baha has to go, you won't want to be in the middle," replied Baasim.

"Oh, ya, I see we don't want to be a prime target just in case Baha needs to take a crap," said Ray, smiling.

"Ray, you couldn't have worded it any better, and when he decides to go," said Baasim, laughing. "Well, he can do that even when on the move, so there isn't any warning."

They were still laughing when Baasim said, "Go, Baha," and they were on their way up the Ken River trail, and Ray was getting excited.

As they were traveling at about 2 to 3 miles per hour, Ray had ample time to take in the beautiful scenery. Sometimes he could even see the Ken River. His mind wandered to his home in California, wondering what Shannon and everybody was doing. He pulled up the locket and opened it; he looked at the picture of his beautiful blue-eyed wife. He missed her so much that he came to wonder if the trip was worth it. Still looking at the locket, he wondered what Shannon meant that the locket contained a not so obvious message that he might find someday.

At New Delhi, Acharya had received the telegram from Baasim. He got a hold of Aadesh and his family and Baasim's family and had them all come over so he could give the families the current news that the telegram contained.

When they were all seated down, Acharya told them, "Well, Ray and Baasim had a little excitement the other day. While on their way to pick up the elephant, a man frantically asked them for help as his wife was cornered by a leopard. They went and Ray shot the leopard to save the woman's life."

"That sounds like Ray can really shoot," said Aadesh. "I can just imagine how things had to be done quickly. I guess those Californians were born to hunt and shoot."

"The story doesn't end there. In the next story, we here can all be thankful to Ray," Acharya said, pausing a little. "When they got to the scene were the dead leopard and the woman was, Ray's alertness saved Baasim's life.

"A leopard was ready to jump on Baasim from the edge of a rock formation 20 feet or so above him. Ray heard a little noise, looked up and saw the leopard, drew his 44 Magnum revolver and shot it, and it ended up dead about 5 feet from Baasim," said Acharya.

"Well, this family indeed can be thankful to Ray," said Aadesh. "I know Baasim must be glad he had an experienced hunter and shooter along on this trip."

"The woman and her husband gave Ray and Baasim a big party to thank them for saving the woman's life," continued Acharya. "She happened to be a leader of the village. This will be the last telegram we will receive until they return from the Ken River," concluded Acharya.

Back at the Ken River trail, things were going fine. Baha was behaving wonderfully. Happy to see the scenery, Ray was pleased to have Baha along. He was starting to get attached to his 10,200 pound friend, occasionally talking to him like he was a human.

"Are you enjoying the jungle and its beauty?" asked Baasim. "The further we go the more beautiful it gets; right now it's getting pretty hot so I think we should stop. Up a little ways from here is a trail that goes to the Ken River, which is about a quarter of a mile west of this road. Thought I would unhook Baha from the trailer so maybe you could take Baha to get a drink of water. He may do a little eating while you head to the Ken River."

"That sounds good; maybe Baha and I could do a little bonding along the way. I am really starting to like Baha, he is a great friend," said Ray.

"I think Baha has got you all wrapped up around his trunk. I am going to stay here and scrape salt off the two leopard skins a couple more time and they're done," said Baasim.

Ray and Baha took the trail that lead to the Ken River, which they did in about 15 minutes. When they got to the water's edge, Baha eagerly waded into the river—it was well over 100 degrees at this time. Ray used the moment to look at the beautiful scenery along the Ken River.

Baha appeared to be really enjoying himself. He was drinking water and using his trunk to squirt water over his body for cooling off and cleaning himself.

Baha was about 10 feet from Ray when he turned his head and trunk towards Ray, and then blasted Ray with a trunk full of water that actually knocked Ray off his feet. Baha then came to Ray and lifted him up with his trunk, as if to say, *Let me help you up*—at least that's what Ray thought. Baha was in a playing mood with his new friend. As he raised Ray up, he decided to drop him from about 6 feet into the water. From there, the two went to have fun with each other. Ray enjoyed it as well, the water cool to his body.

Soon Baha resumed cooling and cleaning himself up.

Ray thought he could use a little wash job on his face. He dipped his head into the water, when, out of the corner of his eye, he saw a crocodile coming full speed ahead towards him. As Ray frantically went to get up, he slipped back into the water, but managed to yell, "Baha! Baha!"

The elephant, however, had already seen the situation, and was on his way to protect his new friend. Baha was with Ray in the nick of time. He intercepted the crocodile using his trunk, grabbed and squeezed him, and flung him into the air—and the crocodile landed about 40 feet up into a tree. Ray was relieved that Baha came to his rescue, but Baha's work wasn't done yet: another crocodile was coming after Ray. Baha intercepted the crocodile and did the same flinging job, sending the second crocodile up into the tree, both crocodiles appearing to be dead.

Baha let out a screeching elephant call, a sound of victory, before giving Ray his elephant kiss. Ray breathed a sigh of relief, and he petted Baha and gave his trunk a hug.

Back at the trailer, Baasim heard the sound and was hoping everything was okay. He thought he better check, so he started running down the trail to where Ray and Baha were. What he saw made him laugh so hard: Ray on Baha's neck, and it looked like he was going to give Ray a ride back to the trailer.

"What have you two been up to—is everything okay?" Baasim asked.

"Everything is okay, thanks to Baha being alert; Baasim, this elephant just saved my life," said Ray.

"What did Baha the beautiful do?" said Baasim.

"Look up into that tree; you will see two dead crocodiles that were ready to have me for dinner."

"Ray, you got to be very alert when you are near or on the bank of the Ken River. Mugger crocodiles are ambushers, especially when you are in the water."

"All I know is Baha rushed to my rescue and threw the first crocodile into the tree, only to have to deal with a second crocodile the same way," said Ray.

Again, Baasim looked at Ray up on Baha's neck. "Whose idea was it for you to be riding on Baha's neck anyway?" he asked, laughing.

"Well, we were starting to head back and I was in front of Baha when he slipped his trunk between my legs. I held on tightly, and he perched me on top of his neck," replied Ray.

"Well, let's get back to the trailer, and then you can figure out how you are going to get down," said Baasim.

"I am sure Baha has it figured out. He probably has done it before—right, Baha?"

Baha let out a screeching sound as if he were saying yes. The three headed back to the trailer. Once there, Baha lowered himself down in such a way that his front leg provided a step that Ray could use to get off easily. Ray went to Baha, gave his trunk a hug, and Baha in turn gave Ray his elephant kiss.

Baasim guided Baha to the trailer and again hooked him up to it. They were ready to travel again and they started up the Ken River trail. Baasim said, "We will travel about three hours before we set up for the evening."

Feeling very comfortable in his seat, Ray was looking around. The jungle started to show itself with monkeys and the beautiful call of the peacocks that brought life to the jungle. Soon they had traveled for about two hours.

"Could you have your 30-30 carbine ready?" Baasim told Ray. "If we see one of those small chattel deer, you could shoot it for our dinner."

Ray was only too excited to shoot some game for dinner; it would also keep his shooting up to par. He made himself on the lookout for the deer while taking in all the creatures all around him, including a water buffalo roaming through the jungle.

"Did you get to prep the leopard skins with some more salt?" asked Ray.

251

"Yes, and they are looking good. Probably one more time and the salting will be done," replied Baasim.

Suddenly, Ray said, "Stop, Baha! Baasim, there is a deer about 100 yards." Ray got off the trailer and positioned himself for a shot, using part of the trailer to steady himself. In time, he pulled the trigger and down went the deer.

"Well, another good shot, Ray," said Baasim. "Let's go get it. We'll dress it out and bring it back to the trailer. We only have another half an hour to go. When we stop I will cut out the best cut of meat and cook it over a fire; hope that sounds good."

After about an hour more of traveling, Baasim told Ray, "This is a good place to stop, close to the Ken River where we can clean up a little. Then we will come back and I will prepare the meat and start cooking." Baasim unhooked Baha from the trailer and the three headed to the Ken River.

"This time I will look for crocodiles," said Ray. "I learned my lesson last time." At the river, Baha had all the water he wanted and sprayed water all over the place—and Ray. When they were all done cleaning up, they went back to the trailer.

As Baasim cut off a nice chunk of meat, Ray gathered and put wood into a special tray equipped with a rotisserie so they could occasionally turn the meat. Ray was impressed with the way Baasim was cooking the meat, and he was getting really hungry. It was only about three o'clock and was pretty hot.

"Ray could you take the rest of the deer to the river so some animal could eat the rest of the deer meat?" said Baasim. "Oh, and take your 30-30 carbine, just in case you run into something and you'd need it."

With only about 40 pounds of meat left to it, the deer was easy to carry, especially as Baasim had it inside a meat bag. The river was only about one eighth of a mile. At the river,

Ray saw a mugger crocodile. He made sure the crocodile saw him before placing the meat on the bank. After about 30 seconds, the crocodile started swimming rapidly to the meat. Ray watched from a safe distance as it devoured the meat.

On his way back to Baasim, Ray heard some voices. Careful not to attract attention to himself, he saw there were two men holding a gun at Baasim, who had his hands up. Quietly keeping himself out of sight, he moved a little closer to see what was happening. Ray remembered Baasim's friend Bishr telling them to be wary of robbers on the Ken River trail—that if they felt threatened, they should shoot them. Ray's biggest concern was the safety of Baasim—how he could shoot one and be fast enough to shoot the other before he could take Baasim hostage.

Ray knew he had to act quickly; just then, a stroke of luck came: there was Baha in such a position that Ray could use Baha as cover while he approached, giving him a good shot at them. Ray felt he would shoot their gun hand; he hoped the other man would pause a moment from the excitement so he could shoot his gun hand or even his arm before any harm could come to Baasim.

Close to Baha with his 44 magnum drawn, Ray quickly stepped out and shot the gun out of one man's hand; not expecting such event, the other turned to shoot at Ray, but Ray proved faster and shot him in the arm, and the man dropped his gun.

"Baasim, are you okay?"

"Ya, Ray, I am okay," replied Baasim. "I thought you were never going to get here. I did get a glimpse of you coming, so I tried my best to keep their attention on me so they wouldn't notice you. I was so relieved when Baha happened to casually move into that position to provide you cover as you approached us."

Ray was now holding his gun on the two robbers. "Don't move. I will finish you off if you do," he told them. He kicked their guns out of reach, and Baasim picked them up.

"What are we going to do with them?" asked Baasim.

"We are going to take them to their vehicle," replied Ray. Turning to the two, Ray said, "Okay, you jerks, what type of vehicle are you driving?"

"A USA military jeep," one replied.

"How many people have you robbed," asked Ray.

"About five."

"Well, I didn't kill you so you can drive; how far is your jeep from here?" asked Ray.

"It's about a quarter of a mile from here."

"Are you Americans?"

"Yes, sir."

"You bastards! Now start walking! Take us to your vehicle, and start walking fast—I am in a hurry to see you leave." Baasim and Ray followed them to their jeep. When they got to the jeep, Ray searched it and sure enough they had a lot of stolen cash. Ray also found three rifles and four revolvers. Ray and Baasim took them, as well as the stolen money.

"Get going! And I don't want to see you again—if I do, you will probably need a mortician! Get the hell out of here."

"Are you going to keep our guns?"

"What kind of a question is that? You must think we just got off the carrot wagon? I will tell you where they are going to be at, though," said Ray.

"You will?"

"Ya—you can find them at the bottom of the Ken River. Now get going!" said Ray.

As Baasim and Ray were walking back, Baasim said, "Well, another exciting day in India's jungle! Boy, that 44 Magnum is hell on people; just the noise will scare the crap out of you."

Baasim and Ray reached the trailer, and there was Baha quietly eating, which reminded Ray. "Baasim, you were just starting to cook the deer meat."

"That's right. It will be awhile before we can resume cooking it. The fire went out. I will start it again, and then we can eat."

It was almost time to go to bed. This would be the first time Ray would be sleeping in the jungle. Ray noticed the cots they would be sleeping on were on each side of the trailer, folded out and about two feet off the ground. Ray certainly admired all the little things the special trailer was equipped with. In time, Ray and Baasim had their dinner of meat and some canned beans.

A moment after their dinner, Ray said, "Well, it's time to hit the sack. See you in the morning, Baasim." Just about that time, Baha came over and gave an elephant kiss to his new friend. Ray smiled and said, "Thanks, Baha."

"Good night and see you in the morning, Ray," Baasim said. "This has been a very exciting hunting trip so far. I just wonder what else could happen to us as we proceed." Baasim paused and casually added, "Ray, you Californians can sure shoot. Again you came to my rescue." With that they retired for a good night's sleep.

CHAPTER 18

OFF TO TIGER COUNTRY

Baasim and Ray were up early the next day. A quick breakfast and they were soon on their way to resume their trek up the Ken River trail.

At this point, Ray was starting to get really excited, although part of him was also getting very lonesome from missing much of Shannon. Again he opened the locket and looked at her picture. As he closed the locket, Baasim said, "Ray, are you missing Shannon? Hopefully we will have some luck and you can get back home a little early."

"That would be great if it could happen that way. We will just have to wait and see how things play out," replied Ray.

"Ray, you need to be on the lookout for signs in another hour. We will be getting into some pretty good tiger country," said Baasim. "We will stop in about two hours. Baha can have his water and we can rest a little."

The jungle was all alive from the peacocks' beautiful calls and all the monkeys roaming in the trees. Looking around, Ray noticed a big, wild water buffalo just off the trail staring at them as they went by. Ray liked the slow speed that Baha was taking, enabling him to pay attention to the surrounding areas while looking for any signs of a tiger—and Baha was doing the driving.

Baasim and Ray were intensely inspecting the sides of the trail for any signs that a tiger may have left. They were approaching the two hours that Baasim indicated as time for break, when Ray suddenly said, "Stop, Baha...!"

"Ray, what's wrong? Do you see something?" asked Baasim.

"Ya, Baasim. I see the shedding of the bark of a tree, which you mentioned is a sign of a tiger marking its territory," replied Ray.

The two moved down and went to get a closer look. Sure enough after examining the tree, they noticed tiger tracks leading to the Ken River.

Since Baha needed water, Baasim unhitched him from the trailer, and the three followed the tiger tracks to the Ken River. When they reached the edge of the river, they could tell by all the tracks that the tiger had visited the river at that spot. Baha took his time in with the water.

The three soon went back to the trailer. Ray and Baasim took out their guns, secured Baha so he wouldn't drift far from the trailer, and then headed back to the river to follow the tiger tracks. As it appeared there had been rain in the area recently, the tracks were easy to make out and follow.

Baasim and Ray spent about an hour following the tracks, which eventually crossed the Ken River trail and heading away from the river.

"We are lucky to find tiger tracks that appear to be pretty recent. Let's go back to the trailer and Baha. We will travel up to the spot where the tracks cross the Ken River trail, then we will make camp and resume tracking in the morning," said Baasim.

"That's sounds like a good plan," confirmed Ray.

Back with Baha and the trailer, Baasim hitched up Baha and they were on their way. At the spot with tiger tracks, they stopped and made camp.

"Ray, could you round up some wood so we could get a fire going?" Baasim said. "We could use it to heat up some canned ham and pork and beans for dinner tonight," said Baasim.

Ray went and gathered some wood for a fire. Dinner was started and before long they were eating. "Baasim, I noticed you have American canned products, like the ones I eat at home."

"I always thought these are the best, so I always have them on hunting trips," replied Baasim. "Well, Ray, you had your first look of real tiger tracks. Hope you are excited."

"I am excited—so what's the plan for tomorrow?" asked Ray.

"We would follow the tracks to see where they would lead us. We will know if they're something we should pursue. Does that sound okay?" Baasim said.

"Sounds good to me. I guess we should hit the sack. Good night, Baasim."

"Ray, could you put a little more wood on the fire? It would be good to have a little light around the camp. And— aren't you forgetting something?" Baasim said.

"I don't think so.... Oh, I know what you are getting at!" said Ray.

Ray got up and went to Baha, gave him a hug on his trunk, and in return Baha gave Ray his usual kiss using his trunk. That had everybody settled in for the night.

After a couple of hours, a loud roar startled Ray and Baasim. They jumped up, only to hear the roar several times more.

"Ray, what you just heard was the mighty roar of the Bengal tiger!" said Baasim. "It is not too far from here. It appeared to come from the direction of the tracks."

They then both went back to sleep.

The next morning called for a quick breakfast. Again, they heard the frightening roar of a Bengal tiger, which sounded close from their location. The tiger appeared to be at the east, the same direction the tracks were headed as Baasim said.

Quickly taking out their rifles and backpacks, they prepared to follow the tiger tracks. Baasim had a special canvas blanket put over Baha's back. The canvas blanket had pouches on each side to carry food and miscellaneous supplies, in case they were to have to stay overnight, or several days, depending on what they found as they followed the tiger tracks.

After about two hours following the tracks, they came to a clearing.

"Let's stop here and do some observing," Baasim said. He could see the tracks were headed across the clearing. "I believe that's a castle about 100 yards across the clearing. It's covered with thick jungle foliage, making it hard to see."

"The castle appears small. Do you think the tiger is using it as a den?" asked Ray.

"This castle was used as protection by clans or tribes when they battled each other. The castle provided enough advantage to the ones using it. But you are right: these castles in the Ken River area are not big like European castles. And I also believe a tiger is using the castle as a den as you said."

Ray took out his binoculars to scan the area; he could barely make out the castle with all the jungle overgrowth. In time, he noticed what appeared to be a dead deer from antlers sticking out of some brush. "Look over there," he told Baasim, pointing out to an area 100 yards right of the castle.

"That appears to be a tiger kill. It's a sambar deer," confirmed Baasim. "They are big; sometimes they can weigh seven hundred pounds. From what I can see, there is a lot more to eat. The tiger will be back to continue eating what it had killed. Ray, this could be a lucky find."

"Well, what's the plan, Baasim?" asked Ray.

"We will stay here tonight," replied Baasim. "We will get into shooting position at dawn, facing the castle and the dead deer. If the tiger shows up, you may just get a shot at it."

"It's about 100 yards to the castle, the same for the dead deer. It should be an easy shot, unless I panic," confirmed Ray.

"Ray, I know how you shoot. You are not the panicky type. It's midafternoon. Let's keep an eye on the castle and the dead deer. It would be a rare case, but the tiger may show up this time of day to eat off the deer. From now on we should be very quiet; we should just whisper to each other to communicate. Remember, a tiger has excellent hearing," said Baasim.

Thus the hunt turned into a waiting game, and time ran pretty fast. At four o'clock, Ray again took out his binoculars to scan the area. This time, he noticed that an area at the foliage appeared to have been pressed to form a path. His experience at trapping taught him this indicated an animal using the path frequently.

Ray whispered to his guide, "Baasim, look at the castle. There is definitely something going in and out of what appears to be the castle entrance. The foliage bears a path in it."

"You are right. By the size of the path, I could say it's something big, like a tiger. You are truly an observant hunter, one of the best hunters I have ever guided," Baasim replied.

Ray scanned the area again, especially where the deer lay. There was still plenty of sunlight, too. Baasim was hidden in a jungle brush where he couldn't be noticed, while Ray was in a little clearing so he could easily observe the area and be ready to shoot if the tiger showed up. Soon, Ray noted some movement at the castle, but he could not make out what it was.

Ray readied his rifle and put his scope on 9 power. The optical quality of his rifle scope was much better than his binoculars. He proceeded to take a shooting position.

"Something is moving around at the castle," whispered Ray, his heart beating rapidly, before he reminded himself to calm down. He sensed this could be the moment he had waited for and dreamed of for so many years.

"Be patient, Ray. If it's a tiger, let him show himself fully, he may have a curiosity problem," advised Baasim.

Ray kept looking at the castle area, and then it happened: the Bengal tiger came out of the foliage overgrowth and showed himself to Ray. The tiger headed over to the deer, intending to eat. Baasim stayed out of sight but he had seen the tiger. The tiger suddenly turned its head and looked in the direction where Ray was. He paused for about 30 seconds and then headed towards Ray; at this point, he was about 75 yards away.

He was now facing Ray directly, and as Ray had his rifle scope trained on the tiger, Ray suddenly noticed something and whispered to Baasim, "Baasim, he has a necklace with a ruby hanging from his neck."

Baasim whispered back to Ray, "Oh, my God it does! This tiger is part of the legend of the Bengal ruby."

Ray still had his rifle trained on the tiger; the tiger kept approaching Ray, slowly.

"Baasim, I can't shoot if he has the ruby necklace. We need to find out if the legend is true. I will shoot him if I think he is going to attack," said Ray.

"Okay, Ray. I will leave the decision up to you, but don't be foolish—shoot him if our lives are at stake," replied Baasim.

The Bengal tiger was still approaching Ray. Then it stopped about 100 feet away, gave Ray a real good look, before making such mighty roar that echoed through the jungle and scared the hell out of Baasim and Ray. However, Ray still managed not to shoot. On the other hand, the tiger stood there as if committing the image of Ray in its memory. Then it calmly turned around and went back to the deer that it killed to satisfy its hunger.

Ray and Baasim had just witnessed the most unique situation that could ever happen on a Bengal tiger hunt: a tiger came to within 100 feet of them, and calmly turned around and walked away from them.

"Baasim, what do you make of what we just went through?" asked Ray.

"Boy, you sure were calm and composed under the situation! Most hunters would have pulled the trigger!" replied Baasim excitedly.

"Another 50 feet closer and I would have decided to pull the trigger. You know, Baasim, your uncle Acharya told me on the airplane that I may have trouble pulling the trigger on such a beautiful animal; besides, it had a ruby necklace hanging from its neck. Which means this tiger is part of the legend of the Bengal ruby; I just couldn't pull the trigger."

"Ray, there is no doubt this hunting trip is full of surprises, and it looks like we are not done yet: if the legend is true, then it follows that the tiger will visit you again," said Baasim.

"You think so? That would be hard to believe," replied Ray.

"I believe he came that close to you to use his senses of sight and smell to always remember you since you were the first human that he had seen; hence, if the legend is true he will visit you again," Baasim said, smiling at Ray.

"Well, it's a little late to head back to the trailer, and Baha is anchored about 200 yards from here. I think we should just spend the night here, since we have all the supplies we need," said Ray.

"Yes, I think that sounds like the best choice we have. We could set up camp were we left Baha."

With that, the two headed back to where Baha was. Ray quickly went up to Baha and gave him a hug; that excited Baha so much that in return, he gave Ray one of his elephant kisses, giving off his screeching sound that indicated he was happy. Ray proceeded to get some wood for a fire to heat up some canned food for their dinner.

In time, the two discussed their plan for the next day.

"I think we should head back to the Ken River trail and pick up the trailer," said Baasim. "From there we'd head south along the river to pursue another tiger. I have not been that far up the Ken River trail before on previous tiger hunts. There is also a village up there that I have never visited. It may be good time to drop in and visit those villagers. Maybe they would know about any recent Bengal tiger sightings in the area."

"That sounds like a good plan, Baasim. After today, I wonder what kind of excitement we will have tomorrow," said Ray.

Soon it was getting a little dark. "Tonight will be a beautiful night in the Indian jungle," said Baasim.

"Why is tonight so special?" Ray asked.

"The jungle will be lighted up with all its beauty by the full moon. It just brings out all the green colors—you just wait and you will see," said Baasim.

Baasim and Ray were soon done eating. They set up their cots, and they were just about ready to hit the sack.

"You are right. The full moon brings out the beauty of the jungle, along with all that sound from animal activity," said Ray.

"Ray, have your 44 Magnum revolver handy, just in case an animal gets a funny idea—you know what I mean," said Baasim.

In time, everything was calm. The jungle was lit up because of the full moon and clear skies; it was as if a light bulb were turned on. Baasim was already sound asleep, but Ray was cherishing the moment as he lay on his cot, taking in all the jungle had to offer at the moment, just so beautiful and so quiet. As he lay there, Ray was thought of his family back home, especially of his blue-eyed brunette wife. He missed her so much, and he hoped she was taking good care of his mom and dad. It was ten o'clock when Ray finally fell asleep.

At twelve o'clock, Ray felt something pulling him out of his sleep. He thought he heard a little sound that resembled the purring of a cat. Slowly opening his eyes, he was terrified—but checked it fast from becoming a full panic—to find the purring sound was coming from a Bengal tiger lying right next to his cot. In a moment, they stared at each other; just then, the tiger gave Ray's hand a lick to confirm he was Ray's friend. Ray was not scared, even when the tiger opened its mouth to reveal carnivorous teeth about three inches long. Ray was very excited about the tiger being there alongside of him. The full moon's light enabled him to confirm that it was the tiger that he had seen previously. It had the necklace with the ruby mounted in gold about 1½ inches in diameter. Ray considered petting the tiger; once he mustered enough courage, he reached over and stroked its neck. The tiger seemed to like it.

Ray suddenly found himself in a different world; he wanted to cherish this special moment with the Bengal tiger. Ray continued to pet the big cat; in return, the tiger put his head towards Ray and gave him a lick on his forehead. Ray felt the bond between the two of them, he was certain that the legend of the Bengal ruby was true, now proven beyond any doubt. Ray leaned a little closer and whispered into the tiger's ear, "I will name you Bengal Ruby."

After that the tiger put its paw on Ray's chest and gave him another lick on his forehead before backing away into the jungle. The bonding of Ray and the Bengal tiger was done, and Ray spent 30 minutes in close contact with his dream animal, the Bengal tiger. Soon, Ray went back to sleep.

Morning arrived and the jungle awakened with all the wildlife sounds. Starting up, Ray couldn't wait to tell Baasim what happened the night before.

"Good morning, Baasim. Did you have a good night's sleep?" said Ray.

"Ya, Ray. I slept like a baby. How about you, did you sleep okay?" replied Baasim.

"I experienced the most wonderful night in the Indian jungle that one could ever ask for," said Ray.

Baasim had a puzzled look on his face. "Ray, what was so wonderful about last night that you sound so excited?" he inquired.

"Well, I slept alongside a Bengal tiger, or you might say he came to be by me. He just happened to pay me a visit while I was sleeping. He awakened me with his purr and then licked my hand," said Ray.

"Before you say anything, I'll say first of all I am not dreaming or kidding. He spent about 30 minutes with me, I petted him and he liked it, he licked my forehead, and I whispered into his ear. Come over where my cot is and I will show you something next to my cot," Ray said.

At Ray's cot, he pointed down to the dirt next to his cot. "Baasim, what do you see in the dirt down by my cot?" asked Ray.

"Holy smokes, Ray, those are tiger tracks! Did he have the ruby necklace hanging from his neck?"

"Ya, he did, so I guess the legend of the Bengal ruby has come to be true. I whispered into his ear that I am naming him Bengal Ruby," said Ray.

"Ray, this hunting adventure is full of surprises I sometimes wonder how it's going to end.

"Well right now we should pack up and go back to the Ken River trail, pick up the trailer, and head south to pursue another tiger that maybe you can shoot for your trophy," said Baasim.

With that they got Baha ready and made their way back to the Ken River trail. They needed around a two-hour trip to get back to the wagon.

CHAPTER 19

RAY ESCAPES DEATH

A fter about two hours, Ray and Baasim finally made it to the trailer. Baasim hitched up Baha and they were now on their way south up the Ken River trail in pursuit of another tiger.

Baasim reminded Ray to be on alert for any signs a Bengal tiger was in the area. "Also have your gun handy and your 44 magnum belted on," he added.

"In about three hours we will stop and give ourselves a little break. It will be pretty hot, probably over 100 degrees. We could go to the Ken River and get refreshed," said Baasim.

"Baasim, do you think Bengal Ruby will pay me a visit again?" asked Ray.

"He will pay you a visit if for some reason you are in danger. If the legend of the Bengal ruby is true, that's when he will show up to protect you. We will just wait and see, although nothing will surprise me anymore on this hunting trip," replied Baasim.

Ray was again looking at the locket with Shannon's picture, wondering how things were going back home. He was missing Shannon so much. Baasim noticed Ray looking at the locket.

"Ray, I know what you are thinking, but I am also missing my family back in New Delhi, so you are not alone," said Baasim.

Back home Saturday morning at the Johnson ranch, Shannon, Paul and Mary, with Denise and Joeseph, were over for breakfast. It had become a tradition for Shannon to have them all over for breakfast on Saturdays. The menu was Portuguese linguica and eggs, Joseph's favorite. It was a good time for all of them to discuss current events around the ranch and the community.

As they were all eating, Shannon said, "I went to Lodi Mold the other day to talk to Fred Sunday and Ray Jensen. I updated them on Ray's last telegram about how he got two leopard trophies after saving the life of a woman and that of his guide. I also mentioned that there would be no more telegrams until they returned from the tiger hunt."

"Well, what did they have to say—were they excited?" asked Paul.

"They were, Dad, but they also cautioned how dangerous the situation must have been for him," replied Shannon. "I told them I would keep them up-to-date if anything else occurred, while also reminding them I should be hearing from Ray after about four weeks, maybe less if he had luck getting a tiger early in his hunt."

"It will sure be good to have Ray back here again. I sure miss my best friend," said Joeseph.

With those words, Shannon found she couldn't hold her own tears back. Her friend Denise held her tightly then, saying, "Shannon, time will pass fast. Before you know it you two will be making love and trying to give grandchildren to Mary and Paul."

At this point, everybody was now in tears. Shannon was surrounded by her closest friends, along with Paul and Mary who she considered her mom and dad. They all calmed down and comforted Shannon some more, and eventually they all left from their Saturday breakfast with Shannon.

Back in India, Ray and Baasim were intently looking for signs of a tiger. After about three hours of traveling, Baasim had Baha stop so they could go to the Ken River to rest and refresh themselves. The river was only about 1/8 of mile in from the trail. At the river, Ray looked carefully around the banks and in the river to see if any mugger crocodiles were around looking for an easy dinner. Ray determined it was safe so he and Baasim made the most of the cool water. Baha was back in his playful mood, spraying water at them.

Baasim decided he and Baha would get ahead of Ray to have the trailer ready for the resumption of their journey.

"I will be there in a little while. I just like to cool off a little longer," said Ray.

"Take your time. You'll need it. It is a very hot day, must be over 100 degrees," Baasim cried back.

After 15 minutes, Ray strapped his 44 Magnum onto his waist and followed Baasim and Baha at the trailer. Along the way, he noticed some tracks off to the side of the trail. Inspecting them closely, he thought for sure they were from a leopard. Looking up, he suddenly saw a leopard looking at him about 100 feet away.

The leopard immediately charged Ray; at full speed, it leapt at Ray from about 15 feet away. Ray thought for sure this would be his last living day on Earth; it was just too fast to give him time to draw his 44 Magnum revolver. Ray's quick response was that he knew the leopard, being in midair, couldn't change direction, so he hit the ground and rolled to the side of the leopard's line of attack. As he hit the ground, he heard a loud roar and a desperate hissing sound from the leopard. Recovering his sense of direction and his revolver now drawn, Ray saw what was happening: a full-blown tiger-leopard fight, and in about 30 seconds, the leopard, soundly defeated, lay dead on the ground.

Ray lay on the ground smiling once he realized Bengal Ruby just saved his life. The tiger slowly approached Ray who was still lying on the ground, lowered its head and licked Ray's forehead, and put its paw on his shoulder before lying down beside him to acknowledge its new human friend. Ray knelt in front of his tiger friend and gave him a big hug, and the two stayed there just enjoying each other's company.

Hearing the commotion, Baasim came running toward the source of the noises, only to stop about 50 feet from Ray and the tiger. Baasim smiled seeing the two together. He realized Ray's dream had come true beyond his wildest imagination, and he had made a friend with a Bengal tiger, his most loved and respected big cat.

Eventually Ray got up; the big tiger sat on its hind quarters, raised its body, and put both paws on Ray's shoulders as if to say goodbye. Ray put his arms around Bengal Ruby and they stayed in that position for about 30 seconds. Bengal Ruby pulled away, gave Ray a big lick on his face, and calmly walked into the jungle and disappeared.

Ray stood there and thinking of the experience. He noticed Baasim standing about 50 feet away. The guide walked towards Ray. "Did you see what just happened?" asked Ray.

"I sure did, Ray. If I didn't see it, I wouldn't have believed it. A wild Bengal tiger giving you, his friend, a hug and protecting you from danger," replied Baasim.

"I can't believe it; it will be exciting to tell your uncle Acharya about how the tiger's actions proved that the legend of the Bengal ruby is true," Ray said excitedly.

"Ray, how are you going to explain to Shannon that you were kissed by someone else?" Baasim said, smiling at Ray.

"Well, I will just tell her the kiss reminded me how much I missed her and how beautiful she is. She will probably say who in the hell was it. And I will calmly say my other love, a Bengal tiger. And then you will have to explain what you saw, so she wouldn't think I have lost my brains," said Ray.

Baasim laughed and said, "Ray, I will tell her it was the most beautiful experience that I have ever, ever, witnessed in all my years of being a hunting guide—a man hugging a Bengal tiger, becoming friends."

After calming down, Ray and Basin went to look at the dead leopard.

"Look, the leopard has the ruby necklace in its mouth," said Ray. "He tore it away during the fierce fight for his life."

"Ray, you might as well take the ruby. Maybe we can show it to the villagers and tell them what happened. I have never been to this village, but I plan to stop and ask if they have seen any tiger activity in the area," said Baasim.

Ray took the gold-mounted ruby and they went back to the trailer where Baha was waiting for them. In no time, the party was back into the Ken River trail.

After a couple of hours of travel, Baasim told Ray, "Look, there is the village I told you about, the one I have never visited."

"Do you think they speak English at this village?" asked Ray.

"In about five minutes we will find out. I will first ask if we could talk to the leader of the village," replied Ray.

Looking around entering the village, Ray thought it appeared pretty civilized. Their living quarters were made out of wood, and he noticed they had a well to draw water from in the middle of the village.

The villagers were looking intently at Baasim and Ray as they entered the village, probably because over 10 feet tall Baha was very intimidating to them.

After stopping Baha, Baasim moved down his trailer seat and walked over to one of the villagers, Ray with him.

"I would like to talk to the leader of the village," said Baasim, addressing the villager.

"Wait here. I will get him," the villager replied.

"Well, that answers my question—they appear to be an English-speaking village," said Ray.

The villager soon came back with the leader of the village who introduced himself as Adjit Singh. Baasim introduced himself and Ray to him.

"How may I be of help to you?" Adjit asked.

"I am a hunting guide. We were wondering if you have seen any Bengal tigers in the area?" said Baasim.

"I am not aware of any sightings, but I have two villagers that may be able to help you," replied Adjit. With that, he sent the villager to fetch the two men who soon arrived with the villager.

One man told Baasim and Ray, "There is a known tiger area located by an ancient castle about 5 miles back. The tiger uses the castle as one of his dens."

"How do you know he is still using it as a den?" Ray asked.

"Well, my partner and I practiced the ancient legend of the Bengal ruby by placing a ruby necklace around the tiger's neck," the man replied.

Ray stood there in amazement, and told the villagers, "I believe we've seen that tiger. We also saw the ruby hanging from its neck, so I chose not to shoot it knowing of the legend."

The villager said, "Have you had any more contact with the tiger?"

"Yes; the first night he paid me a visit while I was sleeping. It was an incredible experience. Today he saved my life from an attacking Indian leopard," replied Ray.

The villagers appeared to be getting a little nervous for some reason, and asked, "What happened today?"

Baasim was also getting a little nervous from the questioning by the villagers, but Ray answered the question.

"He killed the leopard and saved my life, just like the legend said that he will protect the human that he makes first eye contact with."

"So is the tiger still alive?"

"Oh, yes! I would never kill that tiger! He is my friend. But during the fight with the leopard, the gold-mounted ruby was ripped off its neck by the leopard." Ray then showed the ruby to the villagers.

At that point, the four villagers excused themselves for a while and went to talk with each other.

Baasim whispered to Ray, "I don't like the situation we seem to be in right now."

"You think we are in trouble?" asked Ray.

"Yes, Ray. I think we have violated some part of the legend," replied Baasim.

At that point, Baasim and Ray noticed a group of about ten villagers coming toward them.

"Baasim, you are right. Something is going on—I guess we are about to find out what," said Ray.

Adjit said to Baasim and Ray, "I have disappointing news for both of you."

Ray, starting to get angry, said, "What the hell is this disappointing news you are talking about?"

Adjit explained, "Since you possess the ruby that the tiger had hanging from his neck, and since the tiger is still living, you must get the ruby back onto the tiger's neck so the legend may continue. Until the ruby is hanging from the tiger's neck again, you will be retained here at this village."

Ray angrily said, "How do you expect us to do that? That is next to impossible!"

Adjit then responded to Ray's angry comment. "You damn Americans think you are so great! Now see if you can figure out how you are going to get that ruby on the tiger's neck again."

"Well, let me tell you something: Baasim has a brother who, when we don't show up in about four weeks, is going to start wondering where we are, and who knows who he will bring looking for us."

Baasim said, "Yes, my brother knows the route that I use when I guide hunters on a tiger hunt, and he will come looking for Ray and me."

At that point, the villagers rushed Ray and before he could respond, they had taken his 44 Magnum revolver from him. They then showed Baasim and Ray to their designated living quarters.

Adjit said, "You will have all the conveniences that the villagers have, but the living quarters will be well guarded. You will always be watched closely, so don't try to get away."

Ray and Baasim were held prisoners until they could come up with a plan to get out of the village by meeting the demands of the villagers.

"We are really in a hell of a situation here to try to come up with a way to get the ruby back onto Bengal Ruby's neck. Maybe in a few days we will come up with a plan," said Ray.

"Knowing you, Ray, I bet you already have a plan," said Baasim.

"I believe I do. I will tell you about it in morning, and see what you think," replied Ray.

Morning came and, after breakfast, the two went back to their living quarters, sat down, and Ray told Baasim his plan.

"My plan is to go back to the castle ruins where we believe Bengal Ruby has his den. I will camp where we were when Bengal Ruby approached me when I was sleeping, and maybe he will come again to visit me," Ray said.

"Ray, I think that sounds like a fairly good approach. I hope it works," Baasim replied.

"I will approach Adjit and the villagers in the next day or two, to tell them what I plan to do. I believe Bengal Ruby is probably close by, as he is dedicated to keeping me safe. It means he might just follow me when I head to the castle where his den is," Ray said.

"Ray you are always thinking, and that is probably true," said Baasim.

"Anyway we have a plan, and come hell or high water, we will eventually get out of this village," replied Ray.

CHAPTER 20

RAY LEAVES TO FIND BENGAL RUBY

R ay and Baasim were on the third day as captives at
the village. After breakfast, Baasim told Ray he was
going to ask Adjit if they could go to the trailer to get the
leopard skins ready for the taxidermist. As it were, he had
to get the salt scraped off and then turn the flesh side out for
them to dry. Then the leopard skins would be ready for the
taxidermist.

The two went out of their living quarters and asked the
guard if they could see Adjit. "Yes, I will take you to him,"
said the guard.

At Adjit's living quarters, Baasim asked Adjit, "Would
it be okay if Ray and I could go to the trailer so I could
finish the preparations for the two leopard skins; that way,
the taxidermist could mount the heads as a trophy when we
get back."

"Of course that would be fine, but two villagers will have
to accompany you," Adjit responded.

"Thank you; also, we need to get some supplies to bring
back to our living quarters if that's okay," said Baasim.

"That is also fine, but the guards will have to see everything
you want to bring back and approve the items," replied Adjit.

With that, Baasim and Ray made their way to the trailer
accompanied by two guards. Once there, Baasim had the
leopard skins out, scraped the salt, and turned the skin's

flesh side out so they could be dried and later tanned by the taxidermist.

Then Ray and Baasim looked over the supplies they needed to take back to their living quarters. Mostly it was some cloth and general body hygiene items like soap, shavers, and washcloths and towels. They took the items back to their living quarters, closely followed by two villagers.

Inside their living quarters, the two talked about the plan by Ray.

"My plan is to take enough food for two weeks, taking all I need as far as camping supplies is concerned. I will use Baha and that special canvas blanket with pouches on the side for Baha to carry all the supplies."

"Ray, there is plenty of food for that trip, so take what you need. And take both rifles, in case you feel you may need to shoot a deer with your 30-30 carbine, and of course your 44 Magnum revolver," said Ray.

"Baasim, we know they are going to keep you here as a hostage to make sure I will come back for you. Don't worry: I will be back for you unless something happens, and I don't want to think about that. To me you are not only my hunting guide but a good friend, so Baasim I shall return."

"Sounds good to me. When do you want to approach Adjit about your plan?" asked Baasim.

"How about now? I would like to leave in the morning," said Ray.

"Sounds good—I will let you do all the talking to Adjit," said Baasim.

Thus the two went and asked the guards if they could see Adjit. The guards took them to Adjit's living quarters and they summoned Adjit to come outside.

"I have a plan to try to get the ruby around the tiger's neck. I would like to get your permission to go and try my plan," Ray told Adjit.

"Tell me your plan—I am very interested," Adjit replied. Ray described his plan to Adjit. "I plan to take as much as two weeks to try to get the ruby on the tiger's neck. If it's okay, I would like to leave in the morning."

"You Americans are very aggressive and clever people. I think I will grant you permission to leave in the morning. I hope your guide trusts you enough and feels comfortable that he knows you will come back for him," Adjit said.

Baasim smiled and said, "My American friend is trustworthy. I know he will be back, unless he has an accident or some other problem. I hope, Adjit, that you are as trustworthy as my friend Ray is."

"It's settled then; you shall leave in the morning. I do wish you luck," said Adjit.

Ray liked the comment from Adjit; it seemed sincere. In the morning, Ray was ready for his journey to put the ruby on the neck of Bengal Ruby, his new tiger friend. Baasim was with Ray to make sure he packed everything he needed; the guards watched every move that Ray was making.

Baasim was very emotional at this point, and said, "Ray, hopefully I will see you in two weeks or sooner if you have luck finding your tiger friend."

Ray and Baasim said goodbye, and Ray and Baha were on their way to where the tiger was first spotted. Ray felt very confident that he could find the ancient castle ruins again where the tiger had his den.

In California at the Johnson ranch, everything was going just fine. Shannon was home busy doing house cleaning and enjoying her morning. Suddenly the doorbell rang, and it was the mailman with a package to deliver from India. He needed her signature as it was sent guaranteed delivery.

Shannon didn't want to open it until her friend Denise, and Ray's mom and dad were with her. She thus called everyone and invited them over, explaining what she wanted to them.

In about 15 minutes they all arrived at the house. Joeseph happened to be home so he was also present. They went to the living room and sat down.

Shannon was ready with the package.

"Well, here it goes—thank you all for being here," she said, before opening the package. The first item was a letter from Ray that said:

Dear Shannon, I miss you so much. I can't wait to get home and have you in my arms. I mentioned in a previous telegram that I had saved the life of a woman who happened to be the leader of a village and how she wanted to give you a gift so you could always remember what I did shooting a leopard attacking her, saving her life. Shannon, this gift is a big sacrifice for the village: they were waiting for the right circumstance to give this gift to a deserving person, and they felt you, being my wife, would be that person. So Shannon, you are getting something very special. I know you will like it, and I am glad I was part of a lifesaving situation that saved Banhi Sing's life. And please say hello to everyone.

Love Ray
PS. Can't wait to see you again.

Shannon had tears flowing from her eyes after she read the letter. She proceeded to open the package and inside was a small box, with a note attached. She gently took the note and read it.

To Shannon Johnson, Ray showed all the villagers your picture in his locket that he proudly wears around his neck. I can only say this: you are a beautiful, blue-eyed, dark-haired young lady. Your husband Ray will forever be my hero, and a hero to all the villagers that I serve, and for this reason we are giving you this gift in remembrance of what your husband did for me. Accept this gift from all of us in the village. One thing, Shannon: I hope someday our paths will cross. I would welcome both you and Ray as honored guests at our village. Hope to see you sometime. Ray is writing this for me. Banhi Singh.

Shannon proceeded to open the box containing the gift from the villagers. Shannon was getting very emotional, but Denise was right by her side as she opened the lid of the wooden box. As she looked at what was in the box, she couldn't say a word. Tears were flowing from her eyes. She finally calmed down and lifted a ruby mounted in gold necklace out of the box. The ruby was about one inch in diameter.

"What a sacrifice these villagers made to give me such a gift," said Shannon.

Paul came over to Shannon to get a closer look at the necklace

"Shannon, stand up," he told her. When she did, he took the necklace from her and put it on Shannon's neck.

"Ya, Shannon, you look like a Bengal ruby—you, my daughter that Mary and I could never have. You are indeed a beautiful blue-eyed lady as Banhi Sing said in her note to you."

Shannon thanked everyone for sharing such an exciting moment.

"When Ray is back, you both need to pay that village a visit," Paul said.

"I agree, Dad; she wants our paths to cross and we should make that happen. It's the least we can do." Shannon took the necklace off and went to put it in the gun safe.

"Hey, you two amigos, it's a beautiful day—how about you get your 30-30 carbines and go practice your shooting skills?" announced Joeseph. "I don't want you to lose your shooting skills. As I have always said, you never know when you might need them." With that, Shannon and her friends went to practice shooting, and that ended the day at the ranch.

Back in India, Ray and Baha were back on the Ken River trail and traveling for about two hours. Ray always looked around to make sure everything was okay. He was also on the lookout to catch a glimpse of Bengal Ruby who might be following him, though there was no sign of the tiger. Eventually Ray stopped Baha and they went for a drink at the Ken River. This time, Baha couldn't play in deep water from all the supplies he was carrying.

Ray figured it would be another three hours before they reached the castle area. He planned to set up camp at the place the tiger had previously visited him while he was sleeping. Ray noticed the trail that headed east of the Ken River to where the castle was, indicating they were less than an hour away from it.

In time Baha and Ray reached the castle area and found where they had camped before. Ray took everything off Baha and made camp, ready to try to get the ruby necklace back onto Bengal Ruby's neck. The villagers had given Ray a new chain with the ruby attached—if only Bengal Ruby would cooperate and show up so Ray could finish what he came there for.

Ray and Baha had been camped for five days but still there were no signs of Bengal Ruby. Ray had taken walks to the clearing where he could see the castle. He scanned the area with his binoculars, still no trace of Bengal Ruby.

One night while lying on his cot, Ray considered that maybe his plan wasn't going to work. He thus made another plan to try in the morning. The plan was a little more dangerous, but he was going to give it some thought.

After breakfast the next morning, Ray thought some more of his latest plan and decided he was going to give it a try. He grabbed a Coleman camping lantern, his rifle, and his 44

Magnum revolver, along with some ammo, and headed to the clearing where he could see the castle. Ray felt lucky that at least Adjit gave him permission to bring his rifle and his 44 Magnum revolver on this trip. He looked across the clearing; with his binoculars, he could see the path that he thought a tiger was using to go in and out of the castle. When Baasim and Ray were here last time, Baasim thought for sure the tiger was using the castle as one of his dens.

Ray headed across the clearing toward the castle. When he reached the path leading to it, he stopped to think. Going into the castle ruins could be dangerous, but he also felt he had no choice but try to see if Bengal Ruby was inside. Thus Ray proceeded into the castle. He hoped that upon completing his mission, the villagers would let Baasim and him go. He knew it was a chance he had to take.

Ray walked along the path that led to the castle. When he got to what he thought was the entrance, he stopped and considered whether to go into the castle or just leave and be safe. Taking his Coleman gas lantern, he lit the wick and made his way into the castle.

Ray noticed some tiger tracks at the entrance; he had to hope it was his friend Bengal Ruby and not a different tiger. He felt sure it was Bengal Ruby, as tigers are very protective of their territory, and he had seen Bengal Ruby come out on the path that led to the castle. Thus Ray was confident that it was Bengal Ruby's den. Ray soon found himself in what appeared to be a hallway. It was dark in some areas; outside light came in every so often—it appeared to be designed to let outside light in through some openings above. As Ray ventured down the hallway, he noticed rooms to each side, and he ventured into them to look around. It appeared the rooms were used for living quarters by the ancient tribe members. Further down the hallway were rooms with several human skeletons, probably killed during battles.

Ray kept looking around to see if Bengal Ruby was following him. Ray was really hoping for that to happen, but still there was no sign of Bengal Ruby.

The hallway ended at a stairway. Venturing up, Ray came upon a big door at the top. In front of him were hallways going in two different directions away from the big door. Ray opened the door. Inside was a room full of what appeared to be tribal possessions, including gold vases, silver drinking cups, and many other precious metal objects.

He saw what appeared to be an altar, and upon approaching, a large chest on top of it. Opening it, he was greeted by the sight of precious rubies and diamonds inside. Just then, Ray sensed something was in the room with him, but dismissed the thought after looking at the rubies and diamonds again.

And then he had a big smile on his face after he heard the familiar purr sound, the same one he remembered distinctly when the tiger approached him before. Bengal Ruby was the one he sensed in the room with him. He felt the brush in his leg, and almost immediately there were two paws on the altar; Bengal Ruby was now by Ray's side looking at Ray, who was only too overjoyed to see his tiger friend again.

Ray gave the big cat a big hug and the cat gave Ray a big lick on his face; they were united again. Ray knelt down to face his tiger friend, and Bengal Ruby again gave Ray the usual big lick on his forehead, and Ray gave him another hug. Out of a box, Ray pulled the ruby necklace and placed it on the tiger's neck.

With a Buck knife, Ray cut some of the tiger's fur and had it in the same box that previously held the ruby necklace. The tiger's fur would serve as proof to the villagers that he made contact with his tiger friend. Hopefully they would believe he had put the ruby necklace on the tiger's neck and the legend could continue. Ray closed the chest. It would normally be a treasure hunter's dream to find that chest, but

Ray was not there on a treasure hunt; his treasure and love was standing right next to him, his tiger friend Bengal Ruby. Soon Ray and his tiger friend made their way back to the entrance of the castle. Ray closed the big door and left everything in the room as he found it. Outside in broad daylight, Ray took another precious look at his friend Bengal Ruby. Ray was standing and petting his friend. Bengal Ruby stood on its hindquarter and put its paws on Ray's shoulders. Ray gave the tiger a hug as if saying goodbye. Ray felt this might be the last time he would ever see Bengal Ruby.

The tiger let out a monstrous roar as if to say goodbye, and then slipped away into the foliage of the jungle. Ray went back to where he was camped. He greeted Baha with a big hug on his trunk, and Baha gave Ray one of his elephant kisses on his forehead. Ray told Baha, "You and Bengal Ruby are good, beautiful friends. Tomorrow we leave for the village and hope everything will be settled about the legend of the Bengal ruby."

Ray was talking to Baha as if the elephant could understand every word he was saying. He knew Baha could sense what's behind the tone of his voice, and that's all Ray cared about. He was happy and excited at the prospect of being back at the village so his friend Baasim would stop worrying.

After a quick breakfast the next morning, Ray and Baha were on their way back to the village. Ray couldn't wait to give the good news to everybody about getting the ruby necklace back onto the tiger's neck.

CHAPTER 21

RAY HEADS BACK TO THE VILLAGE

A round 45 minutes into their journey, Ray and Baha reached the trail and headed south towards the village. Ray was thinking how happy Baasim would be to see him and Baha, especially after learning that the ruby necklace was back on the tiger's neck. Four hours away from the village, man and elephant stopped for rest and water at the Ken River. The blistering heat meant longer rest time, extending their travel time to five hours on their way back to the village.

Ray hoped his last adventure would put an end to Baasim and himself being held captive by the villagers. While enjoying the beauty of the Indian jungle, he wondered if his trip was coming to a close. Two more weeks and he would have been there six weeks, about the time set for his hunting expedition by SHARMA HUNTING OUTFITTERS.

After 30 minutes refreshing amid the hot, humid jungle heat, Baha lifted Ray back onto his neck and they were on their way.

Along the way, Ray opened his locket and looked at Shannon's picture. He recalled their last night together, making love on that strong bed that Shannon was always worried would break. He smiled for the precious memories that he and Shannon shared. Then he again remembered her words at the airport, that the locket contained some not so obvious information on it. He inspected the locket again, taking special note of the weird-looking writing at the back of the locket. He still could not figure out the information she was talking about. Ray thought the strange characters were nothing but a special manufacturing code.

Time went by pretty quickly and before Ray realized it, the village was in sight. Ten minutes later they were entering the village. After seeing Ray and Baha, some of villagers immediately went to get Adjit and Baasim to tell them Ray was back. Baha knelt down so Ray could get off his neck. Ray gave his elephant friend a big hug and said, "Baha, thanks for the ride. You are beautiful." Happily, Baha let out his screeching elephant sound that could be heard for a mile. Baasim was the first to arrive to greet Ray.

"How did it go, are you okay?" asked Baasim.

"It went good and I am okay. I am real glad to be back with you so you wouldn't have to worry anymore. Now let's see what the village leader would think after I told him what happened," replied Ray.

In time they saw Adjit and the two promoters of the Bengal ruby legend coming towards them.

"We are about to find out what they are going to do when you tell them," said Baasim. He also whispered to Ray, "Did you make contact with Bengal Ruby and have the necklace onto his neck?"

"Yes," Ray whispered back.

"Great! We shall see what they have to say. They are just about here," said Baasim, smiling.

Adjit and the two villagers finally arrived. "Well, Ray, it's good to see you made it back," Adjit said.

"Yes, especially so that my friend Baasim won't have to worry about me getting back to the village."

"Did your plan work as you wanted?" asked Adjit.

"Yes, with a little modification," replied Ray.

Adjit looked at Ray and said, "Well, I must assume you got the ruby necklace around the tiger's neck with that answer." "I did get the necklace around Bengal Ruby's neck," confirmed Ray.

"That sounds interesting. Tell us more," said Adjit.

"For five days I made camp but the tiger never came. Finally I decided I was going into the castle that Baasim and I assumed was Bengal Ruby's den," said Ray.

"Sounds interesting, and exciting," Adjit commented. "Please tell us more," he added.

"Inside the castle and down a hallway I found these rooms with human skeleton remains. Further down the hallway, I came upon a stairway. Taking it up, I came upon a large double door to a room. I opened the door and inside were valuable items, including an altar with a large chest on top of it. When I opened the chest I heard a purr; my instinct told me it was a tiger purr I had known before when he visited me while I was sleeping. It wasn't long before Bengal Ruby was by my side," said Ray.

Baasim was truly amazed by the incredible story they were hearing from Ray; he hoped Adjit was going to believe his friend's story.

"Go on with your story. It sounds interesting," prodded Adjit, now smiling.

"Adjit, you must understand that because of the legend of the Bengal ruby, this tiger has become my friend, and he will protect me from harm. I even think he is watching us right now.

"After he licked my face and I gave him a hug, I took the necklace out of the box that you gave me and placed the necklace on his neck. That means the legend of the Bengal ruby now continues," said Ray.

Adjit looked at the other two villagers. "Well—what do you think of Ray's story?" he asked them.

"How do we know if we can believe his story? There is no real proof," said one of the two.

The response had Ray furious, and Baasim could sense his friend was just about ready to explode.

Baasim thought it was wise to step into the conversation at this point.

"You have to trust what Ray had just told you; without that it could be a lost cause for him. I can tell you he is very trustworthy. I hope that you would understand. Well, Ray, do you have any more to say?" said Baasim.

At this point, Ray had a loud, angry tone in his voice.

"Yes. You jackasses think I didn't expect you to come up with something like this. Well then, let me show you something," he said, revealing the box that had contained the necklace and pulling out the tiger's fur from Bengal Ruby. "I did this purposely anticipating the doubt you would harbor about my story. What do you think now?"

The three conferred with each other. "Ray, I am sorry but your story has too many possibilities for you to mislead us," said Adjit.

Ray was getting madder by the second, and Baasim told Ray, "Let's calm down. Let's see if we could come to some sort of an agreement."

Still furious, Ray asked, "Has any of you been to the castle that I am talking about?"

"Yes, I have been in that castle," said one of the villagers.

"Have you been in the room at the top of the stairs?" Ray said in an intimidating voice.

"Yes, I have been in that room," replied the same villager.

"Did you see the chest on top of the altar?" continued Ray.

"Yes, I have seen the chest and I know what's in it. Can you tell me what's in it, since you say you opened it?"

Still in an angry voice, Ray replied, "Yes—the chest is full of diamonds and rubies."

The villager was quiet for a while. "Well, that proves you were in the room of valuable items," the same villager said finally.

"I left everything as I found it. My only interest was my friend the tiger that I named Bengal Ruby," Ray said.

"Ray, unfortunately you will be retained here until we see the tiger with the ruby necklace hanging from its neck," said Adjit. "Sorry, but that's the way it has to be, and this subject is closed," he concluded.

"Adjit, I believe trouble will be heading to this village because of your actions. I wish you wouldn't be so stubborn, but we will leave this village. Baasim's brother will come looking for us sooner or later, and then you may have a price to pay. This village will lose some dignity in the process, but I hope there won't be any lives taken. But it may come to that, and I wouldn't be surprised if my tiger friend won't be involved in getting me and Baasim out of this village, and that could mean a death to some villagers."

"We will see," replied Adjit, smirk on his face, before walking away.

"That's right, Adjit, we will see," Ray said after Adjit.

Back to their living quarters, Ray and Baasim couldn't be in a more depressed mood. The villagers needed hard proof that the tiger had the ruby necklace back on his neck. Baasim and Ray knew this meant the tiger had to show himself to the villagers.

"I am sorry it didn't work out, Baasim; right now I can't think of what else we could do to leave this village. We will just have to wait and see what your brother will do when we don't show up," said Ray.

"That's right, Ray. It is June 1. Two more weeks and we are supposed to be back from this hunting trip. I think right now my brother is already starting to suspect something has gone wrong," said Baasim.

"Basin, why do you think that?" said Ray.

"My brother knows it usually doesn't take me six weeks to get a tiger— my usual time is three weeks. So I am sure he is wondering what has happened," replied Baasim.

"I guess we will just have to wait and see what happens," said Ray.

Back in California at the Johnson ranch, everything was going smoothly. Paul had got everything planted for the part of the year.

Shannon was out in the yard mowing the lawn when she noticed the mailman coming down the driveway. She stopped the lawn mower and went to meet the mailman.

"Shannon, I have a telegram from India for you," the mailman said after greeting her. Shannon was so excited she could hardly sign for the telegram, but she finally managed and the mailman was on his way.

Shannon saw that the telegram was from Baasim's brother Aadesh who was part owner of SHARMA HUNTING OUTFITTERS. She opened the telegram to read following:

SHANNON I AM SENDING THIS TELEGRAM NOT TO ALARM YOU BUT TO LET YOU KNOW MY BROTHER BAASIM AND RAY HAVE NOT BEEN IN CONTACT WITH ME YET I DO FIND IT STRANGE FOR USUALLY MY BROTHER ONLY TAKES 3 TO 4 WEEKS TO GET A TIGER DON'T BE ALARMED I WILL KEEP YOU UP TO DATE FROM TIME TO TIME ALWAYS AADESH

Feeling anxious about what Aadesh said in the telegram, Shannon chose not to let Ray's parents know about it, not wanting them to worry. She thought everything could be okay.

Shannon gave Denise a call and asked her if she could take her to lunch at the Broiler in Lodi. Shannon needed to talk to her friend. Broiler would be a good place to talk during lunch. Shannon went and picked up Denise and they were on their way to the Broiler.

After they had ordered their lunch, Shannon opened the conversation. "You know, Denise, in two weeks it would have been six weeks since Ray has been gone on his hunting trip. I am so nervous that I have not heard from him again yet," said Shannon.

"Shannon, there is no need to panic. There is still time. I am sure everything is okay in India," said Denise.

"Denise I appreciate your optimism, but I have to tell you about a telegram I just received, and that is why I am starting to get concerned," said Shannon.

Denise had a concerned look on her face and asked, "Who sent the telegram?"

"Aadesh did. He is the brother of Ray's guide," replied Shannon.

"Well, what did he say that was so bothering to you?" asked Denise.

"He didn't want to alarm me, but he said his brother takes only three to four weeks to get a tiger. He says to keep in contact with me in the future," said Shannon.

"It might be too early to be worried at this point. Anyway you know you can count on me to help in any way," Denise assured Shannon.

The two then went on with their lunch. When they were done, Denise told Shannon, "Shannon, if there is a problem back in India you know I will be there for you. As always we will solve the problem together."

"Well, Denise, lets go to the Post Office. It's just down the street. We have to take care of what I mentioned in our conversation over lunch," said Shannon.

"Sounds great, Shannon. Let's go now and get it done," replied Denise.

Their business at the Post Office done, the two friends headed back to the Johnson ranch. They ended their day shooting their 30-30 Winchester rifles for practice.

Back at the village, Ray and Baasim were in their living quarters talking about their situation. Ray was looking at his locket and the picture of Shannon. "If my wife doesn't hear from me in two weeks as the hunt is scheduled to end, it's going to be so traumatic for her. I'm just thankful she has good family support around her. Her best friend, a tough Portuguese gal named Denise, will help her through anything that comes up."

"Ray it's so good to have a close friend like that; sounds like a lifelong relationship," said Baasim.

"They would put their life on the line for each other if the need called for it," said Ray.

"I wish Adjit was more reasonable, but it doesn't look like this situation is going to change anytime soon," said Baasim.

"It's going to take an outside person to come to our rescue; most likely it will be your brother," said Ray.

"I am certain my brother is already concerned about us not being in contact with him. I bet he has already contacted Shannon by telegram expressing his concern about not hearing from us after four weeks since we started this hunting trip," said Baasim.

"I can feel Bengal Ruby nearby watching out for me and ready to come to my aid if my life is threatened. If Adjit could only be sensible, this could be settled and we could be on our way out of here," said Ray.

Ray grabbed his binoculars and went just outside his door. There was a little clearing through the jungle and Ray noticed a rocky cliff formation. He focused his binoculars on the formation, and he couldn't believe what he was seeing: there on top of the rocky formation was a tiger looking almost directly at him, but quickly disappeared. It was about a quarter of a mile, so Ray couldn't tell if the tiger had a ruby necklace on its neck.

Ray quickly went inside to tell Baasim what he had just seen. He excitedly told Baasim, "I am going to go tell Adjit." Baasim and Ray went out the door and asked the guards if they could go see Adjit.

"We will take you to see him, but I hope it's important and not a waste of his time," one of them said.

Once out of his living quarters, Adjit said with a sarcastic voice, "What do you two want now?" Ray was furious at the tone of voice that Adjit used.

"If you saw what I had just seen, I think you would have a concern," Ray replied angrily. "Baasim and I will get out of this village sooner or later."

"What did you see that makes you feel so confident about escaping the village?" asked Adjit.

"About a quarter of a mile away, I had a quick glimpse of a Bengal tiger on a rocky cliff formation," said Ray.

"So what's your point?" said Adjit.

"I believe if I was to try and run out of here right now and some of your villagers were to try to harm me, Bengal Ruby is close by and would kill your villagers. Just like he did with the leopard that tried to kill me. It only took about 30 seconds and the leopard was dead, just like your villagers would be," said Ray.

"Ray, you should try it and see," Adjit said, the same smirk on his face.

"That kind of attitude is going to get somebody killed, but I guess you don't care. I will tell you that someday if Baasim and I don't get help I will probably roll the dice and I believe it will turn out that you will be the loser," Ray said.

"I guess we will see who wins this battle," said Adjit.

"Adjit with your chicken shit attitude you will pay a price, and I will not talk to you about this subject again. Sleep good while Bengal Ruby is lurking around this village just waiting for you to make a fatal mistake. Have sweet dreams, but your time will come and it will come soon," Ray said finally.

Baasim and Ray made their way back to their living quarter and sat down. "Well, Adjit knows one thing. I am not planning on being in this village forever," said Ray.

"I also know one thing, Ray: I wouldn't want to be on your wrong side, and you made it pretty clear what you believe is going to be the outcome," said Baasim.

The two of them relaxed in their quarters for the rest of the day. Later in the day, Ray said, "In about two weeks and still no contact made to your brother or Shannon, the whole world is going to know we are missing. Then we will wait and see what happens. I still believe Bengal Ruby will come to our rescue, or at least be a part of our rescue. We both will just have to wait and see, Baasim. I am sorry I got you into this mess," said Ray.

"Ray, you and I are friends. We are in this together, you just have to always remember that," Baasim replied.

CHAPTER 22

THE PANIC—BUT
RAY GETS A SURPRISE

R ay and Baasim were still being held captives at the village, and there appeared to be no help from the outside to help them get out of the village. The sixth week was upon them, and by this time everyone was expecting to be contacted by Ray and Baasim.

"I guarantee you, Ray, my brother is now in panic mode. I am sure he has telegrammed Shannon on what his plans are," said Baasim.

A few days later back in New Delhi, Baasim's brother and all the family members, including Acharya, were meeting to discuss the situation. "I am deeply concerned that no contact has been made; usually by this time, I would have heard from Baasim," Aadesh said.

"Perhaps it's time to contact the US embassy in New Delhi and let them know about the situation and our concerns. You should also send a telegram to Ray's wife, Shannon Johnson," said Acharya.

"I have already talked to Bob Jones, the consulate at the US embassy," replied Aadesh. "I know him well. It was he who recommended Baasim to Ray for the tiger hunt. He has already given the information to the US State Department, stating that we consider Ray Johnson missing. I have also contacted the Indian government authorities as well as the Department of Big Game. And I have also just sent a telegram to Shannon," finished Aadesh.

"Well, you have contacted all the people that should know," Acharya said.

"My plan is to start my trip in about four days, which would be July 1, to look for them; Baasim left me his hunting plan, so at least I have a starting point. I will start looking for any clues as to what might have happened to them. Hopefully we will find them safe and sound," said Aadesh.

Saturday at the Johnson ranch, Shannon was having her usual breakfast for Denise, Joeseph, and Ray's parents. Afterwards, they went about conversing and drinking coffee while watching the local news. Just then, the news broadcaster interrupted his broadcast.

"I have just received a memo that I must share," he started. "The United States State Department has issued a statement that a California hunter, Ray Johnson, along with his guide Baasim Sharma on a Bengal tiger hunt in India, has been listed as missing by the government of India. Ray Johnson is from the Sacramento Delta. He lives on a ranch just a few miles from the small town of Isleton. If anything else is reported, we at this TV station will keep the community updated," he concluded.

Upon hearing the news, Denise immediately went to Shannon to be by her best friend and provide comfort as tears flowed from Shannon's eyes. On the other hand, Joeseph went to be by Ray's parents who were trying to gather themselves over the news they just heard.

In ten minutes, everybody who heard the news of Ray being listed as missing was calling—Shannon's parents, Denise's parents, and the people at Lodi Mold Inc., including Fred Sunday, Ray Jensen, and Liz the receptionist.

Joeseph's parents were soon at the door to offer any help. Mr. and Mrs. Chin also came right in to give Shannon a big hug, offering any help they could give. Shannon and Ray's parents had calmed down a little. Then the phone rang and Shannon answered it. It was the US State Department calling to explain that the Indian and the US governments were now getting involved, promising to keep the family updated on any new developments. The State Department, however, made it clear they didn't expect any help from the Indian government. A State Department communicator shared with Shannon that the department would assist in any way possible. At this point, Shannon went into the bedroom so she could use the phone inside and talk privately to the person from the State Department.

When Shannon returned, she went straight to Paul and Mary, tears flowing like a river ready to cause a flood. She finally was able to calm down a little as she said, "Mom, Dad—do you think I have lost Ray forever?"

"Shannon, my son is a tough guy. It's going to take a real tough situation for him to give up. We need to be patient in this time of crisis," Paul assured Shannon.

Just then the mailman knocked at the door. When Shannon opened it, the mailman said, "I am so sorry to hear the news about Ray being missing. I have here a telegram from India for you to sign for." Shannon signed for the telegram and came back to the kitchen where everybody was still gathered.

"Well, I have a telegram from India, and since you are all here, I will read it to you all." Shannon then opened the envelope and started to read the message.

SHANNON SENDING YOU THIS TELEGRAM TO INFORM YOU OF MY PLAN SINCE I CONSIDER RAY AND BAASIM MISSING TO LEAVE ON JULY 1 TO TRY TO FIND THEM I JUST LET ALL GOVT AGENCIES

KNOW ABOUT THEM BEING MISSING SHANNON
I PROMISE YOU ONE THING I WILL TRY MY BEST
TO TRY TO FIND THEM OR AT LEAST SEE WHAT
HAPPENED I KNOW BAASIM'S HUNTING PLAN SO
THAT GIVES ME SOME STARTING POINT I WISH
THE SITUATION WAS BETTER BUT IT IS WHAT IT IS
ALWAYS AADESH SHARMA

Shannon stood there teary eyed after reading the message. "Well, thank you all for the support but right now I would like to just take a walk out on the ranch. Denise, could you please come with me, I just have so much to think about," she said. Shannon was so emotional and tears were flowing out profusely. Denise of course was by her distraught friend's side.

Paul went to Shannon and said, "For some reason my mind tells me everything will work out eventually. But right now you two amigos go out and have some private time together. Always remember Mary and I love you both like daughters. Go now and we will see you later."

Paul and Mary watched Shannon and Denise walk out onto the ranch. "Look at those two. They just plain love each other. That's just what Shannon needs right now, one real good friend. We need those two and Joeseph to be by our side in this sad situation," said Paul. "However, I have always been an optimistic person. I believe God has a plan that someday will bring Ray home to us and to Shannon."

"Paul, I know God is looking out for Ray as we stand here. I just know it," said Mary. "He will provide the guidance and wisdom in this very horrible situation." With that, Paul and Mary decided to go home.

Shannon and Denise went to the shooting bench. Shannon stared at the bench and said, "Denise, this spot is where Ray...told me he liked me. I looked up at him...and then he told me, 'In other words, Shannon...I have fallen in love with you.'" Denise hugged Shannon tightly. She could feel Shannon was too afraid thinking of what might have happened to Ray. "Okay, amigo, together we are going to get through this. Come hell or high water we will get Ray back. I just know God will guide us." Both were so emotional that tears just kept flowing.

In time Shannon settled down a little. "Denise, you are such a great friend. I do believe God will find a way to bring Ray back." They resumed their walk around the ranch, occasionally stopping to let Shannon reminisce about those times when she and Ray shared special moments in their early relationship.

They came and stopped on a spot that was so special to Shannon. After looking at the sky a few seconds, Shannon told Denise, "This is where Ray proposed to me. That was the hap... hap... happiest day of my life." She was so emotional she could barely get the words out. "Denise, he has to come back to me so we can continue where we left off. We have to give Paul and Mary grandchildren," she said.

"Shannon, I just know he will be found and be back in your arms." The two resumed their walk. Once they gave each other a high five gesture, as if to indicate there was some sort of agreement between them, before walking again.

They were soon at Paul and Mary's house. Inside they went to see how they were handling the situation of Ray missing. Joeseph was with Paul and Mary trying to help them understand that everybody needed to have a positive attitude about the situation.

Shannon heard Joeseph as he tried to explain, "We need to think that we will see Ray again."

Shannon followed with, "Mom, Dad, my good friend and I were discussing the issue. Denise is convinced we will see Ray again. Let's keep a positive attitude and let God guide us."

From that point on, everybody was thinking more positive. "Right now Denise and I are going to Lodi to send a telegram to Aadesh to let him know we have received his telegram. We would thank him for setting up plans to look for Ray and his brother. I want him to know of our own plans here in California. I will also send a telegram to Bob Jones, the consulate at the embassy in New Delhi. I want to make sure the US government does everything possible to help locate Ray and Baasim. I would also inquire of Aadesh any aid that he might need," Shannon said.

Before leaving for Lodi, Shannon called her parents to let them know that she and Denise would be over in about two hours. She asked her mom to call Denise's parents to ask them if they could come over to their house. They also wanted to talk to them about Ray's situation in India.

At Lodi, Shannon and Denise had two telegrams sent to Aadesh Sharma and Bob Jones, the US consulate at the embassy in New Delhi. From Lodi they proceeded to Shannon's parents. Denise's parents were already there when they arrived. As they walked into the house, Shannon's parent's immediately came to her and gave her a hug, and they all became emotional. Shannon's mom asked Shannon, "How are you handling this situation with Ray being missing?"

"Mom, I am sure we are going to get Ray back. Ray's guide's brother Aadesh Sharma is planning an expedition on July 1 to look for Ray and his brother. We will also do whatever we can from our end to help Aadesh. I have asked the US consulate to give any assistance they could to help Aadesh," replied Shannon.

Denise then entered into the conversation. "I am here to support Shannon all the way through this situation. I too am very positive—somehow, someway, we will get Ray back to California," she said.

"Well, knowing you two, I believe you will do whatever it will take to get Ray back. I just know you two together have always been determined to succeed in whatever task you set your mind to," said Denise's father. The six of them were out of the house, Shannon and Denise heading back to the Johnson ranch. All of them were still crying as the two said goodbye. "I am so sorry to have to put you all through this, but sometimes life is tough. Well, we have to get back and see how Paul and Mary are doing. I know reality is really starting to set in about Ray being missing," said Shannon.

Along the way, Shannon and Denise shared each other's thoughts about what else they could do under the situation. As the conversation kept going, they ended up with a big smile and gave each other a high five, as if they both agreed with each other's thoughts. They pulled into the ranch house driveway and went in to visit with Ray's parents.

Ray's parents seemed to be doing better at this time. That they had to live with the news of Ray being missing started to sink into their minds. "Dad, Mom, I will keep you updated as things happen, about any future plans, and if you need anything please give me a call," said Shannon.

"Paul and I need you both in our lives now more than ever. Thank you for being by us," replied Mary.

"Mom, Denise and I will be by you and support you until this situation with Ray is resolved. We both love you dearly. And when Ray gets back to us, Ray and I have some unfinished business to attend to," Shannon replied.

"What kind of business are you talking about?" Paul asked.

"That of giving you and Mom grandchildren, which will be our daily priority when he gets back," said Shannon.

Paul and Mary smiled and gave Shannon a big hug. "Dad and I appreciate your positive view. We can't wait to have grandchildren. And I know you two will get things done when God guides you through this situation," Mary said.

Once at Shannon's house, Denise bid Shannon goodbye. As Denise started to walk home, Shannon said, "Hey, amigo, thanks so much for your support."

Meanwhile back at the village, Ray and Baasim were told they had to do certain tasks in order to earn what they were getting from the villagers.

When told about the duties, Ray told Baasim, "I don't mind doing work to earn our keep. I never wanted to be a freeloader, unfortunately we are here against our will, and that just plain ticks me off."

July was approaching still nobody showed up to rescue them, a fact that started to bother Ray and Baasim. "We have to be patient in a situation like this. I know my brother has not forgotten us," Baasim reminded Ray.

"You are right. Your family appears to be so united, and I just know they are planning something to come and look for us," replied Ray.

One day Ray went out to get water from the well so he could shave, his beard getting uncomfortable. As he was washing his face and getting his shaving soap ready, he felt like looking at the picture of Shannon in the locket. Again the picture brought back wonderful memories. As he was doing so, he noticed the writing on the back of the locket as it appeared in the mirror. Looking closely, he finally managed to read the message from Shannon. He smiled broadly as he read the whole message written backwards that the mirror rendered normal and easily readable.

Ray decided against telling Baasim the locket message; he thought some information were too personal to share with Baasim.

Ray was shaved and feeling refreshed as he walked and sat down by Baasim.

"You look very happy—anything I should know about?" asked Baasim.

"I saw the tiger on the rock formation where I had seen him before while I went to clean myself at the well. Didn't have my binoculars but I know it was a tiger. I just couldn't see the ruby necklace on his neck," replied Ray.

"That's interesting. The tiger is doing its job and looking out for you. I believe you are right thinking that someday he's going to get us out of here," said Baasim.

"I believe that day is getting closer to reality," replied Ray.

"You sound so confident about us getting out of here. I certainly hope you are right. Should we go tell Adjit about the tiger sighting?" asked Baasim.

"No. I told him last time we talked I would not talk to him about it again. He will know when the day comes, and then I will remind him of my words. Adjit just may have to learn the hard way," said Ray.

CHAPTER 23

ADJIT GETS A SURPRISE

It was the first of July and still no signs of Baasim's brother Aadesh attempting to approach the villagers looking for Ray and Baasim. Ray, however, was not concerned; he knew Aadesh would show up sooner or later.

It was too hot and humid around July. One night around ten o'clock, Ray was awakened by loud talking outside. Apparently, something had happened that caused some villagers to get very excited.

Ray woke up Baasim and they went out to see what had happened. The village area was quite visible from a full moon at this time.

After they asked around, a villager explained what happened. "A Bengal tiger roamed around the village area as if looking for something, though he didn't seem to want to cause any harm," said the villager.

Ray looked down at the ground and told Baasim and the villager, "Look, the tiger tracks stopped at our entrance door. I bet I know why—he wants to know where I am."

"Yes, I am sure his keen sense of smell told him you were inside our living quarters, and that satisfied him and he left," replied Baasim, smiling.

"Hey look who is coming over," said Ray. "Adjit must be wondering what has happened with all the commotion, maybe this incident will bring him to his senses and let us leave the village."

"I wish you were right, Ray, but I highly doubt he is going to let us go. I don't think he has any senses. I guess we will soon see what he has to say," replied Baasim.

"What has happened to cause all the villagers to be so excited?" Adjit inquired after reaching their place.

"Just my tiger friend came looking for me; scared the hell out of some villagers as he roamed around here," replied Ray.

"How in hell do you know he was looking for you?" said Adjit arrogantly.

"Well, it appears he stopped right at my door for a while," said Ray.

Just then the villager guarding Ray and Baasim's living quarters arrived. "I saw the tiger, Adjit, and he definitely stopped here at Ray's entrance. I observed him from my living quarters after I saw him roaming through the village area."

"Well, what did you see? And why did you leave your guarding position?" asked Adjit.

"Adjit, you have the nerve to even think I would stay when an over 500 pound tiger is heading my way? You got to be insane to ask such a question. I feared for my life. Why don't you leave these two go before some of us in this village get killed? And by the way, the tiger did stop at the doorway, like the tracks indicate, and sniffed the air for Ray's scent. And then the tiger left," said the guard.

Ray was smiling after he heard the villager call Adjit insane. Ray knew Adjit did not like that remark. Adjit sent the villager back to his living quarters. "Don't come out again until I call for you," he called after him.

"Adjit, if you were a wise leader, you would take the advice of the villager and leave us go before someone gets killed," said Ray.

"I run this village and no, you will not leave until I say you can," replied Adjit angrily. "Oh, by the way, Baasim, where is your brother? Seems he would be here by now to rescue you two if he cared."

"My brother will be here, and then you will see anger, and you will be forced to let us go," replied Baasim.

"Baasim, don't threaten me with such talk. I don't scare easily," replied Adjit.

Ray went up to Adjit and got face-to-face with him. "Adjit, help is going to come, and it's going to be here sooner than you think. This is not a threat; it will be a reality and I hope no harm has to come to anyone in this village. I consider you a stubborn horse; in other words, I consider you a jackass, and you may have to pay a price because of your attitude," said Ray.

Hearing Ray's words, some of the villagers became nervous. They came to advise Adjit to let the captors go to keep everyone safe in the village.

"Don't worry, these two are fill of hot air," said Adjit. "We are very safe in this village. I promise you that. It is late, let's get some sleep."

As everybody headed to their living quarters, Adjit assigned a new guard at Ray and Baasim's quarters. He regarded the other guard's comments very disrespectful so he relieved him of his duty.

"Adjit, you are not a leader of this village. I would call you a dictator," said Ray. "Your power over this village will soon leave you if you are not careful. Go to sleep, but always remember my tiger friend is around and close by."

"I have to laugh if you think that scares me," replied Adjit, and soon as he finished, a fierce, loud roar rolled over the village and scared everybody, except Ray and Baasim.

Ray then yelled out to Adjit, "Have sweet dreams, Adjit, if you can even sleep with the eye of the tiger watching over this village!" In a sarcastic voice, he added, "Hey, Adjit, maybe you need a guard at your door look out for any big cat roaming around, so you could sleep well tonight." Another loud roar came from the tiger and by now the village was starting to get in a panic, for fear of a tiger attack on someone. The next morning Ray and Baasim ate their breakfast outside in the village eating area. They talked about the tiger's visit the previous night and the roars that could be heard for miles. They wondered if Adjit would change his mind, as some villagers were now concerned for their safety.

"Hey, Adjit is heading this way," whispered Ray. "Maybe he has some good news for us, although I doubt it, but we will see."

When Adjit reached the place where Ray and Baasim were eating, he told them, "Well, did you both have a good sleep last night?"

"We both slept great, but how did you sleep? I know you had a lot to think about," replied Baasim with a smirk.

"You think the tiger incident put any fear in me; well, you are wrong, but it did cause me to make a change," replied Adjit.

Ray thought perhaps Adjit had come to his senses. "And what is this change you are considering?" he asked.

"You will be confined to your quarters with minimum outside privileges. Two villagers armed with guns will guard you henceforth. They are the only ones I have given guns to, being loyal to me. They are trusted villagers and supporters of my leadership," announced Adjit.

Ray was getting angrier by the second. "So basically you just took a step backwards, putting you and this village in more trouble."

"I feel a lot safer with you both confined to your quarters; you have caused a lot of trouble," said Adjit.

"You don't know what trouble is yet, but it's coming your way." In an instant Ray blurted out to all the villagers, "You all need to talk some sense to your leader and convince him to let us go before something serious happens!"

Ray's action made Adjit so angry he quickly ordered the guard to take Ray and Baasim back to their quarters. "They are to remain there except for eating and other personal duties. And only one of them can be outside at any time," barked Adjit.

Inside their living quarters, Ray and Baasim talked about the new situation they found themselves in.

"Well, Baasim, looks like we have made no progress towards getting out of this village. Hopefully help will be coming," said Ray.

"Ray, I know my family will not abandon us," said Baasim.

"I just know our own families are communicating with each other about us being missing and having no contact with them by now," confirmed Ray.

Night time before Ray and Baasim retired for the night, Ray thought he would mention something to Baasim. "Before I came here to hunt for the Bengal tiger, I told Shannon that I had a feeling something else might happen that would take the place of a trophy of the Bengal tiger," he said.

"When we get out of here, I am certainly willing to keep on hunting for your trophy," replied Baasim.

"I got to get acquainted with my tiger friend. I love Bengal tigers, and I know their population has gone down dramatically," reflected Ray.

"What are you leading up to with this conversation?" asked Baasim.

"When we get out of here, I am going back to the US with a plan to promote the preservation of the Bengal tiger; to ensure that the tiger will always be alive on this earth. It's the least I can do for the animal I love. I could never kill Bengal Ruby. We have made extraordinary connection with each other. That big cat is in my blood forever. He is my protector and I want to be his protector," said Ray.

"Ray, you have just encouraged me to also stop taking clients to hunt the Bengal tiger. They truly are a precious animal," encouraged Baasim.

"I remember your uncle Acharya telling me on the plane how, after looking through my rifle scope, I might have trouble pulling the trigger on such a beautiful animal. At that time I had considered that I probably wasn't going to get a Bengal tiger trophy. When Bengal Ruby came into my life like he did, I made up my mind what I would rather do for the big beautiful cat. I want to help preserve this species. And it's time to get started on that project and it's not too late," narrated Ray.

"It is getting late. Let us go to sleep with such good thought for the day. I hope I can be part of the tiger preservation— good night, Ray," said Baasim.

The next day, Ray and Baasim realized what their new limited privileges meant so far as making the day as boring as it could be.

Just then, Ray and Baasim suddenly heard a loud screeching sound. "That's Baha; something has got him really excited," said Baasim. They pulled the window flap to the side to see if they could see what was going on.

"I don't see anything, but something definitely excited Baha," said Ray.

Five minutes later there were a lot of villagers talking and they too appeared to be excited. And then Baasim heard a loud voice, and the person said, "I need to speak to your village leader, could you get him it's urgent and I want him here now."

Outside, a villager went to get Adjit to see a visitor who had asked for him. Baasim and Ray couldn't see who was doing the talking, but Baasim with a smile and teary eyes told Ray, "I can tell it's my brother's voice." With that, they gave each other a hug.

"Baasim we will get out of here, won't we?" asked Ray.

"This is the start, but it is certainly encouraging," confirmed Baasim. They listened intently to make sure they knew what was going on.

Adjit introduced himself to Aadesh and Baasim's Uncle Acharya.

"What can I do for you, and why are you here at this village?" said Adjit.

"We are looking for my brother Baasim Sharma who is a hunting guide and his client who is from California, USA. I am Baasim's brother Aadesh, and this is my uncle Acharya. This is a picture of them both. They are listed as missing. Have you seen them?" asked Aadesh, handing Adjit the pictures.

"No; we at this village have not seen them," replied Adjit. "I am sorry to give you that news but that's just the way it is."

Ray and Baasim, with their ears to the window opening, were thinking Adjit just made a big mistake.

"Are you absolutely sure you haven't seen them?"

"I couldn't be more certain. I don't like people who think I would lie to them about a matter like this," Adjit replied.

Aadesh in an angry and loud voice told Adjit, "Adjit...Adjit, I don't like being lied to about this and I have two good reasons to believe you are lying to me."

"What are these so-called two good reasons that you have?" Adjit replied.

Aadesh answered, "What is Baha the elephant doing just 100 yards from here shackled to a tree, and the hunting trailer with supplies is also close by."

"The elephant just wandered in one day and we kept him," said Adjit.

"You are really lying and you know it. You could at least have given that information about the elephant wandering into your village, but you had chosen not to tell me," replied Aadesh.

"I just forgot about it," Adjit said, a smirk on his face.

"Well, what I am about to tell you is going to wipe that chicken shit smile right off your face," replied Aadesh.

Baasim and Ray, still listening very intently, wondered what Aadesh was about to tell Adjit.

"Well, what is it that you have that is a compelling evidence that your brother Baasim and Ray are here in this village?" asked Adjit.

"Adjit, we have been observing this village for four days using binoculars, and we have actually seen Baasim and Ray in the village area." Adjit was not smiling anymore; instead, he had a concerned look on his face.

"I told you I knew that smile would melt off your face. So we want them released—are you willing to hand them over?" Aadesh asked.

"No. I am not letting them out of this village, and I am not going to be intimidated by just you and that old guy you call your uncle," replied Adjit.

"Adjit, it's a bad decision for you and your village. I will be taking Baha with me and I have his son Baha Jr. At 18000 pounds, the two of them can easily destroy this village if I give the order. We will be back here tomorrow at twelve noon. Hopefully you will have changed your mind by that time."

"Adjit is so hardheaded," said Ray. "Your brother handled the situation beautifully, and Adjit was caught off guard with Baha being close by. Aadesh nailed it calling Adjit a liar when your brother said he had seen us while observing the village."

"My brother will get this job done. He is a pretty good pistol shooter and he has shot 30-30 Winchester rifles," said

Baasim. "He can get a lot of shots off with one of those old western type guns—you know, the ones those famous actors would use in western movies. I think they were known as the gun that won the west."

"We will just have to wait and see what happens tomorrow at twelve noon. It is a shame Adjit is going to have to learn the hard way," said Ray.

CHAPTER 24

HIGH NOON AT THE VILLAGE

R ay and Baasim were excited the next day knowing Aadesh was coming back to the village at twelve o'clock to try and get them released from the village. They knew this was going to be a very tense situation, and wondered how Aadesh was going to convince Adjit that he should free them.

When Baasim asked the guard about breakfast, the guard said he and Ray need to take turns having one. Baasim went first. When he returned, he had words for Ray.

"The villagers are sure nervous about today. They know my brother is returning and they fear the worst losing their life in a fight to release us," said Baasim.

"Did Adjit show his face when you were out eating?" asked Ray.

"No, Ray, but I can tell you he has lost a lot of respect from the villagers. I believe his days as a leader are going to end over this situation. We will just have to wait and see," replied Baasim.

Ray was so anxious to be released. At the moment all he could think of was home and his beautiful wife, along with his mom and dad.

"Baasim, it's almost high noon. Things should start to happen soon. I certainly hope nobody has to die." Just then, Ray and Baasim heard villagers talking.

"Ray, I believe my brother has arrived and he is right on time," said Baasim. He and Ray proceeded to listen intently at the window opening to hear everything that was said. They couldn't see anybody as one of the living quarters was blocking the view of the village courtyard.

Ray and Baasim then heard Aadesh ask a villager. "Go get Adjit. I want to speak to him—and tell him to hurry. He knows what I want and my patience is running thin."

Ray saw the villager head to Adjit's living quarters. In time, Adjit came out to meet Aadesh.

"Look, he has a holstered hand gun on his hip," said Ray. "Baasim, this doesn't look good. It appears Adjit is not going to give in, or at least not yet."

"My brother is a very good shot, and my uncle Acharya can hold his own when it comes to handling and shooting a gun."

Adjit finally made it to where Aadesh was and in an angry voice told Aadesh, "Well, you made it back exactly like you said. My answer is still the same: Ray and Baasim are not leaving this village and that's final."

Aadesh responded angrily, "In your opinion you say that is your final answer. Well, you see in my opinion, I am taking my brother Baasim and my friend Ray out of this village, and that is final."

Baasim and Ray knew things had gotten deadly serious at this point.

"Aadesh, how do you plan to free them? You are only two and we are many," spat Adjit.

"Adjit, I don't believe your villagers want trouble," replied Aadesh, and in one instant gave the command, "Come, Baha!" and the elephant, along with Baha Jr., stood by Aadesh's side.

"What do you plan to do with those two giants?" asked Adjit.

"I could ask them destroy this village," Aadesh said, before directing his words at the villagers, "Do you want your village destroyed when there is a much simpler solution to this problem, which is just free Ray and Baasim."

Baasim and Ray took in all the angry words going back and forth between Adjit and Aadesh. It appeared Adjit was not going to give in. Then there was a silence for about two minutes.

"Maybe Adjit is starting to give in and come to his senses," suggested Ray.

"I doubt it," said Baasim.

Adjit then broke the silence and said to Aadesh, "I see two people coming this way. Do you know them?"

"Ray why are you are smiling?" asked Baasim.

"I have a gut feeling I know who the two people are, but let's wait and see. I tell you we will be freed from this village," replied Ray.

"I know them, but they will introduce themselves to you once they get here. I believe they will convince you to change your mind," replied Aadesh.

"Well, we will see, but nobody is going to change my mind," replied Adjit. As the two people got closer, Adjit could see the two people were women. "I can't believe you would think these two females are going to change my mind. Ray and Baasim are as good as prisoners," declared Adjit.

"Well, Mr. Adjit Singh, I have heard a lot about you. Let me introduce you to my friend, Denise Alexander, and I am Shannon Johnson, Ray's wife. I have heard that you were a stubborn leader, and you do appear to live up to your reputation."

At this time, Ray and Baasim found themselves really listening to what was being said.

"Baasim, I knew it was going to be Shannon and Denise. I finally got the message she had printed on back of the locket.

It was all printed backward. The mirror gave it away while I was shaving," said Ray. Again they turned their attention to what was going on outside.

"So you are Ray Johnson's wife. I have to laugh if you two women think you are going to free Ray and Baasim from this village," said Adjit.

"Baasim, I bet my wife's beautiful blue eyes are now turning red. Adjit is about to get a lesson," said Ray.

"Adjit, I see you have a holstered sidearm on your hip. You must be expecting trouble," Shannon baited Adjit angrily.

"I can handle any trouble you are going to try to give me," replied Adjit.

Smiling, Shannon said, "Oh yeah, really," and instantly Shannon cocked the rifle hammer and in lighting speed shot the handgun right out of Adjit's holster. "Now, Adjit, you won't be using that pistol against me. You don't appear to be smiling—what's wrong?" Shannon quickly put another cartridge in her Winchester 30-30 rifle. "Denise, Aadesh—when we use any bullets, reload as quickly as possible. I want all guns fully loaded; if we have to, we might have to kill some people to bring Adjit to his senses."

Adjit appeared to be shaken by what had happened but showed no signs of giving in to letting Ray and Baasim go.

Denise asked Adjit, "What are those containers on the table to your right?"

One of the villagers answered Denise, "They are water jugs."

"Well, Shannon, there are eight. You take the left four and I will take the right four." With that, they shot all eight in six seconds, and then quickly reloaded their rifles so they had full loaded rifles that held seven rounds.

"Adjit, you don't seem to be smiling much—are you worried about something?" Shannon said, smiling. Shannon was thinking of the next step to take.

Shannon yelled out, "Ray, have you been listening to our conversation? Are you and Baasim okay? You both will be out of this village today, I promise you both."

"Shannon, it's so great to hear your voice again. Hey, I did get your message on the locket!" replied Ray.

"Don't make promises you can't keep!" Adjit told Shannon.

"I don't make promises I can't keep. I know that the guard at Ray and Baasim's living quarters is armed with a gun—tell him to drop the gun onto the ground," ordered Shannon.

"I will do no such thing. You will not bully me into releasing Ray and Baasim," replied Adjit.

"Adjit, it's over, tell the guard to drop his gun," insisted Shannon.

"No! No! No!"

Getting really mad at this point, patience wearing thin, Shannon said, "Adjit, you shouldn't wear sandals."

"Why, what wrong with sandals?" replied Adjit.

Smiling, Shannon replied, "Oh, nothing wrong with the sandals—it's what in them that really bothers me."

"What the hell bothers you?" asked Adjit.

"That ugly big toe; unless you order your guard to drop his firearm, I am going to shoot your big toe off; don't worry, it's a lot less painful than amputation," said Shannon.

Denise found herself almost laughing at the big toe take. She was wondering how Shannon came up with that scheme to convince Adjit to tell his guard to drop his gun.

Adjit finally did give the order to his guard to drop his gun to the ground.

"Ray, did the guard drop the gun to the ground?" yelled Shannon.

"Yes," replied Ray.

"Honey we are coming to get you and Baasim," Shannon said. "I will be giving instructions before we make our way to your quarters."

Adjit still made no attempt to let the situation be solved in a peaceful manner. He was at this time about twenty feet in front of Shannon.

"Acharya, Aadesh, and Denise: let's start moving forward," Shannon instructed. "If anybody pulls a firearm, shoot him or her." Turning to the villagers, she said, "You villagers know how we can shoot so if I were you I wouldn't try using a firearm. We have been well trained with these 30-30 Winchester carbines. As we move forward, you all will move backwards; if you don't we will shoot to injure you—hopefully not kill you."

There appeared to be some resentment to Shannon by some villagers. But now the four of them were starting to go forward, with Baha and Baha Jr. also following. They had now advanced about twenty feet.

Denise noticed some of the villagers appeared to be very scared "Hey, Shannon, you really scared the hell out of these villagers! Everybody seems to be backing up with no hesitation—even Adjit," she said.

Shannon noticed that the pace of the villagers going backward was getting faster. It was then she felt something brush against her leg. Looking down, she told Denise, "We just gained another support in our effort to free Ray and Baasim. Denise, look down, he is between you and me," announced Shannon.

Denise was totally petrified after she saw what was between her and Shannon. "We have a Bengal tiger between us—he must know Ray," she said.

With the tiger now on the scene, the rescue party made it to Ray and Baasim quarters easily with no further resistance from Adjit or any villagers. Shannon made it to the inside of the quarters followed by Bengal Ruby. Shannon went to Ray immediately and gave him one of those arousing kisses. For his part, Bengal Ruby went on his hindquarters, put his face next to theirs, and gave them each a big lick, sensing Shannon was special to Ray.

Ray's two loves were together with him for the first time. Outside, Acharya, Aadesh, and Denise kept guard over the situation. In time, Baasim made it outside to greet his uncle and brother. It was a big reunion. Happy times were back.

Soon they were ready to depart the village. Ray had some parting words to the villagers.

"I am happy that nobody had to die here today. Adjit, do you now see the ruby necklace around the tiger's neck? I told you I put it back around his neck. I am not a liar, and the legend of the Bengal ruby has been proven to be true. I didn't get the Bengal tiger trophy that I came here for, but I got to touch and hug a Bengal tiger in the wild, which is much more precious than a trophy. I say goodbye to you all," declared Ray.

Adjit called the attention of the people. "Ray Johnson and Baasim, you taught me a lesson that sometimes you have to put trust in people. I didn't, and I am sorry for what I put you through at this village." He went to Ray and Baasim and gave them a hug. "Because of my wrongful deeds in this situation, I resign my position as leader. We should all vote for a new leader. I must say you all were very lucky that the Bengal tiger came onto the scene when he did," he said.

Shannon was quick to respond to Adjit's words. "Uh-oh—no, no, Adjit, you were the lucky one. The tiger is the one that made you change your mind. Let me tell you that if you didn't change your mind, I was very much prepared to kill you and anybody else that got in the way of us freeing Ray and Baasim. I hope you understand that, Adjit," she said.

323

Looking down, Adjit replied, "I understand Shannon Johnson. I guess you were right. Ray, you have a great and devoted wife. Again, I am sorry for putting you through all this grief."

"Well, we will all head back to New Delhi now, so let's all get the hunting trailers hooked up to Baha and Baha Jr.," said Ray, just relieved this part of his trip was over.

As they were hooking up the trailers to the elephants, the four men had a conversation; afterwards, it appeared they had come to some type of agreement.

Ray, Shannon, and Baasim took the trailer being pulled by Baha. The rest took the trailer pulled by Baha Jr.

As they were about to head north on the Ken River trail, Ray said, "Shannon, give Baha the go command."

"Go, Baha," said Shannon. "Go Baha—why isn't he going?"

"Go give him a hug on his trunk," explained Ray, smiling. "It's what he expects of somebody new giving him a command. Don't forget to also say 'Baha, you are beautiful.'"

Shannon did as Ray instructed and Baha gave his screeching elephant sound of approval. Shannon went back to the trailer seat, gave the "Go, Baha," command, and they were on their way north down the Ken River trail.

"Ray, we didn't get to say goodbye to Bengal Ruby," said Shannon, concern in her voice.

"In about another hour we will come to a trail that crosses this one. As it is very hot today, we will stop and refresh ourselves along with the elephants in the Ken River. Then we will go to the area where I first saw Bengal Ruby. Maybe we will see him again and give him a hug."

Arriving at the cross trail, they diverted to the Ken River a short distance away. Reaching the riverbank, they all went down off the trailer seats.

"Wait till I make sure no mugger crocodiles are around," said Ray. After he confirmed the place was safe, the elephants were unhooked from the trailers. "It's okay to get into the river," said Ray. They proceeded to enjoy the cool water and all the splashing and squirting of water by the elephants that were in the mood for play.

While their companions enjoyed the water, Ray and Shannon strayed a little further from the rest. Shannon grabbed Ray and gave him one of those earthshaking kisses. "Honey, we need to make love. We have got to do it somewhere, I am like a female dog in heat," she said.

"Shannon, you haven't changed; in about an hour I have a plan." Ray was smiling big time. They returned to the group and everybody prepared to go back onto the trail.

They eventually crossed the Ken River trail. Ray turned to Shannon. "We will camp at the place I first met Bengal Ruby. It's only about a mile away. There I am going to take you for a little adventure trip."

"Will we be alone?" asked Shannon. Baasim smiled at the remark.

"Baasim, why are you smiling?" asked Shannon.

"I am just so happy you and Ray are finally together. I take it you both need some private time.

"By the way, where did you and Denise learn to shoot those 30-30 Winchester carbines? My brother said you two were fast and accurate. Aadesh was very impressed," said Baasim.

"Ray's friend Joeseph, who is Denise's husband, trained us both," replied Shannon. "He wanted us to be able to defend ourselves living as we do in the country. He always said you never know when and where you might need good shooting skills; well, today was the day we needed them."

"Shannon, with all the excitement I forgot to ask how Mom and Dad were doing," said Ray.

"When they found out you were listed as missing, they were so worried they kept themselves updated with the local news channels," replied Shannon.

It was about three o'clock when they reached the area where they would camp. Everybody helped getting the camp ready. Denise walked over to be by Ray and Shannon, put her arms around them, and said, "It's so good to be here together with you," she said. "You two have any plans right now," she added, smiling.

"Ya—I am going to take Shannon on a little adventure trip," replied Ray.

"I love you both. I know you need some private time together," said Denise.

Ray took Shannon's hand, went and took the Coleman lantern, and then asked Baasim, "Do you have the leather bag that we talked about earlier?" Baasim went to get the leather bag and gave it to Ray. Ray strapped on his holstered 44 Magnum revolver, just in case he needed it for protection.

Ray turned to everybody. "Shannon and I are headed to the castle ruins for a little exciting adventure trip; see you in about two or hours," he announced.

Denise looked at Shannon, winked at her, and said, "Have fun Shannon. I know you will."

Ray guided Shannon to the clearing. "Shannon, look across about 100 yards ahead. That is one of Bengal Ruby's dens. One day he walked out from the castle and made eye contact with me. That was the start of the Bengal ruby legend," he said.

"Acharya told me all about the legend and how, once the tiger with a ruby necklace on its neck made eye contact with the first human that it saw, it would always protect that person and be that person's friend," replied Shannon.

"Bengal Ruby saved me from an Indian leopard attack. During the fight, the necklace was torn off his neck and I found it on the ground. When we came to Adjit's village and I told them about it, they kept me and Baasim captive until I would get the necklace around Bengal Ruby's neck again."

"So how did you find Bengal Ruby again? That must have been a challenge for you?" said Shannon.

"They decided to let me go, but kept Baasim as a hostage while I went to look for the tiger. I eventually replaced the necklace around the tiger's neck. We will visit that same spot in just a little while. I will show you how I ventured into the castle and stumbled into a room with such number of valuable items," said Ray.

"Ray, why didn't Adjit let you go?" asked Shannon.

"He didn't believe my story. The two villagers who practice the Bengal ruby legend said I had to stay at the village until they could have proof that the necklace was back on the tiger's neck," explained Ray.

Ray and Shannon crossed the clearing to the castle entrance. When they reached it, Ray had his Coleman lantern lighted. "Well, Shannon, you are here with me. I love you so much and your blue eyes are still so beautiful. At one point I thought I would never see you or my family again," admitted Ray.

Shannon smiled at Ray and gave him a kiss and said, "Let's go into the castle. I am getting anxious."

Into the castle they went and down the hallway. Ray showed Shannon the rooms with human skeletons in them, explaining how battling tribes and clansman produced those skeletons. They finally came to the stairway. He took her up to the landing and they soon faced the door to the room with the valuable artifacts.

Ray opened the door and they both went into the room.

Looking around the room, Shannon couldn't believe all the items that were made out of silver and gold. "There must be at least a thousand items in this room; I can't even imagine how much these items are worth," she said.

Ray took Shannon by the hand and took her to what appeared to be an altar. "Shannon, see that chest on the altar?" asked Ray.

"Yes, I see it; even it is made of silver. Can I open it?" asked Shannon.

"Sure—go ahead, but be ready for a big surprise," said Ray.

Shannon opened the chest. "Ray—it's full of diamonds and rubies! I have never seen so many diamonds and rubies in one spot," she said.

They turned to each other and hugged and kissed. Just then Ray said to Shannon, "I believe we have a visitor."

"I hear a sound; it's like a cat purring or something," said Shannon.

Shannon felt a nudge on her thigh, looked down, and saw Bengal Ruby. He was between Ray and Shannon.

"Ray, he came to tell us goodbye," said Shannon.

"This is the same exact spot where I put the ruby necklace back onto his neck. I thought he would show up. I wanted you to see the situation I was in," said Ray.

Shannon and Ray faced each other and embraced and kissed. Bengal Ruby stood on his hindquarters and put his face next to their faces, rubbed his face against theirs, and both Ray and Shannon gave him a big hug. And then the big cat left the room.

Ray turned to Shannon. "I brought this leather sack to take about half of the jewels in the chest. It's not for us; on our way back to New Delhi, we will make a stop and then you will see another part of my adventure to hunt the Bengal tiger," said Ray.

Soon they left the room, retracing the path back to the entrance and outside. Once there, Shannon said to Ray,

"Look over there, that's a nice lush green grass area. Let's go have some quite time together."

Ray already knew what was about to happen. At the grassy area, their love for each other took over and they made love for the first time after about three months of being apart. When it was over, they looked up at the blue sky, and Shannon said, "It is so beautiful here in the Indian jungle."

"That's what you get when you are in tiger country," Ray said, smiling. "Well, we better get back to the camp."

On the way back a thought occurred to Shannon. "You know, while you were gone I talked to the doctor about not getting pregnant, and he started me on a pill that has helped others to get pregnant. It would be wonderful if I was to get pregnant here in the Indian jungle," she said.

Crossing the clearing, they could see Denise waiting for them. When they got to her, she went and gave them a big hug. She winked at Shannon and said, "Did you have a good time?"

Ray and Shannon both replied, "Yes, we sure had a great time alone together!"

"Well just moments ago I got a surprise of my life. I couldn't believe what I was seeing," Denise said, smiling

"Well, tell us what happened," said Shannon.

"I was standing here when I heard a purring sound like that of a cat. I looked down and there was Bengal Ruby. I mustered the courage to give him a hug and he gave me a big lick on my face. And then, Ray, I told him, 'Bengal Ruby, what big teeth you have.'"

Shortly, Bengal Ruby was amongst the three of them; he got up and looked at them, nudged them with his body, and then left to go into the jungle.

An emotional Ray said, tears in his eyes, "I wonder if we will see Bengal Ruby ever again."

The three then made it back to camp. Denise had shot a small deer so Baasim and Aadesh were busy cooking dinner.

Short conversation among the group came after dinner, but it had been such a tiring day that they all said good night to each other and retired for the night.

CHAPTER 25

THE JOURNEY TO CHHATARPUR

A fter a quick, simple breakfast the next morning, the group prepared for the trip down the Ken River trail to return Baha and his son Baha Jr. to their owner. They reckoned the owner must be wondering if he would ever see Baha again, along with Ray and Baasim. Everybody was happy and excited that they all finally were safe and together.

However, Baasim reminded everybody to put their guns in the rack behind the seat, for you never know what you might come across in the jungles of India.

"The elephant dealer is about twelve hours away. We would set up camp after about six hours," he said. They were traveling north on the Ken River trail.

Time was flying by and it was such a nice cool day that they just kept going at a moderate pace. When they had been on the trail for about six hours, Baasim said, "We will look for a trail that will take us to the Ken River. We will set up camp and then take the elephants to the river so they can get refreshed."

Just then, Ray noticed something. "Baasim, is that where we were confronted by the two robbers?" he said.

"Yes, Ray, that's the place," replied Baasim.

With a surprised look, Shannon said, "Somebody tried to rob you? Ray, that must have been scary."

Baasim smiled at her. "Shannon, your husband took care of the situation with no problem; he also taught them a lesson and sent them on their way. He confiscated their money and any other stolen property they had in their possession. He also shot and wounded one of them slightly so he would remember that crime doesn't pay," he said.

They finally reached the trail that Baasim had mentioned; the two elephants pulled to the side of the trail where there was a clearing and everybody got busy and started to set up camp.

Baasim turned to Shannon and Denise. "Maybe you two sharpshooters could get us a small deer for dinner...?" he told them.

Denise answered, "We would love to try! Shannon and I are really born to hunt."

Baasim smiled. "You go east on this side trail. Go quietly and you will come to a clearing. There is a lot of deer in this area that you gals should have no trouble getting a shot. Remember we are depending on you for dinner."

Ray went to Shannon, "Honey, this is starting to seem like home."

Denise, smiling, said, "Ray, being around you and Shannon certainly makes it like home—except I don't have Joeseph here." Denise was pretty emotional at this point and tears were flowing.

Shannon and Ray went to Denise and gave her a hug. Shannon said, "Ray, my best friend had no reservations coming with me to get you, and Joeseph didn't put up any resistance. It was all complete dedication to help friends that needed help, sort of like your parents, Ray."

Ray went to Denise and said with a smile, "Denise, in a couple of weeks we should all be home in California and enjoying life." Ray paused a little and then went on to say, "And maybe we can all work on having children."

"Well, Ray and Shannon I ... think, I think ... I may be...."

With joy in her face, Shannon said, "Denise—are you telling me you are pregnant?"

"Ya, I believe I am. I am three weeks late with my menstrual period, so I am in the early stages. When we were on the plane to India, I already felt that I was pregnant." Denise was crying and then continued to say, "First telegram home I will let everyone know."

Ray said, "You two go on your hunt and try to get a deer for dinner. What great news, Denise. Joeseph is going to be so excited to hear he is going to be a daddy. You both have fun—and Shannon, make sure you carry most of the deer when you get one; hopefully after we take the elephants to the river I will try to come and find you to help you carry the deer. What a day filled with good news!"

Ray went back to the men and they all headed to the Ken River with the two elephants to get refreshed. When they were done at the river and started back for the camp, they heard a rifle shot.

"I think we have our dinner. We better get a fire going. I am going to go and try to help the two hunters," said Ray.

As Baasim gathered firewood, Ray left to find Shannon and Denise. He found them just about finished dressing out the deer.

"Well, I shot my first animal in India. Let's get back to camp and start cooking dinner," a smiling Shannon said.

Ray carried the small deer, which was about 50 pounds, on his back and they all headed back to the camp. At the camp, Ray skinned the deer and prepared it for cooking over a fire. They placed the meat on the special rotisserie that Baasim had brought along. It was still early; it would take about two hours to cook over the open fire.

Around seven o'clock they took their places for dinner. "Baasim, you sure put the right spices on the meat. The flavor is out of this world," said Denise.

"Thank you, Denise," replied Baasim. He turned to everybody. "Tomorrow we have around six hours before we reach the elephant dealer and drop off our two friends," he said.

"I know I will really miss my big elephant friend, Baha the beautiful," said Ray, smiling. "Oh, everybody, I must tell you how Baha saved my life at the Ken River when two mugger crocodiles tried to attack me; it was a close encounter with death."

"Ray, you sure had some excitement on this tiger hunt; maybe someday you should write a book about it," said Denise, smiling.

"You know, I got to the point on this hunting trip wherein I didn't know what to expect next," said Baasim. "I think it's time we all retire and get a good night's sleep."

Pulling out the special cots from the trailers, they all retired for the night. As everybody was just getting settled, there was a loud roar that echoed through the jungle.

"What was that?" Shannon said.

Ray held Shannon close to him and said, "That was a tiger; who knows it might have been Bengal Ruby saying good night." They all then went to sleep.

After a quick breakfast of fried Spam and some heated canned pork and beans next morning, Ray gave Shannon a kiss and told everybody, "By the way we had a silent visitor last night. He left tiger tracks by my cot. Bengal Ruby wanted to say goodbye." Ray turned to Denise. "Denise, how are you feeling? We need to keep you and the little one healthy," he said.

"Don't you all be worrying about me. I am doing fine. What really makes me feel good is that I know part of Joeseph is here with me," said Denise.

Baasim heard Denise. "What do you mean part of Joeseph is here with you? Oh—do you mean you are pregnant?" he asked.

Shannon smiled and put her arms around Denise. "Ya, everybody: my friend Denise is pregnant and going to be a mother," she said.

Smiling, Acharya went to Denise and said, "What a great surprise for all of us! Did you know before you travelled to India?"

"No, but after I arrived at New Delhi I realized I may be pregnant; now I am definitely sure of it," said Denise.

The trailers were hooked to the elephants, and the party was soon headed down the Ken River trail to take the elephants back to their owner.

"You know, it always amazes me when an animal senses that it is headed home," said Baasim. "They pick up such speed that at this rate we will make better time than I first estimated. We will just go straight to the elephant dealer and we can have lunch there. He always serves a good meal to his customers."

Shannon and Denise were with Baasim, and Ray was with Aadesh and Acharya.

"Acharya ... with all the excitement, I haven't been able to talk to you. I apologize and there is no excuse for my behavior. I do want to thank you for coming to help rescue Baasim and me," said Ray.

"Ray, I consider you as part of the family. When I met Shannon and her friend Denise, it wasn't hard to come along. Your mom and dad are lucky to have such a nice daughter-in-law and her friend Denise around them," replied Acharya.

"Dad and Mom consider them as daughters—the daughters they could never have," said Ray.

Denise and Shannon were immensely enjoying the beauty of Indian jungle with all the animal sounds, especially the squawking of the peacocks that were visible everywhere. Around twelve o'clock they pulled into the elephant owner's yard.

The owner came out to greet his customers. "I am so glad to see you all back here safe and sound!" he said. "Let's unhook the trailers and give the elephants some food and water. I have lunch prepared. Please follow me to the dining area."

After lunch, the party returned outside got their vehicles fueled up and hooked to the trailers. They were soon ready to hit the road.

They thanked the elephant dealer for the use of his animals. As for Ray, he walked slowly in the direction of Baha, Shannon and Denise following him. They knew Ray was going have a hard time saying goodbye to Baha, his 10,000 pound friend.

"Baha, you are indeed beautiful," Ray emotionally addressed the elephant. Hugging his trunk and looking up his eyes, Ray said, "I have to say goodbye now. I will never forget you. You saved my life when those mugger crocodiles wanted me for lunch. I doubt we will ever see each other again, so Baha give me a kiss that I can remember."

As Ray stood back, Baha put the tip of his trunk on Ray's forehead, gave him a kiss, then raised his trunk high into the air trumpeting his loud elephant screeching sound as if to say goodbye. Ray, Shannon, and Denise then made their way to join the others.

Shannon took Ray into her arms and gave him a kiss. "I know it was hard to say goodbye to Baha. The two of you have bonded so well like we did. The difference is I will be with you until death do us part," said Shannon. Ray smiled at his beautiful blued-eyed wife.

Ray, Shannon, and Denise took the Land Rover that Baasim was driving. Before taking off, Baasim told everybody, "We are going to the city of Chhatarpur, which is about three hours away. We will eat lunch at my favorite restaurant. Then we need to telegram the governments of India and the US so they'll know Ray and Baasim had been rescued and are okay and in good health."

"I know Ray, Shannon, and Denise are also anxious to send a telegram to California, Denise especially to announce that she is pregnant," he added. "I can't imagine the kind of reaction after all these news made it to all the families."

The two Land Rovers then hit the road. In about three hours they reached Chhatarpur and proceeded to Baasim's favorite restaurant.

"You will like the food here. Last time I had curry chicken and it was great," Ray told Shannon and Denise.

As the waiters at the restaurant knew Baasim and Aadesh, they welcomed them. Once they were seated, the waiter said, "Baasim, we are all glad to see you. We heard how you and your hunting client went missing."

"That's a long story, but we are here now and we are all safe and happy to be amongst friends," replied Baasim. They made their orders and had their lunch. Afterwards, Baasim said, "Well, time for the Post Office and take care of the telegrams."

At the Post Office, Baasim took care of the telegrams to the governments of both India and the US as he promised.

Friday morning at the Johnson ranch in California, Joeseph was over for breakfast. He had taken it upon himself to spend time visiting Mary and Paul knowing how they needed to have somebody give them some support during this difficult time, with their son missing in India and now Shannon going after their son. They couldn't help wondering if they would ever see Ray or Shannon again.

After breakfast, Joeseph told Mary and Paul, "We have to think positive and just plain trust in God that he will return everybody back to us; then we can go on with our lives."

"Joeseph, I don't know what we would do if you were not here daily to give us support during this tragic ordeal,"

Paul replied, tears rolling down his face. "But I know God has a plan, so we just have to accept what he has decided," he concluded. Mary appeared to beside herself, but Joeseph managed to calm them both.

They were looking at the TV news when the newscaster said, "Ray Johnson and Baasim Sharma are still missing in India. At the moment, there are no positive developments concerning their fate."

"I know this news is hard to take, but we have to keep a positive attitude," Joeseph quickly reminded them.

Just then, the newscaster said, "Oh my God, we just received new information! The United States Department of State has just received a telegram from India. Ray Johnson and his guide Baasim Sharma have been rescued from a village that held them as captives. They are now on their way to New Delhi, and everybody is safe and in good health, including the rescuers—Aadesh and Acharya Sharma, Shannon Johnson, and her best friend Denise Alexander. That's about all we know at this time. We at this station will keep you updated if any more news comes to us."

Joeseph, Paul, and Mary found themselves hugging each other for joy at the sudden turn of events. As expected, the phone calls kept coming from all concerned friends and relatives, showing how much they were supporting Paul and Mary. The three couldn't have been more relieved sitting at the living room.

Just then the doorbell rang. Mary at the door saw it was the mailman.

"Mary, I have a telegram that you need to sign for. It's from Ray in India. I bet those words bring joy to your heart, and of course I am so happy for you and Paul," said the mailman.

Mary signed for the telegram and hastened back to the living room. "Well, this is a telegram from our son, Paul," she announced happily. The loving parents had tears of joy knowing their son was indeed safe and alive. "Here, let me read the telegram," Mary said.

HI MOM AND DAD WE ARE ALL SAFE AND NOW TRAVELING TO NEW DELHI WE WILL HAVE A MINOR SIDE TRIP ON THE WAY I LOVE AND MISS YOU BOTH IT WAS NICE THAT SHANNON AND DENISE COULD COME AND BE PART OF THE RESCUE TEAM JOESEPH THAT 30-30 WINCHESTER TRAINING CAME IN HANDY FOR MY RESCUE WILL TALK TO YOU ABOUT IT WHEN I GET HOME SHANNON SENDS HER LOVE TO YOU ALL JOESEPH DENISE HAS SOMETHING TO TELL YOU HI HONEY I MISS YOU SO MUCH I HAD TO DO FOR MY FRIEND WHAT I KNOW SHE WOULD DO FOR ME THAT'S JUST HOW WE AMIGOS ARE JOESEPH HONEY IT WAS SO GOOD THAT I HAD PART OF YOU WITH ME HERE IN INDIA YES JOESEPH YOU ARE GOING TO BE A DADDY CAN'T WAIT TO GET HOME LOVE YOU DENISE HEY JOESEPH MY BEST FRIEND CONCRATULATIONS ON YOU GOING TO BE A DADDY I WILL SEND A TELEGRAM WHEN WE GET TO NEW DELHI TO LET YOU KNOW OUR TRAVEL ARRANGEMENTS AND TIME LOVE YOU ALL RAY

Mary and Paul congratulated Joeseph on his upcoming role as a dad.

"Paul, Mary—God did us all a big favor today. Not only were Ray and his guide rescued, but I am also going to become a father!" Joeseph said emotionally. "Well, I better go give my mom and dad the news of them becoming grandparents," he added. Thus he said goodbye and quickly went to see his parents.

Back in India, the two Land Rovers were approaching the highway to New Delhi. "We will take a little side trip to surprise Shannon and everybody else. It's about 30 minutes away," said Ray. The men knew what this side trip was all about.

Turning into a side road from the main highway and heading south, Ray told Shannon, "I promise you and Denise will enjoy this little side trip."

CHAPTER 26

THE TRIP BACK TO NEW DELHI

"Ray what's this trip all about? Why is this so special?" asked Shannon.

"Just wait and see, honey. You and Denise will enjoy this occasion. I am sure it's going to be fun," replied Ray.

After about 30 minutes, Shannon noticed they were approaching what appeared to be a village. "Ray, we are in a village, and the people seem to be real excited—what is going on? Have you been here before?"

"Yes—Baasim and I have been at this village before." Ray went to give Shannon a kiss and pulled the mounted ruby out from her shirt; she had it inside her shirt in order to protect it. "Shannon, welcome to the village that gave you the necklace after I saved Banhi Singh's life. They are great people."

"Ray, there seems to be a crowd forming. A man and a woman are leading the crowd and heading this way," observed Shannon.

"Well, those are Banhi and her husband. They are probably surprised to see me again so soon," replied Ray.

Shannon wasted no time—she jumped out of the Land Rover and headed right towards the crowd where Banhi and Baahir were, giving Banhi a hug.

"Well, Shannon, you are even more beautiful than the picture Ray had in his locket. I never thought our paths would cross so soon. What a great surprise! I must give Ray a hug," Banhi said, becoming very emotional after seeing Ray.

"Banhi, it's great to see you again and be amongst friends! If you haven't got wind of it, Baasim and I were held captives by a village not at all like yours," Ray said.

Just then, Banhi noticed Denise. "Wow, and who is this beautiful young lady?" she said.

"Banhi, this is my best friend Denise Alexander," Shannon said. "She came with me to look for Ray and Baasim after they went missing. She is a dear friend. She came with no hesitation to help me find Ray and Baasim," added Shannon.

Banhi approached Denise, looked at her, and said, "Denise, there is something about you that I feel is special." With that she gave Denise a hug and held her tight." "We are having a special feast tonight. All of you will be our special guests," she went on to announce. The villagers started clapping to acknowledge Banhi's announcement.

Ray then explained everything that had happened to him and Baasim after they left the village to continue their hunting expedition.

"I can't believe anybody would treat you and Baasim in such a manner," Banhi remarked after hearing the story. "Anyway we will celebrate tonight and feast on roasted pigs cooked over a fire. This feast will be to honor your return to our village. I want Shannon to sit on my right and Denise on my left—I have something special planned for tonight."

Ray, Shannon, and Denise walked around the village talking to the villagers. "These villagers are all so niece and friendly—and they all speak great English," Shannon told Ray.

"That's because Great Britain at one time had a lot of influence in India," explained Ray.

It was time for the feast. Banhi and Baahir motioned for everyone to be seated so they could start the ceremony. Baasim, Aadesh, Acharya, Ray, Shannon, and Denise were seated at the head table with Banhi and Baahir.

Banhi stood up and called the attention of everybody.

"We are all gathered here today to honor our returning guests and thank them for coming back to visit our village. I want to thank you Ray for thinking of us and bringing your wife Shannon and her friend Denise so we could meet them. Of course, your Indian friends are also greatly welcomed at our village," declared Banhi.

Ray stood up and offered his own thoughts. "It was just the right thing to do. You were all so kind and generous to give Shannon such a memorable gift. I know Shannon would want to say thank you for such a gift—for the sacrifice this village had made to give her such a gift," he said.

Shannon understood too well it was her turn to speak. "I always have your gift with me. Ray explained in a telegram what had happened. If I wasn't here today, I would have made a special trip to visit you all and thank you for such a memorable gift. I will forever cherish the gift, and I know it came from your heart. Right now I think Ray has something more to say," said Shannon.

Ray asked Banhi and Baahir to stand up before turning to everyone. "Recently at a village along the Ken River, my guide and I were held captive over the legend of the Bengal ruby. I won't go into detail but they just wouldn't believe me. They insisted that Baasim and I would be held captives until the situation with the Bengal tiger was resolved. After everybody lost contact with Baasim and me, they came up with the rescue party to come and look for us. Fortunately that turned out to be good for everybody, and so here we are today amongst family and friends," he concluded. Turning to Baasim he said, "Baasim—maybe you have something to say?"

Baasim stood up and addressed the villagers. "Because this village is made up of such kind people, my friend Ray came up with a special way of expressing his gratitude to all of you. He asked me, my brother Aadesh, and Acharya my uncle for permission to give this village a special gift. He felt the three citizens of India with him could explain to the Indian government, why this special gesture needed to be done," he said.

Shannon again thanked them for her necklace before going on to say, "After we left the village Ray and Baasim were held captive, Ray and I went into an old castle that served as his tiger friend's den. In a special room full of precious objects that Ray discovered earlier, the tiger came to us and showed how much we meant to it by licking us all over our faces. After the tiger left, Ray had me open a chest filled with such diamonds and rubies.

"Ray told me he wanted to give this village a gift. Because he felt this village deserve something to honor your loving attitude and acts of kindness and generosity to others, I now hand to you this leather sack containing some of the diamonds and rubies from the chest. He hopes this will help some way in bettering the lives of the people in this village" concluded Shannon before handing Banhi the leather sack while giving her a hug and a kiss.

Baasim spoke again. "My friend Ray left half the diamonds and rubies for the other villagers despite how they treated us. He felt they were only led by a bad leader, and that some of them were probably good people. That's how my friend Ray thinks. Fortunately the said leader resigned and the villagers had a chance to vote for a new leader. The leader did apologize for not believing Ray. Beyond any doubt, my friend Ray is a kind, generous, and loving man," he said.

An emotional Banhi stood up and said, "Look at these two beautiful women sitting next to me. Shannon, Denise—will you please stand in front of me and face the villagers," and the two did as Banhi requested. Banhi went on to say, "You know this village gifted Shannon the ruby necklace for what Ray, her husband, did by saving my life."

Everybody was starting to wonder what Banhi was planning next.

"My people, you once gave me a similar necklace to honor me as your leader, and I am wearing it right now." Everybody went dead silent as they watched Banhi reach over Denise's head and put what was her necklace around Denise's neck.

Denise and Shannon faced each other tears flowing, before turning to Banhi, Denise hugging and kissing Banhi while stumbling for words to say. "Banhi … I can't … I can't keep … this," she finally managed to get out.

"Denise, you can—and you will keep the necklace; it couldn't have been given to a sweeter woman who would do anything for her friend Shannon. From what I understand, you came with Shannon showing no hesitation to help get Ray back into Shannon's arms. I hope the two of you will always have good memories of this village as you wear the necklaces," Banhi said.

At that point, the villagers clapped and sang what appeared to be a song rightly fitting for what just took place.

Soon, Banhi announced, "It's time for the feast and conversation on this joyous occasion," so everybody took to their food and drinks and had fun.

Late into the evening, Baasim announced, "Well, I think it's time we all retire; we still have a big trip to New Delhi tomorrow." With that, the six of them went to the camping trailers, pulled their cots out and, after saying good night, went soundly to sleep.

The next morning, Ray and his group went to join the villagers for breakfast. Ray knew the time had come to bid goodbye. Ray, Shannon, and Denise went to be with Banhi and her husband Baahir.

Ray called the attention of the villagers and started to give a little departing speech. "We all want to thank you for your gracious hospitality and the precious memory of the ruby necklaces that you gave Shannon and her friend Denise. We will all remember this occasion forever, and the story will be passed down amongst our families," he said.

Banhi went to Ray, stood before him, looked up into his eyes, and said, "Ray, we must all remember and never forget." Turning to Shannon and Denise, she told them, "You, too, should always remember that there is only one reason I could give you the ruby necklaces—the day Ray took a shot that saved my life is the reason I am still here today."

Shannon then with emotion and tears said, "I don't know if our paths will cross again, but I know one thing: I am glad we came to this village and I am here right now to enjoy and remember this moment."

Ray then said, "Goodbye, and may God be with you all. I came to India to collect a Bengal tiger trophy; instead, I will go back to California and promote the preservation of the Indian Bengal tiger, and my guide Baasim, has agreed to that project here in India. Together we hope to make a difference in keeping the Bengal tiger from becoming an endangered species."

In time they walked to their Land Rovers and waved goodbye as they drove off on the way to New Delhi. Ray, Shannon, and Denise were riding with Baasim.

"Ray, make sure you have your 44 Magnum revolver with you. We never know what we might encounter on the highway to New Delhi," Baasim said. "The same for you, Shannon and Denise—have your Winchester 30-30 carbines in the vehicle, too. I don't expect trouble but one never knows," he added.

The two Land Rovers were soon going down the highway, Baasim following his brother Aadesh, and uncle Acharya.

After about two hours, Baasim said, "We will stop at a city named Gwalior for fuel and something to eat; afterwards it will be about four hours away from New Delhi."

"It's great to hear the name New Delhi again. What time do you think we will get to New Delhi?" Ray asked Baasim.

"We should be there around five o'clock. We will get you checked into the Hotel New Delhi. You can all relax and do what you want. I know Aadesh and myself want to go be with our families," replied Baasim.

At the city of Gwalior they had fuel and a simple lunch at a little cafe, before they were on the road again to New Delhi. Along the way, they saw Aadesh's land Rover come to a stop.

"Ray, something is up with Aadesh's Land Rover."

"You are right, Baasim," replied Ray. "Two men are making them get out of the vehicle. Shannon, Denise, make sure your carbines are loaded," said Ray.

"Yes, we have them loaded," Shannon answered.

"It looks like it's a holdup," said Denise. "Look, one of the men is coming to us. The other has Aadesh and Acharya with their hands up. It definitely looks like a holdup."

The man approached the Land Rover on the side of Ray, who had already rolled down his window. When the man got to the Land Rover, he told Ray, "You all get out of the vehicle—and I mean now! Now!"

"Sir, we can't do that. If we do, it will be over your dead body," replied Ray.

The robber laughed and said, "What the hell are you talking about over my dead body? You must be joking!"

"Oh, no, I'm not joking," replied Ray, pulling and aiming his 44 Magnum at the man's head. "Does this look like a joke? I recommend you tell your partner he better put down his gun."

"Why, I will shoot you first and then my partner will shoot your other friends and you all will be dead," said the man.

"You better look around. Behind me in the rear seat is a 30-30 carbine pointed right at you. You shoot me and you are dead—right, Denise?" said Ray.

"Ya, Ray, he will be dead, as will his partner. Shannon has him in her sight," replied Denise.

Ray didn't know Shannon had quietly moved out the other side and had the other robber in her sights, ready to shoot to kill.

Ray told the robber, "Are you ready to die? We will shoot to injure you and your partner unless you shoot me, then its shoot to kill. Shannon, Denise, do your job."

Almost simultaneously, Shannon and Denise shot both the robbers' gun hands and the robbery attempt was over. Ray ordered them to get going unless they wanted to pay a visit to a mortician.

The traveling party came together, relieved that nobody had died in the incident.

"Now you've all seen how Ray takes control and gets the job done," said Baasim. "Thanks to you gals; without much communication, you knew your job from the beginning."

"Well, in India this is just all in a day's work—right, Baasim?" said Ray, smiling.

"Right, just all in a day's work when you have Ray as a client," replied Baasim.

With that they were back into their vehicles bound for New Delhi. Around five o'clock they were at the New Delhi Hotel.

Baasim turned to Ray. "Tomorrow morning I will meet you here," he said. "You can then make reservations for your flight home. We can visit the US embassy here in New Delhi. Later we will all have dinner so Shannon and Denise can meet our families," he added.

"Sounds good, Baasim. See you in the morning. And hey, I am paying for the dinner—make sure your uncle understands it's something I have to do. My dad and mom would want me to do it," said Ray.

"Okay, Ray. It will be fun to have everybody at dinner," replied Baasim.

The next morning, and Baasim and Ray went to the airport and made all the flight reservations. The route was similar to the one coming over, with all the same stops. The arrival date was July 24, about four days away.

Baasim took Ray, Shannon, and Denise down to meet Bob Jones, the consul at the USA embassy. After showing appropriate identification, they were escorted to his office and introduced to Bob Jones. The first thing Bob said was, "Ray, you and your guide sure had an exciting adventure. Now you are safe and probably anxious to get home to California."

"That's right. At the moment Baasim and I want you to know that we have something in mind, and maybe you could use your influence to help us," replied Ray.

"What is it that you need me to do?" Bob said.

"You know I came here to hunt a Bengal tiger for trophy. I didn't get the trophy, but in a way I got something more valuable—touching and interacting with a Bengal tiger. I decided I would like the US and India to enter into a program that would preserve and protect the Bengal tiger from becoming extinct," said Ray.

"I will be more than happy to start a program like that," replied Bob. "I will contact the Indian government and our government to see how to get started." After concluding the meeting, they all said thanks and went back to the hotel.

"I will go pack your container and put all your belongings in it, and prepare it for air freight," said Baasim. "You all use the rest of the day to enjoy New Delhi. I will be back to pick you up for dinner at about six o'clock."

Ray, Shannon, and Denise used the hotel telegram service to inform Ray's parents of the traveling plans, flight number, and arrival times so Joeseph could make the necessary arrangements to pick them up at the San Francisco airport. When that was done, they decided to go back to their room and just relax and wait to have dinner with the Sharma families. Ray and Shannon went to their room after they asked Denise to meet them at five o'clock in the hotel lobby.

It was a perfect time for Ray and Shannon to be alone and they did make the most of it. At five o'clock they met Denise at the lobby, enjoying conversation while waiting to be picked up.

"Ray, I believe you were made for an adventure like this. Someday you ought to write a novel about this adventure," said Denise.

"You know, Denise, you might be right, but one of my biggest adventures was when I happened to meet this gal sitting next to me," replied Ray. "To me, that was an adventure worth living for."

Just then they then noticed Baasim and his family coming into the lobby, followed by Aadesh and his family.

Introductions were made all around before Ray noticed something. "Where is Acharya?" he asked.

"He is going to meet us at the restaurant," Aadesh replied. With that they were off into the vans and made their way to the restaurant.

After Baasim asked the receptionist to take them to Acharya, they were duly escorted to the table where he was. They had a wonderful time conversing with each other before eventually ordering their dinner.

When it was over, Ray asked for the check, but the waiter told him, "This dinner is on the house."

Ray asked with a puzzled look, "Why is the dinner on the house?"

"Sir, the Sharmas are precious people to us. We understand you saved Baasim from being killed by an Indian leopard, and that's the reason," the waiter explained.

Ray looked at Acharya. "Did you have anything to do with this?" asked Ray.

"A few visits ago at this restaurant, I did mention that we learned through a telegram that you had saved a village leader as well as my nephew Baasim from a leopard attack. That was all I said, so I am just as surprised as you, but it is fitting for you to receive this dinner as a token of our family appreciation," replied Acharya. "Just look at those two boys; they would be without a father if you hadn't been alert and a good marksman when you needed to be. Thank you, Ray," he concluded.

Soon the dinner was up and they left for the hotel. At the lobby they said goodbye, tears falling all around. Ray managed to say a few parting words.

"This was a trip of a lifetime. It is so great to meet you, the Sharma families, and of course, Acharya. I don't know what lies ahead but I will keep in touch, and if you all could ever make it to California, we would all look forward to seeing you. Thanks for everything you have done, it's all been great," he said before turning to Baasim. "I guess we will see you in the morning to take us to the airport. Goodbye to you all."

Morning came and Ray, Shannon, and Denise were down at the hotel lobby waiting for Baasim. They didn't wait long and soon they loaded their luggage into a van and were off to the airport. At the TWA ticket counter they checked in their luggage. Flight #315 was called for boarding and they all went to Baasim and gave him a hug.

"It's been a pleasure to have you as guide and now a great friend," said Ray. "Please try to come and see us in California.

I will keep in touch with you about our joint project to start preserving the existence of the Bengal tiger."

"Thanks, Ray. Our friendship will always be there, and my family is forever grateful for you saving my life," said Baasim. Turning to Shannon and Denise, he said, "Thank you two for helping free Ray and me from that village. And Denise, you have fun with that little one you have inside you. Let me know when you give birth, my family will be so excited."

Shannon went to Baasim and said, "Ray could not have picked a better guide. Thank you also for protecting my husband."

"Shannon, when you and Ray have a little one, please let me know. We will all be so excited to hear the news," replied Baasim.

Shannon hugged Baasim and whispered something to him. He looked up with a big smile, and they soon made their way to board their plane on the way to San Francisco, California.

CHAPTER 27

THE JOURNEY HOME WITH A SURPRISE

O n their way to the plane, Ray, Shannon, and Denise
were all smiling and talking about their adventures in
India.

"Just think we will all be home in a few days and enjoying
life on the farms," said Ray enthusiastically. "And Denise,
you and Joeseph will become parents. That's got to be so
exciting!"

"Ray, Shannon—thank you so much," said Denise.

"For what, Denise?" said Shannon.

"Well, the two of you brought Joeseph and me together,
remember?" replied Denise.

"Ya, I remember, Denise." The two friends reached across
the aisle and held each other's hand firmly as if to say, *Our
friendship is tightly bonded.*

Back in California at the Johnson ranch, Paul and Mary
had just finished lunch when they heard somebody knocking
at the door. It was the mailman with a telegram. The mailman
said, "Mary, I have a telegram from India for you to sign.
By the way, I just heard on the news that Ray, Shannon, and
Denise are now on the plane and coming home. It's been a
long time coming—you and Paul have a good day, see you
all later."

Mary went back into the kitchen and said, "Paul did you
hear? The news said Ray, Shannon, and Denise are on the
plane and on their way home!" Mary opened the telegram to

see all the flight information. She called Joeseph and gave him the details.

Joeseph came right over, gave Mary and Paul a big hug, and said, "Mom, Dad, it's been a long wait to get them all back, but they will be here soon, and I can't wait to see them all! Mom, what was that flight number again?"

"It's TWA flight #315; arrives at two o'clock on July 24."

"Mom, that flight number is Ray's birthday; must be a lucky number—what a coincidence! I can't wait to pick them up and have Denise back home." Joeseph emotionally added, "Mom, Dad, it was so hard for me to let Denise go, but it just had to be. My friend was in trouble and her friend needed help. I also wanted to go along but I just couldn't."

"Joeseph what kept you from going?" asked Paul.

"I thought it was my place to take care of you. It was a hard situation to go through, and you have always been like a mom and dad to me," he said, getting close to them.

"And you are like a son to Paul and me. Thank you for your concern for us. It's going to be great to see all their faces again," said Mary.

Back on the plane, time was going by pretty fast and before they knew it, they were on their last leg of the trip and heading to San Francisco.

Denise and Shannon had aisle seats across each other; Ray next to Shannon was fast asleep. Shannon pulled out a pen, wrote a note, and handed it to Denise.

After reading the note, Denise looked up with a big smile. She whispered to Shannon, "Really, really, Shannon, what a blessing from God...!" They reached across the aisle and held hands tightly again, an indication of their strong bond as best friends.

The captain announced that they would be arriving at San Francisco airport in 30 minutes. Ray was awake at this time.

"Hey, we are almost home. What a great feeling when we finally get to see Joeseph!" he said.

"I will second that. I can't wait to give him a big kiss and a hug," Denise said, smiling.

The TWA airplane soon touched down on the runway at the San Francisco airport. Ray was smiling. "Well, you two, we made it back to California and it feels good!" Just then, Ray started to get emotional, and Shannon noticed it.

"Ray, what's wrong?" she asked him.

"I just remember all the things that happened to me in India and the friends I made, especially my tiger friend Bengal Ruby. I wonder if I will ever see any of them again. Oh well, time will tell and only God knows the future," he said.

"The important thing is you had a great experience and lots of good memories. Those are worth so much. I believe someday we and some of your friends like the Sharma families will get together again," she said.

When the passengers were advised they could disembark the plane, the three of them made their way to the terminal. Denise was being very emotional at this time, her tears flowing at the thought of seeing her husband Joeseph again. At the TWA terminal they saw him immediately, and Denise and Joeseph embraced each other as if they wouldn't let go. Finally Joeseph gave Ray and Shannon a hug, greeting them with a lot of emotion.

"I am so relieved to finally see and touch you all again. Welcome home!" he said. "Let's get your luggage be on our way to Isleton. Our families are all waiting to welcome you back!"

Soon they had their luggage loaded into the 1960 red Impala. Joeseph promptly started the trip home to the Johnson ranch, a 90 minute drive. At Isleton they saw how active the town was this summer, a lot of it involving boating and water skiing on the Sacramento River. "Well, this is home," commented Ray. Three miles further they pulled into the Johnson ranch, where all the families were at hand to welcome them home with plenty of warm hugs and tears of joy.

Ray immediately went to his mom and dad and gave them the longest hug while whispering to them, "Mom, Dad, at one point I didn't know if I was going to ever see you again, but here we are together and we can now continue our life on the Sacramento Delta. It's so good to be home."

At last the families were once again united after a lot of joy was passed around. Ray's dad prepared some steaks for dinner and everybody was seated and eating when he called the attention of everybody. "This is a joyous occasion for all the families to be united once again. We should all be grateful that God found a way to bring everybody home," he said.

"Paul and I are so blessed to have Shannon, her friend Denise, and Joeseph in our lives," Mary managed to add, pausing before she continued, "When Ray and his guide were listed as missing, I could sense that Shannon wasn't going to sit by and do nothing. I also knew her friend Denise was going to be by her side. Joeseph could tell his friend was in some sort of trouble, and Paul and I knew they were planning something."

"The plan took my precious daughter-in-law and her friend to India to find my missing son," Paul said. "Mary and I knew how much of an emotional burden the families took upon themselves seeing Shannon and Denise leave in order to find my son."

"But here we are, God answered our prayers and we should all give thanks for the outcome," Mary concluded.

"During this whole episode, God granted something very special to the Alexander family: Denise is pregnant with a child. So congratulations are in order," Paul said, and everybody gave a round of applause, extending all the goodwill to Joeseph and Denise.

Just then, Denise stood up.

"Okay Shannon and Ray, please come and stand by Mary and Paul." Likewise, Denise asked Elizabeth and Bob to come up and stand to the side of Shannon. "Well, to Joeseph's and my parents, what you see here is a family that had a dream; that dream has now come true, for this family that you see standing here are going to have a new role in life."

Ray was wondering what Denise was leading up to.

"Mary, Paul; Elizabeth and Bob, your new role will be...." Denise had to collect her emotional thoughts before she continued to say, "My best friend in the whole world is pregnant; you are about to be grandparents! Ray, congratulations! You are on the way to being a father!" Denise let out finally.

The announcement made for a big happy family affair on the Johnson ranch. Shannon knew her best friend wanted to make the announcement. Everybody was joyfully fired up at the turn of events.

Ray whispered to Shannon, "Honey, it happened in the jungles of India at the entrance of the castle, at Bengal Ruby's den!"

"Ya, Ray; that was a wonderful moment in our lives, and we should remember it forever," confirmed Shannon.

"Well, what an outcome to Ray's adventure to India!" Joeseph happily said. "In about nine months our two families will start to raise our children on these two ranches in the Sacramento Delta." A thought suddenly occurred to Joeseph "Knowing my friend Ray, he is probably already making plans to order a Marlin 39A 22 rifle for the kid. I can guarantee it."

"That's right, Joeseph, and I am sure your coming little one will be right alongside ours. What a future it would be if I may say so," said Ray.

"I have one more item I must share with all of you," Joeseph started. "You all know how I had trained Shannon and my wife to shoot 30-30 Winchester carbines, and they became so good at shooting those rifles," he concluded.

"Ya, Joeseph, you wanted to make sure Denise and I could protect ourselves out here in the country," Shannon replied, "but after all that's happened to us, I sometimes wonder if that was the real reason," she finished.

"Shannon, you probably had a right to wonder; as a matter of fact, I did have another reason for the training the two of you went through," Joeseph replied, smiling. "When Ray told me he was going to India for a Bengal tiger hunt, I realized he could get into trouble over there. If that happens, I know Shannon was going to do all she could to get him back, and with my wife Denise, too. Seeing all that, I decided they had better be able to defend themselves under any situation they could find themselves in."

"Joeseph, you should have been there to see their performance," said Ray, smiling broadly. "I tell you it was great; you trained them well."

Around four o'clock in the afternoon, everybody was on their way. Ray and Shannon remained with Ray's mom and dad.

Shannon went to Mary and Paul. "Ray's trip to India was all worth it. We made good friends, and now Ray and I are going to give you a grandchild," she said.

When Mary hugged Shannon, she just couldn't let go, "That was a big surprise! Paul and I can't wait for your delivery day so we can hold our grandchild in our arms! Shannon, it will be a great day when you give birth," Mary enthused.

"Well, we haven't even been home yet," said Ray. "We will see you tomorrow. We have to get home now and unpack."

Once inside their house, Ray said, "Everything looks the same. Shannon, thank you so much for coming to India. I am glad you went and met some good people and my tiger friend Bengal Ruby."

"What a beautiful animal Bengal Ruby is! It's too bad we will never see him again," Shannon said.

"You are probably right, but I will always remember him and tell the story," said Ray.

"Ray, we got a lot of catching up to do. See, we still haven't broken the bed. You know how it is... I am starting to feel like a dog in heat," teased Shannon.

"Shannon, you haven't changed one bit, and I wouldn't want you to," replied Ray, smiling. "I feel like I am the luckiest man on earth to have you in my life."

With that they retired to the bedroom. The next morning, Friday, Ray and Shannon prepared for the day's activities. First, they realized they had to get some groceries. Then the phone rang, and Ray answered it. It was Ray's mom inviting them over for breakfast and they accepted.

At the door, Shannon said, "Mom, thanks for the invite; we just realized we have to go shopping. We have no food in the house."

"Well, we are having linguica and eggs—does that sound good to you two?" Mary said.

Shannon gave Mary a hug and said, "Mom, it's just like old times—except Joeseph is not here with us...."

Just then they heard a voice. "Did I hear my name mentioned?" It was Joeseph, with Denise; Mary also invited them over for breakfast."

"This is starting to look like normal times. It feels so good to have everybody here!" Paul said.

After breakfast, Denise and Shannon made Monday appointments with a doctor for their pregnancy.

Ray called Fred Sunday at Lodi Mold to ask if he could return to work on Monday.

"Most certainly! We will see you Monday morning. We are all glad to hear all of you are back home," replied Fred.

Ray and Shannon were soon off to Isleton for grocery shopping, making time to drop by and say hello to Mr. and Mrs. Chin, who greeted and hugged them warmly.

"Ray, we were so afraid we might not see you ever again!" said Mr. Chin. "But hearing that Shannon and Denise were heading to India to find you sure took care of our worries. It is so great to have you back!"

After shopping, they headed back to the ranch. Later, they drove out to the field to see the tomato crop was already harvested. The corn looked good for that time of the year.

Ray went to work on Monday, while Shannon and Denise went to the doctor for a prenatal examination. After confirming their pregnancy, the doctor told them they would probably have a delivery date of late March for Denise, and early April for Shannon.

Shannon and Denise were soon back home with all the good news, happy at the knowledge that they would give birth within a month or less of each other.

Life on the Johnson ranch quickly returned to normal. One Day Shannon gave Mary a call and asked her, "Mom, would you be available to help me and my mom with the nursery for your grandchild?"

"Oh, Shannon, I would love to help in any way possible!" replied Mary.

"I'd pick you up before driving to Lodi to pick up my mom. We will have to go shopping for curtains, a baby crib, blankets, and think of new colors for the room. I already called my mom. I will be over to pick you up, and we ladies can have some fun," said Shannon.

After putting down the phone, Mary turned to Paul and excitedly said, "Paul, Shannon kept her promise to include me in helping with the nursery! We are heading to Lodi."

That set the nursery project in motion, taking top priority among things that had to be done. In two weeks it was completed and ready to accept the new addition to the family.

Time moved fast, and all attention was on the two young mothers-to-be who just grew bigger and bigger. Late March Denise was a little overdue and should give birth at any time.

It was Friday night; Ray and Shannon were home watching TV when the phone rang. Ray answered it and on the other line was Joeseph. "Hi, Joeseph, what's going on?"

"Ray, Denise and I are heading to the Lodi Memorial Hospital; I believe Denise is going into labor. I will see you later. I will let you know the progress that Denise is making," said Joeseph.

"Good luck. Stay calm, everything will work out," said Ray. Turning to Shannon, he announced, "Shannon, Denise and Joeseph are going to the hospital; it appears Denise is in labor."

After several hours, the phone rang again. Ray ran to answer it, and sure enough it was Joeseph.

"Hi, Joeseph, how are things going? Oh, you are now a father to a baby girl! Is Denise okay? Is the baby okay?" said Ray.

"Ray, everything is okay. Denise was in labor for only three hours and then, wow, what an experience! We have a little girl, and she weighed 8 pounds, 10 ounces. Her name is Annie Renae."

"Shannon and I will be there tomorrow to see Annie and visit with Denise and you. See you tomorrow morning," said Ray before hanging up the phone.

Saturday after breakfast, Ray and Shannon were on their way to Lodi. As they were driving, Ray told Shannon, "If little Annie likes shooting, I am going nickname her little Annie Oakley. Do you remember when I first told you about Annie Oakley?"

"Ya, Ray, I remember. I will never forget those early days of our relationship," replied Shannon.

Standing before Denise's room at the hospital, they first peeked in the doorway. Shannon saw her friend holding her little girl, and Joeseph was sleeping. Shannon quietly went to Denise and gave her friend a hug. It proved to be a difficult thing to do; Shannon herself was just a week or so away from her delivery date, and she looked like she was ready to burst.

Shannon and Ray looked at little Annie with amazement. "You two have a beautiful little girl," said Ray, smiling. "When she gets older I will give her a Marlin 39A 22 rifle. A name like Annie rightly deserves it."

Now awake, Joeseph smiled. "Ray, only you would think of doing something like that," he said.

At that point, Shannon was compelled to sit down. "What's wrong, honey?" a worried Ray asked.

"It's probably nothing," replied Shannon.

They were there 30 minutes when Shannon had another bout with biting pain. "Oh," she muttered, "Ray, let's walk down to the nurse's station."

"Why, honey, what's wrong? Are you starting to get labor pains?" asked Ray excitedly.

"I don't know. Since we are here, I could ask," said Shannon.

As they made to leave the room, Shannon told Denise and Joeseph, "It's probably nothing. We will see you in a little bit."

Denise told Joeseph, "I think she is going to deliver her baby. Her due date is not that far off anyway."

At the nurse's station, Ray and Shannon told the nurses what was happening. They immediately took Shannon in and examined her. The nurse came out and told Ray, "We are calling the doctor in. Shannon has dilated extensively. Mr. Johnson, you can go to the waiting room. We will keep you informed; from my experience, it won't be long for you to be a daddy."

Ray went to the waiting room, and Joeseph came in. "What's happening, Ray?" Joeseph asked.

"The nurse just told me I am going to be a daddy. The doctor is on his way," replied Ray.

"Ray, I will be right back! I am going to tell the news to Denise," Joeseph replied.

A little later, Joeseph sat down with Ray, who proved to be a very nervous father-to-be. Soon a nurse came to tell Ray, "Things are moving rather rapidly. Shannon asked for you, so please follow me."

At the predelivery room, Ray went to Shannon and gave her a kiss. The doctor came in and explained, "The birth is just a little premature, but there is nothing to worry about. Ray, it would be better if you go to the waiting room. Give your wife a kiss before we proceed to the delivery room."

Ray went back to the waiting room where Joeseph, Denise, and little Annie waited with him. After about 45 minutes the doctor walked in. Ray shot up immediately.

"You are a proud father of a healthy baby boy. Mom is in great shape and everybody is doing well. He weighed 7 pounds 15 ounces, quite handsome, too. In about an hour you will be able to see him and mom."

Ray excitedly turned to Denise and Joeseph. "Boy, that was quick! You will be the first to know—his name is Tiger Cody."

Gathering his thoughts together, Ray realized he had to call Shannon's and his parents. He thus quickly went to the nurses' station and used their phone to make the calls, briefly explaining to them how things happened so quickly, and they all seemed to understand.

Shannon and her baby boy were finally brought to their room. The nurse called Ray so he could get a look at his new born son. Denise, Joeseph, and Annie were also there and everybody settled down to be calm and relaxed.

In time, Ray's and Shannon's parents showed up to see their new grandson. They were all one happy family ready to get on with the next phase of their lives.

Thus two ranches on the Sacramento Delta became home to Tiger and Annie, two new lives on the way to start their own paths.

CHAPTER 28

SHANNON IS WORRIED AND SCARED

E verybody, especially the grandparents, was excited at the Johnson and Alexander ranches. Tiger and Annie were two months old.

Ray kept in touch with Baasim every month. A telegram from Baasim told him to pick up the container with his belongings at the air freight terminal at the San Francisco Airport.

The next day, Ray and Joeseph went to the freight terminal and found there were two containers. One was Ray's original container, the other unknown to him, but they loaded both and returned to the ranch. After unloading the containers, they proceeded to open the second container. Inside they saw the trophy head mounts of the two Indian leopards that Ray had shot while saving Baasim and Banhi's life from the two leopards.

Ray quickly mounted them on the wall, one on each side of the fireplace mantel. They each had an engraved plaque that said, THANKS RAY FOR SAVING OUR LIVES ALWAYS BAASIM AND BANHI.

Ray coordinated with the California San Diego zoo of the project to protect the Indian Bengal tiger from becoming an endangered species. The zoo administrator told Ray he could see no problem if they received a tiger; they could very easily introduce it into a breeding program. In the end, Ray was to ready to receive a Bengal tiger from India whenever they could trap one and bring it to the United States.

Ray sent a telegram to Baasim and told him everything that he would need to do. Baasim replied he was working on the project, but it would probably take a year or two. He indicated that the government of India was definitely interested in the project.

In 1967 Tiger and Annie were six years old. They grew up the best of friends doing everything together. Ray's dad would take them out where they could play and have fun, and get as dirty as one could ever imagine.

One Saturday around ten o'clock in morning, the phone rang and Shannon answered it.

"Oh, hi Mom, what are you up to? Oh, there is someone to see Ray and me? We will be right over. Okay, Mom, I will make sure to bring Tiger and Annie. I'll have Denise and Joeseph come also, see you in about 15 minutes or so."

After hanging up the phone, Shannon gathered Ray, Tiger, and Annie who had stayed overnight with Tiger. With Denise and Joeseph who came after she called them, they walked to Ray's parent's house.

As they approached, Ray noticed a big truck towing a low bed trailer with a covered enclosure on the side of which was some writing.

"Ray, our friends from India are here," Shannon said.

"How do you know, Shannon?" said Ray.

"The sign on the trailer says 'India and USA program to save the Bengal tiger. Thanks to Ray and Baasim, a tiger named Bengal Ruby will have a home at the San Diego Zoo in southern California.'"

With that they all ran inside, where Acharya, Baasim, and his brother Aadesh were waiting for them. What followed was a round of warm hugs, smiles, and excitement from everyone.

Ray was first to ask. "Is *that* Bengal Ruby in the cage on the trailer?"

"Ya, Ray. It took a while but I wanted you to see your friend again," replied Baasim. "Let's all go out and raise the side cover to the cage to see his reaction."

Outside everyone stood by the trailer as Baasim raised the cover. Bengal Ruby immediately saw Ray who stood close to the trailer and offered his paw to Ray through the cage's steel bars. Man and tiger brought their faces to the cage bars and the tiger gave Ray a lick on his face. Ray reached through and petted the tiger's neck, and the reunion was done. The tiger never forgot Ray.

An emotional Ray stood by Shannon; he was beyond himself at seeing his friend again, and he was so happy to have started the Bengal tiger preservation program between the US and India.

Ray's parents couldn't believe their eyes when Ray reached in to pet the tiger.

"Dad, Mom, please, don't worry. I know this tiger. When he acknowledged me first as he did, I knew he remembered me and was thus safe to pet," said Ray to his parents.

As Tiger and Annie had not been told about Ray's adventure in India, the adults proceeded to explain to them the amazing story of the tiger named Bengal Ruby. .

"It's time for lunch," said Mary. "We have a very special Portuguese lunch today. It's called *soupas.*"

"Can't wait to eat lunch!" said Joeseph. "This food is great, and I am sure you all will like it." With that they went into the house and sat down to eat.

After a while, Baasim commented, "Mary, this is definitely a good traditional Portuguese food. I can see why Joeseph was excited."

"I know Mary is a good preparer of fine food," said Acharya. "I remember having so many meals here each time I went to fish when I was in college."

"Those were great times, Acharya," said Paul. "You held Ray when he was four years old and ended up meeting him on the airplane trip to India. Then your nephew Baasim was to be his hunting guide. What a surprise."

"Mary, Paul, you were so kind to insist I stay for dinner every time I was here. I had to come here with my nephews so I could thank you for everything. I also want to say that you have a fine son. Shannon and her friend Denise I will remember forever after we encountered the village that held Ray and Baasim captive. Those are the memories my nephews and I will remember forever," Acharya said.

"Joeseph, you did a good job training these two gals to shoot those 30-30 Winchester carbines," said Aadesh. "They demonstrated their ability to the villagers, especially to the village leader."

"I just thought Shannon and Denise might need good shooting skills someday. I guess that was the day at the village," replied Aadesh.

Paul was beside himself after hearing what Acharya said about Ray, Shannon, and Denise.

"You all should know that Mary and I think the world of Shannon," Paul said. "We consider her like our own daughter. Someday when I am gone, Ray will be in good hands with Shannon by his side." Turning to Shannon, he said, "And Shannon, someday you know you will look back and I won't be there; when that happens, you will just have to go on."

Shannon could only hang her head. She understood too well what Paul was talking about. At this point, everybody went stone quiet looking at Shannon, who was so emotional, with tears flowing.

Shannon got up, stood behind Paul and Mary, and broke the silence, "I am sorry for my emotional state at this time. Everybody around this table knows how wonderful these two are, how they bring so much love and kindness to us all, including the whole Isleton community."

"Shannon please, you don't have to cry," Mary said.

Shannon was really having trouble to say anything, but she did manage to say, "Dad, Mom, I know I will have to go on, but... but you know it's going to be hard to set foot on the ranch. I will always have memories of working alongside Dad, maybe looking down remembering how we were there irrigating a crop, and then looking around and he's not there."

Acharya reflected and finally spoke, "Shannon, of course there is going to be grieving period. It may take a long time, but it's normal. Right now you give Mary and Paul joy in their hearts showing how you love them and will miss them when they are gone. But you and Ray will go on in life, the grieving period will end, but the memories will always be there, and that's what close families are about."

"Well, as we are sharing some very personal thoughts, I also want to share some important information with Ray," said Baasim.

Ray noticed that Baasim was getting very emotional while attempting to talk. "Baasim, what's the matter? Is something wrong?" asked Ray.

"No, nothing is wrong, Ray, but you are such a friend and I am so proud that India has asked me to deliver this very special message to you," replied Baasim.

Shannon and Ray anxiously waited to hear what Baasim was about to say.

"When I told the India Big Game Commission about our hunting adventure, of how much you wanted to collect a Bengal tiger trophy but made friends with Bengal Ruby instead, they were so impressed, especially when I told them you wanted to look into preserving the Bengal tiger species by beginning a breeding program here in the USA," Baasim said.

"Baasim, thank you so much. Did they like the San Diego Zoo for such a breeding program?" said Ray.

"After looking into it, they came to agree the zoo was one of the finest in the world. So, yes, that's where we are taking Bengal Ruby. They feel he will live at least five more years," said Baasim.

Baasim paused a little and then continued to say, "There is more to the message. The government of India wants you to have Bengal Ruby as a trophy when he dies. Our government will shoulder the taxidermist cost, and you will receive the ruby necklace that hangs around his neck. By giving you the necklace, they feel you will always remember the legend of the Bengal ruby and the beautiful jungles of India."

Acharya joined the conversation by saying, "Well, it's been good to visit the Johnson ranch again, and I am glad, Ray, that my nephews could meet your parents. But now I think we will have to be going as we still have a long trip to San Diego."

Outside, Ray knew he had to say goodbye to Bengal Ruby, and man and tiger made contact with each other again.

"Baasim, thanks again for bringing Bengal Ruby to California. I thought I would never see him again, and now someday he would be my trophy. It would bring great memories, and this story would be told many times. You all have a safe trip," said Ray.

"Dad, could Annie and I pet the tiger?" It was Tiger.

Ray lifted Tiger and Annie level with the cage, careful to observe Bengal Ruby's response at seeing Tiger and Annie being held by him. When he thought it was safe, he let the two kids pet Bengal Ruby for a little while. He didn't want to push it; after all, Bengal Ruby was a wild animal.

When it was over, Baasim lowered the side cover of the cage. Everybody said their goodbyes and they were off to take Bengal Ruby to his new home at the San Diego Zoo.

Everyone started to head home, Shannon walking with Denise. "It is so wonderful how Ray was rewarded for his effort for starting a program to save the Bengal tiger, receiving the tiger after it's mounted by a taxidermist," Denise said. "Shannon, you and I will also remember this famous tiger and how he came to know us. It's such a great remembrance for a truly great adventure."

The two families said goodbye and Joeseph, Denise, and Annie proceeded to their house a little ways away.

Time marched along as it always did, and soon it was 1972. Tiger and Annie at eleven years old already had hunting permits, and Ray had bought them Marlin 39A 22 caliber rifles. They made a habit of hunting cottontail rabbits, and they learned how to dress them out before putting them into the freezer. Like two peas in a pod, the two couldn't resist each other's company.

Shannon immensely enjoyed herself helping Paul with his farming operation, still thinking the world of him and Mary.

One day Paul asked Shannon to take the H-Farmall tractor to hill some corn. They were getting ready to furrow irrigate the corn. Paul was going to make a V ditch by following Shannon atop a D4 Caterpillar tractor with a V ditch plow. They would then use siphon pipes to run water down the rows of corn from a V ditch filled with water.

Driving the H-Farmall tractor, Shannon looked back to see Paul was not behind her, the D4 Caterpillar tractor still close to the ranch shop.

Shannon immediately turned around, tears flowing, especially after seeing her father-in-law on the ground. She jumped off the tractor and knelt down to him; his eyes were open and he had a smile on his face.

Shannon held his head in her arms and asked, "Dad, what's wrong? Are you going to be okay?" Shannon was devastated looking at Paul's condition.

Paul could hardly talk, but he did manage some last words for Shannon. "Shannon, this is when we will part. I think the Lord has picked this time for me to leave. Please take care of Mom, Ray, and Tiger. I know you will. Shannon, thank you so much for being the daughter that I could never have. Tell Ray to take care of you, for you are truly one of kind." Paul paused a little before managing just enough to whisper his final words to Shannon.

Shannon was holding Paul in her arms and crying as she watched his eyes close for the last time. Paul Johnson, the father- in-law that she so loved, had died in her arms. Shannon just sat there with him; suddenly Tiger, Annie, and Mary showed up. Tiger saw the situation from the kitchen window and promptly told Mary that something was wrong outside. They then rushed out to see what had taken place.

Mary was devastated to learn that her husband had died. "Oh, Shannon, did you get to talk to him before he died?"

"Yes, Mom, I did. He bid me to take care of everybody and thanked me for being the daughter that he could never have. Mom, Mom, Mom—what are we going to do without Dad? It's going to be tough around here," cried Shannon.

Tiger came to his mom, put his arms around her, and said, "Mom, Annie and I will help you get through this hard time. It's going to be hard for everybody. We need to call Dad at work so he can get home. He's going to be devastated."

They went to the ranch house and Shannon called Lodi Mold Inc. Liz the receptionist answered the phone, and Shannon told her what had happened. Liz said, "Shannon, I will tell Fred Sunday to call Ray to his office before we tell him. One of us will offer to drive him home."

Liz called Fred Sunday and told him what had happened. Fred called Ray to his office. Liz was seated down when Ray came in. "Well, how is everything going today?" said Ray.

Silence.

Liz got up and went to Ray. Ray then sensed something was wrong. "What's wrong, Liz? Did something happen at the ranch?"

"Yes, Ray. Your dad has died."

Silence.

"I told Shannon one of us will drive you home," Liz went on to say, holding him tightly.

"No, no, that's okay. I think I will need that little drive to get all the past memories about my dad through my mind. He was the best friend and dad a son could ever have," Ray said.

"Your dad died in Shannon's arms," Liz said.

"That is about the best thing that God could have arranged, Dad dying in the arms of the person he loved so much. She was like a daughter to him. I will be okay; I will drive home and do a lot of thinking on the drive home," said Ray.

Mary had already called the funeral home in Rio Vista to let them know that Paul had died, and asked them to come to pick up her husband. The family would be down to make the funeral arrangements later.

About 30 minutes later, the funeral personnel arrived and took Paul to the Rio Vista funeral home, which was about seven miles away. Shortly after, Ray arrived and went immediately to both Shannon and his mom and gave them both a hug.

Shannon was very emotional and teary eyed as she told Ray, "Honey, what are we going to do without your dad? I don't think I can survive without seeing or talking to him."

Tiger came to his mom and dad. "We can all survive. My grandfather would want us to go on and be strong in a situation like this," he said.

373

Mary heard tiger's words and responded, "That's right, Tiger, and your grandmother will help get everybody through this grieving period. Shannon, we will survive this episode in our lives."

Shannon then thought that she had better call Denise. So she did get Denise on the phone and told her what had happened.

In 10 minutes Denise and Joeseph walked through the door. Denise went to Mary and gave her a hug. In a very emotional tone of voice she said, "I will miss Paul immensely. You all know you can count on Joeseph and me to help you with everything."

"And I am going to help Tiger get through this tough period in his life," Annie added. "Losing a grandfather like his is a big change in his life." For some reason she went to Tiger and gave him a hug and a kiss on the cheek and told him, "Tiger, you can always count on me, remember that." And then Annie gave him another kiss, but this time on his lips.

Shannon and Ray looked at each other, thoughts running through their mind. In the end they just passed it off, knowing Annie and Tiger were such close friends.

The next day Ray, Shannon, and Mary went to the funeral parlor and made all the arrangements. The funeral was to be on a Thursday.

As they drove home, a lot was going through Ray's mind. Knowing he had to make some decisions, he decided to share his thoughts by saying, "You know, Mom, I think I am going to have to turn in my resignation at Lodi Mold, Inc."

"Yes, Ray, I believe you will have to help Shannon run things, and it's time to turn over the reins to you. Dad and I had already talked about that. One more thing: your dad was very successful at investing so I will not need any ranch income. Therefore, all the income from the ranch will be yours and Shannon's," said Mary.

Shannon tearfully told Mary, "We will always be here for you. I hope you know that."

They arrived at the ranch and Mary got out of the car. Ray walked her to the door, gave her a hug, and said, "We are all going to miss Dad. I know it will be hard on you living here without your longtime partner. Mom, I will see you tomorrow."

Thursday the day of the funeral came. It turned out to be a well-attended funeral, followed by a reception at the Catholic Church in Isleton. When it was over, Ray, Shannon, and Tiger along with Annie took Mary home.

They gave Mary a hug and Tiger said, "Grandma I will be here as often as I can," before giving her a big hug and a kiss on the cheek, and they all left for their homes.

Shannon said, "You know, Ray, I wonder how long your mom is going to last without your dad by her side." Shannon paused a little and then added, "That Christmas letter that your dad once wrote to you is now a reality. As we walk as family, we will all look back and your dad will not be there. That letter will always be on my mind, something your dad and I often shared with each other."

CHAPTER 29

RAY AND SHANNON
OWN THE RANCH

P aul was put to rest and the family was trying to get back to normal. Shannon and Ray were now running the farming operation. They had tomatoes and corn to take care of, and it was time to handle the irrigation the crops. It was busy time on the farm.

Ray called Lodi Mold shortly after his dad's death, advising Fred Sunday that due to the new circumstances, he had to resign from his position. Fred completely understood and expressed that he would truly be missed.

About four weeks after Paul's death, Mary had Ray and Shannon come over to talk over some family matters. At the kitchen was Mary smiling and welcoming them with a hug.

Mary said, "My son and daughter, what I have here is something very special." Getting very emotional, Mary could hardly speak.

Ray looked at her and commented, "Mom, should we come back another time?"

"No, no! It's just a happy time in my life. But I do wish Paul was here to enjoy the happiest moments that I am about to enjoy. He so wanted to do this, especially after you married Shannon. He talked about it often to me, as what a joy this day would have been to him," explained Mary.

Patiently, Ray and Shannon waited for their mom to finish what she was about to say.

"Well, you two: here is the deed to the ranch; it's all yours— Dad and I just couldn't wait for this day to come," said Mary finally.

The two went to Mary and hugged her and thanked her for such a special gift.

"Mom how are you getting along without Dad around?" asked Shannon.

"Some days are really hard. I just miss the kindness that Paul would bring to everybody he knew," Mary replied.

"Mom, you must have taken your ways from him," said Ray, smiling.

Shannon was really emotional as she told Mary, "Mom, why do you think I called you both Mom and Dad the first time I ever met you. The two of you have that loving attitude, and it shows with everybody that you come in contact with."

Ray and Shannon gave Mom one more hug before going off to the fields to irrigate the corn and tomatoes. They seemed to have everything completely under control.

Shannon returned home ahead of Ray so she could cook dinner. Ray stayed to finish the siphon pipes to furrow irrigate the corn. Back at home, he greeted Shannon with a kiss as she was busy cooking dinner.

"Ray, I just received a phone call from the San Diego zoo administrator. He said Bengal Ruby had passed away. He wanted you to know that Bengal Ruby had sired eight tiger cubs and that you should be proud of your effort to save the Bengal tiger from extinction," said Shannon.

"Did he mention anything about Bengal Ruby being mounted as trophy?" asked Ray.

"Yes, Ray; he said it's already being processed as we speak, and it should be delivered in about a month, along with the ruby necklace," replied Shannon.

"I think we should mount him on the wall between the two leopard trophies," said Ray.

"That sounds good to me; it would be a fine remembrance of your trip to India," said Shannon.

The three of them were now getting ready for dinner. Ray said, "Tiger, I almost forgot—Grandma called and said to come over tomorrow for breakfast. She said she had a surprise for you, and to bring Annie so she could share in the surprise."

"You know, Dad, it's been hard without grandpa around. Annie and I sure miss going out in the field with him. Dad, did you know he taught Annie and me how to drive his pickup? It was funny how Annie could hardly see out the windshield. I will call Annie after dinner and tell her about breakfast in the morning at Grandma's, and maybe after breakfast we could go hunting," said Tiger.

"You and Annie are twelve years old and you still like to hunt with each other—the best of friends. Tiger, a person always needs a real close friend in life, someone who can always give you support and advice when needed. I hope your friendship will always be there," said Ray.

"You know, Dad, I am sure we will always be friends till the day we die."

After dinner, Tiger called Annie about breakfast at Grandma's, and hunting afterwards.

That night when Ray and Shannon were in bed talking, Ray brought up the subject about Annie and Tiger being such close friends. "You remember that little talk I had at dinner with Tiger about him and Annie being such close friends? He says he thinks the world of her and he feels they will be fiends forever. I hope that is true," said Ray.

"I have also given a lot of thought about Tiger and Annie. They will be starting high school in a couple of years. Annie being so cute, I just know she will be asked out by other boys, and I think it's going to break Tiger's heart when it happens, and I know it will happen," said Shannon.

"Well, honey, we just have to let life go on and see how it all works out," replied Ray.

The next morning, Annie showed up to go with Tiger for breakfast at Grandma's and to find out what she had for surprise. As the two walked in at the old ranch house, Mary was as joyful as ever to see her grandson and Annie.

Mary went to Annie and said, "Honey, I believe you are getting cuter by the day—don't you think so, Tiger?"

"Ya, Grandma, she sure is cute and I must say nice," replied Tiger.

"Well, let's sit down and have some breakfast," said Mary.

Once the three of them were seated down, Tiger said, "After breakfast, Annie and I are going to go hunting."

"On that subject, I talked with your dad and told him you could drive your grandfather's pickup anywhere on the ranch, and that includes the Alexanders' ranch also. That would make your hunting a little easier."

"Grandma that is so great! Grandpa had taught Annie and me how to drive his pickup."

"I know, Tiger. Paul told me he had let you drive his car," said Mary.

At that point, Annie went to Mary and whispered something in her ear.

"Oh, Annie, you need to give it some time," said Mary, smiling.

After breakfast, Mary handed the key to Tiger and the two were off to their hunting expedition. Along the way they came across Ray and they stopped.

"You two now have a little transportation. I hope you treat the privilege with a lot of respect—that's what your grandpa would expect," said Ray.

"I know Tiger sees it that way, and I know he's thinking right now about his grandpa," said Annie, leaning over and giving him a kiss on the cheek. With that they were off hunting again. They had rabbits dressed out for the freezer at the end of the day.

Annie was so excited about the special day. After they said goodbye and she started for their house, she looked back, smiled at Tiger, and said, "Tiger, did you have a good time?"

"Ya, Annie, I did. You are really fun to be with," replied Tiger.

One day, a special delivery arrived at Ray's house. Shannon who was home received the trophy of Bengal Ruby, along with the ruby necklace.

Once Ray came in from the field and Shannon told him, they opened the wooden box—and before them was his tiger trophy. Tears flowed freely from both of them. The trophy embodied a big part of their early relationship, and they would never forget it.

Shannon held Ray close to her. "My best memories of Bengal Ruby was when we were in the castle looking at the jewels in that chest. He came between us and gave us both a lick on our face, like he had accepted me."

Ray got busy and prepared the wall above the fireplace to mount the trophy of Bengal Ruby.

When Tiger walked into the house, Ray told him, "Tiger, go and look above the fireplace."

Tiger went and looked with amazement at the beautiful specimen of the big cat.

"Dad, someday you have to sit down and tell me what happened in India, how Bengal Ruby became central to your adventure there," said Tiger.

"Tiger, you will know everything about that adventure trip to India," replied Ray.

One Saturday, Annie and Tiger thought they would go hunting again, so they hopped in the pickup and stopped by to see Grandma. They pulled into the yard and went into the house as they usually did.

"This is strange," Tiger said. "Grandma is usually here to greet us." They looked around until they were in her bedroom. Just then, Annie immediately took Tiger into her arms. She could see Tiger's grandma had died, but he hadn't noticed yet.

"Annie, Annie... has my grandma died?" said Tiger.

"It certainly looks like it, Tiger. We better go and call your mom and dad," Annie replied.

Once Ray and Shannon arrived, they patiently collected their thoughts together.

The first thing that occurred to Ray was to call the funeral home in Rio Vista to prepare Mary for burial. Six months after Paul died, Mary was put to rest alongside her husband.

As time passed, the farm operation continued to prosper. Shannon and Ray became very good farmers. They proved to be so successful they even bought a neighboring farm. They could only hope that someday, Tiger would want to continue the family tradition.

The year was 1979. Shannon and Ray had been married twenty years. Tiger was seventeen years old, an incoming senior in high school along with his longtime best friend Annie. Everything was moving right along and soon Tiger would have to pick a college.

One night at dinner, Ray asked, "Tiger, have you decided what college you would like to attend?"

"I am thinking of UC Davis," replied Tiger.

"Have you thought about a major?" asked Shannon.

"Yes, Mom. I would like to major in Agriculture. I want to follow the family tradition. I love seeing things grow and get them harvested for market. To me it's a rewarding profession," replied Tiger.

Ray was now smiling. "Well, I can't tell you how excited your mom and I are about that major. You don't know how it would make us proud to see you someday be managing this operation," he said.

"Tiger, has Annie shown an interest in any colleges?"

"I don't know, Mom. We haven't talked about it very much, but I am sure her parents would want her to get a college education."

Getting a little curious, Shannon asked, "Tiger, do you and Annie still get along as best friends?"

"Oh, yes Mom. I believe she will be my best friend for life. I can't see that ever changing."

"That's good to hear, son," replied Ray, smiling.

"One thing for sure: Annie is a beautiful girl with a lot of class and wonderful parents," Shannon said with a concerned look.

"Yes, Mom, she is really cute. I like Annie a lot. Like I said, I believe we will be friends forever," replied Tiger.

Later in bed, Shannon said, "Only time will tell what Tiger and Annie's relationship will be. It may turn out to be pure friendship, nothing else. I guess that's okay. I just hope Tiger doesn't get hurt someday." With that they went to sleep.

CHAPTER 30

RAY AND SHANNON
IN LOVE WITH LIFE

L ife on the ranch for Ray and Shannon was wonderful; there were even times it was getting better by the day. It was August and high school was to start in a couple of weeks. One day, Tiger went to Annie's house after finishing some field work. Approaching the house, he noticed an unfamiliar car parked in the driveway. Tiger knocked at the door and Annie's mom answered, greeting him with a hug.

"Is Annie home?" asked Tiger.

"Yes Tiger, come on in. She is in the living room," said Denise.

Tiger thought Annie's mom acted a little uneasy towards him, like she wasn't her natural self.

At the living room was Annie with a boy and she introduced Tiger to Jeff Gomes. Tiger knew Jeff, and he suddenly felt out of place in the situation. He had never seen Annie close to another boy before.

Looking devastated, Tiger told Annie, "Well, Annie, I thought you might want to go to the movies tonight, but I guess you already have plans."

Annie had to be truthful and told Tiger, "That's where Jeff and I are going tonight. We are going to see the movie *King Solomon's Mines.*"

385

Tiger was holding up pretty good under the awkward situation. In her bedroom Denise listened to everything. She felt bad seeing what Tiger had to go through, she knew that's life, and it can sometimes be cruel.

"Well, you both have a good time at the movies," said Tiger. "I will see you later, Annie." Tiger then started to walk home.

In the meantime, Denise snuck outside and caught up with Tiger, grabbing him while tears flowed from her eyes. "This had to be so hard for you. I am so sorry, Tiger, you are like a son to me. I wish it could have happened differently."

"It's okay, Mom, some things are just meant to be, but Annie and I will be friends forever, I can guarantee that," Tiger said before heading home.

As Denise made her way back inside the house, she realized Tiger just called her "Mom." Back in the living room, Annie asked, "Mom, your eyes are all red—is there something wrong?"

"No, no, just a case of allergies that came on very quickly."

"Mom, I never knew you had allergies."

Dinnertime at the Johnsons, Ray, Shannon, and Tiger sat talking about today's events around the ranch. Shannon noticed Tiger was not very forthcoming with conversation. "Tiger, is anything wrong? You seem so low-keyed tonight."

"I am just tired, Mom. I'll probably retire early tonight for the big day tomorrow," replied Tiger.

"That's right, we start picking tomatoes tomorrow," said Ray.

As Tiger lay in bed, Shannon and Ray thought something must have happened today, but what was it? Just then, the phone rang. It was Denise. She explained what had happened and wanted to know how Tiger was doing. Shannon explained that she and Ray sensed something happened to account for Tiger's weird mood at dinner. Shannon thanked Denise for calling and letting them know what transpired that day.

In their bed, Ray said, "We knew something like this was going to happen. Annie is such a pretty girl bound to attract boys."

For a time, Tiger and Annie didn't have contact with each other. Tiger kept himself busy with the tomato harvest until it was done.

One Saturday morning, Annie called Tiger and asked him to come over for breakfast. Tiger readily accepted, walking in as usual after he reached Annie's house.

As they were eating, Joeseph said, "Well, the tomato crop is in. That has to be a big relief."

"Ya, it sure is," Tiger responded.

Denise brought up the subject of school. "Well, you two are seniors this year. Soon you'll be off to college. Tiger, have you thought about where you might go?"

"Yes. I would like to attend UC Davis and major in agriculture," replied Tiger.

"I am leaning towards UC Davis, too. I want to be a farmer," said Annie.

After breakfast, Annie told Tiger, "I thought before we start school this year we should have a shootout match at the shooting range. We would use our Marlins 39A 22 caliber rifles. Are you up to it?"

"Annie, are you up to it?" teased Tiger.

After picking up what they needed, the two were off to the shooting range. Once there, they had the shooting bench in order and set up the targets.

There were to be five targets and five shots for each. Score would be based on where the bullet hit the target. Each target was worth a maximum fifty points. Annie was sitting on Tiger's right.

"You shoot first. I will go next," Tiger said.

"Get ready, Tiger, I am in the mood to get you today!" said Annie.

They shot very well; after four targets, their score was tied at 200 points, which was perfect shooting.

"Well, Annie, this is your last target. Shoot carefully." Annie took aim and shot a 10.

"You sure are going to be hard to beat today," commented Tiger.

"Let's just say I am destined to win this match today," said Annie.

"You know, Annie, I believe you might be right." Then Tiger shot another ten. At this point, he was really smiling.

As they went on for target number five and as Annie was about to shoot, Tiger said, "Before your last shot, I have something I have to tell you, Annie."

"What do you want to tell me, Tiger?" Annie replied, not taking her eyes off the target.

"Annie, this is our last year in high school and I thought...."

"Tiger, what are you trying to say?" said Annie, eyes still locked on the target.

"Annie ... over the years we were the best of friends, doing everything together during that relationship. I like you so much, Annie," said Tiger.

"Tiger, what are you trying to tell me?"

"Annie, I have fallen in love with you. I don't know if that's what you wanted to hear from me, but I had to tell you, so you would always know how I felt."

There was no response from Annie; her eyes still glued to the target, she finally made the shot. Still not looking at Tiger, she said, "I just shot a ten—mission accomplished!"

Tiger didn't know what to think. He could not read her mind, no emotional sign. "Annie, I am sorry if I have offended you. I would never want to hurt you in any way." Afterwards, Tiger noted wet spots on the old wood on the shooting bench. *So Annie was crying*, Tiger thought, *maybe that is a good sign,* or he just didn't know for sure what the tears meant.

"Tiger—Cody Johnson—you know how many years I have waited to hear those words," Annie said finally.

The two embraced and kissed like there was no tomorrow, the first time their lips met in such a romantic way. "Tiger, you made my day. I finally got you. I know we will have a wonderful future on this ranch in the Sacramento Delta. I told you I was destined to win this match," said Annie.

Just then, they heard a car coming down the road along the cornfield. "It's Mom and Dad on their daily drive."

Approaching the new couple, Shannon said, "Annie, have you been crying?"

"Ya, Mom. It's just that your son just told me that he loved me."

The remark had Shannon crying out of joy in no time. Tellingly, she said, "Annie, I thought this would be the day those words would come out."

"Mom, your plan worked. It didn't take long."

Shannon happily turned to Tiger. "I have your grandma's diary here. Do you remember the day about seven years ago when she gave you the keys to your grandpa's pickup?"

"Ya, Mom, I remember very well," replied Tiger.

"Here is what the diary says: 'Today, Annie whispered to me, "Someday I will get Tiger to tell me that he loves me." And I told Annie just be patient." Annie was crying, as that day had finally come.

"This shooting bench has a reputation for bringing those words out. It did for us, and Annie, it did for your parents also," said Ray.

Shannon and Ray were soon on their way back to their house. Along the way, Shannon moved close to her husband. "This day reminds me of our own courtship days," she said affectionately. "Those were great memories, and we will always remember those days."

After the target range, Tiger and Annie found themselves riding around the ranch and talking. "Annie, after we graduate high school next year, we should plan on getting married and then attend UC Davis," Tiger said.

"Where would we live?" asked Annie.

"I thought of asking Mom and Dad if we could live in my grandparents' house, and then we could commute to college. Annie, it's only about 40 minutes away. Does that sound like a plan?"

"Tiger, I can't wait to get married! And yes, that seems like a good plan." Tiger and Annie were truly excited about their future plans.

Arriving at Annie's house, they explained to Annie's mom and dad what had just happened.

Denise said to Tiger, "I even felt sorry for you when you saw Annie with Jeff Gomes. I am so glad it worked out well in the end."

"Well, I guess I did a good job of fooling everybody," said Annie.

"What do you mean fooling everybody?" asked Tiger.

"Tiger, Jeff Gomes was a setup guy to get you to make a move for fear of losing me," said Annie.

"My mom did the same thing to my dad," said Tiger, smiling.

"Indeed, it was your mom who gave me the idea—and work it did well and fast, only took a couple of weeks," said Annie.

"Well, I will have to thank my mom," said Tiger.

On the way out, Annie gave Tiger a kiss that he would not forget. This was indeed a great day for Tiger and Annie.

After the kiss, tiger told Annie, "That was a very arousing kiss, Annie."

Annie smiled at tiger as she told him, "I learned from your mom that a woman should always arouse her man with a kiss."

"Annie, you sure seemed to learn a lot from my mom." Tiger smiled and left for home.

Tiger greeted his mom with a hug and kiss, and went and gave his dad a hug. "Mom, Dad, I didn't know if that's what Annie wanted to hear today. But it was, and Mom you gave her the idea of having a guy pretend he was interested in her to get me to make a commitment for fear of losing her. I have to say it worked, and thank you," he said.

"Tiger, I could tell by Annie's actions when you two were sixteen years old that this was becoming more than a casual friendship. Because it was a friendship of that kind, it would be hard for you to take it one more step. I knew Annie wanted a deeper commitment, and when I read what she whispered into grandma's ear, I knew I was right," Shannon said, smiling.

"Mom, Dad, thanks so much for helping to make this the happiest day of my life."

Ray, Shannon, and Tiger went on to talk about the marriage plan and the part about moving into his grandparents' old house.

"You and Annie can have the house, but I believe we will do some updates to fit today's standards before you could move in," said Ray.

"Annie and I want to have a very small and simple wedding—just family and a few friends," said Tiger.

Time ran swiftly. Shortly after graduation, Annie and Tiger were married. They moved into Paul and Mary's house which was completely modernized. Afterwards, they enrolled at UC Davis University and commuted to school every day.

One Saturday, Ray and Shannon had Joeseph, Denise, Tiger, and Annie over for dinner. When it was over, Ray asked everybody to go into the living room. Ray wanted to tell Tiger and Annie a little history about how life at the Johnson ranch had gone for twenty years. Of course, Denise and Joeseph were already aware of much of what Ray was about to say.

Ray began with how he fell in love with Shannon after meeting her at the student lounge at college. He said that at the shooting range, he got her interested in shooting and, eventually, hunting. Ray affectionately narrated that part at the shooting range where he told Shannon he had fallen in love with her.

He told everyone how he had to be upfront with Shannon of his love for the Bengal tiger, of his desire to go hunting in India for a tiger trophy. Ray recalled how Shannon bade him to go to be true to the call of his passion.

"How did the family take it when you were going to leave Mom to go hunting?" Tiger asked.

"With the help of your mom, everyone came to see that I just have to do it," replied Ray.

"Dad, tell us about your hunting trip in India. It all sounded like it was a very adventurous and dangerous trip," said Annie.

"Indeed it was, to such a point that Baasim, my guide, would often wonder what excitement the next days would bring us."

They were all sitting in front of the fireplace where above it was the trophy of Bengal Ruby the tiger. Ray pointed at the tiger. "The tiger was the reason the hunting trip took place."

Ray narrated how he spotted the tiger and how he and Baasim tracked the tiger to an ancient Indian castle.

"He was in a castle—wow!" Tiger exclaimed.

"Yes. Baasim and I felt it was his den. I waited patiently, my rifle focused on what appeared to be a path going in and out the castle.

"Eventually he came out and saw me. I had him in my crosshair, and I noticed he had a ruby necklace around his neck, which meant he was part of the legend of the Bengal ruby," said Ray.

"Why didn't you shoot him?" from Denise.

"On the airplane trip to India, I met Baasim's uncle Acharya who told me about the legend. Acharya went on to tell me, 'When you have a tiger in your crosshair, you may find you cannot pull the trigger. They are such a beautiful animal,' and that's exactly what happened—I couldn't bring myself to pull the tiger," elaborated Ray.

"Dad, do you really believe in the legend?" asked Annie.

"Well, the tiger did everything that the legend described, and he became my friend, even saved my life from an attacking leopard. And he also helped in the release of Baasim and me from the village," said Ray.

"But you know, I have another thought about the legend," continued Ray. "When I had my rifle aimed at him, he was only 100 feet away. We looked at each other for quite a while before he finally left. Looking back, maybe he felt my compassion for him, and he just wanted to return the favor." Ray paused a little before continuing.

"We will never really know the answer, but I do know I was licked in the face by a wild tiger, as was your mother later during their attempt to rescue Baasim and me. Not too many humans have been licked in the face by a wild tiger."

As Joeseph and Denise stood and prepared to leave, Tiger told his dad, "Annie and I would like you to write a book so someday your grandchildren can *read about* your courtship with Mom and your adventures in India."

Ray smiled. "Yes, maybe someday I might just do that. I believe it's a good idea," he concluded.

Just then, Annie went up to Ray, smiling. "Dad I don't know what your title will be, but the ending should include this memory. Also, you are about to be grandparents—I am carrying Tiger's child."

Everybody was filled with joy to hear the great news.

Ray was full of tears as he held Shannon tightly. "Shannon, right now I feel that I am the luckiest man alive to have you in my life. I could never let you get away that day when you walked into the student lounge with that short red dress." Ray paused a little and collected his thoughts. "And now we just heard we are going to be grandparents—what a joyous day!"

With the tiger and leopard trophies above the fireplace behind them, Ray and Shannon stood facing Tiger, Annie, Denise, and Joeseph.

Shannon was starting to get emotional and Ray could sense it.

"Shannon, what's wrong? We should all be in a happy mood right now after the news we just received," teased Ray.

"It's not about being sad; this has truly been a truly happy meeting with Tiger and Annie and our best friends Joeseph and Denise." Pausing awhile to compose herself, Shannon went on to add, "I now want to tell you something that I have never shared with anybody before." Another pause.

"Years ago, Ray's dad died in my arms. Because I loved the man so much for his loving attitude in life, let me tell you I will remember that moment in my life forever."

Everybody was intensely listening to Shannon, wondering what she was leading up to. They could sense it was going to be something very special.

"Before he died, he managed to whisper to me his last loving words. I will remember those words as if it happened just minutes ago."

"Mom, what was it Grandpa whispered to you?" Tiger finally let out.

Shannon grabbed Ray's arm firmly, and Ray really wondered what she was going to say. Shannon looked up at Ray, tears running down her face, and Ray knew the words she was about to say were really special. Ray gently put his arm around her and held her closely for support.

"Paul's last words were, 'Shannon, you and Ray—please try to have another child so Tiger can have a sister or brother to look after. It would be good for him.' With that he closed his eyes for the last time. He was a great man in my life, and I still miss him—and Mary."

Denise could tell Shannon had more to say.

"Ray and I have been trying for years to have another child. The doctor told me the other day that at forty-four, chances are pretty slim for me to get pregnant. Ray, I am really sorry."

"Shannon, what are you sorry for—we tried hard," replied Ray.

"Ray, I am sorry that we couldn't have a baby—sooner," said Shannon.

The statement didn't sink in right away, but Ray then thought about what Shannon had just said.

"Honey! Honey! You mean you are pregnant...?"

"Ya, Ray ... you are going to be a daddy for a second time. Tiger is going to be a big brother, and Annie is going to be a sister-in-law. We are going to have a bundle of joy roaming around in about eight months, along with the grandchild from Tiger and Annie."

Ray was beside himself at the revelation.

"This has indeed been a night for great news. Well, as we all go our separate ways tonight, I will tell you this: someday I will write a novel." Ray paused a little, gave his wife a big kiss, and added, "Look up behind me." Looking up at his beautiful tiger trophy, he concluded with, "I believe the title of the novel should be..."

The Bengal Ruby
The End

CPSIA information can be obtained
at www.ICGtesting.com
Printed in the USA
FSOW02n1744220915
11427FS